PRAISE FOR *THE MO*

'*The Mother* is a gripping, insightful and compelling with the issue of coercive control. Jane Caro's deep re are evident on every page. The characters are beautifully drawn and extremely real. Truly, I could not put this book down. It will spark fierce debate about how we should punish perpetrators, and support victim-survivors. I gasped out loud at some of the plot twists, and wept at the end. Every Australian should read this book. Choose this for your next book club, and talk about it with your family and friends.'
TRACEY SPICER, journalist and author of *THE GOOD GIRL STRIPPED BARE*

'Chillingly authentic, dark and exhilarating, a domestic revenge tale for any mother who's ever wondered how far she would go to protect her children.'
JUANITA PHILLIPS, journalist

'How refreshing to read something so human and honest and so firmly entrenched in the perspective of women subjected to abuse and coercive control. To feel what those women have felt. To gain insight into their experience. And especially not to have their sufferings blunted or Hollywood-ised. *The Mother* is devastating, frightening and heartbreaking, but also compassionate and empowering. It felt so convincing and real. With incisive clarity and insight, Caro shows how pressure builds on those who are oppressed and fearful. A deeply moving portrait of the shattering emotional impact of abuse on women and their families.'
KAREN VIGGERS, author of *THE LIGHTKEEPER'S WIFE*

'In her passionate and compelling novel, Jane Caro tells the vivid and heart-stopping tale of a young family in danger and the mother who will do anything to save them. I couldn't put it down. Passionate, vivid and unsettling, this heart-stopping tale of a family in turmoil had me transfixed.'
SUZANNE LEAL, author of *THE TEACHER'S SECRET*

Jane Caro AM is a Walkley Award-winning Australian columnist, author, novelist, broadcaster, advertising writer, documentary maker, feminist and social commentator.

Jane appears frequently on *Q&A*, *The Drum* and *Sunrise*. She has created and presented five documentary series for ABC's *Compass*, airing in 2015, 2016, 2017, 2018 and 2019. She and Catherine Fox present a popular podcast with Podcast One, Austereo 'Women With Clout'. She writes regular columns in *Sunday Life*.

She has published twelve books, including *Just a Girl*, *Just a Queen* and *Just Flesh & Blood*, a young adult trilogy about the life of Elizabeth Tudor, and the memoir *Plain-speaking Jane*. She created and edited *Unbreakable* which featured stories women writers had never told before and was published just before the Harvey Weinstein revelations. Her most recent non-fiction work is *Accidental Feminists*, about the fate of women over fifty. *The Mother* is her first novel for adults.

THE MOTHER
JANE CARO

ALLEN&UNWIN
SYDNEY · MELBOURNE · AUCKLAND · LONDON

First published in 2022

Copyright © Jane Caro 2022

All rights reserved. No part of this book may be reproduced or transmitted in any form or by any means, electronic or mechanical, including photocopying, recording or by any information storage and retrieval system, without prior permission in writing from the publisher. The Australian *Copyright Act 1968* (the Act) allows a maximum of one chapter or 10 per cent of this book, whichever is the greater, to be photocopied by any educational institution for its educational purposes provided that the educational institution (or body that administers it) has given a remuneration notice to the Copyright Agency (Australia) under the Act.

Allen & Unwin
83 Alexander Street
Crows Nest NSW 2065
Australia
Phone: (61 2) 8425 0100
Email: info@allenandunwin.com
Web: www.allenandunwin.com

A catalogue record for this book is available from the National Library of Australia

ISBN 978 1 76087 966 2

Set in 13/18 pt Granjon by Bookhouse, Sydney
Printed in Australia by SOS Print + Media

10 9 8 7 6 5 4

The paper in this book is FSC® certified. FSC® promotes environmentally responsible, socially beneficial and economically viable management of the world's forests.

To my mother, Kate

To Angela
March 2023

Really think you'll like this book

PROLOGUE

'Can I help you?'

The man behind the counter looked surprisingly ordinary. She didn't quite know what she'd expected—some sort of gangster vibe, perhaps. *What a cliché*, she chided herself. There was nothing of Robert De Niro or Harvey Keitel about this inoffensive bloke, nor was he a fat, aggro-looking MAGA type. He was neither Middle Eastern nor Italian nor Eastern European, as far as she could tell. He was just a sales assistant in the kind of shop she had never thought she would enter.

She tugged the collar of her puffer jacket higher around her face and smiled apologetically. 'I'm just looking, thank you.'

He raised an eyebrow at her response and she blushed. A gun shop wasn't like the upmarket boutiques she was used to, and 'just looking' was probably not an acceptable response here. In a boutique it meant 'give me time', and that was exactly what she needed—time to absorb her surroundings, to calm down enough to do what she had to do.

The door of the shop opened again, and another customer entered—a man who looked much more at ease in these surroundings than she felt. The new customer met her gaze and she looked away quickly, afraid she might be recognised. It was an irrational fear—no one knew her in Wollongong; that's why she'd come here.

She stood back from the counter and gestured to the sales assistant that he should serve this new customer first, but the bloke who had entered—older, big-bellied and wearing a cap with a logo of some kind on it—decided to be chivalrous.

'No, the lady was here first.' The man in the cap walked to the back of the shop, examining the rows of lethal weapons displayed in locked glass cabinets.

The sales assistant smiled at her, his manner as mild and professional as if he were selling her a coffee. 'Made up your mind yet?'

She had the urge to turn on her heel and run, but she knew that if she did, she would not come back. It was now or never. She put her hand in her bag and felt for the official papers that allowed her to purchase a firearm legally. She had ticked all the boxes—and there were a considerable number of boxes to tick. Then, summoning all the faux confidence of her rich lady persona, she stood up as straight as she could and said, 'I'd like a Smith and Wesson nine-millimetre, please.'

'You got the paperwork?'

Miriam handed over her Permit to Acquire and her firearms licence. To the man's credit, he checked them both carefully.

'That all seems to be in order. I'll fetch the gun for you. We always have them in stock. They're popular with sporting shooters, especially women.'

He turned and went through a door at the back of the shop. Miriam looked at the guns lining the walls behind her. They must be for display purposes only.

The cap-wearer sensed her looking in his direction and he turned and smiled at her supportively, giving her the thumbs-up. 'Good on you, love. I hope it helps.'

He thinks I'm traumatised, Miriam realised as she stared at his denim-clad back, *and so I am.* Somehow this recognition soothed her; she did not quite understand why, but whereas before she had felt like a complete alien in this strange place, now she felt a little more like she belonged. *The hunters and the prey*, she thought to herself. *We're all one or the other in here. Or both.*

PART ONE

CHAPTER 1

'It doesn't fit properly, and I hate it!'

Allison was in tears as she marched down the hallway to the family room and threw a large dress bag onto the couch. She then cast herself theatrically down beside it and sobbed noisily into a bolster.

Miriam felt a wave of irritation. Why did everything involving her younger daughter have to be so dramatic? Miriam had battled hard over the years to control her own emotional reactions to life's inevitable upsets. Because it didn't come naturally to her, she admired restraint and despised its opposite. Perhaps that was why her youngest daughter's behaviour so often got under her skin.

She took a deep breath. 'Don't be silly, darling. It looked beautiful at the fitting last week.'

Miriam was now sitting beside her daughter, perched on the few available inches of couch, stroking her back in what she hoped was a comforting manner. Ally didn't bother to lift her head. *Do tears stain?* Miriam wondered. Was Ally wearing mascara that might run? The couch was pale cream and had cost a bomb. Miriam wished her daughter had picked an older piece of furniture on which to cry so extravagantly.

'I was trying to convince myself it did, but I didn't even like it then! I thought it'd look better when it was tighter.'

'And I am sure it does.'

'No, it doesn't! I told you—it doesn't fit!' Ally spat the words at her mother as if all this was somehow her fault.

Repressing her answering spurt of rage, Miriam reminded herself this was merely pre-wedding jitters. 'Here, let's try it on in my bedroom and see.'

'No! I never want to see it again.'

Ally kicked at the bag, and it slid silkily to the floor. Miriam's stroking became a rather firm pat between the shoulder blades.

'Allison, darling, you are not twelve. You are getting married tomorrow and you are going to have to wear something, and this is the only wedding dress you've got.'

Though she was doing her best to sound calm and reassuring, Miriam felt a lurch inside her belly as she thought about the wedding day ahead. Her anxiety wasn't caused by nerves about last-minute details, or even the tantrum about the dress. In her usual fashion, Miriam had everything sorted down to the last pale pink rosebud. No, it was an uneasiness that had been there ever since her youngest daughter had announced she was marrying Nick, a young man whom Miriam and Pete—and Allison, for that matter—had only just met. But it wasn't the short time they had known him that worried her; Miriam had taken an instant liking to her daughter's new lover. Tall, handsome and charming, he reminded her of Pete in some indefinable way. They didn't look alike, but maybe it was something about Nick's smile. Whatever it was, she liked him. When the couple announced they were getting married only a few weeks in to their whirlwind romance, Miriam had felt relieved. She was sick of the assortment of musicians, hippies and other dropkicks her beautiful, smart and talented daughter had brought home, all of them so obviously her inferior. Nick was different. In the handsome vet, Ally had at last found someone who was her match. What worried Miriam was not that they hardly knew each other—it was that Ally would somehow do something to stuff it all up.

She had always felt more protective of her younger daughter than her elder. Even as a child, Fiona had been robust and even-tempered. Allison, on the other hand, was sensitive, delicate, easily frightened. She liked everything to be predictable, familiar, and she hated surprises. She was the kind of little girl who hid behind her mother's legs when asked to say hello to other grown-ups. She'd sucked her thumb until she was midway through primary school, a habit that had led to much expensive orthodontic work. Even when she grew up and became a surprisingly independent teenager, Miriam had worried more about Ally than she had about her sister. Allison had found her mother's anxiety oppressive, and reacted by becoming sullen and withdrawn. Rightly, Miriam admitted to herself, Ally had understood that her mother's protectiveness stemmed from a lack of confidence in her younger daughter's ability to cope.

Miriam scooped up the dress bag and ushered the sobbing bride-to-be up the hall. While a tear-stained Allison stood in front of the full-length mirror in her parents' bedroom, Miriam bent down behind her and painstakingly fastened the fiddly, cloth-covered buttons that snaked down the back of the form-fitting wedding dress. Allison's sobs were abating. When the last button was done up, Miriam rose to consider her daughter. As she had known would be the case, beautiful Allison looked, well, beautiful.

'Oh,' Allison said, between sniffs. 'It looks better in here.'

'It looks stunning, and it fits like a glove. Here, let's get it off you and back in the bag. We don't want any marks on it.'

And Miriam bent back down and returned to those bloody buttons. The bridesmaids could do them up tomorrow.

<hr />

The wedding of Allison and Nick passed faster than Miriam had thought possible. All that preparation, fuss and money (Pete never stopped updating her on the running total—it was their pillow talk every night) over in a few exciting and emotional hours.

Miriam was pleased to have met Nick's parents at last. She and Pete had suggested they should get together before the big day—go out to dinner or something—but the Carruthers hadn't been available. And it wasn't as if there was much time between the engagement and the wedding. Miriam had exchanged a few conventional remarks with Nick's mother, Sally, after the ceremony about how lovely Ally looked, how lucky Nick was, though there wasn't time for much more than that, because so many people wanted to speak to the mothers of the bride and the groom. And the wedding planner was constantly sidling up to Miriam to consult on some issue or other. It wasn't until dinner was underway at the reception—held in a marquee in the backyard of the bride's family home in Greenwich, on Sydney's North Shore—that she had a chance to sit down and take stock.

Liam, Fiona's husband, was acting as MC, and after a nod from the wedding planner, he took the floor. He began by asking Nick's dad to open the formal proceedings. Miriam put her dessert spoon down—her mother-of-the-bride dress had required Spanx, to her horror—as Maurice Carruthers got to his feet. Tall like his son, with a shock of thick white hair and a moustache, he appeared much older than his wife, and older than either Miriam or Pete, too. His manner was courtly, old-fashioned, very much of a different generation.

'Thank you for that kind introduction, Liam. It's certainly a pleasure to be at this wonderful occasion, watching my son marry such a beautiful bride. I can't help wondering how a no-hoper like him managed such a catch.'

Oh Christ. Miriam sat back in her chair. *Not a humblebrag, surely?* No one ever said anything like that about their child unless they meant the exact opposite. But she tittered politely, along with the rest of the guests. She watched Nick play along with the gag, pulling a self-deprecating face.

'You'll need to keep a careful eye on her, son, or else she'll be off with someone else!'

Miriam looked at Pete and raised an eyebrow. That remark seemed a bit inappropriate. Pete gave her his 'calm down' look. She supposed he was right. Wedding speeches were notoriously awful, made by people trying desperately to be funny.

'I intend to, Dad!'

Nick was laughing as he put his hand on Ally's back. She smiled up at her new husband adoringly. She did look fabulous, Miriam thought with pride.

'And I would like to thank the bride's parents, Pete and Miriam, for hosting this wonderful occasion. In fact, I think we should all be upstanding and raise a glass to the Franklin family for their kindness and generosity, not least in letting their beautiful daughter become a Carruthers!'

'Duffy-Franklin family!' interjected Nick.

Neither Miriam nor Fiona had changed their name. Miriam had always been Miriam Duffy, Fiona had always been Fiona Franklin. Miriam was delighted that her new son-in-law had corrected his father and acknowledged her so publicly. She caught his eye and raised a glass to him as a thankyou. He grinned back.

Nick's dad acknowledged the interjection with a nod. 'I stand corrected—apologies to our lovely hostess. The *Duffy*-Franklin family.'

Scraping their chairs, the guests rose and duly made the toast. 'The *Duffy*-Franklin family.'

Were some members of the party placing a slight emphasis on the word 'Duffy' as Maurice had done? Miriam didn't care. She'd done all the bloody work for this wedding and was paying for half of it. As Nick had clearly understood, the least they could do was acknowledge her by name.

Maurice Carruthers spoke for a further few minutes—after asking them all to be 'downstanding' following the toast, which also made Miriam roll her eyes—but as he didn't say anything particularly clever or revealing, Miriam was left with no more sense of him than she'd had before. Mrs Carruthers did not make a speech, even though she had been asked. She'd made it clear to Ally that she'd rather poke her own eyes out with a fork. 'Mum's terrified of public speaking,' Nick had explained to them later. 'She leaves all that stuff to Dad.'

Miriam and Pete made a speech together. They told stories about Ally's childhood—having carefully checked with the bride that she was comfortable with the ones they had chosen. They'd been burnt before.

'Ally was a great disappointment to us,' Pete was saying, pulling a sad face, 'even as a very small child. She was so prosaic. Nothing like my good lady wife . . .'

Miriam looked around in confusion at this point, as if he must be hiding the good lady wife somewhere behind her—a bit of business that brought a loud laugh. *Good*, she thought, *the guests have had just enough champagne.*

'. . . who is much given to flights of fancy.' Their family and friends laughed appreciatively. 'Ally was so allergic to anything different or unpredictable she insisted on calling all her toys by the most straightforward names possible. Her teddy was, well, Teddy. Her clown was Clowny. Her sheep Sheepy and her doll—well, what do you think she called her doll?'

'Dolly!' the guests called back.

'Nope.' You could hear the pleasure in Pete's voice; the audience had fallen into his trap. 'She called her doll Raggy because she was . . . rather ragged-looking. We got her second-hand at a fete and—to Ally's credit and her mother's embarrassment—she loved Raggy best of all, despite her being so grubby. In fact, that was Raggy's middle name. Despite her unprepossessing appearance, she enjoyed the magnificent moniker of Raggy Grubby Franklin!'

'Raggy Grubby *Duffy*-Franklin, surely?' It was Nick again.

Everyone roared. Miriam grinned widely and took the mic from Pete.

'Thank you for a second time, Nick. It's nice to know there's one member of this family who appreciates me.'

The remark was perhaps a little more pointed than she'd meant it to be. All she'd intended was to pay Nick a compliment, not have a dig at her daughter. She hoped Ally had not taken it that way.

Ally's new surname was a bone of contention. Unlike her sister and mother, Ally had decided to take her husband's name.

'I'm still a feminist, Mum,' Ally had declared, when she'd told her parents. 'But Nick's dad feels really strongly about it. He's old-fashioned and Nick is his only son. Nick couldn't care less, of course, but why upset Maurice if I don't have to?'

What about upsetting me? thought Miriam, but she kept her mouth shut.

'And anyway, I've got Dad's name, not yours, so what difference does it make?'

Nevertheless, when the celebrant had announced that Nick and Ally were now Mr and Mrs Nicholas Carruthers, Miriam had winced. It wasn't so much that Ally was rejecting her surname that upset her mother; it was the fact that by doing so her daughter was rejecting her values. And that hurt.

Once the formal proceedings were over and the band they'd hired started to play, it was too noisy to talk to any of the guests. Most of the young ones were dancing while the older guests were getting as far away from the music as possible. Miriam spent a moment or two trying to make conversation with Nick's father. She needed to get over the resentment she felt about the surname thing. She knew it was trivial. She *knew* it was. But the fact that Maurice's feelings were seen as more important than hers rankled. To her relief, as neither of them could hear themselves think and had to repeat everything twice, yelling at the top of their voices, they eventually gave up and just stood and watched the dancing. Standing there, Miriam suddenly realised she was exhausted and couldn't wait for the whole thing to be over.

❦

It seemed like hours of drinking and dancing and shouted small talk passed before Ally finally walked down the stairs, ready to get into the limousine that would take the bridal couple to the honeymoon suite at the Park Hyatt. Her daughter looked so radiant with happiness that the normally unsentimental Miriam had to blink away a couple of tears.

Ally must have noticed, because she immediately went over to her mother and hugged her hard.

'Thank you, Mum, for everything. I really appreciate it. Especially how wonderful you have been, even when I . . . well, you know, acted like me.'

It was unusual for Ally to make any kind of acknowledgement of Miriam's efforts, and her words made Miriam choke up a second time.

'I am the happiest woman in the whole world tonight,' Ally told her.

Miriam nodded and smiled. 'Of course you are, darling—everyone can see that.'

The bride turned and hugged her father. Pete, always the more demonstrative parent, was weeping openly. Nick hung back, giving father and daughter space to say their goodbyes. Eventually, Miriam decided to intervene.

'Come on, darling,' she said, reaching for her daughter's elbow and gesturing towards the door. 'The car's waiting.'

Ally pulled back from her father, laughing through her tears.

Nick stepped forward and took Ally's arm from Miriam, steering her outside.

They got into the waiting limo, and Ally wound down the window and beckoned her parents over for one final hug. Miriam caught the eye of her new son-in-law over her daughter's shoulder and smiled. He smiled back. It was as if they were silently passing Ally between them, from her mother's care to his.

～

'Thank God we only had two daughters!' Pete collapsed into an empty chair.

The last guest had gone, and Pete and Miriam were sitting amid the detritus in the lounge room. They'd had the reception at home, in a hired marquee in their garden, ostensibly to save money, although—after doing the sums—it didn't seem to have cost any less than hiring a venue, as they had for Fiona.

Despite her tiredness, Miriam had enjoyed the wedding. It was lovely to see both her girls looking so happy. She was proud of them, proud of herself, proud of what she and Pete had created together—their home, their family, their long and stable marriage. She had come a long way, she thought, looking around at her messy but still glamorous surrounds, from that Housing Commission cottage in the backblocks of Allambie Heights. Thanks to Gough Whitlam's education reforms, she'd been the first in her family to get a university degree. Just a humble Bachelor of Arts, majoring in history, but she'd gone to Sydney Uni and that was where she'd met Pete. She would never have met a man from his background otherwise. She raised a glass of warmish champagne.

'To Gough Whitlam, without whom none of this would have been possible.'

Pete pulled a face. 'You're not going to tell me your poor little rich girl story again, are you? How you escaped from the slums of the Northern Beaches?'

She pulled a face in return and drained her glass. 'No, I am not. Don't be such an old grump, Peter Franklin. The wedding was a triumph. It went off without a hitch or even a cross word. And it's wonderful to see both our daughters settled, and with two such lovely men. I confess I've had my doubts about Ally's ability to pick blokes in the past, but I could not be more delighted to be proved wrong.'

'Another daughter would have bankrupted me.'

'Us, if you don't mind.'

'What if they divorce? Will we have to cough up again?'

'Oh, for God's sake, they've only just wed. Don't wish divorce on them quite so soon. Here, have another drink and cheer up.'

She poured them each another glass from a half-drunk bottle of champagne sitting on a side table nearby.

'You're cheerful enough for both of us,' her husband observed. 'You look like the cat that has swallowed the cream.'

Miriam stretched her tired limbs in a rather catlike fashion. She did indeed feel rather smug.

'And why not?' she replied. 'It's our time now, old man. Our time! We can let their husbands worry about our daughters from now on while we enjoy ourselves. And I have no qualms about bankrupting you to do that.'

'Us, if you don't mind.'

She laughed out loud and took a swig of the champagne. She suddenly felt a wave of deep affection for her husband. She loved him, she loved how easily they bantered with one another, and she loved the life and family they had established together.

'I love you, you old bastard,' she told him.

'Right back at you, Mims.'

CHAPTER 2

'Hi darling, it's just me, ringing to see how you are getting on. It's just a boring, rainy Sunday down here. Call me when you can.'

Miriam put down the phone and picked up the book she'd been reading. She had lost count of the number of voice messages she had left for Ally. The newlyweds had been home from their honeymoon for a couple of weeks, but apart from a snatched chat over the phone shortly after their return, Miriam hadn't heard a word from her youngest daughter. This was classic Ally. Whenever there was something new and exciting going on in her life, she forgot everything and everyone else. *Even her old mum*, Miriam thought, ruefully. *Especially her old mum, perhaps.*

And Ally did have a lot of new things going on, Miriam had to concede. Nick was a country vet and straight after their honeymoon he and Ally had left Sydney to live a three-hour drive away in Dungog, where Nick had been offered the opportunity to join a growing practice. Miriam was used to seeing both her daughters regularly. Fiona and Liam lived just ten minutes' drive away with their small daughter, Molly. (Molly had been a very cute but somewhat unpredictable flower girl at the wedding, suddenly taking fright, dumping the petals from the basket she was carrying in the middle of the aisle, bursting into tears and running away to bury her head in Miriam's lap.) Until she married, Ally had lived a little further away, in Ultimo, on the other side of the Harbour Bridge, but her neighbourhood had some of the best restaurants in Sydney, many of them cheap and quirky, and Ally's parents were always happy to pop over for a meal. Miriam had felt a real pang when Nick and Ally had shared their plans in the lead-up to the wedding.

'I'll miss you and Dad, Mum—of course I will, but it's only a few hours' by car, or on the train, and I'm sure we'll be up and down all the time. You don't need to worry.'

'I'm not worried,' Miriam said. 'I understand that this is a good move for Nick. But what will you do, darling? I am not sure there's much call for economists in Dungog.'

Ally, for all her emotional fragility, was an academic powerhouse. She'd blitzed school and university, winning academic prizes every year. Fiona had sung solos at all their high school speech nights, but Ally had always won the awards. She had been working for Deloitte for a couple of years now, and by all accounts they thought very highly of her. Miriam was sorry to see her successful daughter walking away from her career to follow a man. *But it's Ally's life*, she reminded herself, *and she can do what she chooses.*

As if sensing the reason for her mother's hesitation, Ally said, 'I've decided to use my time as a country vet's wife to get a PhD. I've already sorted out a supervisor at Newcastle Uni. If I'm lucky, I might even get some sessional work there lecturing and tutoring in the Economics faculty.'

Miriam felt relieved. This was the independent, self-motivated Ally she admired. She was glad that side of her had not disappeared completely in the rush of new love.

Ever since her daughter met Nick, Miriam had noticed a change in her. She was in love in a way her mother had never seen before. The two of them were always in each other's company. Nick had moved into Ally's unit almost as soon as they'd met, and Miriam couldn't now recall if she'd seen her daughter alone since. Miriam missed spending time as just the two of them. Ally wasn't as easily confidential as Fiona, but she would open up occasionally and she saw the world in a different way from her mother and sister. Miriam felt she often learnt things from her brainy, plain-spoken youngest and she valued that.

Miriam tried hard not to feel sorry for herself. She was genuinely delighted that Ally had found such a terrific partner, but she had never felt as secure about her relationship with Ally as she did with her eldest daughter, and that made it hard for her not to worry. Not about Ally—she was sure Ally was blissfully happy. She was worried about herself and her place in her daughter's life. Miriam had always seemed to have an uncanny ability to say precisely the wrong thing at the wrong time. All she wanted was to have the same kind of easy relationship with Ally as she had with Fiona, but try as she might, she blew it. No sooner did Miriam start to feel she and Allison were on better terms than she'd say something without thinking, feel her prickly daughter's defences go up and watch their relationship go backwards.

Miriam's guilt about her failings as a mother were easily triggered by her youngest daughter. She hadn't been around enough when Ally was young. She'd been too focused on building her own real estate business. Delighted, in fact, to have something more interesting to occupy her than the drudgery of motherhood. She'd fobbed sensitive, clingy little Ally off onto others not just too often, but with too much ill-disguised relief.

Whenever she had these thoughts, however, her feminism would kick in. How come Pete never felt any guilt about his parenting? He'd been just as busy as Miriam—busier, in fact. He never turned up to school concerts, whereas Miriam would move heaven and earth to get to them. She'd even sat dutifully in Ally's class twice a week to help with reading, surreptitiously looking at her watch as some poor little mite faltered through *The Very Hungry Caterpillar*, wondering how late she could be for her next open house. But men got a free pass. Not just from society but from their own kids. Granted, Pete had been a hands-on father in comparison to most men of his generation, but his smallest effort got rave reviews, while all Miriam remembered receiving was criticism, no matter how much she did. Criticism she now levelled at herself, she conceded ruefully.

The feminist in her might have agreed that mothers were judged too harshly, but it didn't help. She didn't like the mother she had been with Ally. She didn't much like the woman she was when she was with her daughter now, and that self-consciousness made everything worse. It was why she was either too pushy or too distant. She cursed herself daily for having revealed her disappointment over Ally changing her surname. What did it matter what Ally called herself? She didn't really believe Ally had become a Carruthers just to please her old-fashioned father-in-law. She was head over heels and wanted the whole world to know. Changing her name was one way she could do that. But try as she might, Miriam still felt the sting of rejection.

'Maybe this explains it,' Pete said. He was sitting in an armchair, reading an article on Facebook.

'Explains what?'

'Why Ally was so determined to change her name.'

'Mind reader!'

Pete grinned and Miriam grinned back. She loved her husband's smile. In fact, she now remembered, one of the reasons she had warmed to Nick so quickly was that he had the same kind of whole-of-face smile as her husband. Mind you, she reminded herself, Pete often gave her that smile when he was about to tell her off for something.

'Anyway, this article says that women of your generation didn't want to take their husband's name because they were fighting to make a place for themselves—as themselves, not as some bloke's wife or mother—whereas this generation are confident of their place in the professional world but have lost confidence in their ability to be wives and mothers, so they're compensating.'

'Huh!' Miriam snorted derisively. 'Sounds like a whole lot of mansplaining to me.'

Despite her gruff response, Miriam was touched. As always, Pete was trying to comfort her. He was the calm, stabilising influence in their relationship. She knew he worried about her volatility sometimes—*like I do about Ally's*, she thought—and sometimes, maybe as Ally felt with her, his efforts to soothe her and keep her on an even keel annoyed her, though she knew he did it because he loved her and this was one way that he showed it. She pushed back against him most of the time, as a way of holding on to . . . what? Herself? Her nature? Who she was? But she also understood that having sane, centred Pete to push against was what kept her from falling down.

'It's written by a woman,' Pete countered.

'So? Women can mansplain. They do it all the time.'

'Oh well, it makes sense to me.'

'Did it ever worry you that I kept my name?'

'Not for a second. Anyway, I did change your name—you're always Mims to me.'

Miriam gave an ironic little laugh at his pet name for her. 'Just as well I like it.'

'Not sure you had much choice.'

Pete returned to his article and 'Mims' (*funny how I never think of myself by that name*, she thought) went back to her book.

∽

'They're madly in love. They're not interested in talking to their parents. They know we'll always be here, grateful for any crumbs of attention they scatter our way. You're overthinking it.'

It was later the same day. She and Pete were sharing a glass of wine and a bowl of soup—pea and ham, one of his specialities.

Pete knew her too well. Even though she had assured him that she was neither worried nor upset by Ally's silence, he was not fooled.

'I'm just missing her, that's all,' Miriam said. 'And I want to get to know Nick better. Don't you? I mean, I like him very much—he seems warm and easygoing, and he's a vet! What's not to like? But we hardly know him.' An idea struck her. 'Why don't you call Nick? He's hardly going to dodge a call from his father-in-law.'

Pete shrugged. 'I haven't got his number. Have you?'

'No. I thought you did.'

'Nope.'

'Can you call him via the vet clinic at Dungog?'

'That'll look a bit drastic, don't you think?'

'Maybe I'll try Ally at the uni,' Miriam mused.

'Is she even working there yet?'

'How should I know? I haven't spoken to her since the wedding, apart from that one brief call.'

'Has Fiona?'

Of course! Why hadn't she thought of that?

'You are a genius, Mr Franklin.' Rising to collect the soup bowls, Miriam kissed her husband on the top of his head.

'I know. That's why you married me.'

'Must be. It certainly wasn't for your looks.'

'Weren't we fortunate that we found one another, then, two such hideous freaks of nature? No one else would have had either one of us!'

Miriam stuck out her tongue, but one of the things she loved about Pete was his playfulness. It rarely failed to cheer her up.

Miriam called her eldest daughter from work the next day.

'Do you know how Ally is?' she asked, after a few minutes' talk about Molly.

'Fine,' said Fiona. 'I think.'

'What do you mean?'

'I've only spoken to her a couple of times since they moved into the new house.'

'Lucky you. I've hardly spoken to her at all.'

'Don't worry, Mum. It's just love's young dream. They're wrapped up in each other. They're not like me and Liam. We'd been together so long before the wedding we were more like an old married couple than newlyweds. Ally and Nick are just the opposite.'

'Can you give her a call? I think she's deliberately not picking up when I ring.'

'I'll try her tonight.'

The next day, Miriam received a text from her youngest daughter.

Sorry Mum, been flat out painting the house. Call me at work tomorrow.

Then another message popped onto her screen with a landline number. That struck Miriam as odd. She almost texted back, *What's wrong with your mobile?* but stopped herself just in time. That was the sort of thing Ally might see as either a criticism or being nosy. Instead, she merely responded with: *What's the best time?*

10, was the answer.

Later she wondered why it had taken so long for the penny to drop. Work? What work? Had Ally started tutoring at the uni already? No matter; she'd find out all about it the next day—if her daughter answered the phone, of course.

※

'Ally! How are you?'

Miriam had rung her daughter promptly at ten as instructed and, to her relief, Ally had answered immediately.

'I'm fine. And you and Dad?'

'Just the same as always. Your Dad is still a sarky bastard.'

'And you still always rise to the bait!'

Miriam laughed. She wasn't going to rise to the bait now.

'How's married life?'

'Well, we haven't called our lawyers yet.' Her voice was a touch grim.

Miriam didn't know what to say to that.

'Mum, I'm *joking*—it's fabulous. Better than I could ever have imagined.'

Miriam exhaled. Ally and Pete often laughed about how literal she and Fiona were. It made Miriam feel small and a bit stupid at times. She didn't know how it made Fiona feel. Water off a duck's back, probably.

'But you're working!' Miriam remembered. 'Where? At the uni?'

'No, not yet. I'm just helping out on reception at the vet clinic. One of the girls is on maternity leave.'

Again, Miriam was struck silent. Her brilliant daughter was answering the phone at a country vet clinic? She was surprised at how horrified she felt. *You're a snob, Miriam Duffy*, she told herself.

'But what about Newcastle Uni? Your PhD?'

'Like I said, Mum, not *yet*. I didn't say not *ever*. My potential supervisor is away for a few weeks and I can't see him till he gets back. I have an appointment, though. It's all under control.'

Miriam could tell by the edge in Ally's voice that she had once again put her foot in it.

'Of course it is, darling,' she said hastily. 'And anyway, it's completely your business. But tell me about Dungog and your new house. Dad and I thought we might come up and visit you one weekend soon. As you said, it's not far.'

They chatted for a while, and it was only after Ally had hung up—she'd had to answer a call on another line—that Miriam realised they hadn't pinned down a date for the visit. Never mind; now she had the landline number at the clinic, it'd be much easier to stay in touch.

She'd also meant to ask if there was something wrong with Ally's mobile—hence her daughter's request that she call on the clinic's landline—but had forgotten. And then a horrible thought occurred to her—if Ally used the work line, it was easier to keep the call short and get her mother off the phone with an excuse like the one she'd used just moments before. That thought made Miriam feel like shit.

∽

'Mum! You shouldn't have! There was no need!'

'Of course not, but I just felt like sending you something lovely.'

'Well, they *are* lovely! Really gorgeous—so gorgeous they got me into trouble!'

Miriam had felt so rotten after their unsatisfactory phone call the day before that she'd decided to make amends properly. She'd ordered a very expensive bunch of flowers to be delivered to Ally the next day. She'd even put 'Mrs Allison Carruthers' on the card, as a subtle peace offering. The arrival of the bouquet had managed to do what nothing else had so far: it made Ally pick up the phone.

'Got you into trouble? How?'

'I'm joking. Nick pretended to be jealous.'

Miriam chuckled. 'Never hurts to keep husbands on their toes.'

'But that's not why you sent them.'

'Of course not. I sent them for no particular reason. Just felt like it.'

'Bullshit. You never do anything without a reason.'

'I'm—we're—your dad and me—we're just missing you, that's all.'

'That's nice, but I am not missing you.'

Miriam laughed. She'd forgotten how much she enjoyed Ally's humour. And somehow the fact that her daughter wasn't soft-soaping her made her feel less jumpy.

'Nor should you be. You need to be enjoying your gorgeous husband without a thought of your ageing parents.'

'Yup. I'm doing that. Exactly that.'

'I'm not surprised. Nick clearly adores you. He seems really lovely. In fact, Dad and I would like to get to know him better, which is why I wanted to talk to you again about coming up for the weekend soon. We won't put you to any trouble. We can stay in an Airbnb, and I promise we'll make ourselves scarce—but it would be great to see you both and your new place.'

'Our new place isn't much to write home about; it's just a creaky old weatherboard. But it's spacious, and affordable on Nick's salary. I'll think about a date. Nick is often on call on weekends, though.'

'Well, let me know the next one he has free and we'll organise it for then.'

Miriam could feel her tension rising. Once again, it seemed as if Ally was coming up with excuses, trying to fob her off.

'Okay, I'll get back to you. And thanks again for the flowers. Love you, Mum.'

The phrase sounded like a dismissal. Not so much 'love you, Mum' as 'enough now, Mum'. Despite the flowers and the chat—two chats by this time—Miriam had never felt further apart from Ally, not even when her daughter had been living in New York as an au pair in her gap year between school and uni. Ally had been so horribly homesick at first, she'd rung every night and sobbed down the phone. Unable to do anything about her daughter's misery at such a distance, Miriam had dreaded her calls then as much as she yearned for them now. *Careful what you wish for*, she thought to herself as she put her phone back in her handbag.

'I feel like she's avoiding me—*us*.'

Miriam was sitting up in bed, laptop on her knees, supposedly paying some bills, but she couldn't concentrate. Beside her, Pete was scrolling through Facebook again.

'She probably is,' he agreed, 'but that's fair enough. They're just happy and in love. Let her go, Mims. That's the way to get her back. Here, look, she's just posted these . . .'

Pete passed her his phone and she looked through a series of photos of Ally and Nick on what looked like a bushwalk through beautiful rainforest.

'See—she's glowing.'

And Miriam had to admit her daughter and her new husband looked not just spectacular but spectacularly happy. The comments below from friends, many of whose names Miriam recognised, reflected the happiness the camera had recorded.

'You're right. I'm just being silly. She's a grown woman and she's newly married. I need to back off and give her some space. I just hope she doesn't forget us entirely.'

'She won't. We'll always be here whenever we're needed and we'll fade into the background when we're not. That's how it works.'

Pete yawned and plugged his phone into the charger beside his bed, took off his specs and put them carefully in their case.

'Night, Mims. I've set the alarm for six; I have an early meeting.'

He patted her on the bum under the covers, as he had done every night that she could remember. Then he rolled over onto his side with his back to her. She could tell by his breathing that he was asleep in an instant. Miriam yawned too and closed her laptop. The bills could wait until tomorrow. It took her longer to get to sleep than her husband. She ruminated on things. He didn't. *Not that there is anything to worry about*, she reminded herself. What was it her 2IC, Prisha, had said to her at work when she'd been complaining about Ally not returning her calls? That you are only as happy as your unhappiest child? Well, if that was the case, Miriam should be blissful.

CHAPTER 3

'See you tonight.'
Pete popped his head around the bathroom door the next morning and Miriam stopped blow-drying her hair to blow him a kiss. It wasn't even 7 am.

'Shall we go to Sushi Ya for dinner?' she suggested. She had a big day ahead of her too. Four viewings and a couple of potential listings, plus meetings with her sales staff and the young woman who managed the Duffy Real Estate website. She wouldn't be home in time to cook anything. 'Unless you want to throw together a spag bog or something.'

Spag bog was another of Pete's specialities. His version was always much nicer than hers. She still did not quite understand why.

'Japanese sounds good,' he said.

'I'll book a table—'

But she was talking to the closed door. He had gone.

She was at work, just about to leave the office for a viewing—literally grabbing her jacket and bag—when her mobile vibrated. She considered not answering it, as she was already running late, but the thought that it might be Ally calling made her rummage through her bag to find her phone. But it wasn't her daughter.

'Hi, Miriam, it's Mark from BPF. I work with Pete.'

Pete was a partner in a firm of architects. He'd been the junior partner originally; now he was the senior. B and P had both retired long ago, and only F remained.

'Oh yes, Mark, of course.'

Miriam had met Mark several times. He occasionally brought plans over on weekends for Pete to review and they'd have meetings in their lounge room. Miriam was vaguely resentful of the interruption to their weekends and evenings—after all, real estate agents don't get many of those off—but she was always polite to the younger man.

'What can I do for you?' she asked now.

She was glancing at her watch. She couldn't keep potential buyers waiting outside a locked door.

There was a pause. Pete's colleague sounded breathless over the phone, almost as if he'd been running.

'Mark? What's happened? What's going on?' She could hear the edge in her voice. *This better be bloody serious*, she thought, *giving me a fright like this.*

Her sharp tone did the trick.

Mark took a deep breath. 'Um . . . Pete has collapsed. He's in the ambulance now, on his way to Royal North Shore.'

A vivid picture of Pete falling in a heap like a puppet after its strings were cut flashed into Miriam's head.

'Collapsed? How do you mean collapsed? Is he alright?' She felt bewildered now, she was having trouble processing what Mark was telling her.

'Um . . . I don't know. It seemed pretty serious. I think you should get down there straight away.'

'But what happened?'

'I don't know. One minute he was standing up, next minute he was on the floor. Hopefully the hospital can tell you more.'

'Okay . . . thanks for calling me.'

She was not exactly alarmed; not yet. Pete had been rushed to hospital once before with a suspected heart attack. It had been years ago, when the kids were young. She'd arrived at Emergency in a spin, two little girls in pyjamas in tow, each with a Tim Tam shoved in her mouth. ('A sometimes food,' Fiona had said, eyes wide. She'd grabbed it quickly before her mother could change her mind.) After hours of waiting in the ward, trying to keep two fractious and exhausted little girls quiet and entertained, Pete'd been diagnosed with an anxiety attack and sent home. He'd been sheepish about the whole thing afterwards.

This is probably another false alarm, she assured herself. Nevertheless, she would take Mark's advice and head straight to the hospital. She hurried into the outer office. Prisha was on the phone. Miriam gestured at her to hang up.

'Sorry, but Pete's collapsed and has been rushed to Royal North Shore by ambulance. Can you cancel all my meetings for today and farm out the viewings to Laura and Kim? I have a second viewing at the Sera Avenue place in'—she glanced at her watch—'*fuck*, fifteen minutes.'

Thank God for Prisha. She'd been working for Miriam since the early days. She was sensible, reliable and knew the business backwards.

'Of course. Is Pete alright?'

'I don't know. Nevertheless, it's probably best to write off the whole day. You know what hospitals are like. I'll keep you posted.'

※

She phoned the girls from the car (a real estate agent always has Bluetooth) to tell them what little she knew.

Fiona, of course, picked up immediately. 'I'm on my way,' she said.

Ally, equally predictably, did not answer, so Miriam had to leave yet another voice message.

'Ally, it's Mum. I don't want to worry you unnecessarily, but Dad's collapsed and is in Emergency at Royal North Shore Hospital. I'm on my way there now. That's all the info I have at the moment. I'll ring again when I know more.'

She soon turned into the hospital car park (despite her best efforts to remain calm, she later received two speeding tickets for that ten-minute drive), and managed to find a parking space without too much trouble—never a given. Striding into Emergency, she approached the nurse behind the glass partition with a cool and professional smile.

'Hi, I'm Miriam Duffy. My husband—Peter Franklin—was brought here by ambulance a little while ago.'

'Just a moment.' The nurse reached for the phone. There was something about her expression that Miriam did not like.

Another nurse appeared almost immediately and ushered Miriam along a corridor and into a small room. This surprised her. She'd expected to be taken into the Emergency ward, like last time, and led to Pete's bedside. She wanted him to smile at her sheepishly and say, 'Sorry, Mims.' Instead, she was in this cold little waiting room, furnished with the institutional version of comfortable chairs. She didn't sit. She walked to the window and looked out at the multistorey car park. She was trying and failing to quell the sense of dread that was rising in her belly when she heard the door open behind her.

'Mrs Franklin?'

She didn't turn around immediately. She felt if she could just stay in this moment for as long as possible, staring at a red car driving around and around looking for a parking space, she could hang on to her old life for just a little bit longer. She didn't 'know' anything yet. Maybe it was better that way.

'Mrs Franklin?' It was a woman's voice. Gentle—too gentle—but insistent.

Miriam turned. As always, these days, she was surprised at how young the doctor was. Everyone now—police, politicians, even the goddamn prime minister—seemed barely out of high school. She and Pete joked about it.

'Won't you sit down?'

Miriam gripped the windowsill behind her with both hands and shook her head.

'I'm Dr Chiang,' the woman said. 'I attended your husband when he arrived. Are you sure you won't sit down?'

Miriam shook her head a second time.

The doctor took a breath. 'I am afraid there was nothing we could do. He was dead on arrival. To be honest, I think he died instantly. He was gone by the time he hit the floor.'

Miriam nodded mutely.

'It was a massive aneurysm. A bleed to the brain . . .'

'I know what an aneurysm is.'

The girl-doctor nodded apologetically. 'He'd have felt nothing.'

Nothing? She wanted him to have felt something! Fear, anger, despair, pain—yes, fuck it, pain! How dare he just slide out of her life, their family, their marriage and feel nothing? How dare he? She was going to have to feel something, all of them would, and the pain was going to be excruciating and never-ending.

But then, just as quickly as emotion had overwhelmed her, it disappeared and she didn't feel much of anything anymore. She felt the way you do when you fall and really hurt yourself. You get the nauseating stab, then the injury goes numb—but you know you are in for it when the numbness fades.

'Mrs Franklin? Are you alright?'

Miriam nodded again.

'Is there anyone I can call for you?'

'My daughter—Fiona—she's on her way. She'll be here any minute.'

Oh God. She didn't feel she could face Fiona right now—or anyone. She couldn't bear to have to deal with Fiona's pain. She'd have to feel something then. But there was no stopping her—or it—whatever *it* was that she could sense stampeding towards her. Oh, to be back watching that little red car.

'She'll be brought straight here when she arrives.'

'Can we—I mean—can we see him?'

She had to see Pete for herself. That was the only way she could be sure any of this was real.

'Of course. I can take you to him now. Or would you prefer to wait for your daughter?'

Miriam wanted to see Pete straight away, but how could she tell Fiona her beloved father was dead while they stood over his cooling corpse?

'I'll wait for her.'

'I'll wait with you, if you like.'

And yet again, all Miriam could do was nod. For the first time, there were tears in her eyes. It was the woman's kindness that got to her. But she coughed the tears away; she could not cry now. She didn't know why she was so determined to hold everything together, to keep her emotions in check. Was it for Fiona's sake? Or for her own? Or was it just the habit of a lifetime?

*

'DADDY!'

It was Fiona's gut-wrenching scream, the way she sobbed the name she had not used for her father since she was a little girl, that finally dragged proper tears from Miriam. Yet she wasn't sure who she was crying for. Was it Pete? No, not Pete. She was still absurdly, unreasonably angry with Pete.

Was she crying for herself, so suddenly a widow? She tried the word out in her head for the first time and shuddered. No, she didn't think of herself that way. Not yet. She was crying for her child, for Fiona, and the terrible pain she was suffering. The two of them sat huddled together in that cold, institutional little room and wept. The kind doctor sat next to them, but not too close, hands folded neatly in her lap, eyes cast down, waiting patiently.

After a few minutes they stood and were led along the maze of corridors in the hospital to the room and the bed that held Peter.

'He's here,' said the doctor, unnecessarily.

As she went to pull back the sheet that covered him from head to toe, Miriam had a wild thought that the body would not be her husband's, that the face revealed would belong to some other man and she would discover that it had all been a dreadful mistake. But it was Pete, of course, unmistakably—and yet strangely—him. She'd thought he'd look like he was sleeping but he didn't. She had never seen him so profoundly still. The sight of his body made Fiona shake with sobs, but Miriam was again dry-eyed. She put her hand up to Pete's cheek to touch him and recoiled. He was still warm. She looked at the doctor, startled.

'It takes a while,' the doctor said, knowing what Miriam was asking.

She's done this before, Miriam thought, then she jumped, startled by the Fitbit vibrating on her wrist. Both the doctor and Fiona reached for her. *They're worried I am going to faint*, she realised. She waved the vibrating Fitbit on her wrist. 'It's my phone . . .'

As always, she had to rummage through her bag to find the bloody thing.

It was Ally. 'Mum? Is Dad okay?'

Miriam could hear the fear in her youngest daughter's voice. Her courage failed her. How could she tell this fragile daughter the terrible news? It had been hard enough with Fiona, face to face. In fact, Miriam had hardly had to say anything. Fiona had taken one look at her mother and the doctor and known.

Miriam put her hand over the phone. 'It's Ally.' Anything to delay the inevitable.

'Do you want me to tell her?' Fiona's voice was thick with tears.

Miriam shook her head. She was the mother. It was her job. She would tell her daughter the worst.

She whispered the words as if lowering the volume might somehow lessen their impact. 'I am so sorry, Ally, but . . . he's dead.'

There was a gasp at the end of the phone, as if someone had just punched Ally in the stomach.

Miriam's instinct was to offer comfort, but she had none. 'I . . . I wish there was an easier way to tell you . . .'

'What do you mean, dead?'

'He had a massive aneurysm. It killed him instantly. The doctors say he would have felt nothing.'

There was a long silence at both ends of the phone. Miriam could almost feel her daughter trying to comprehend the news. It was what she was trying to do too.

'Will you come?' Miriam asked, her voice breaking. In that moment, it sounded like she was the child asking for help. Help she knew no one could give.

CHAPTER 4

'Sit here, Mum.'

Fiona pointed towards a seat in the centre of the front row. All week, Miriam's eldest daughter had insisted on treating her mother as if she'd lost her marbles as well as her husband.

'Yes, thanks for that. How would I ever have found my seat without you?'

She saw Fiona stiffen, and felt momentarily guilty, but she didn't really care. Yes, they were all red raw, but her own pain was so overwhelming she did not have room for anyone else's. Everyone and everything seemed too much for her now. Except Molly. Her granddaughter's needs were the same as they ever were. There was no undercurrent. She could deal with those.

'Sonny! Sonny!'

Even her new son-in-law was grating on her. While they waited for the funeral to start, he was hissing at his wife from the row behind. For a moment, she couldn't work out who he was referring to, then she remembered her son-in-law had given Ally a new nickname.

Unlike the change of surname, this new name pleased Miriam. She saw it as a very good sign. As Pete had pointed out, he had given her a pet name when they became a couple. When he had called her 'Mims' it was proof of affection, of intimacy and partnership. Tears pricked as she realised that no one would ever call her Mims again. She bit her lip hard.

The funeral was about to begin. The music had started playing on the sound system, the volume turned up just a little too high, but it brought everyone to order, including Nick. Whatever it was that had been so urgent would have to wait.

After the first few notes, people recognised Nancy Sinatra's 'These Boots Are Made for Walkin" and began to laugh. Even Miriam managed a smile. The song was the one Pete had played to the girls when they were little and, as the familiar riff began, she was struck by a vivid memory of little Ally, clutching her Raggy, demanding 'Boots' and stomping her feet enthusiastically alongside her father whenever he'd popped it in the cassette player. The force of the recollection drew an involuntary dry sob from Miriam. Ally turned to her mother immediately. She took Miriam's hand and gave it a squeeze. Ally's own hand was dry and papery.

Miriam was staring straight ahead. On her left sat Fiona. On her right Ally. Behind them Liam was struggling to entertain Molly, who had decided she wanted her mum. On the other side of Molly sat Nick. It was a secular funeral in the chapel of the crematorium, so the room was warm, comfortable and utterly anonymous. It had all the ambience of a hotel conference room. Instead of hard pews, the mourners sat in upholstered chairs. They could look at the well-manicured gardens through the wall of glass that ran down one side of the room. The gardens were so well cared for even the plants, shrubs and flowers seemed to have been clipped of all their personality. Miriam found herself longing for a few dead leaves littering the perfectly mown lawn, or even some weeds poking their defiant heads up through the grass, but there was nothing. Everything was so perfect it was unnatural. On the TV screen attached to the wall above the podium (no pulpit for cheerful atheist Pete) photographs of her deceased husband scrolled endlessly, a record of his journey through life. From chubby baby in black and white to the most recent shots of them together in Tuscany last year. It was the same collection they'd used at the party for his sixtieth a few months ago. They'd both been so full of optimism then about what the next few years had in store.

'We're in the youth of our old age,' she remembered saying in the speech she had made. 'We're going to have all that fun we've been denying ourselves as we've built our businesses and cared for our family. The world is our oyster!' Oh God, if only she had known.

But she wasn't really looking at the photos, not properly. Her eyes might be open, but she wasn't really taking anything in. As she had for days, Miriam felt stunned, not really present in her own life at all. The only thing that brought her back into herself was her constant, low-level irritation at everything. Loud noises made her jump but people tiptoeing around her and speaking in hushed tones made her snarl. Poor Fiona copped most of it. Miriam would normally have felt guilty about taking advantage of her older daughter's good nature, but not now. She couldn't make the effort.

The chapel was filled to overflowing with mourners; Pete had been a popular and successful man. Dry-eyed still—she had not wept since the hospital—she stared blankly as their friends and family filed into their seats. The chairs were lined up on two sides of a makeshift aisle down the centre of the large room. *Which side for the bride and which for the groom?* she thought sardonically. And the funeral did feel like a macabre parody of a wedding. The same hush. The same obsequious ushers (Pete's nieces and nephews) showing people to vacant seats and handing out the order of service. The same sense of repressed emotion.

Even when the mourners began to line the walls once all the seats were taken, she remained numb. She supposed she'd have felt bad if there had been a small turnout, but it was beyond her to derive any pleasure from the regard in which her husband had been held, or to feel any sympathy for those who also grieved. The only face that did cause her to feel something—and it was a spasm of pure pain—was that of the poor fellow from Pete's office, Mark, who had phoned her with the news of Pete's collapse and so catapulted her into this strange half-life she now occupied. Had it only been a week ago? It felt like a lifetime. The pain she'd felt at the sight of Mark had been so intense, she had clutched at her chest, afraid for a moment she was having a heart attack. Once she regained her self-control, she almost regretted that she had not been struck down. It would have been so much easier to follow Pete into oblivion than struggle on alone.

The music had stopped now, and the funeral celebrant stood up. (*Celebrant? Was that what you called it at a secular funeral?* Miriam wondered. Odd the silly thoughts that popped into one's head at times like these.) The celebrant was an old friend of Miriam and Pete's from university whose day job was as a relationships counsellor, and she hit just the right note—sympathetic, kind but not cloying. She even made the occasional joke. Miriam smiled when the others laughed but she wasn't really listening to what Brigit was saying. If she did, she might have to acknowledge exactly what she had lost, and she could not do that. Not yet. Instead, she sat in a kind of bleak stupor. Enduring. Resentful. Hostile. The part of the service she dreaded most was afterwards, when she would have to talk to people and bear the weight of their sympathy.

A more sombre song now: 'And So It Goes' by Billy Joel. She supposed that someone must have got her to approve the playlist at some point—Fiona most likely, and she had probably been yelled at for her trouble—but Miriam had no memory of it. The song was a tear-jerker, alright, and Miriam heard people all around her beginning to cry, but not a drop fell from her own eyes. As the song ended, Liam and Nick got up from their seats and went to the back of the room. Molly protested so furiously that she got handed over everyone's heads to her own mother, where she was shushed and eventually placated with a muesli bar that Fiona fished out of the bottom of her bag. The only person Miriam could bear touching was Molly, but her small granddaughter mostly kept her distance. Miriam's need was so great, even a two-year-old could sense it. Miriam satisfied herself with a quick caress of Molly's arm, which the child ignored.

After Molly had settled down on her mother's lap, everyone turned to look at the doors at the back. *The bride has arrived*, Miriam thought, and kept staring straight ahead, but Fiona nudged her mother, gently and firmly.

Molly tried to help. 'Look, Nanna!' Her voice was piercing. 'Poppy is in there!'

Miriam turned her head. *Sometimes you could give kids too much information*, she thought.

The pallbearers were holding Pete's coffin, waiting to walk down the aisle—just like bridesmaids. The music began and they started to move, trying to keep pace with David Bowie's 'Changes'. *All those lyrics about facing the pain . . . Really?* thought Miriam. Perhaps Fiona had been rather too creative with the playlist.

Miriam snapped her head back to the front, unable to cope with the sight of the coffin, but not before she had registered the pallbearers. Duncan and Greg, Pete's best mates all the way through school, at the front; his two sisters in the middle, sobbing openly; and Nick and Liam bringing up the rear. *Why not Ally? Why not Fiona?* she wondered. But they were on either side of her, arms around her waist and shoulders, crying piteously. *They wouldn't have been up to it*, she acknowledged, *just like me.* Yet even in the face of her daughters' grief, Miriam remained mostly numb. What was wrong with her? The only emotion she could really feel was anger. Anger that all these people should live while he did not.

She got through the rest of the funeral somehow. People were kind and forbearing with the new widow, not expecting much from her, thank God, but her professional sales training kicked in anyway. She smiled and nodded at the appropriate times, but with little real feeling.

When the funeral and the awful wake were finally over, and they were in Liam's car heading home, she was overcome by a weariness she had never experienced before. Every muscle ached and every movement felt as if she were pushing through treacle. She closed her eyes and rested her forehead against the passenger window. All she yearned for was oblivion. She didn't care if she found it via sleep or alcohol or tranquillisers. She never wanted to think about that funeral again—or any of it. They said that funerals offered closure or some such new age rubbish. Well, maybe they did if the person who had died had reached a grand old age, or if they had succumbed to a long and drawn-out illness, but Pete had been hale and hearty one minute, stone dead the next, and Miriam simply could not take it in.

*

The day after the funeral, Liam picked up Pete's ashes from the crematorium, as arranged.

He came into Miriam's lounge room holding a plastic shopping bag. 'They're in here.'

Then he extracted a truly hideous blue plastic urn and held it out towards his mother-in-law.

Miriam recoiled from it as if it were on fire.

Fiona was quick to snatch the urn away. She held it in both hands, her face crumpling, as if it had just dawned on her that the remains of her father were inside.

'Why don't you put it down?' Ally spoke gently.

'Where?' Fiona looked around the room and then put the urn reverently on the mantelpiece.

'Don't put it there!'

Miriam spoke sharply, and Fiona burst into tears.

'Just for now, Mum,' Ally said. 'We'll find somewhere better for it later.' She put her arm around her sister.

Miriam had not meant to make poor Fiona cry, so she just nodded wordlessly.

Later, once Fiona and Liam had finally left and Ally and Nick had gone to bed, Miriam took the ghastly urn down from the mantelpiece. She carried it upstairs and shoved it right to the back on the middle shelf of the linen cupboard.

*

The next morning, she got a stepladder from the garage and lugged it through the house towards the stairs. She made slow progress. She had to stop every now and then, as the bloody thing was both heavy and awkward.

'Hey, Miriam, let me help you with that.'

Nick, who was making a pot of tea in the kitchen, stepped forward and took hold of the ladder with both hands. Miriam gave him a long look. This was something she'd meant to do on her own, but she knew she would struggle to get the ladder up the stairs. She let Nick take it and walked on ahead.

'Where are we going?' he asked.

'Just follow me . . .'

'Here,' Miriam said when they reached the linen cupboard, gesturing for Nick to lean the ladder against the wall. She retrieved the urn and began to climb the ladder.

'Wait,' said Nick, reaching for the urn. 'I can do it.'

Miriam gripped the object closer to her chest and turned away, like a child in a playground trying to stop a bigger kid from snatching her toy.

'No, I will do it.'

Nick backed off and just held the ladder steady so she wouldn't fall. She climbed until she could reach the very top shelf, the one she could not reach normally, and that was where she put the urn with Pete's ashes. *Let it gather dust in there.*

To her relief, Nick said nothing. He merely waited until she had climbed back down, then he picked up the ladder and took it away. As far as she knew he never said anything about it to anyone either. She was very grateful for that. She could not explain her intentions because she did not understand them. She had just followed her instinct.

∼

From that day on, every time Miriam passed the linen cupboard on her way to bed, she had a weird, goosepimply feeling. It felt as if Pete's ghost was shut up in there, scratching feebly to be let out. He'd always been a bit claustrophobic. Sometimes she wondered whether she should fetch the ladder and liberate her husband's remains. But Nick and Ally had gone back to Dungog, and the idea of wrestling with the ladder on her own was enough to stop her. Anyway, it didn't matter. Pete was not in the linen cupboard. He wasn't anywhere.

Every morning she woke and for a few blissful seconds Miriam felt just as she always had. Then the knowledge of her terrible loss descended, and she grieved all over again. She almost understood—for the first time ever—why Adam and Eve had been thrown out of the Garden of Eden for eating from the tree of knowledge. Ignorance really was bliss, or it was for those few seconds.

Going to bed was the opposite, and Miriam put it off for as long as possible—not just because she had to walk past the linen cupboard. After as many glasses of rosé as she dared—she left a little in the bottle just to reassure herself she had not yet become a complete alcoholic—she finally crawled into what now felt like a vast expanse of empty bed and curled up into a ball. (*Should I buy a king single? Or is too soon?*) Every time she closed her eyes, the whole experience—from Mark's phone call to viewing Pete's body—played out in her mind. Only after she'd watched the hospital sheet settle over Pete's lifeless face for the millionth time could she fall asleep. When she woke a few short hours later, and reality descended on her with the weight of all the sorrow in the world, she lay and fumed at her fate. How dare Pete leave her this way? How could this have happened? What was she to do now? She, who had not been on her own for more than a few days since she was a girl? How could she carry on? What earthly good could she be to anyone now?

For months, she went through the motions. She went to work, even sold a few houses. *Thank God for Prisha*, she thought, not just daily, but over and over. Her 2IC's knowledge of the business saved Miriam more times than she wanted to count when things got neglected or fell through the cracks. Like Fiona had at the funeral, Prisha nudged her along, gently but firmly, and helped Miriam to feel that her work was a kind of lifeline. When she was thoroughly absorbed in balance sheets or nutting out sales copy or negotiating the best possible price for a client, she forgot about her loss. Those moments of forgetting made her feel both relief and guilt. Had she really loved Pete as much as she thought she did, if she could be so easily distracted?

&

'Coffee?'

Prisha was standing at her office door, putting on her jacket.

'Lovely, thanks.'

'And a friand?'

Miriam had developed a sweet tooth since Pete's death. Only dessert and alcohol comforted her now. And Molly—reading her granddaughter a story, singing her a song, persuading her to give her grandmother a kiss, snuggling up beside her to watch *Bluey* and spoiling her (well, both of them) with a sugary treat was all she looked forward to now. Molly soon stopped asking for Poppy. Fiona explained that Poppy had died and was not with them anymore, an explanation that only partly satisfied Molly.

'But where has he gone?'

'He's nowhere, darling. He isn't alive anymore.'

But this was an answer that did not compute.

'Has he gone to another country—like Melbourne?'

'No, Mol. He isn't anywhere.' Fiona sighed with a mix of exasperation and sorrow. 'God, I can see why people believe in one,' she said to her mother. 'A god, I mean. It'd be so much easier if I could tell her he'd gone to heaven or something.'

But at least Molly didn't ask Miriam how she was in a stupid voice or pull a 'kind' face or pat her sympathetically on the arm. Molly treated her grandmother just as she always had and that was a relief. And as time went on, she asked where Poppy was less and less, until she stopped altogether—an omission that filled Miriam with both relief and pain.

Prisha was still standing by the open door of Miriam's office, eyebrows raised. She was patient with her boss, who quite frequently got caught up in her thoughts and lost the thread these days.

Miriam pulled herself back into the present. What was it Prisha had asked? That's right: she'd offered Miriam a friand. 'I shouldn't, but I will.'

Miriam had had to do up her skirt with a safety pin that morning. A few weeks ago, she would have been horrified. Today, she couldn't give a fuck. She could get as fat as a barrel now. But she still went for her morning walk, even without Pete. It helped clear her head and shake off the restless night, and she liked passing the other walkers, who she only knew well enough to exchange nods. Like Molly, they required nothing more than a wave and a smile. Everyone else wanted something—for her to get 'closure' (that awful word), for her to comfort them, for her to appreciate their kindness and compassion. It made her feel sick.

Sometimes she repeated her hour-long walk in the evening, stomping along with her head down. According to her Fitbit, her daily step count was up the wazoo. Even so, she could no longer to do up her skirts.

The Fitbit vibrated on her wrist, as if on cue, and for a moment she stared at it dumbly. But it just meant her phone was ringing. She didn't have to rummage for her mobile this time; it was sitting on her desk under a few papers.

'Hello, Miriam Duffy.'

'Mum, it's me—Ally.'

Despite still being deep in the angry funk that had overwhelmed her since Pete's death, Miriam still felt a thrill of delight that her youngest daughter had made contact without being prompted.

'Ally!' she responded with real warmth. 'It's lovely to hear from you.'

'Sorry I haven't called sooner.'

And there it was—the undercurrent of guilt, which was not what Miriam had wanted at all. For once there was no hidden agenda in her pleasure at hearing Ally's voice. It was just what it was.

'I have news.'

Miriam stiffened. She now lived in constant anticipation of the worst, especially if the news was delivered over the phone.

'What news?'

She tried to keep the anxiety out of her voice. No doubt she failed.

'I'm pregnant.'

Miriam took a deep breath. This was the last thing she had expected to hear. This would be a grandchild Pete would never know and who would never know Pete. The loss of all those years of life that should have been his and hers now felt even greater. This good news—because that's what it was, she reminded herself—felt like a body blow. She gathered herself as best she could and answered with what she hoped was enthusiasm.

'Oh, darling! That's wonderful . . . or, at least, I hope it's wonderful.'

'Well, yes, it is—of course it is. Nick is over the moon. But . . . it's earlier than we intended, or than I intended, anyway, so I feel a bit overwhelmed.'

'That's only to be expected. Having a baby is a huge deal . . . life-changing . . . and if you weren't planning on it, no wonder you feel a bit out of your depth. And we're all still in shock. How far along are you?'

'Twelve weeks. I didn't want to tell anyone until I was sure it would stick.'

Not even me? thought Miriam. *Not even your mother? Not even when your dad died?* But she knew better than to say these things aloud.

'Very sensible.' Then she risked giving voice to the pain that was clawing at her. 'Your dad would have loved this news.'

'I know. I wish he was here. I miss him all the time.'

'Me too.'

And then mother and daughter were silent, but in a good way, it seemed to Miriam. They were sharing something awful but also genuine and uncomplicated—their loss and grief.

It was Miriam who spoke first. 'How are you feeling?'

'Okay . . . fine. I feel a bit wobbly in the morning but great most of the time now.'

'Shall I come up for the weekend?'

'No, no. No need.'

'I know, but I'd like to. I've missed you, and I'm lonely rattling around the house all on my own.' As she said this, Miriam silently cursed herself. Ally might read that as pressure.

'Oh, I'd love you to come, Mum, really I would, but Nick's working on weekends.'

'Well, that's a shame, of course—I'd love to see him—but it's you I really want to see. And I daresay he comes home in the evenings . . .'

'Not always; it depends on what he has to deal with. Cows are like people—birth complications can happen at all hours.'

'No matter. If I see him, that's a bonus. If I don't, at least I'll get to see you. And—I've been missing you.' Miriam heard the wobble in her voice and felt the tears pricking at her eyes. If Ally took her emotional display for pressure, that was just too bad. She could not bear to spend another silent weekend alone. She wanted, desperately, to see this much-loved, if sometimes difficult, daughter.

'And I've been missing you too.' Ally's voice was also thick with tears. 'But the house is still a bit of a renovator's nightmare . . .'

'That's okay. I don't have to stay with you. The last thing you need is a house guest. I could stay in an Airbnb and we could just hang out in beautiful downtown Dungog, or you could take me for a country drive and we could just catch up and chat. I haven't seen you since Dad's funeral.'

Miriam felt bad about how sad and needy she sounded, but it seemed to be just what Ally wanted to hear. Her daughter's voice was warm and eager.

'Would you? That'd be awesome! I'd love to see you and there are lots of great Airbnbs around here. Do you want me to ask around about a decent one?'

'That's alright. I'll google it and find one that's available. I'll finish work early on Friday and drive up.'

'Perfect. Thanks, Mum. I can't wait to see you.'

※

When Prisha returned with her coffee and friand, Miriam could not contain her excitement, or her anxiety.

'She probably just feels sorry for me.'

'Or perhaps losing one parent makes you value the remaining one a bit more than you used to.' Prisha popped the last of her cake in her mouth.

Miriam wiped her sticky fingers on the paper serviette that came with the food. 'I can always rely on you to bring me down to earth.'

'Anyway, it doesn't matter why she wants you to come, just be pleased that she does.'

Prisha was right. Miriam realised she *did* feel pleased. She was looking forward to something for the first time since Pete had died.

CHAPTER 5

Just like its photo online, the Airbnb in Dungog was a charming little convict-era pink-brick cottage with pretty white gables. What the photo had cleverly managed to conceal was its lousy location, wedged between the railway line and the Dungog IGA. The supermarket was rather incongruously called 'Lovey's', as if it catered for a flamboyant crowd of thespians and interior designers rather than the motley crew of local residents currently trundling their shopping trolleys towards their battered and dusty four-wheel drives.

Miriam hoisted her overnight bag out of the boot of her car. The name of the supermarket had amused her, and the mild spurt of pleasure made her wonder if she was starting to 'move on', as everyone seemed to expect her to. Or maybe it was just the prospect of a weekend with Ally that had cheered her up. Her daughter was meeting her for a drink at the craft brewery on the main street in an hour or so, so whatever it might have lacked in the way of views, the cottage was at least conveniently located.

As she put the kettle on and opened the curtains in the small open-plan kitchen/lounge room, she also realised—to her surprise—how nice it felt to be away from her own home. The house she had shared with Pete had reminders of him saturating every surface. The house smelt of him, for a start. A peculiar leathery scent had permeated every piece of clothing he owned due to how much time he spent in his beloved old Merc. He had fussed over its cream leather upholstery so much, it looked as good now as on the day he'd bought the car home from the showroom a decade or more ago. The Merc was sitting in the garage at Greenwich now, gathering dust. She'd have to sell it, she supposed. She sighed.

This pink cottage held nothing of Pete and, although she clung to memories of him in the big house on the North Shore, his absence here was a relief. She could almost pretend that he was waiting for her at home. Despair followed that thought, of course, because he wasn't and never would be again, but she was able to push the feeling aside quite quickly.

As she sat in a chintz armchair sipping tea from a delicate rose-patterned cup (the owners might be taking this 'quaint cottage' thing just a tad too far), she had to admit she felt better. She hadn't realised just how tightly she had been holding every muscle in her body until she had allowed herself to relax. She wondered whether she should take her tea and sit on the wicker chair out on the little front verandah and contemplate the cars coming and going from Lovey's car park, but decided she was happy where she was. A shaft of sunlight was shining through the window, warming her gently, and she felt quite sleepy. It hadn't been a particularly long drive, but she hadn't realised how bone-weary she was until now. *What delicious sleepiness*, she thought. *I can't remember the last time I felt like this.*

She must have nodded off in the overstuffed armchair, because when next she opened her eyes it was darker, and the air coming through the open window was chilly. She got up and closed it quickly, then she ran her hands through her hair to wake herself up. Her unexpected nap was hardly surprising given how poorly she had been sleeping recently, but it was the first time she had nodded off so easily at any time of day since Pete had died. She looked at her watch with a lurch of panic. She had just ten minutes to get to the brewery in time to meet Ally. She'd meant to change and put on a bit of make-up. It was frightening how much she had aged in the last few months, and make-up helped to disguise it (to her own eyes anyway), but there was no time for that now. She quickly ran a brush through her hair, grabbed her warm jacket and stepped outside.

⁂

Dowling Street, Dungog was a main street in the classic Australian country town tradition, wide and straight, with parking along the edges and a cenotaph in the centre of the roundabout. Shop awnings covered most of the footpath, keeping it dry in the rain and cool in the heat. There was a bottom pub and a top pub, and the older residents gathered at one or other of those, but the tourists, weekenders—of whom there were increasing numbers—and new residents frequented the craft brewery and, even at 5 pm, the place was pumping. 'It's the only brewery in town,' Ally had said. 'You can't miss it.' Ally had been right. Miriam just had to follow the noise.

As she drew closer, she saw Ally leaning out from one of the outside tables and waving. Even at this distance, she felt a small shock at the sight of her youngest daughter. Ally looked pale and was wearing a baggy sweatshirt. She looked like she'd pulled on whatever was lying on the floor to go to the laundromat, not like she was stepping out on a Friday night. *But*, Miriam reminded herself, *she's only going out with her mother. No need to dress up or make an effort for me.* She was not sure whether that thought pleased her or depressed her. *Just as well I didn't wear any make-up*, she thought.

Mother and daughter greeted each other with affection, falling into each other's arms. For a beat or two, this filled Miriam's bruised heart to the brim, and then, without even thinking, she went and put her foot in it by pointing at Ally's sweatshirt.

'Bit premature, isn't it?'

Miriam could have bitten off her tongue as soon as the words were out of her mouth. Whatever possessed her to comment on Ally's appearance so soon? They'd literally just stopped hugging one another, which they'd done for rather longer than usual, with Ally almost clinging to her mother in a way that Miriam found delightful and yet also vaguely alarming. Maybe that was why she'd blurted out such a critical remark—she needed, for some unfathomable reason, to re-establish a distance between them. She saw Ally's expression change and her heart sank.

'What's premature?' Ally demanded.

Well, she was in it now . . . 'The baggy jumper. You can't be more than thirteen weeks and you're not showing at all.'

'All my other clothes are a bit tight these days. This is the only thing I feel comfortable in . . . Why? Don't you like it?'

'No, no, it's fine. Sorry. I just got a bit of a surprise. You actually look thinner to me.'

'I've lost weight in my face, but I've gained it on my tits and my belly. I feel a bit self-conscious about it, actually. I just want to cover it up.'

Now Miriam felt worse. Of course she did. Fastidious, elegant Ally had always worked hard to maintain her willowy figure. *Trust me to go straight to the sore spot*, thought Miriam.

'No need,' she said. 'You look marvellous. You always do.'

A few nearby drinkers turned to look at them. Miriam had spoken more loudly than she had intended. Her uneasiness had come rushing back—and then some.

'Don't bullshit me, Mum. I feel like shit, and I look like shit.'

'You're feeling sick?'

'Mostly in the morning, but in the evening I'm knackered. Honestly, poor Nick. His new wife is either throwing up or asleep.'

'I'm sure he doesn't mind.'

'Of course he minds! He's really nice about it. Keeps apologising, as if it's his fault—which it bloody well is—but he wouldn't be human if he didn't mind. And I mind too. I mind a lot.'

'Are you sorry you got pregnant?'

'No, not really. We want kids. I'm just sorry it happened so quickly. It would have been nice to have more time together first.'

Time together. That was what she and Pete would never have again. The thought brought with it a wave of grief that made Miriam feel faint.

'Mum! Are you alright?'

Ally extended a hand, her expression anxious.

Miriam forced herself to smile. 'Yes, fine, fine. Sorry. It happens sometimes. Funny things, anything really, can make me think of your dad.'

'I'm a brute, honestly. I am so sorry. Here's me rabbiting on about morning sickness, when—well, you know . . .'

'Don't apologise, please. You have lost as much as me.'

'No, I haven't. A dad is different from a husband. I see that clearly now.'

'Anyway, life goes on. New life in particular.'

Miriam didn't want to talk about her loss. It was all too raw. She wanted to have a good time, to forget, as far as that was possible.

'I suppose you're sick to death of people giving you advice?' she said. 'Eat dry biscuits as soon as you wake, that sort of thing?'

Ally nodded vigorously and pulled a face. 'I've eaten so many dry biscuits my mouth feels like the Sahara. Speaking of dry mouths, what can I buy you to drink? Before I got knocked up, I really liked the porter.'

'I'll be guided by you. I am not really a beer drinker, as you know.'

'They sell a rosé, if you'd rather.'

'Nope, when in Dungog, do as the . . . what do you call people from here?'

'No idea. Dungogians?'

'Do as the Dungogians do, then.'

It wasn't a particularly funny remark, but it eased the tension, and they both laughed.

Ally went to order their drinks—mineral water for her—and Miriam had a chance to observe her surroundings. They were sitting on an open verandah outside the brewery and the breeze had intensified. Miriam zipped up her puffer jacket and tucked her chin into her scarf. The temperature had dropped and she was grateful for the gas heater above their heads. The crowd was mostly young—well, younger than her, anyway—and a weird mix of private-school country types (moleskins and expensive woollen zip-neck jumpers) and farm and mine workers (high-vis, Blundstones and tatts). Regardless, many of the patrons seemed to know one another and the bar was buzzing with greetings, banter and shouts of laughter. It pained Miriam to notice that no one smiled or hailed her daughter as she wound her way back through the crowd holding their drinks above her head. Even with both her arms high in the air, there was no sign of any baby bump. Her boobs were definitely bigger, though, and Miriam remembered how painful they had been during her own pregnancies. Poor Ally.

'Have you met any nice people since you've moved here, love?'

Miriam took a sip of her beer and found—to her surprise—it was very good. It had a warm, dark, ground-coffee flavour.

'I've been a bit preoccupied.' Ally gestured towards her non-existent belly.

'What about at the vets?'

'Yeah, the girls there are lovely, but they've all got small children, so there's no way they'd be at the brewery on a Friday evening.'

Ally always seemed to know what her mother was thinking, especially if she felt it was in any way anxious or critical.

'That's nice. It's good to know other mothers when you become one yourself.'

Miriam smiled encouragingly at her daughter, but Ally's expression remained neutral. She tried again.

'And what does the doctor say about your nausea?'

'I'm feeling a bit better this week. I couldn't hold any food down for the first few weeks or so, but it's okay now. And the baby is developing normally, according to the twelve-week ultrasound.'

'Do you know what you're having yet?'

Miriam felt a spurt of excitement. She remembered how delighted Pete had been when Fiona and Liam rushed over to tell them that Molly would be a girl. He adored his daughters and was over the moon that he'd have another female member of the family to fuss over. 'I don't know what I'd do with a boy,' she remembered him saying as he raised a glass of champagne to toast the new member of the family. Honestly, he was the best feminist of all of them.

'Yes, we do, but Nick and I have decided not to tell anyone. We think it's more fun to surprise everyone on the day.'

Miriam's excitement died as quickly as it had flared. *You're not even going to tell* me, she thought, hurt. *Not even your mother, who could really use a bit of hope for the future right now.* But, looking at Ally's face, she decided to resist the temptation to play this for sympathy. She was determined not to derail the conversation. Instead, she pulled a brightly wrapped and beribboned parcel out of her tote bag.

'Fiona and I got you this.'

Ally's face lit up as she accepted the gift. She leant forward and kissed her mother on the cheek. The affectionate gesture made Miriam a bit teary. *We're both so fragile*, she reminded herself. *I must not forget that—we're both grieving.* She wiped her eyes unobtrusively as she watched Ally tear at the pale green wrapping paper. *She's still opening gifts the way she did as a little kid*, she thought. *She might be on her way to being a mum, but she's mostly still a little girl.*

'Oh! It's gorgeous!'

Ally held up the canary yellow baby-gro. It had small ducks picked out in pale grey on the pockets and had cost an arm and a leg. Why a baby needed pockets, Miriam had no idea.

'It looks impossibly tiny!'

'It's actually a single zero, for a six-month-old. Fiona said it's better to get something that's too big than too small.'

'Exactly my reasoning.' Ally tugged at her sweatshirt, pulling it out from her body.

Miriam winced inwardly, berating herself again for having spoken without thinking. Ally was still stewing about it, obviously.

'Very sensible, darling. I am sorry. I must learn not to make personal remarks!'

'But then you wouldn't be you, would you?'

Miriam didn't know what to say to this, so she took another large mouthful of the delicious beer. It was disappearing rather quickly, she noticed.

Ally, placing the baby-gro carefully back in its wrapping, leant forward confidentially and put a hand on her mother's knee. 'But how are you? Are you coping? I keep thinking of you all alone in that great big house and wish I could be there to keep you company.'

'You can be there, anytime. My door is always open to you.'

'I wish I could. But don't deflect, Mum. You're always doing that, and you haven't answered my question. How are you? I mean *really*.'

Am I? thought Miriam. *Do I always deflect the conversation back to Ally?* Maybe that was something worth thinking about. She took a deep breath, surprised at how hard it was to be honest about her own feelings.

'I'm . . . coping, I guess. Oddly, I feel much better being here—in Dungog, I mean. I was almost dreading coming away. I was looking forward to seeing you, of course, darling—but I haven't done much since the funeral except go to work, and it felt strange to be packing a bag and making plans. But now I'm here, I feel'—Miriam looked about them as she searched for the words—'a bit more like I'm back in the land of the living somehow.'

And as she said it, she realised it was true. Ever since Pete had gone so brutally and so suddenly, she'd felt half-dead herself.

Ally was nodding. All the tension between them had disappeared.

'I miss Dad all the time. When I think of him it hurts, right here.' Ally put her hand up to her chest and pressed on it. Tears welled up, then rolled down her cheeks. She brushed at them with the end of her sleeve.

Miriam put her hand on her daughter's arm and leant in close. 'Yes, that's how I feel—exactly. I hadn't realised that when people talked about being heartbroken, they meant it literally and not metaphorically. It does feel as if my heart has cracked in two. As if there's a wound in it.'

'I can't imagine how much worse it must be for you. I've got Nick, and bugalugs on the way. That's what we call h—' Ally caught herself just in time and grinned at her mother. 'The baby. But you've lost your life partner, your soul mate, everything!'

'It's worse than that! I've lost the man who put the bins out and changed light bulbs and unpacked the dishwasher and cooked the best spaghetti bolognaise I have ever eaten and ordered the wine and kept our finances under control and cleaned the goddamn shower recess every time he used it! You should see it now. There's mould on the grouting I suspect will never come off. He'd have had a heart attack—if he hadn't had an aneurysm already!'

Ally took a sharp breath and paused, as if unsure how to react, then she started to laugh. Her mother joined in. It might have had an hysterical edge, but it felt good.

'He would've too. Can't you get the cleaners to tackle it?'

'What? Mr and Mrs Once-Over-Lightly? That'll be the day.'

'You should get new cleaners, Mum.'

They'd had this conversation before, but Miriam didn't care enough about the dust gathering in the corners or the mould in the shower to fire the nice Korean couple who had been cleaning the Greenwich house for so long. When Pete was alive, he'd taken care of what they'd missed. Now it was just ignored. Her cleaners were getting older and slacker. Well, so what? So was she.

The conversation moved on to other, safer topics. They reminisced a lot about Pete and their life as a family of four, when the girls were children and life was so much simpler— or so it seemed to Miriam now. Miriam had another of the delicious craft beers. The brewery was clearly a business that took what it was doing seriously.

'How's Julie?' Ally asked.

Julie had lived next door to them for decades and had been widowed herself a few years previously. When they were younger, Miriam and Julie had little in common, disagreeing on politics, religion and education. Miriam thought Julie was ridiculously conservative, while Julie thought Miriam a trendy leftie. But the older they had become, the less those differences seemed to matter, and now the two women were quite close. The Trump presidency had frightened Julie out of some of her more conservative ideas, and the son she was proudest of had come out as gay. To her credit, that had opened Julie's mind to new ideas in a way that nothing else had. Miriam also wondered sometimes if the death of her husband, Graeme, had allowed Julie to form her own ideas. That thought led to another. What would Pete's death do to her and her ideas and beliefs about the world? Nothing? Or everything? Miriam did not pursue that insight. It was for another day. Instead, she groaned and raised both eyebrows in response to Ally's question.

'She's rescued a greyhound!'

'She's done what?'

'Lachy put her up to it.' Lachy was Julie's gay son.

'Bloody hell!'

'Awful, skinny, jumpy thing. It has to wear a muzzle whenever it goes out and I won't go around anymore unless she locks the bloody thing up. It jumps up on me and practically looks me in the eye!'

They both laughed.

'Excuse me, ladies. I'm glad to see you're having such a good time.'

A man with one of those ornate, Victorian paterfamilias beards that were so fashionable was standing beside them. *If you are so glad to see us enjoying ourselves*, thought Miriam, *why are you now interrupting?* But she stayed silent and smiled politely.

The bearded man introduced himself. He was the head brewer and he was doing the rounds of the tables, explaining all about his range. The two women listened courteously as he launched into his spiel. He had rather broken their mood, though, so when at last he moved on to the next table, they finished their drinks and made their way a few doors up the road to the only bistro in town. There, Miriam decided against a bottle of wine—there wasn't much point with Ally not drinking—and instead ordered a gin and tonic and the steak. When Ally gave her a look—Miriam had never been much of a steak eater—she realised she was in a slightly hysterical mood. Perhaps the beer had made her tiddly.

'I know, I know, but it's cattle country around here, isn't it? And when in Dungog . . .'

'Do as the Dungogians do . . .'

And they both laughed for a second time. Was it a release of tension? Deflection? Who knew? Who cared? It was fun.

'I'm so sorry Nick isn't joining us.'

Ally had explained that Nick was on call, so they'd have the night to themselves.

'Yeah, me too. Country vets' hours can be a pain in the arse. He told me to give you his love and said that he's looking forward to cooking up a feast for you tomorrow night.'

Miriam smiled with genuine pleasure. Whatever else Ally was dealing with—unplanned pregnancy, morning sickness, a new town where she knew no one and, of course, bereavement—at least she had Nick.

Their meals had arrived and she sawed at her steak. It was tough and a bit overcooked, but the chat potatoes were delicious. She was now on to her second gin and tonic and definitely a bit drunk, but she couldn't give a flying fuck. She was newly bereaved, a fucking widow for fuck's sake (Pete always said he could tell when she'd had too much because she started swearing like a trooper), and the only upside she could see was that her misery gave her permission to eat and drink and behave as badly as she liked. Well, permission with everyone except Ally. She was still wary of upsetting her youngest, despite the mostly successful evening they'd had so far.

'What does he end up doing when he's on call?'

'All sorts of things, but around here calving is the big thing, apparently. He's probably pulling a calf or something in a freezing paddock somewhere.'

'Pulling a calf?'

Miriam had hardly spent a day in the country in her life, apart from a family holiday when she was a teenager. Oddly enough, they'd spent that holiday not far from Dungog.

'That's what they have to do if the calf gets stuck in the birth canal. Sometimes they use a tractor.'

'Yikes! Rather him than me.'

'Rather the cow than me.'

Miriam was popping another potato into her mouth, and almost choked on it as she burst out laughing. Once she'd stopped coughing and spluttering, she took a breath.

'I'd forgotten how fucking funny you can be, Allison Franklin!'

'Carruthers, Mum, but thanks.'

Buggery bollocks, thought Miriam. *I hate that name.*

She took another deep breath and then swallowed the last of the potato.

'Are you worried about giving birth? It's not as bad as people like to tell you. Just keep your options open so you can get pain relief if you need it. Have you thought about support people and all that? I mean, apart from Nick, of course.'

Miriam had been second support person when Molly was born. Pete had been green with envy. She'd have been only too delighted to do the same for Ally.

'Haven't thought about any of that yet. I was just making a joke.'

Ally was on the defensive again. Miriam backed off.

It was warm in the bistro. There was a crackling fire in the corner burning enormous logs, and Miriam had shed her puffer jacket. She picked up the dessert menu as the waitress took their plates away.

'Shall we have something really sticky and sinful for afters?'

'You go ahead, Mum. I'm feeling a bit stuffed.'

Ally did look tired. Miriam cursed herself for being so inconsiderate.

'Do you think I could have it takeaway?'

'Of course. I'll organise it.'

Ally stood up to attract the waitress's attention, and Miriam fished out her credit card. That was just the sort of excuse to leave the table that Pete had used when he wanted to pay the bill for everyone without the usual fuss and objections.

'My shout, darling.'

'Are you sure, Mum? That's very kind.'

While Ally ordered her a slice of lemon tart to take away, Miriam ignored the rest of the second G&T and reached for the tumbler of water. She did not want to ruin tomorrow with a hangover.

When the waitress returned with the tart in a plastic container, Miriam and Ally put on their coats and hovered by the door—reluctant, perhaps, to finally part . . . or so Miriam hoped.

'Where did you park?' Miriam asked.

'Oh, I sold the car.'

Miriam looked at her daughter. She was full of surprises at the moment.

'Why? Surely you need one more than ever out here.'

'We can't really afford to run it, what with us being on one salary . . . and with a baby coming.'

'One salary? I thought you were working at the vets?'

'Oh, no, that's voluntary. I'm just helping out when they need an extra pair of hands.'

They were standing outside now, facing a deserted Dowling Street, hunched up against the cold.

'But you should be paid for your work. And you should have your own money. It's feminism one-oh-one. A man is not a financial plan.'

'Don't lecture me, Mum.'

'Sorry, sorry, I didn't mean to . . .'

'I know.' Ally sounded annoyed.

'I'm sorry, love, but cut me some slack. I know I'm not as good at the parenting thing as your dad was, but I am here, and I love you very much.'

Ally smiled at her then and hooked her arm through her mother's. 'I know, Mum. I've never doubted it for a minute. I am okay, honestly, I'm just a bit scratchy. After all, my dad is dead, I'm unexpectedly pregnant, I feel sick as a parrot and I've moved to a new town where I don't know anyone. It's just a lot of changes in a very short time. Thank God for Nick. He's the only thing keeping me sane.'

Miriam looked down the deserted street. 'Do you need me to drive you home?'

'No, I've booked the only Uber in town. It'll be here any minute.' Ally looked at her phone. 'It's just turned into Dowling Street.'

Miriam could see the headlights coming towards them. For some unaccountable reason, the sight of them made her feel completely alone.

Maybe it was because Ally was going home to her husband, while Miriam knew that from now on, she would always be going home to no one.

CHAPTER 6

Miriam's first thought when she woke the next morning was to thank God she had not finished that second G&T. Mercifully, she did not have a hangover.

As she lay between the floral sheets (what else?) contemplating the day ahead, she longed for her husband. She'd have been really looking forward to a day exploring the countryside if only Pete had been with her, and he would have taken care of everything. He'd have had a plan and maps of what they must see and where they should go. Instead, the day loomed ahead of her—long, strange and lonely.

She had not realised while he was alive just how much she relied on his ability to take charge. She wished—oh, how she wished—she had not taken him for granted and that she had told him why he was so important to her. She knew he knew he was loved, but did he know *why* he was loved? She couldn't remember ever telling him that, and it was too late now. Of course, she did still talk to him whenever she was on her own—in the shower, making breakfast, straightening up the bed, even cleaning her teeth. She did it at home and she did it here, but her voice just bounced off the walls. Often, she talked to him about Ally, but Pete no longer had any answers. She would have to find those for herself.

Miriam had suspected she would spend Saturday on her own. She hadn't wanted to ask what Ally was doing because she was being very careful not to crowd her. She had wondered last night if Ally might inquire what she intended to do the next day, but her daughter had not brought it up. Now, resisting the temptation to just lie there and mope, Miriam rose, showered, dressed and, after a leisurely breakfast on the rose-patterned china, and with Pete's organisational example in mind, she googled the local points of interest.

Half an hour later she drove out of town to the hundred-year-old Chichester Dam. She followed the winding road down to the park at the bottom of the weir, set among heavily wooded hills, and sat for a while gazing out at the scenery. Like Google had said, it was picturesque, but there was no real point to her being there, except to kill time, and she was not used to doing things on her own. The longing for her husband she had felt when she woke multiplied tenfold. For as long as she could remember, Pete would have been with her at a place like this, carrying her along with his curiosity and enthusiasm. Now she had to motivate herself. It was hard. It was lonely. She sat and shed tears over the huge hole Pete's death had left in her life, even when she was doing simple things that she was meant to enjoy, like going for a walk in a beautiful spot. Then she pulled herself together, dried her eyes and got out of the car.

She wandered along the dam wall and stood for a while staring at the wide, blue sky reflected in the expanse of water below. But the clouds scudding across sky and lake could only hold her attention for so long. Eventually she found a bush path that skirted the water's edge. As she walked, conscientiously trying to appreciate the beauty around her, she was also aware she was doing something for no good reason. She felt conspicuous in her aimlessness, even though there was no one else there to see. When the path narrowed to a track, she decided not to walk any further into the increasingly dense forest. No one knew where she was. If she got lost, how would anyone find her?

Miriam knew she was being silly and overdramatic, but after only fifteen minutes or so, she turned around and retraced her steps to the car park. Cursing how slowly time seemed to be moving, she climbed back into her car and drove on. She was filled with grief and misery but also a kind of resentful self-pity. The intense fury at Pete for daring to die had passed, but she was still angry with him for leaving her. She knew it was irrational but that made no difference. Here she was in the middle of nowhere, and not only did no one know where she was, no one cared.

It was a pretty drive. The winding road she followed clung to the side of the Williams River through rolling farmland, but she hardly noticed it. She was too busy stewing over the unfairness of everything. In a little less than an hour she had reached the entrance to the Barrington Tops National Park. Without anything else to fill the daylight hours that stretched endlessly before her (thanks, Pete; thanks, Ally), she had decided to return to the site of the country holiday of her childhood. It was close enough, and where else did she have to go?

In 1973—or was it '74?—she had visited the area with her mother, stepfather, brother and stepsister. They'd stayed at the famous old Barrington Guest House. She remembered big smoking fires, a dark, wood-panelled interior and a door guarded by a gigantic carved bear. She'd looked it up online that morning, hoping her memories of the fabulous Devonshire teas they'd served could be repeated. No such luck. According to her Google search, the place had burnt down years before and had never been rebuilt. Nevertheless, she remembered it had a beautiful setting and a huge, crystal-clear swimming hole. They'd still be there. She'd found a thermos in the pink cottage and brought her own tea and some gingernut biscuits the hosts had left for her. They weren't scones, but they'd do. She'd take them down to the swimming hole and have an impromptu picnic . . . alone.

The bitumen ended once she entered the forest and she drove slowly along the dirt road to another car park. She had little memory of it, but it looked like it must be the same one that had been there the last time she'd visited. It had survived, at least. It was not as well tended as it had been decades ago, perhaps, but she was relieved to see a couple of other cars parked against the collapsing post-and-rail fence. Miriam pulled up beside them. Reassured by the presence of others, she decided she would walk the rest of the way. There was a barrier across the entrance warning against trespassers. She hesitated for a minute, then decided to press on anyway. She was a real estate agent. She'd use that as an excuse if anyone challenged her.

The potholed driveway leading to the guest house was just as she remembered it, but the horse paddock and stables that had once stood on the left were long gone. She remembered how excited she and Carmen had been when the horses had trotted up to the fence to greet them as they arrived. She and her stepsister had been grumpy after the car journey, complaining loudly about the weight of their bags, but the horses had lifted their mood. The horses had whinnied and, when the girls were close enough, snuffled at their pockets in the hope of a carrot or apple or something. She and Carmen had been both delighted and nervous—giggling and shying away if the horses got too insistent and their muzzles came too close. Now, more than forty years on, Miriam stopped for a minute or two, the better to remember, but there was nothing left to see, just a fallen fence post or two rotting in the long grass.

Looming above where the stables had once stood, a clutch of two-storey wooden cabins had been built on the escarpment. They had not been there, she was sure, when last she'd visited, even though they were by no means new. All of them looked a bit shabby, a bit neglected, as if they stood empty for long periods of time. Time shares most likely, she thought, assessing them with a professional eye.

When she got to the end of the driveway there was little left of the old guest house. The remnants of the once-massive brick chimney, and a few yellow plastic strips with KEEP OUT printed on them fluttering in the breeze. The ruins were fenced off, but she spotted a few old twists of police tape tied around a tree. Miriam raised an eyebrow at that and wondered if there had been questions over how the fire had started. Google had told her the cause was an electrical fault. *That old chestnut*, she thought to herself.

She looked at the collapsed chimney. It must have stood in the central dining room. Now there was just weedy grass, tall saplings and scrabbly bushes surrounding the old bricks. The paddock, like the time shares, looked sad and neglected. Miriam remembered it as being alive with holidaymakers. There had been tame kangaroos lazing about on the grass and an aviary of brightly coloured birds, but there was no sign of any of that now. She remembered kids charging around, free to wander, while their parents sat about talking, playing cards or reading the newspaper. By today's standards, the parents of her childhood had been positively neglectful. They hadn't bothered with sunscreen, hats, insect repellent or even proper shoes. They'd never asked where their children were going, she remembered, they just ran wild, and that was why it had been so much fun.

Her mind was full of all the things that had seemed so firm and solid to her as a child and now were gone. Her mother and Boris, her stepfather, were both dead—in Boris's case unlamented, at least by her. Even her brother, Michael, and stepsister, Carmen, while still alive (as far as she knew), were no longer part of her life. Neither of them had attended Pete's funeral, for example. (*Did I invite them?* she wondered suddenly. She'd been in such a fog she could not remember.) Michael lived in Singapore, doing something fancy and incomprehensible in an investment bank, while Carmen had married a bikie—to her father's horror—and, the last Miriam had heard of her, was living in the boondocks of Townsville. Miriam hadn't seen either of them since they'd gathered for her mother's funeral, God knew how many years ago.

Back in 1973—if that's when it was—they had been a family of sorts. Carmen usually lived with her mother, Boris's ex-wife, Rysia (Miriam was astonished that the woman's name had popped so easily into her head), but she often spent school holidays with her father and his second family. Miriam had loved Carmen in those days. She'd been—what? about six?—with blonde curls and enormous blue eyes. Teenage Miriam had seen her as the little sister she'd always wanted. She'd loved her brother, she supposed, although she couldn't remember ever feeling very positive about him. There was something dark around her memories of Michael, though she had no idea why. At sixteen—seventeen?—he was a morose adolescent with little time for his sisters, but she couldn't remember him ever being worse than grumpy.

'Must you always be so annoying?'

He was always growling at her, even if all she had done was sit down for breakfast or lain down on the flokati rug in the lounge room to watch TV. It was as if any space she took up was too much space. She'd fought back, of course, using the only weapon she had—her relative weakness as a younger sister. She'd used it to try to enlist her mother on her side.

'Michael's being mean to me!'

'Michael, stop being mean to your sister.' A useless response, as all of them knew.

'I hate you!' she'd hiss at him, teary with impotence.

'I hate you too,' he'd reply, grinning in triumph.

He was kinder to Carmen, but only when no one was looking. Her brother had never changed, as far as Miriam was concerned. He'd been spectacularly grumpy and unpleasant at their stepfather's funeral, not bothering to conceal how little he wanted to be there, despite their mother's obvious distress. Even the ever-charming Pete had been unable to coax a civil word out of him. Adult Michael had behaved just like the entitled adolescent of old, despite being a father himself and, apparently, a big deal professionally. He'd glowered at the other mourners. It had the desired effect. Everyone had left him alone.

Sister and brother exchanged cards at Christmas, although Miriam was sure Ming, Michael's wife, sent them. Did she miss him? No. Maybe the idea of him. If they had been closer, maybe he could have been a comfort to her now. But it was no use pining for what might have been. He had his life and she had hers. Or she used to.

She was walking down the track to the swimming hole, or 'Crystal Pool' as it appeared to be called now, but she wasn't paying much attention to her surroundings. She was lost in the past.

She tried to remember her mother as she was on that holiday, but she could not. She always felt guilty about the woman who had given birth to her, probably because Carol had died a shadow of her former self, unrecognisable due to the ravages of dementia. Sometimes Miriam took out old photos of her mother to try to replace the image of the wizened child she'd been at the end with a picture of the vital young woman of Miriam's childhood. It did no good. Carol was fixed in Miriam's mind as the bewildered, whimpering shell of a person she had been when she died. That was one reason why Miriam was so pleased she'd remembered Rysia's name. In the back of her mind, she was always alert for signs that she too was succumbing to Alzheimer's. She recalled how her demented mother had irritated her, how impatient she had been with her sometimes, how relieved she had been to pack her off to a home for the frail and aged. If she did succumb to Alzheimer's, she hoped her own daughters would show more compassion.

I am impatient with neediness, Miriam thought, with a flash of insight. *It makes me uncomfortable. I pull away from it. Allison is the same. That's why when I push for intimacy, she retreats from it. I taught her how to do that and now I am suffering the consequences.* Miriam laughed ironically at her own stupidity. *Maybe that's also why I'm so relieved that Nick has taken her off my hands. We have always brought out the worst in one another. Maybe Mum and I were like that too. Maybe that's why I always feel so bad when I think about her, dribbling in her chair with a blanket over her knees in the common room of that awful home we shut her up in.*

As their mother declined, Miriam remembered how angry she had been with Michael for not being there, for not helping, for being safely overseas in Singapore.

Her mother had loved her two children, but the only person she had really adored was Boris. God only knew why. Miriam had hated her stepfather; hated him with an intensity that had lasted long past her adolescence, long past his own death. She could feel the hatred again now, in this place, at this minute. He never actually did anything to her. It was just that whenever they'd been in the same room—something she'd tried to avoid as much as possible—he'd given her the creeps. She supposed it was inevitable that she'd remember him again in this place, where they had spent that one holiday. A cloud went over the sun, and Miriam shivered in her puffer jacket.

Poor old Boris, she thought now. He'd been saddled with supporting two families on a fairly average wage. That's why they'd had to live in the Housing Commission place in Allambie. Miriam remembered how ashamed she had been walking home from school, when she'd turned left into the estate while all her friends went straight ahead to the more salubrious houses in the new developments. Miriam had blamed Boris for their poverty, even though she had always known that wasn't fair.

Boris had repelled her even as he lay on his deathbed, hooked up to wires and machines, a victim of mesothelioma. She'd tried to feel pity for him, but she'd failed. When he'd gasped out his last and the nurse had finally closed his protuberant eyes while her mother sobbed her grief into his lifeless chest, Miriam had felt nothing but relief. She still didn't know why she hated her stepfather. Jealousy, she supposed. *Poor Mum. I must have been a very difficult daughter*, Miriam thought. She had more sympathy for Carol now.

'Can't you at least try to be nice to Boris, for my sake?'

She remembered her mother was always asking her that sort of question. Teenage Miriam had just folded her arms and shaken her head.

'What has he ever done to you?'

Fourteen-year-old Miriam did not reply, just shrugged.

Her poor mother had sighed with frustration. 'It's not Boris you should be mad at—it's your shoddy excuse for a father who deserves it.'

That just made her hate Boris even more. She had no memory of her real father—he'd left when she was very young—but she still resisted seeing goggle-eyed Boris as some kind of replacement, perhaps because that was what her mother seemed to want.

'Boris is staring at me!'

'Don't be ridiculous, Miriam!'

Boris had large, droopy brown eyes in a fleshy face. It was easy to accuse him of staring and his eyes did disturb her. Just as her brother resented her taking up any space at all, so Miriam had resented the presence of Boris. Even looking at her was too intrusive. It was as if he wanted something from her that she could not give. That was why meeting Pete had been such a delight. His love had been light, warm and undemanding. She had returned it as much for that reason as any other. He gave her space and made her feel better about herself. (Damn, she must not think about him like that, it only made her want to cry.) All her other experiences of love had weighed her down. Pete's love had lifted her up.

Shaking her head to rid herself of the ghosts of Boris and her mother, Miriam continued walking down the steps carved into the river rock that led to the swimming hole. She and Carmen had spent wonderful afternoons in the freezing-cold waters of the Williams River on that long-ago holiday.

It was too cold even to contemplate swimming, but there was a group of people having a picnic on the rocky beach— the owners of the other cars, she assumed—and so she walked further along, away from the prime position they had claimed. She found a log she could sit on fairly comfortably and unpacked her thermos and the gingernuts. She wished she'd brought a sandwich or something as well. She was hungry.

The river was just as she remembered it. Deep and wide, with slow-moving greenish water flowing past the cliffs that lined either side. Above was the rainforest, thick and impenetrable. Moss and lichen covered the lower trunks and whole ecosystems of bird's nest ferns, staghorns and orchids filled the tree branches as high as she could see. Birds shrieked and chortled and twittered, their calls echoing off the rocky outcrops. She could also hear the occasional plop of things moving in the river—catfish, frogs, eels. She and Carmen had been terrified of the eels. Now she was glad they were still around. It meant the river was healthy.

She drank her tea and ate half a packet of gingernuts, flicking the crumbs to a spot where the birds could find them. Then she just sat for a while, watching the water eddy and flow around the river rocks. The cliff opposite was sheer, the water deep and slow-moving below it.

She and Carmen had loved yelling rude words from the riverbank and hearing them come echoing back. Michael had sneered at them for being juvenile as he pranced about in his boardies, flicking his blonde hair back in a vain attempt to get some of the older girls to notice him. They never did. The only one of them the glamorous girls paid any attention to was Carmen, because she was 'soooo cute'. Their attention, while it lasted, had made Carmen an unbearable show-off, no longer interested in her daggy stepsister. When tagging along had become tiresome, Miriam had escaped to a spot like the one she was sitting in now. The occasional bark of laughter she could hear from the picnickers who were now out of sight took her right back.

Despite Carmen's temporary defection, Michael's scorn and her mother's neediness, Miriam had enjoyed the holiday. It was easy to keep away from Boris. And when the older girls got sick of Carmen, which they did fairly regularly, the two of them went happily back to mucking about in the river. She and Carmen had gone for a trail ride every afternoon. Carmen had wangled the weekly fee out of her dad, and insisted that Miriam had to join her, as she could not possibly go alone.

Miriam could almost hear the creak of the leather saddles and smell the warm, salty animal aroma of the horses. Hers had been a chestnut called Jimmy and Carmen's a palomino called Magnolia. Again, she couldn't believe she had remembered their names so easily. 'Fuck you, Alzheimer's!' she said out loud. The words echoed back to her across the water, and she looked in the direction of the picknickers and covered her mouth. She heard nothing. Maybe they'd left or had not noticed.

She was enjoying her memories now. *What had made that particular holiday so memorable?* she wondered. The lack of parental supervision? The ease of maintaining a distance from Boris? The long, warm, busy days filled with other kids and interesting and unusual things to do? All of that, no doubt. But looking back on it, she thought it was Carmen who had made it special. She had loved having a little sister to teach, guide and protect. (*I must look up her address in Townsville*, she thought, *and see how she is doing.*) Or maybe she just remembered the holiday so well because she was back here and surrounded by so many reminders.

After a while, Miriam's bum began to ache from sitting on the uneven log and she decided it was time to leave and go back to her little pink cottage. It wasn't until she was backing her car out of the overgrown car park that it dawned on her she had spent large chunks of the afternoon without thinking obsessively about Pete. This place belonged to a time long before she had ever met him. Perhaps that was what had made the memories so bearable.

❧

That evening, dressed smartly and wearing full make-up, she drove out of town to Ally's place. It was easy to find. There really weren't many opportunities to make a wrong turn in the back blocks of Dungog, and she'd made herself wait until the last moment to leave. Desperate as she was to speak to another person—she'd realised she had not said a word to anyone but herself all day—she did not want to seem needy or over-eager.

Ally and Nick were living in a small weatherboard cottage at the end of a long straight driveway. Even in the fading light she could see it had been newly painted and that the young couple had made a stab at taming the garden. The house looked cosy and well cared for, with yellow light streaming from its windows and wood smoke rising from the small brick chimney. She parked her car behind Nick's jeep and stepped out onto the gravel. *I shouldn't have worn heels*, she thought, looking down. She walked up onto the wooden verandah, a good bottle of red under her arm. Then she stopped. Her real estate agent's trained eye had picked up a feature she hadn't expected to find on a charming little cottage like this in the middle of nowhere. Above the front door was a state-of-the-art camera, part of a sophisticated security system. It was the sort of thing you might see at the entrance of an upmarket house in the city, protecting all the valuables within. It looked out of place here.

Before she could knock, Nick—who must have heard her tyres on the gravel—threw open the door, a huge and welcoming smile on his face. 'Miriam! We're so glad you're here.'

Delighted by the warmth of his greeting, she immediately felt at home. Pulling a face, she pointed up at the camera.

Nick gave a self-deprecating grin. 'I know. It's totally OTT, but one of my clients gave it to me as a thankyou for saving his prize bull. He even came and installed the bloody thing, so I couldn't exactly say no. We've never turned it on.'

'Why didn't you put it up at the vet surgery?'

'Because he gave it to me, not the business. Buggered if I was going to give it to them! Anyway, they've already got CCTV. I should probably sell it on eBay, but I don't want to seem ungrateful.'

'Fort Knox!'

'Hardly. Come on inside, where it's warm.'

They stepped into the narrow front hallway, also newly painted, and Nick held his hand out to take her coat.

'Sonny! Your mother is here.'

Ally poked her head around the doorjamb of what was presumably the kitchen. She grinned at Miriam. 'Hey, Mum. Go through to the lounge room—the fire is lovely. I'll bring you a drink. Nick's preparing dinner.'

And a good job he'd made of it too, Miriam thought as they gathered around the table a little while later to enjoy roast chicken with all the trimmings followed by an old-fashioned apple pie with custard.

'It's just like the meals they used to serve at Barrington Guest House,' Miriam commented.

'Where?'

'Oh, just a place where I went on holidays when I was a girl. I went back there today.'

'Never heard of it.'

'No, it burnt down years ago.'

Miriam waited for either of them to ask her to tell them more, but they didn't. *The young are so rarely interested in the doings of the old*, she thought, and another wave of missing Pete flooded through her. He would have been interested. He would have listened. He would have wanted to know. With effort, she swallowed her hurt feelings and concentrated on scraping the last skerrick of custard from her bowl. Then she put down her spoon and leant back in her chair.

'That was wonderful—a real country-style roast dinner.'

'When in Dungog . . .' said Ally.

'Do as the Dungogians do,' Miriam finished, and they laughed.

'Dungogians?' queried Nick.

'Well, what do you call people from around here?' Miriam asked.

'I don't know. The locals often refer to the place as Dead Dog. There's even a cafe by that name in town. It's a funny little place, but we're happy here, aren't we, Sonny?'

And Nick looked at his wife with such affection that Miriam had to glance away. It felt intrusive to watch. She also felt a stab of pure envy. *No one will ever look at me like that again*, she thought. *Not ever.*

'Blissful!' said Ally, and she got up from her chair and put her arms around her husband's neck to emphasise the point.

'I should hope so!' Miriam said. 'It'd be a bit sad if you were anything else at this stage of your relationship.'

She stood up and began to gather the dessert plates, but Ally held up a hand to stop her. 'No, Mum, leave it—let me.'

'I'll do it.' Nick stood up.

'That's not fair,' said Ally. 'You cooked the meal.'

'So what? You and Miriam should catch up. It'll take me no time.'

'Nick's very hands-on,' Miriam observed as she joined Ally on the couch by the fire.

'Yeah, it's great. He reminds me of Dad. He doesn't see jobs as male or female. They're just jobs that need doing and he's happy to do them.'

'As it should be.'

'I'm teaching him to make spaghetti bolognaise. Dad's recipe.'

Miriam's heart lurched a little.

Nick joined them at that moment. Gesturing to Miriam's empty glass, he said, 'Shall I fetch another bottle?'

'Not for me, obviously.' Ally was on mineral water.

'And don't open one on my account,' Miriam chimed in. 'I have to drive.'

'Not a lot of RBTs round here. Anyway, I'd like another.'

Nick opened a second bottle and poured Miriam a hefty slug, which she ignored.

'And speaking of driving, you know how you told me that you can only afford to run one car at the moment, Ally? Well, I had a brainwave today while I was out exploring.' She picked up her glass and took a small sip. 'Your dad's car—the beloved Merc—is just sitting in the garage gathering dust. I was thinking I ought to sell it, but the idea of handing it on to strangers just feels disloyal somehow . . . and then I thought, why not give it to you?'

'Oh no, Mum, that's far too generous.'

'It's not generous at all. You'd be doing me a favour. Relieving me of yet another thing I have to sort out—and it's exactly what your dad would have wanted.'

'It's very kind of you, of course, but we couldn't possibly—'

Miriam cut Ally off. 'I insist, especially with a baby on the way. What if you're out here on your own and Nick's in the boondocks somewhere out of range—pulling a calf, or saving the life of a prize bull or whatever—and something goes wrong? You need a car, and I have a car that needs an owner. Problem solved.'

'Well, it would make life much easier, especially when the baby comes, and even before then—like when I have to go to Maitland to see the obstetrician . . .'

'I think it's a brilliant idea, Miriam,' Nick said. 'We hated having to sell Ally's car, but we really needed a new bed and a couch, and my salary is not, well, not yet what I hope it will be one day.'

'I only have one condition,' Miriam told them.

'What's that?' asked Ally cautiously.

'You have to look after Dad's cream leather upholstery. It's what he would have wanted.'

'Done!'

And for a moment, Miriam felt elated. Another problem solved and her daughter would benefit. Then, just as suddenly, she felt bereft. Another piece of Pete gone; another confirmation that he was never, not ever, coming back.

Miriam picked up her glass and drained it dry.

CHAPTER 7

Theodore Nicholas Peter Carruthers—Teddy, Ted—was born on a Thursday in the first week of October.

'It's a boy!' Nick announced joyfully over the phone.

'Oh, congratulations! And everything went well, Ally is okay?'

'A bit sore, poor darling. It dragged on a bit, but she got there in the end.'

'And the baby?'

'Three point one kilos and gorgeous. Yelled his lungs out as soon as he emerged.'

Nick sounded giddy with delight. His excitement was infectious and Miriam felt overwhelmed by joy.

'I can't wait to see him!'

'I'll text you a photo.'

'No, in person—I'll come as soon as I can!'

Miriam had not waited until she drove to Maitland, however, to talk to Ally. Nick had asked her not to call until the next morning, to give Ally a chance to sleep. At 9 am on the dot, she called her daughter and, for once, Ally immediately picked up.

'Did I wake you?' Miriam asked.

'Don't be silly!' Ally snorted sardonically. 'This is the place sleep forgot! I've been awake for hours.'

'It's lovely to hear your voice, and congratulations on Teddy. Is he gorgeous? And how are you? How did it go? Are you alright?'

'I'm better today. I was wiped out yesterday. And Teddy is lovely. But, Mum! What a trip! It was nothing at all like I expected.'

It never is, thought Miriam, despite all the books, prenatal classes and YouTube videos.

'Tell me all about it, darling. Every gory detail.'

Ally giggled and launched into a blow-by-blow description of the birth. As is the case with most births, it was not without its complications. Miriam listened quietly as her daughter talked. She remembered her own need to do the same, particularly after Fiona's traumatic arrival, which had included suction and more stitches than she now cared to recall. She had needed to tell every detail to anyone who would listen—which turned out to be her own mother. Carol, she recalled guiltily, had listened as patiently as she was listening now. *I was not fair to my mother*, she realised. *Perhaps we never are. Mothers get the negative download their offspring dare not tell anyone else. There's no need to charm your mother*, she thought, *which is both a compliment and a burden.*

How Miriam wished she could have been at Teddy's birth, even if just to offer encouragement. To her great regret, Nick and Ally had decided they did not need a second support person.

'Nick's practically a doctor anyway, Mum,' Ally had told her over the phone, 'and helping an animal give birth is not really all that different from helping a human do it.'

That comparison had caused Miriam to raise her eyebrows so high they threatened to leave her face.

'What I mean is, he's not the usual clueless new father who needs someone there to hold his hand.'

'Whatever you want, darling. This event isn't about me.'

Perhaps Miriam's voice had betrayed her, because Ally added, 'I'm sorry if you're disappointed, Mum.'

Miriam had pulled herself together. *Don't be so self-pitying, woman*, she'd imagined Pete saying to her.

'Oh, Ally, don't give it another thought! I won't. I'm just so excited for you both and I cannot wait to meet my new grandchild and find out if it's a him or a her.'

'It's a him.'

Miriam had remained silent for a beat or two. Ally had surprised her. She had been resigned to not knowing. She was delighted, both by the news and the confidence.

'That's fant—'

'Don't tell anyone,' Ally broke in. 'I shouldn't have told you. Nick and I agreed.'

'I won't breathe a word. And everyone will know in a few weeks, anyway. But, thank you for telling me. I feel very privileged.'

'You are my mum. I always felt mean, not telling you, particularly after Dad . . .' Ally's voice had sounded small and wobbly as it trailed away.

'Yes. He'd have loved all this,' she'd said.

'I can't wait to meet my new grandchild,' she said again now, when Ally had finished her recount of the birth. 'I'll see you this evening.'

※

Miriam was tired and frazzled by the time she squealed into a parking space outside the small regional hospital in Maitland. She'd driven hell for leather from Sydney in Pete's Merc, leaving the minute her last meeting ended. She would leave the car with Ally, and Fiona could drive them both home on Sunday night. She'd been terrified a breakdown, roadworks (they never seemed to finish the M1 before they started digging it up again) or an accident might make her miss visiting hours. She made it by the skin of her teeth.

When she entered Ally's room, however, it was crowded with people she did not know, all of whom appeared to be related to Nick. For a moment, standing at the door, she wondered if she had the right room. The faces that turned to look at her were obviously wondering the same. It was the sight of Nick, towering above everyone else, that reassured her she was in the right place. He smiled and gestured for her to come in.

'Get out of the way, you lot. Grandma has arrived.'

Miriam wasn't sure how she felt about being called Grandma in front of a bunch of strangers, but she took his welcome in the spirit in which it was intended. As she pushed through the crowd, she caught sight of Maurice, Nick's dad, sitting in a visitor's chair by the window. He looked a bit lost. She nodded at him but he appeared not to recognise her.

'Mum!'

There was such emotion in her daughter's voice that Miriam's uneasy feeling of being an outsider disappeared. She managed to elbow the last person out of her way.

'Oh, Ally! Well done. How wonderful.'

She leant forward and kissed her daughter, being careful not to bump the sleeping baby Ally held close to her chest.

'Would you like to hold him?'

Would she! She held out both hands.

The warm weight of this mysterious little person felt immediately familiar. Holding her grandson in her arms, she felt an uncomplicated joy she had not felt since Pete had died, almost a year before.

In fact, the squishy, purple-faced newborn reminded her of her husband. Whether this was due to her desperate need to see him reborn in her grandson, or an actual resemblance, she did not know. And she didn't care. He was a boy, he was related to Pete, also a boy. That was all the resemblance she needed. One male had left the world, another had entered it. She would cherish Teddy as much for that as anything else. And even though she wasn't remotely religious (the word 'spiritual' made her squirm) or into the supernatural at all she did have an odd feeling, as if Pete had patted the little boy on the head and sent him on his way before he arrived. Anointed him, almost. She knew this was silly, but the idea gave her comfort.

She looked at the black hair standing straight up on the top of his head and took a deep breath. The delicious smell of milky newborn took her back to her own early days caring for a baby. *Motherhood's like riding a bike*, she thought. *You never forget how.* She stared at Teddy with delight for some time before she remembered that it was Ally she was here to see.

'He's beautiful, darling. I think I see your dad in him.'

She had not realised that Nick's mother was hovering just over her shoulder.

'Do you think?' Sally asked. 'He's the image of Nick as a baby. Here, I've got a photo.' She began rummaging in her bag.

Miriam turned her head slightly and managed to smile, but she felt irritated. *Let us have our moment*, she thought. *It's my daughter who has done all the hard work.* She didn't bother to focus on the photo the woman gave her, although she took it politely.

'Really?' she replied, handing it back. 'I can't see it myself.'

No wonder—her reading glasses were in her bag.

With the little boy in her arms, Miriam leant towards her daughter. 'You know, I did feel a little frustrated, not knowing if the baby was a boy or a girl, but now he is here, I can see why you kept it a secret. It makes him even more of a lovely surprise.'

Ally looked at her mother and widened her eyes. 'Thanks, Mum.'

Miriam felt closer to Ally than she had for ages, but Nick's mum was still at her shoulder.

'You're nicer than I am,' she said. 'I was furious with them for not telling me.'

The smug delight Miriam felt at being the only parent who had been confided in was petty, juvenile and mean. She knew that, but it didn't stop her taking pleasure in it.

Sally was standing as close to the baby as she dared without actually ripping poor Ted out of Miriam's arms. *This woman has a problem with personal space,* she thought, as she took a step backwards.

～

Walking back to her car a few minutes later, she felt ashamed of herself. When had she become so territorial? Why did she feel so possessive about her daughter and, now, her grandson? Maybe this was some sort of weird response to losing Pete. Maybe that loss, still so raw, had made her desperate to feel special. She didn't come first with anyone anymore, she knew that, but she'd be damned if she'd be demoted to second.

On the recommendation of Prisha, whose sister Diya lived in Maitland, Miriam had booked rooms at Maggies in Bolwarra. It was only a few kilometres from the hospital, walkable if she felt energetic. Fiona would be joining her the next day.

Maggies turned out to be a rambling weatherboard cottage set in a pretty private garden. Prisha was as proficient at recommending accommodation as she was at everything else. There was no restaurant, although breakfast was provided, but—thank God—there was a bar. Miriam dropped her bag in her allocated room (quaint with an iron bedstead) and made her way to the lounge. It was a large room with generous couches, a piano and a crackling fire. She was the only guest enjoying its comforts at that moment, so she settled back on the nearest couch with her iPad and ordered champagne.

When it arrived, she poured a glass and raised it in a silent toast to Theodore Nicholas Peter Carruthers. It was a pity to be toasting the family's newest member on her own, but Fiona hadn't been able to get away. Still, they'd have a nice day together tomorrow, hopefully spent with Ally and Teddy—and Nick too. The next day was Saturday, and although country vets worked all hours—as Ally was fond of reminding her—it would be nice to spend more time with her new son-in-law. Really, she still hardly knew him. *I must get to know him properly, the way I do Liam,* she thought. *He is the father of my grandson.* Mind you, there would be plenty of time for that. Nick and Ally were still clearly besotted with one another and wanted to spend all their time together, but the demands of a newborn might make the presence of a helping hand in the form of a mother-in-law more desirable. The important thing was that both her daughters were happy in their marriages, and she was happy for them.

Other people's marriages were always a mystery, she mused, thinking wryly of some of her girlfriends who had married men she could not stand. It was Carmen's choice of husband that had led to them losing touch. He'd disliked Miriam on sight, rightly suspecting she did not approve of him. Pete always told her she was a terrible snob. Worse, he found her pretensions hilarious, given he was the posh one and she'd been raised in a Housing Commission home. She hadn't liked it when he'd teased her about that.

Carmen's husband had whisked her away straight after their rushed (shotgun, they called it then) wedding and she'd hardly seen her stepsister since. And then there was Prisha's marriage. Her husband said very little, and when he did speak it was always in a formal manner. He seemed disapproving to Miriam. And he treated Prisha as if she was a servant and he was her boss. Fetch this, do that, pour the other. *I* am *her boss*, thought Miriam, *and I would never treat her the way he does.* Prisha just accepted it. *Perhaps it was cultural*, Miriam thought, and then admonished herself for being racist as well as judgemental.

Miriam had just poured a second glass of champagne and was scrolling idly through her emails, trying to avoid getting caught up with work, when her phone rang. Glancing at the caller ID, she saw it was Ally.

'Hello, darling,' she said.

'Did you tell anyone Teddy was a boy?' Ally demanded. 'Before he was born, I mean?'

The accusation, so unexpected—and so unfair—took Miriam's breath away. She sat up straight. 'No! I didn't tell a soul. I promised I wouldn't and I didn't!'

'Not even Fiona?'

'Not even Fiona. Why? What makes you think I did?'

'It's not that I *think* you did, I'm just worrying that you did. They're different.'

Not very, thought Miriam, but she held her tongue. 'Well, even if I did, would it have really been so bad?'

'Yes! I shouldn't have told you. Nick and I agreed, and I broke the agreement. It's the first secret I've ever kept from him and . . . I don't know, I'm just feeling guilty and ashamed about it. I feel like I betrayed him.'

'Don't you think you're overreacting a little bit? Just come clean. Tell him you told me. I'm sure he won't mind. It's hardly a hanging offence, telling your mum—your *bereaved* mum—the gender of your baby.'

'That's not the point! I just shouldn't have told you, that's all. I broke the deal. Me.'

Miriam could hear a note of hysteria in Ally's voice. 'Are you alright, darling?'

'Yes. No. I don't know.'

'It can be very unsettling having a new—'

'I DON'T KNOW ANYTHING ANYMORE!' Ally wailed.

Poor Ally—it sounded as if she had a case of the baby blues.

'Do you want me to come?' Miriam asked. 'I can be there in a few minutes.'

Thank God she'd only had a few sips of the second champagne. She reached for her handbag with one hand, fumbling with the bloody iPad with the other, while pressing the phone to her ear with her shoulder.

'I . . . don't . . . know . . . if . . . they . . . will . . . let . . . you . . . in . . .'

Miriam could just make out the words between sobs.

'Let me worry about that. I'll be there asap.'

She grabbed the champagne bottle as she rushed out the door, ramming the cork back in as hard as she could. They would need all the help they could get.

⁂

When she arrived at the hospital, she squared her shoulders and marched through the automatic doors. Pete had always said if you want to get in somewhere, walk in like you own the place. Her purposeful stride only slightly undermined by the champagne bottle under her arm, she paused at the front desk, ready to do battle. It was deserted. She almost felt deflated as she hurried to the lift.

She paused outside the closed door of Ally's room, steeling herself for whatever state she might find her daughter in. Then she took a deep breath and entered—to see the happiest little family in the Hunter. Ally was sitting up in bed, pale but otherwise calm. She was holding Teddy, who was wrapped in a spotless white baby blanket. Nick stood beside them both, his hand resting on Ally's shoulder, grinning from ear to ear. It was as if they were posed for a photograph.

'Miriam! Thank you for coming so quickly. A girl really needs her mother at a time like this.'

'I'm so sorry.' Once again, Miriam felt like an intruder. Perhaps she was the one who was overreacting. 'I thought you'd be on your own, Ally.' She considered her daughter more closely and saw how anxious she looked. 'Are you alright, darling?'

Ally nodded, but big tears ran down her face.

'I think you have a case of the baby blues,' Miriam said, wanting to comfort her. 'It happens to us all. It's hormonal.'

Ally nodded, but the tears kept falling.

'I'm sorry I worried you.'

'Don't be silly. That's what I'm for.'

'And it's also what champagne's for!' Nick added, reaching for the bottle in her hand. 'Here do you want me to . . .? Oh, I see it's already open—even better. And, sorry, all we have is water glasses. They don't run to champagne flutes in this establishment, so I hope they'll do.'

'Are you sure you're alright, darling?' Miriam asked, her attention still on her daughter.

Ally's eyes were red and her chin was trembling, but she said, 'I'm fine.'

Miriam was not convinced, but before she could say anything, Nick handed her a glass and passed one to Ally, who took it and smiled shakily at them both.

'Sorry. I feel like an idiot now.'

'Don't be so hard on yourself,' Miriam told her. 'Pregnancy and childbirth are huge! They change your body, your life, everything. I think the fact that all that women do is shed a few tears in response rather than go bonkers is extraordinary!'

'Some of them do go bonkers.'

Both Nick and Miriam let that scared little remark pass but not before they'd exchanged a worried glance. Miriam changed the subject.

'Has your milk come in yet, Ally?'

Ally nodded her head and began to cry properly. Miriam was sympathetic but she also felt relief. This was a misery she could understand. She remembered the torture vividly. That alone would explain the wailing.

'Are they very painful?'

Ally kept crying and nodded even harder.

'It's awful. Did they give you cabbage leaves?'

Ally pulled down the neck of her nightie to reveal the leaves cupping what Miriam knew from bitter experience would be tight, red, painful breasts.

Nick opened his eyes wide. 'Cabbage leaves? And the medicos look down on us vets! I must try cabbage leaves on a cow with mastitis next time. Who knew?'

'They put the leaves in the freezer,' Miriam explained. 'They cool your breasts down without being uncomfortably cold. And lactating women can't take many drugs, for obvious reasons.'

'Except Panadol.'

'Panadol doesn't even touch the sides of the agony of having two burning hot rocks on the front of your chest. You blokes don't know you are born.'

'Well, Teddy certainly doesn't seem to have a clue he has been.'

Nick said this so tenderly, Miriam felt suddenly teary herself.

'He's very sleepy. Is that normal?' The anxiety in Ally's voice was heartbreaking.

'Totally normal, darling. He is a perfect little baby in every way.'

'May I have a cuddle?' Nick looked around for somewhere to put down the champagne bottle and glass he was still carrying.

Ally passed Teddy to her mother. Nick came up to her, arms outstretched. Miriam resisted the temptation to hold onto the baby. 'Here you go, Dad.' She passed him to his father.

Nick took Teddy gently and carefully.

Then it was Miriam who burst into tears. She'd said those exact words more than thirty years ago to her own husband when Fiona had been born, and the memory had caught her unawares.

'I'm so sorry,' she said to her son-in-law and daughter, when she'd blown her nose and composed herself. 'I was just thinking about Dad and how much he would have loved this little boy.'

CHAPTER 8

'I don't like him.'
Fiona had arrived at Maggie's an hour before.
'That's a bit harsh!' Miriam objected. 'You just don't know him yet.'
'I don't like him. Nor does Liam.'
Miriam's heart sank. Ally was having a hard enough time already without her sister taking a set against the husband she loved so much.
'Well, keep it to yourself. Your sister adores him.'
Mother and daughter were sharing a pot of tea in the garden while they waited for hospital visiting hours. Miriam had just finished telling Fiona about the previous evening. How desperate Ally had sounded over the phone. The surprise of finding Nick there when she'd arrived. That's when Fiona had blurted out her dislike of her new brother-in-law.
Miriam felt like she had enough on her plate already. She had woken in the middle of the night and had nauseating thoughts about post-partum psychosis. Miriam couldn't banish her anxiety

about how this difficult daughter of hers was coping. That sad little remark Ally had made about some new mothers going bonkers had gone around and around inside her head. Thirty years ago, Miriam had a friend who'd developed the condition after the birth of her first child, and it had been terrifying to watch a normally sensible woman become paranoid. She was convinced she was being spied on and that people were out to kill her. Miriam could not bear the thought of something like that happening to her daughter. After watching her mother succumb to dementia, Miriam had a fear of madness, of losing control.

'She got herself in quite a state about breaking the pact she'd made with Nick that they'd keep Teddy's gender to themselves, crying about how she'd betrayed him. It was completely out of proportion. I mean, it's not even an important secret. Everyone knows his gender now, only a few weeks later.'

'Lots of people are weird about revealing the baby's gender these days, Mum. They even have gender reveal parties.'

Miriam was horrified. 'You're kidding?'

'I'm afraid I'm not.'

'Anyway, whether I thought her secret was important or not, I would never have told anyone!'

'Well, you certainly never told me.'

Shit, now Fiona felt excluded. *I may never forget how to be a mother*, Miriam thought, *but sometimes I wish I'd never learnt in the first place.*

'How could I tell you? I was sworn to secrecy.'

'Would you like me to freshen the pot?'

The woman who ran the guest house was standing by their table. They had been so absorbed in their conversation they had not noticed her approach. Miriam nodded. The tea had gone cold. After the woman had gone, Miriam changed the subject.

'Anyway, why don't you like Nick? He always seems perfectly charming to me, and your sister obviously adores him.'

Fiona sighed. 'Maybe I'm not being fair. I mean, you're right, I don't know him very well. Perhaps it's because the pair of them are so bloody gorgeous. I never feel dumpier or sillier than when Nick is around. Or shorter!'

'It's not like he can help being so tall.'

But Miriam sympathised with Fiona about how it felt to be short around tall people. Fiona had inherited her lack of height from her mother.

'And he never actually looks at me. I'm not pretty enough, I suspect.'

Ally had been blessed with all the looks in the family, it was true. Fiona was shorter, stockier and had an intelligent face rather than a conventionally pretty one.

'Men who judge women on their looks are fools.'

'There are lots of fools around then, Mum.'

It hurt Miriam to think that her clever, efficient and warm-hearted oldest daughter felt overlooked and undervalued. Sometimes it was hard not to hate men as a species. But then she remembered Pete and lovely Liam and, of course, Teddy.

'Whatever else Nick may be, I don't think he's a fool.'

Fiona just gave her mother a doubtful look. Miriam was starting to feel irritated. It wasn't like Fiona to wallow in self-pity.

'Cut him some slack, Fi. He just doesn't have eyes for anyone but his wife.'

'Sonny?' Fiona said the name in a sarcastic voice.

'Your father always called me Mims—don't knock it.'

Fiona still didn't look convinced.

Miriam tried another tack. 'I'm not sure looks do their owners any favours, anyway, not in the long run. I know a lot of miserable beauties.'

'You did all right.'

'I've never been beautiful.'

'Look in the mirror, Mum: you are bloody gorgeous. You always have been.' Fiona sounded almost cross with her mother, in the same way that fat people are often irritated by slim people who complain when they've put on a couple of kilos.

Miriam's instinct was to protest—she genuinely did not see herself as beautiful—but she held her tongue. *I am getting so much better at keeping my mouth shut*, she thought, *and I guess that's a good thing. I didn't think I had any more growing up to do at my age, but it seems I was wrong.*

'There is absolutely no need for you to envy anyone, Fiona. You're the one who has got it all worked out—wonderful, supportive and loving partner, gorgeous daughter and an interesting job. I think they used to call that "having it all".'

'Nobody has it all worked out, Mum, and no one can have it all.'

Miriam felt a stab of anxiety. She relied on Fiona being steady. She couldn't deal with both her daughters being a mess at the same time. Christ! She was the one who had lost her husband! They ought to be looking after her, not the other way around. But, she reminded herself wearily, she was the mother and they were the children. She took a deep breath.

'Are you okay, Fi?' she asked gently. 'Is everything alright?'

'Everything is fine. It's just . . . everyone thinking you've got it all worked out is another way of making you invisible.'

'You're not going to start competing with your sister over who is the most fucked up, are you?'

Fiona gave a bark of laughter. 'Fair call. No, I am not going to compete with Ally for that honour. She's welcome to it.'

Miriam took hold of Fiona's hand across the table and gave it an affectionate squeeze. She could empathise with her oldest daughter. 'It's not fair, is it? It's the problem children who get the attention. Mind you, if you have another baby, you may find out how bloody hard it is to get the balance right.'

Miriam suddenly thought about her brother. Like Fiona, Michael had been the sensible one, the one their mother had relied on to just deal with things. She felt an unexpected rush of sympathy for him. Perhaps it wasn't entirely his fault he was so prickly.

Fiona sighed at the mention of another child. It was a bit of a sore spot between her and Liam. He wanted another, while Fiona, who had a demanding job running a large not-for-profit, was hesitant.

'Mu-u-um!'

She sounded just the way she had when she was fifteen and Miriam had prodded her to do her homework.

'No pressure, no pressure.' Miriam looked at her watch. 'We should head off to the hospital.'

The freshened pot arrived. They both looked at it.

Miriam reached for it. 'Another cup? I'll be mother.'

'As if you could ever be anything else.'

When the two of them arrived at the hospital, Ally's bed was again surrounded by people Miriam did not recognise. They seemed like a whole new batch of hangers-on to Miriam, but maybe she had not looked very carefully the day before. She saw Sally Carruthers sitting on the chair next to Ally's bed, cradling the baby. She looked around for Nick's father, but Maurice was nowhere to be seen.

'Hello, Miriam,' Sally said. 'And Fiona! How lovely! Look, Sonny, your mother and sister are here.'

It felt to Miriam as if they were being treated like strangers in need of an introduction. As if the Carruthers owned that hospital room. *I'm being territorial again*, she thought. *I have to stop it. It won't help Ally feel safe if her mother and mother-in-law are at loggerheads.*

'Hi, Sally,' Miriam said, and gave the woman a big smile.

Fiona was carrying their joint gift. It was large and so she used it to help push her way through the other visitors until she reached her sister. Looking at the other gifts piled on a table, Miriam could see it was the only parcel not wrapped in blue. She felt absurdly proud of the Franklin-Duffys, as if wrapping a baby boy's present in fire engine red was a revolutionary feminist act or something. Fiona put the gift on Ally's knee and leant in to give her a kiss.

'Well done you. Molly made the card. The picture is of a teddy bear.'

It was as well she had explained, as otherwise it was just a lot of colourful blobs in the middle of the card.

'I think she's convinced that's what you've given birth to.'

'It's a gorgeous picture,' said Ally. 'I'll put it up on Teddy's wall. Give Mol a big hug for me. And I'll get her a teddy called Teddy for Christmas.'

Ally seems happier than she did last night, thought Miriam, who was watching her unobtrusively. That was a relief.

'She'll love that. Here, can I have a cuddle with the genuine article?' Fiona turned towards Nick's mother and held her arms out for the baby, but the woman didn't respond.

Ally leant towards her mother-in-law. 'Sally, can Fiona have a hold?'

Sally pulled a face. 'Do I really have to hand him over?'

She looked as if she might refuse to give Teddy up, but Fiona was already taking the baby and the woman let him go. What choice did she have? They couldn't have an actual tug of war. Not for the first time, Miriam admired Fiona's quiet determination. She had always been a bit of an irresistible force. It's why she was so good at raising money for her not-for-profit. Whether Fiona wanted her to or not, Miriam did think her eldest daughter was okay. Better than okay, in fact.

Having sorted out who got to hold the baby, Ally began to unwrap the present. Inside was a large and very expensive teddy bear—the classic kind with golden brown fur, short limbs and a melancholy expression.

'Oh!' exclaimed Ally. 'Look, Teddy, he's bigger than you are!'

Miriam was relieved to see a flash of the Ally of old in her pleasure at the gift. There was no sign of the dreaded baby blues now.

Nick walked into the room carrying a tray of coffees. He did a double-take at the sight of them.

'Oh, hi, Miriam . . . Fiona. I'd have got coffee for you too if I'd known you were coming.'

'Of course we were coming! We didn't visit Maitland for the waters.'

'Is there a spa in Maitland?' one of the hangers-on piped up.

Miriam could not believe anyone could be that stupid.

'I have no idea. It's just an expression.'

She turned her gaze to Nick. He had perched on the end of the hospital bed and was passing the coffees around. As always, he seemed cheerful and relaxed. Miriam wondered what it was about him Fiona didn't like. *She is probably a bit jealous*, her mother thought. It was understandable; Nick had replaced them all in Ally's affections.

'No worries,' Miriam assured him, 'we've just had tea. How are you this morning? Did you manage to get some sleep?'

'Thank you, yes. What about you, darling?' Nick patted Ally's leg under the blanket. 'Did the Tedster keep you awake?'

'The night nurse took him into the nursery along with all the other babies and only brought him back for his feed. She said I needed all the sleep I could get.'

'When are you going home?'

'A few days yet, apparently, even though the paediatrician checked out Teddy this morning and said he was fine.'

'Why can't we take you home now then?'

Nick was already standing up and looking around the room as if preparing to grab all of Ally's things and hustle her out the door. Miriam smiled at his eagerness.

'I have to see my obstetrician and get my stitches looked at before he'll give me the all-clear. And he's not back in the hospital until Monday.'

'Sonny was cut from here to next week, weren't you, poor darling?'

'Teddy has a very big head . . .'

'Like his father! They had to cut him out of me with chicken snips!'

Sally seemed to regard this nauseating interjection as a huge joke. Miriam just felt a bit queasy.

❧

That night, over an extremely good dinner at a winery in Morpeth, Miriam prodded Fiona about the reasons for her antipathy towards her sister's new husband.

'I told you, Mum—he makes me feel invisible. Why would I like someone who hardly seems to notice I'm there?'

Miriam wasn't sure why she felt so defensive on Nick's behalf. Or was it on Ally's behalf? She didn't know.

'He hasn't got eyes for anyone but Ally at the moment,' she reminded Fiona. 'Surely that's to be expected?'

'He pays attention to you.'

Miriam had to concede the point. He did.

'Maybe that's why I *do* like him, then. He's kind to me. I appreciate that. I've been a bit lonely since Dad died and it's nice to have a man recognise that.'

Fiona immediately looked stricken.

'Oh, Mum, I'm so sorry. Of course you're lonely. You always seem so together to me, I forget sometimes . . . and I shouldn't.'

I always seem so together to her and she always seems so together to me, Miriam thought, *when both of us are probably struggling more than we want anyone to know.* Now she leapt to her daughter's defence.

'Of course you should! I don't want you treating me like some kind of basket case! I want us to be just as we've always been, you and me—open, honest, easy. You comfort me more than you could ever know just by being you.'

Miriam leant forward and put her hand over Fiona's. She was suddenly overwhelmed with pleasure at having this daughter of hers all to herself. It hardly ever happened anymore. Fiona was so busy juggling daughter, husband and demanding job that Miriam only got to see her with the full tribe in tow. Not that she minded. She loved Liam. He was quiet but warm and easy company, and, of course, Molly was the light of her life—but it *was* wonderful to have Fiona all to herself.

'It's lovely to have this time with just me and you.'

'Yeah, you're right. I should make more of an effort to come and see you. After all, it's not like you're far away.'

'No, no, that's not what I mean at all. I don't want to become a duty, not ever. I am fine, really I am. Work keeps me sane, and I've got Julie and Prisha. Worrying about your sister is an old habit; don't take it too seriously. Even without your father it's still situation normal . . .'

'All fucked up!' Fiona laughed.

'To be honest, I've actually been worrying about your sister a lot less since she married Nick—another reason why I'm predisposed to liking him.'

'You were worried about her last night.'

'Yes, but you saw her today. She was her old self. It was the baby blues, perfectly normal. Even you got a bit teary a few days after Molly was born.'

'Good God! It seems I am human after all!'

Miriam let her elder daughter's sarcasm go.

'But cut Nick some slack. He makes your sister very happy.'

CHAPTER 9

Nick made Ally so happy, it seemed, that within only a few weeks, Miriam was back where she started, ringing and leaving messages and hoping that her daughter would eventually return her call. She tried not to take it personally, but it almost felt worse this time. Mind you, everything felt worse now because Pete wasn't around. Quite apart from her grief, she had no one to complain to and no one to keep her feet on the ground. It was also worse because she was so desperate for news of her grandson. If she was lucky, they managed a quick chat a couple of times a week. She knew the early weeks of motherhood were busy and exhausting, but sometimes she could not help feeling a bit hurt and a bit shitty that Ally kept her—her own mother—at such a distance. The calls they did have always ended in the same way.

'Sorry, Mum, got to go. Teddy's woken.'

Sometimes—red-letter days—Ally showed Miriam her grandson over FaceTime. She loved seeing him—sleeping, awake or yelling his lungs out, she didn't care—but she ached to hold him and get to know her grandson in the same way she knew Molly. But Duffy Real Estate kept her very busy. And Fiona had been true to her word and visited her mother, usually with Molly, more often than she had and that helped. She could complain to Fiona. In fact, she sensed that her elder daughter rather enjoyed hearing her sibling being criticised. But, she suspected, the real reason she accepted the small amount of attention Ally was prepared to give her was that, as always, she was wary of pushing Ally too hard. But she missed her daughter, her grandson and her solicitous son-in-law.

She had not even seen Ally, Teddy and Nick at Christmas. As the newest member of the practice, Nick was the vet on call over the holiday weekend.

'Can't you pop down for New Year's instead? We could take Teddy to see the early fireworks.'

Miriam felt real distress when Ally rang to tell her they could not come to Sydney to join the rest of the family. It was going to be a miserable Christmas anyway. The first without Pete.

'He's on call then too.'

'Well, can you and Teddy come down for a day or two? We'll miss you . . . I'll miss you terribly. You have the Merc now.' Then a rustling, and for a minute Miriam thought Ally had hung up.

'Hi, Miriam, it's Nick. I want to apologise on behalf of us all for not being able to join you at Christmas. My parents are pretty pissed off as well, I can tell you.'

Miriam was taken aback by how abruptly Nick had taken control of the call, but she tried to stay polite.

'I daresay, but can I speak to Ally again please, Nick?'

'Sorry, it's not a good time right now. Teddy is due for a feed. Sorry again, Miriam. We'll make it up to you, I promise.' And then he hung up.

'Honestly,' Miriam said to Prisha one lunchtime as they shared their usual sushi on either side of Miriam's desk, 'you'd think my daughter and grandson were living in London or Paris rather than just a few hours' drive up the road.'

'You should just go and see her. Why are you waiting for permission?'

Prisha was right, of course. Dungog was not a gated community. If she wanted to drive up there on a weekend, she could. And yet she didn't.

Sometimes, unreasonably, she blamed Pete for the loss of Ally. Just as Miriam had always had an easier relationship with Fiona, so her husband had been more in tune with Ally. If only he was still around, Miriam was sure it would have been much easier to stay in touch. And there was something else that was disturbing her. As the months turned into a year after Pete's death, she became aware that she was slowly losing the sense she'd had of his presence in the big house in Greenwich—although, to her secret relief, his ghost still hovered around the linen cupboard. Miriam kept scratching at her memories of Pete, as if letting him fade at all from her consciousness was an act of betrayal; as if forgetting about him, even for just a little while, was like letting him die all over again.

Despite what she had said to Fiona, the house in Greenwich had never seemed emptier or more silent. She could hear it creaking and groaning in the night as its old timbers expanded and contracted in the weather. She could hear the faint hum of the fridges in the kitchen and basement and the occasional churn of the dishwasher (a machine she only had to put on every second or third night these days). On the weekends, she relied on talk radio to create an illusion of company, and in the evenings Netflix, Stan and the ever-reliable ABC kept the silence at bay. But when she turned them off and went upstairs to bed, the quiet wrapped itself around her like a blanket. Except it wasn't a warm and comforting blanket; it was damp, itchy and smothering. The silence was within her and without her. And she was not used to it. This house had always been full of people. It was built and designed to be full of people. She had loved the distractions of family and friends and housework and the demands of a complicated and busy life. She had not had to face herself and her own thoughts for as long as she could remember. Now they hammered at her, deafening her through the quiet.

She found herself revisiting the past more than she ever had, recalling what her mother had been like before the Alzheimer's had claimed her, and thinking about creepy Boris. She even dug up a couple of old photographs of her real dad. There weren't many. Miriam's mother had been his first wife and Michael was his eldest child. She didn't remember much about him because he'd left them when she was still very young. He had married again, but she, Michael and Carol had never had anything to do with either Charles Duffy or his new wife. She did not even know if he had more children. She might have a half-brother or half-sister out there she knew nothing about. That was a disturbing thought.

Miriam had never really missed her dad or even thought about him much. *I wonder why not?* she mused, as she looked at the old black-and-white snapshots. One showed a man with his hand on the shoulder of a little blonde girl (herself, she guessed) as they stood on the beach, and another, hand-coloured, was a photo of him and her mother on their wedding day. Both images were so old-fashioned they looked as if they came from another century. As indeed they had. That was all Miriam had left of Charles Duffy, the man who had given her his last name and half his DNA. She put the photos away in the envelope in which they were stored and wondered why she felt absolutely nothing when she looked at them—not even curiosity. Then she put the envelope in the old shoebox where such memories were stored and shoved it back where it belonged, on the top shelf of the linen cupboard, next to Pete's ashes. She felt almost disgusted with herself as she closed the door.

'Christ!' she said aloud. 'Stop being so maudlin!'

She spat the words into the silence. Like everything else she said or thought in that house in the last year, they were swallowed up whole.

Should she sell the house? she wondered. Downsize, as she'd helped so many of her clients do successfully? At work—thank God for work—she occasionally came across an apartment or semi that she thought might suit her nicely, but she never took the next step. Should she ask Julie to move in with her? Now, that really was a desperate thought. Live with that bad-tempered greyhound? Never. No, she'd rather sell the house.

She probably should, but she didn't. She was still stewing over this decision, when a new turn of events pushed it aside. Out of the blue, Ally announced she was pregnant for a second time.

⁓

'Christ, Ally, that was quick! How far along are you?'

'Twelve weeks.'

'Twelve weeks!'

Miriam did the maths in her head. Teddy was only four months old. Ally and Nick simply could not have waited the recommended six weeks before having sex again. This shocked Miriam. It would never have crossed her mind that you could disobey your doctor's instructions.

'But . . . but . . .' Miriam was stuttering, wondering what on earth she could say, when Ally cut her off.

'Don't, Mum. It's none of your business. Anyway, aren't you going to congratulate me? You're getting another grandchild! That's good news, isn't it?'

Miriam swallowed hard. *Well, it might be, if I ever saw the one I've already got*, she thought, and then she swallowed again. She really was getting better at keeping some thoughts to herself.

'Yes . . . yes, of course. It's wonderful news, of course it is. You just took me by surprise, that's all. I wasn't expecting that you'd be expecting.'

It was a lame joke, but it was the best she could manage. Miriam felt bad. She should have kept her shock to herself and been more supportive of her daughter. When would she learn not to react without thinking? Particularly with Ally. She'd only been putting her foot in it regularly with her youngest daughter for . . . oh . . . about thirty years! But her clumsy attempt to lighten the mood seemed to have done the trick, as the tension eased.

'Thanks, Mum. It took me a bit by surprise too. A second contraceptive failure! Clearly my kids are just in a hurry to be born.'

Ally gave a sharp, bleak little laugh. But at least she was laughing and not crying. Miriam tried to raise another one.

'To have one contraceptive failure could be considered a misfortune, to have two looks like carelessness. Apologies to Oscar Wilde.' Then she laughed at her own joke.

Ally was silent for a moment. Then she said, 'Or deliberate.'

At least, that's what Miriam thought she heard Ally say. She'd spoken so quietly, Miriam couldn't be sure.

'What? Sorry, darling, bad line. You'll have to speak up.'

'Nothing, just thinking aloud. I have to go. Teddy has woken up.'

Miriam felt a surge of something like panic. She did not want to let Ally go after sharing such momentous news. And what had her daughter meant by 'deliberate', if that was what she had said? Maybe she'd said 'or an idiot' . . . or something.

'Wait, don't hang up yet. Let me come up and stay with you. It's hard enough with a new baby without being pregnant as well. I can take a few days off work and help out.'

Miriam was already mentally calculating how to rearrange her week.

'Great idea, but not right now. Maybe in a few weeks. I'll get back to you about it.'

'But why not now? Now's when you need the help. Remember how sick you were last time? It's often worse with the second . . .'

'Like I said, I'll get back to you. Gotta go.'

'No . . . wait . . . let's make a date now. This makes no—'

Miriam was speaking to a dead line.

'Shit! Shit! Shit!' She swore at her phone as if it was somehow responsible.

'It's not the phone's fault.' Prisha was standing in the doorway, holding a spreadsheet.

'Must you always state the bleeding bloody obvious?'

'And it's not my fault either.'

Miriam felt the fight go out of her. She stared at her friend. Then, much to her own surprise, she began to cry. Prisha stepped into the room and closed the door to the outer office so no one would hear, but Miriam was beyond caring. She, who was usually so careful of her dignity, so determined to stay in control, was finally overwhelmed by her emotions. As Prisha lowered herself into a chair on the other side of the desk, it all poured out. The loss of Pete, the distance between her and Ally, her loneliness, the lack of contact with her grandson, even the tension with Fiona. All of it. She'd had no idea how much misery she had been carrying.

'I just don't know what to do! I can't seem to say or do anything right anymore. Especially with Ally, but even with Fiona. I always knew Pete was a better parent than me, but I didn't think I'd ever feel quite so useless. Ally seems to be actively avoiding me.'

'I doubt that.'

'It certainly feels that way.'

'Maybe she has postnatal depression.'

'Maybe. But how would I know? She won't talk to me.'

'Have you spoken to her husband? He might be worried too.'

'No. It would feel like I'm going behind her back.'

But Miriam was struck by her friend's advice. She had a lot of respect for Prisha. She was calm where Miriam was volatile, and full of common sense. And Prisha seemed able to keep a sense of perspective about what was going on that Miriam felt she had lost. Of course, Ally was not Prisha's daughter. Prisha's children were primary school-aged and seemed to cause little trouble. She occasionally complained about Arkesh studying too late into the night, as if that was any kind of a problem! Whenever Prisha's kids came with their mother to the office—if they were sick or school holiday care had fallen through—they seemed like nice little boys, if very quiet. When her own daughters had done the same as children, they'd been much more distracting and difficult. They'd complained about being bored all day. She'd only managed to keep them quiet by doling out chocolate bars and chips and letting them play video games. Different strokes for different folks, Miriam had told herself at the time. Now she just felt she'd completely failed at motherhood whereas Prisha had made of it a resounding success.

Miriam felt ashamed of her parenting, but also of her tears, which now seemed melodramatic. 'Perhaps I have an iron deficiency or something,' she said.

Prisha actually laughed. 'Or perhaps you are understandably upset about everything that has happened to you in the last year or so.'

But what good was that? She couldn't give in to her misery. If Ally really was depressed, she needed her mother to be the way Prisha was—calm, unruffled, practical—not blubbering all over the place. But she'd never been that kind of mother. She was as bad as Ally—jumpy, brittle, quick to take offence.

'You are very like her, you know.' It was as if Prisha had read her thoughts.

Miriam groaned. 'I know, I know. That's why I'm so useless. If only Pete was here! He didn't get hooked in the way I do. He could talk me down. He would know what to do.'

'You don't know that. But if he *was* still here, you probably wouldn't be so upset, because you wouldn't be grieving, and nor would Ally.'

That was such an astute observation it brought Miriam up short. It wasn't only she who was grieving, Ally was too—and Fiona. No wonder they were all a bit rubbish with one another.

'You are a good mother, Miriam. Stick with your instincts.'

Miriam smiled at her friend. 'Thank you, that's kind. I am doing my best, but I was a pretty dodgy mother even when I had Pete, and now that I have to do all the parenting on my own . . .' A sob caught at the back of her throat, but she chose defiance over self-pity. 'Parenting! Hah! Why am I even bothering? My children are adults with children of their own. I should be off the bloody hook at last.'

Prisha grinned at her. 'That's why you're a good mother, Miriam. You'll never be off the hook. I doubt any of us ever are.'

'Tell me about it! I get so furious with Pete sometimes, exiting the way he did, just at the wrong time.'

'I am sure he'd rather he was still here, however complicated things get.'

'If he was here, like you said, they wouldn't be so complicated. Even if he didn't have all the answers, he'd be someone to talk to about it and we could support one another. I could get out of my own head. I feel . . . so alone.'

Miriam gulped down the tears that threatened to undo her a second time. She did not speak again until she felt steadier.

'I feel like I am a million miles away from Ally and Teddy, and I guess this new baby too, when he or she arrives, and I can't bear the thought of losing anyone else. Not after Pete! I can't bear it.'

Now Miriam was crying again. In fact, the tears were streaming down her face.

Prisha sat quietly. She didn't move, offer comfort or say anything.

Somehow, that seemed to give Miriam permission just to release her pent-up emotions, crying in a way she couldn't remember doing for years. When she eventually calmed down, she felt oddly better, although her eyes were sore and her nose was dripping, and she was sure she looked a sight.

'Can I get you some water?' Prisha asked.

Miriam blew her nose and gave a rueful laugh. 'Thanks, yes—I probably need some after all that. Can you get dehydrated from crying? Sorry.'

'No need to apologise. You are very hard on yourself, you know.'

'You missed your calling. You should have been a therapist.'

Prisha grinned and fetched a bottle of water.

Miriam took a long drink. She spilt a little down her chin. *I must still be a bit shaky*, she thought, as she wiped at the dribble with the back of her hand.

'I should be celebrating. The arrival of a new member of the family is good news, not bad.'

Prisha shrugged. 'Some babies are born into fortunate circumstances, some are not. That's just the way of things.'

'You're not a Buddhist, are you?'

'No, common, garden-variety Hindu. Not a very observant one, either.'

'Because you sounded positively Zen, just then.'

'I think most of the world's religions have similar ideas.'

'You'd know more about that than me.' Miriam rubbed her face with her hands. 'Anyway, there's no use crying. I just have to get on with things.'

'You might want to fix your make-up a little bit before you do.'

Miriam stuck out her tongue.

༄

That night, alone in her large and echoey house, watching something dull on TV to kill time between dinner and bed, Miriam thought more about Prisha's suggestion. Should she call Nick? Maybe he was worried too. Perhaps they could join forces and support Ally together. Or would ringing him be seen as intolerable interference by her youngest? She genuinely could not decide. Ally seemed very clear that she wanted her mother to give her space; maybe she should do just that.

Her indecision made her anxious and she got up off the couch and paced about, holding her phone. Nick's number was in her contacts and she got it up on the screen. All she had to do was press the phone symbol to make the call, but she didn't. She could not bring herself to. The sick feeling in the pit of her stomach kept telling her that calling him—however sensible and reasonable it sounded—was a really bad idea.

༄

The next day, she was on her regular morning walk when her phone rang. She pushed her earbuds into her ears, assuming it to be the call she'd been expecting about an offer, and looked at the screen. The caller ID brought her up short.

Had she conjured him up? Had she accidentally called his number while hesitating over the idea last night and he'd seen the missed call? Then her heart really leapt into her throat. Maybe he was calling because there was something wrong—with Ally? With Teddy? With the baby? The only time Nick had ever called her before was to tell her about Teddy's birth. It must be an emergency.

'Hello?' She knew she sounded as scared as she felt.

'Miriam? Hi. It's Nick.'

'Nick! Is something wrong? Is everyone alright?'

'Alright? What do you mean?'

Obviously he hadn't anticipated that his call would send her into a panic.

'I mean, has there been an accident or something?'

'Oh! No, no, everyone's fine . . . well, I am a bit worried about Sonny, actually.'

'Worried how? The pregnancy?'

'No, that's progressing fine. I just wondered . . . sorry, there's no nice way to say this, but has Sonny ever had any mental health problems? You know, in the past?'

'Mental health problems? What do you mean?'

Miriam felt cold all over. Nick was voicing her worst fears.

'She's not herself at the moment and I'm worried about her.'

Miriam was immediately on the defensive. 'It's not surprising, is it? She's pregnant again and so quickly! She's got a four-month-old to care for. Her father died a year ago, she's newly married, she's given up the career she loved and moved to a new town. That'd be enough to make anyone "not herself", surely?'

Miriam knew she sounded hostile but Nick stayed calm.

'Yes. She's had a lot to deal with, I agree, but this seems different. She's crying all the time, losing her temper, and the house is a tip.'

'Well, tidy it up, Nick,' Miriam said impatiently. 'You've got two hands. That's something practical you could do to help.'

She was walking along the path she followed every morning in Greenwich Point Reserve. It promised to be a beautiful day, but she wasn't looking at the scenery. Her agitation made her pick up her pace.

'Yes, yes, of course I do what I can, but it's just not like her, that's all.'

'You didn't know her when she was a teenager.'

Despite her own worries on that score, Miriam was still reluctant to collude with her son-in-law about her daughter's mental health behind Ally's back.

'Anyway, I just wanted to know if she'd had any issues in the past so I could tell her doctor,' Nick said.

'Her doctor?'

'Yes, I've booked her in to see a psychiatrist.'

'A psychiatrist?' She really must stop repeating everything he said. 'Is she on board with that?'

'She hasn't much choice. The baby health centre nurse insisted.'

That took the wind out of Miriam's sails. It sounded as if Nick was right and there really was something wrong with Ally. Post-partum depression would make sense under the circumstances. If that's all it was. Miriam felt a chill at the thought of psychosis. She stopped walking and leant against a stone wall bordering the path. She tried to catch her breath and calm down.

'Oh. Okay. Sorry, I've just walked up a hill.' Her breathing calmed a little. 'As far as I know, Ally has never had any mental health issues. The usual stress around exams at school and uni, but otherwise . . .'

Miriam paused as a vivid memory of a mulish teenage Ally sprang into her head. She remembered her daughter refusing to eat, mute with misery, locked in her utterly chaotic room. She remembered how worried she and Pete had been about her. 'Usual stress' was understating it, but she still couldn't bring herself to tell her daughter's secrets, not even to her husband.

'Thanks, and one more thing . . . Could you come and stay for a few days? I have to go to a very inconveniently timed conference and I really don't want to leave Sonny alone right now.'

For a moment Miriam was delighted. His invitation was exactly what she wanted. Then she had another, much darker thought. Only the day before, Ally had put her mother off.

Why had Ally not wanted her to come? Maybe she feared that Miriam would be her usual judgemental and critical self and just make her feel worse. She must have totally fucked up her relationship with her difficult daughter, even more than she had feared. Miriam felt sickened by herself, but nonetheless she stepped up. What choice did she have?

'Of course I'll come. When?'

CHAPTER 10

Miriam had just about managed to squeeze a week's work into three days. Inconveniently timed conference was right. Thursdays and Fridays were often her busiest days wrangling hopeful buyers and sellers after open houses on Wednesdays and before those on Saturdays. Nevertheless, whatever she had not been able to get done, she had left in Prisha's capable hands, but she felt guilty about it. It wasn't as if her 2IC didn't already have enough to do.

'I owe you a pay rise,' Miriam said, as she handed Prisha a pile of paperwork.

'Yup, I reckon you do,' Prisha replied, grinning, as she took it.

'We'll talk about it on Monday, when I get back, I promise.' Miriam was already heading out the door.

'I'll hold you to it, you know,' she heard Prisha call out after her.

She smiled to herself. At least her colleague was direct and uncomplicated, unlike the rest of her totally fucked-up life.

But the minute she was in her car and had started the engine, she forgot about Duffy Real Estate and the busy days ahead for her staff. All she could think about as she drove through NorthConnex and onto the M1 was her daughter and the size of the crisis she might find. Would Ally be rational? Was she taking proper care of Teddy? Would Miriam be able to help her or, given their past difficulties, was she the very worst person for the job? But who else was there?

And another thing she had been ruminating over. The last time she'd talked to Ally on the phone, had she heard her right? Had she really said this second pregnancy was deliberate? Deliberate on the part of whom? Or had Ally called herself an idiot? Or did she mean Nick? The worst thing about the throwaway remark was that she would never know what her daughter had said or what she meant by it, because she knew—only too well—that she could never, ever ask. Yet every time she tried to think about something else she found her thoughts circling back. Surely Nick would not want to get Ally pregnant deliberately against her will? It must have been Ally's depression speaking; perhaps she was becoming delusional and paranoid. That was the worst thought of all.

※

By the time Miriam arrived at the little weatherboard cottage in Dungog, she was a wrung-out rag.

Ally opened the door to her mother's knock. She looked thin and tired, and her hair was a bit of a mess, but otherwise she seemed more or less herself. Miriam almost felt deflated.

She wasn't actually sure what she'd been gearing up for. Some sort of raving lunatic?

'Hi, Mum.'

'Oh, darling.' Miriam dropped her bag and gave her daughter a hug. 'Are you alright? Nick said you haven't been well.'

'No. No, I haven't.'

'Where is Nick?'

'Oh, he left this morning. It's just me and Teddy—and Teddy, thank God, is finally out for the count.' The relief in Ally's voice was palpable. 'Whatever you do, don't make a noise.'

Miriam and her daughter tiptoed through the door. Miriam winced when an old floorboard creaked. When she spoke, it was in a whisper.

'Is he a bad sleeper? Lack of sleep can make you feel like you are going mad.'

'Depends on the night, but how *he* sleeps isn't the problem. It's me, I just seem to have lost the knack of it anyway.'

'I remember that! I'd finally get you off to sleep at some ungodly hour, and then I'd lie awake staring at the ceiling.'

Ally seemed too depleted even to react.

'You're in here.'

They'd been walking down the narrow hallway and Ally had opened the door into a small but neat spare room. There was a bunch of old-fashioned roses in a jug on the bedside table, filling the air with fragrance.

'They're lovely!'

Miriam lowered her face into the bright flowers and drank in their heady scent.

'Nick picked them for you.'

'That's kind.'

Again Ally hardly reacted; she really looked dead on her feet. It was still early but it was obvious what Ally needed and it wasn't to make conversation, not even with her mother. Maybe especially not with her mother.

'Go to bed, love. I've got everything I need. Even if you can't sleep, you need to get all the rest you can.'

'Well, I will, if that's okay. I'm buggered.'

'Yeah, I'm dead on my feet too. See you in the morning.'

Miriam realised she was still talking to Ally in hushed tones, as if to an invalid. *Of course*, she reminded herself, *I didn't want to wake the baby. Nevertheless, I must stop tiptoeing around her. That would drive me crazy, if it was me.*

∽

Miriam had braced herself for a pig sty, and got up early the next morning determined to get stuck into any housework that needed doing, but the house was neat as a pin. Either Nick had taken her suggestion that he clean it himself to the nth degree, or Ally had gone to a lot of trouble to tidy up for her. She almost felt flattered. She made herself a cup of tea and sat in front of a window to read the Sydney paper on her phone, instead. When Ally did get up, to respond to Teddy, Miriam was glad to see she looked a little better than she had the night before.

'How did you sleep?'

'Better.'

'I heard Teddy a couple of times.'

'Yeah, but because Nick's not here, I fed him and put him in bed with me. That usually sends him off.'

'Why can't you do that when Nick is here?'

'He can't sleep with Teddy in the bed, and he has to go to work . . .'

'Looking after a baby is work!' Miriam was bridling.

Ally put her hand up. 'Leave it, Mum.' And Miriam left it.

'Well, I'm glad you had a better night. I got up to do some housework, but there was no need. Did you clean up especially for me?'

Ally frowned. 'No, the house usually looks like this.'

Where was the 'tip' Nick had mentioned? Miriam wondered.

'You were never this houseproud when you lived at home.'

'I'm not a teenager anymore, and Nick's very particular about things being clean and tidy. His medical training, I think. He has a horror of mess and germs.'

'He's a vet! Not a surgeon.'

'Turns out there's not much difference—we're all just mammals. Here, would you mind holding Teddy for me? I haven't had a shower for days!'

'Mind? Are you kidding? Come here, gorgeous.'

It was lovely holding a baby again, and her grandson was a particularly beautiful specimen. Miriam spent a contented half-hour playing peekaboo with a mildly interested but somewhat confused baby. She did succeed in making him giggle by blowing raspberries on his belly. *How Pete would have enjoyed this*, she could not help thinking, but even that stray thought did not spoil her pleasure. By the time Ally emerged from the bathroom, washed, hair up in a towel and dressed, he'd fallen asleep on Miriam's shoulder, little head by her ear, and she had fallen in love.

Ally was feeding Teddy on the couch later that morning when there was a knock at the door.

Miriam was surprised by how startled she was at the sound. *I'm nervous as a kitten*, she thought, *waiting for something awful to happen*. Yet so far, apart from Ally's obvious exhaustion, everything had seemed fairly normal.

'That'll be the mental health nurse,' Ally said. 'I forgot she was coming.'

Miriam got up to answer the door, pausing first to adjust the cushions she'd arranged around her daughter so she could rest both her back and the arm that held Teddy's weight.

'What's a mental health nurse?' she asked.

Ally lifted one shoulder. 'Who knows? My shrink arranged it.'

Miriam winced inwardly at the word 'shrink'.

She opened the door to find a perfectly ordinary looking woman standing on the verandah. She wasn't wearing any kind of uniform, just jeans and a patterned shirt. The only indication that she was there in a professional capacity was the lanyard around her neck.

'Hello, I'm Louise Sarkov, the local mental health nurse.' She held her hand out in a confident and businesslike fashion.

Miriam took it. Louise had a firm handshake and a warm, dry hand.

'And I'm Miriam Duffy, Ally's mother.'

'Ally?' The woman frowned. 'I'm here to see Sonny.'

'Sorry, her husband calls her Sonny. She's Ally to her family. Anyway, she's just feeding the baby. This way . . .'

As they walked into the lounge room, Miriam tried to see Ally the way the nurse might. Her daughter looked pale and thin, with dark smudges under her eyes. She was dressed in the baggy clothes she'd worn during Teddy's pregnancy and there were milk stains on the front of her t-shirt. But she looked cosy and comfortable surrounded by the cushions, with Teddy's dark head resting on her hand as he grunted and snorted his satisfaction at being fed. If you didn't know any better (and weren't a mental health nurse), it was a picture of maternal bliss.

Yet here was this stranger whose job it was to pry into Ally's affairs, and Miriam wasn't sure what she should do with herself while this visit unfolded. Ally's mental health was private, even from her mother. Miriam should probably make herself scarce.

'Would you like some tea? I'll make you a pot and then I'll put Teddy in his stroller and go out for a walk. He could use some fresh air and so could I.'

Ally looked a bit stricken at this suggestion, and Miriam wondered if she had done the wrong thing, but the nurse positively beamed and somehow radiated reassurance.

'That would be lovely. White with one.'

'Nothing for me, Mum.'

Ally's voice sounded small and scared, and Miriam felt like she was abandoning her child, just as she had when Ally had disappeared through the international departure gates with a tearful wave on her way to New York for the au pair job. The way Ally had sobbed, you'd have thought she was heading off to her execution, not the most exciting and glamorous city in the world. Miriam looked around the small lounge room. How her daughter's life had changed.

She soon found herself pushing a sleeping Teddy along the long country road where Ally and Nick's house stood. It wasn't the prettiest part of Dungog. It was a bit flat and a bit weedy. The sort of land that Pete—who'd come from a farming family—used to call hardscrabble. And there wasn't a footpath, so Miriam had to push the stroller along the rough gravel shoulder.

Fortunately, there also wasn't much traffic, just the odd four-wheel drive whooshing past and disappearing over the hill. Miriam fixed her eyes on the mountain range to the west and the clouds that had gathered above it. Maybe there would be rain later. It certainly looked as if it was raining on the Tops. It was a pleasant morning. Cool enough for a cardigan but not cold. Teddy was tucked snugly under his baby blanket.

There weren't many other houses on the road and those there were had a neglected, down-at-heel air that signalled people doing it tough on low rents. Miriam found herself trying to calculate exactly what the residents were likely to pay. It was an old habit she'd developed from her early days in real estate. After half an hour or so, she passed the driveway of a rundown house with an unkempt garden. A derelict couch sat on the propped-up verandah and a few sad-looking kids' toys were scattered about the front. There were a couple of rotting car bodies down the back that had been there for some time, if the weeds around their wheels were any guide. *A knock-down, land-value-only proposition*, thought real estate agent Miriam as she walked past.

Miriam had never understood how people could live in rural areas, even hardscrabble country like this, and just leave a broken-down car to rot where it had drawn its last rev. It was a very North Shore reaction, she knew, and she admonished herself for it. She was startled out of her reverie by a furiously barking cattle dog charging down the driveway at her. Her instinct was to run; she'd always been slightly frightened of dogs, and this one certainly didn't look friendly. But she had an utterly helpless human child to protect, so instead she moved to stand between the baby and the threat.

'Shoo! Shoo! Go away! Leave us alone!'

She waved her hands at the creature in what she knew was a totally ineffectual manner. The dog was jumping up and down in front of her, baring its teeth and growling.

'Abbey! Stop that, you mongrel! Get back here.'

Thank God! A man had emerged from the shed beside the crumbling house, wiping his hands on a rag. Abbey turned and ran back to her owner, issuing a few more warning growls on the way. Miriam found she was shaking, and then Teddy started to cry. She hoisted him out of the stroller and held him close, though whether it was to comfort him or herself, she wasn't sure. When Abbey reached her owner, the man bent down and began to fondle the animal affectionately. This infuriated Miriam. Her fear became anger.

'You should keep your dog under control!' She used her rich lady voice, the one she'd learnt at uni, hanging around with all the posh private school kids.

The man looked up at her, unmoved. 'You're not from round here, are you? Well, Abbey is. You're on her territory.'

'I'm on a public road!'

'Abbey doesn't give a shit about that. She's a guard dog; she's just doing her job.' Then he looked back at the dog who was now sitting on her haunches, tail thumping enthusiastically. 'Good dog.'

There was something shockingly deliberate about the way he reached into his pocket and pulled out a dog treat. It felt like he'd made a rude gesture. Miriam was just wondering how to respond, when he looked up and pointed at her.

'I'd cross to the other side, if I were you.'

Then the dog and its master went back into the shed, leaving Miriam open-mouthed. She hugged Teddy closer and he stopped crying. Then she turned the stroller around awkwardly with one hand and took the man's advice, crossing to the other side of the road. Gathering her dignity as best she could, Miriam marched rapidly back towards Ally's house, glancing nervously behind her as she went.

'I hate this place.'

She said this to Teddy, who was sucking the edge of his blanket. His clear blue eyes looked back at her gravely. When she felt they had reached a safe enough distance, she stopped and strapped him back into his stroller.

'I HATE this place!'

She yelled the words as loud as she could, sure the man with the dog could not hear her.

*

'That's a very fancy security system they've got there.'

Miriam stopped and looked up at the camera attached to the verandah post opposite the front door. She'd almost forgotten about it. She was holding the door open for the nurse, who was just leaving.

'It was a gift to Nick for saving a farmer's calf or bull or something.'

'Why is it pointing at the door, not the gate?'

Good question, thought Miriam. She hadn't noticed that before.

'I don't know. Perhaps Nick's buggered it up. He's a vet, after all, not a security camera installer. He says they've never turned it on.'

'Ah, I see.' The mental health nurse smiled at Miriam and put a hand on her arm. 'It's great you're here. Sonny needs support right now.'

'Is she alright? Is there anything I can do to make things better for her?'

'Keep doing what you're doing. She relies on you.'

Does she? thought Miriam, as she closed the door behind the woman. *That's news to me.*

When she walked back into the lounge room after putting Teddy in his cot she asked Ally the same question the nurse had asked: 'Why is the security system pointing to the front door instead of the gate?'

'Nick said he isn't interested in who comes through the gate—it's who comes to the front door that worries him.'

'Oh. Right. He doesn't seem the nervous type to me.'

Ally looked at her mother as if considering what to say next. 'No, I know.'

Now Miriam felt as if she might be the crazy one. What was going on here? Ally almost seemed to be implying that Nick was the problem. Was that paranoia, or the truth? Miriam had a million questions she wanted to ask but, as she was slowly learning to do, she kept her mouth shut and just sat still.

After a long pause, Ally began to speak. 'He seems convinced that I'm about to run off! As if I could, with Teddy and another on the way. It's ridiculous, but he gets in these moods sometimes and there's just no convincing him.'

'He always seems completely calm and reasonable to me.'

'Oh, he is, he is. Most of the time. It's just . . . anyway. No one's perfect. I mean, look at me. I'm a mess.'

'You're not a mess. You're exhausted, bereaved, a new mum who is also unexpectedly pregnant. You're doing brilliantly, considering.'

'That's what Louise said.'

Miriam just nodded, waiting to see if Ally would say more.

'I've only made one real friend since I've moved here and it's a bloke—Jeremy, who works in the cafe. But he's flamingly, outrageously gay and Nick is still jealous! It's ridiculous; Jeremy makes no secret about his sexuality. I've told Nick over and over that even if I did fancy Jeremy, he wouldn't touch me with a ten-foot barge pole; he's much more likely to fall for Nick. It does no good. And I need a friend. I need someone to talk to who doesn't fly off the handle one minute and cover me with kisses the next.'

'Is that what Nick does?'

'Yes. He blows hot and cold and I never know what's going to set him off. Something he laughed at one day will have him throwing plates the next.'

Miriam suddenly felt nauseated. She wondered for a moment if she was coming down with a stomach bug, but the spasm passed.

'Throwing plates?'

'No, not exactly.'

'But?'

'Oh, he got annoyed about some mess on the kitchen bench— he was trying to do something and it was in his way. He swept it all sideways without thinking, and a plate fell off and smashed on the floor. It was nothing, an accident.'

This was a side of Nick Miriam had never seen.

'He rang and asked me if you have ever had mental health issues . . .'

'Did he? He said he was worried about me.'

'Why? Have you given him any reason to worry?'

'I dunno. I'm not myself, that's for sure.'

'When he rang and asked me to come and stay . . .'

'Maybe I have got a problem,' Ally burst out. 'It's just that I'm so tired and the morning sickness is much worse this time, and my brain feels so foggy and . . . and is it any wonder that sometimes I forget things or remember them wrong, or have trouble working out what's real and what isn't anymore. What if I *am* mad!'

'I don't think you're mad,' Miriam said carefully, 'but you're clearly not happy.'

Ally's eyes filled with tears. Miriam just wanted to throw her arms around her, but she restrained the impulse. She tried to do what Prisha had done for her and just concentrate on what Ally was saying.

'Sometimes I am, sometimes I'm not. You know me, Mum. I'm difficult. I always have been. You're always on tenterhooks with me, and I know I can be a bitch sometimes. I get hurt really easily. Nick's trying to help me with that. He's really good at reminding me to be nice to people and not to take offence too easily. It was his idea to ask you to come while he's away, for example. He said it was important that we work on our relationship—you and me, that is. He made me see how lonely you must be, with Dad dying, and told me I needed to be nicer. But it's hard, because we used to be so happy, before I stopped coping.'

Miriam felt ashamed. Ashamed of being judgemental, ashamed of the conversations she and Fiona had had about Ally behind her back. Ashamed of her self-pity, as she'd focused on how Ally had made *her* feel without thinking about how Ally felt. She had been a bad mother to this fragile daughter of hers. She always had been. Then she caught herself. Once again, she was turning her focus onto herself. This wasn't about her or her mothering. *I did what I did, good or bad*, she thought. *Too late to change it now.*

'You've just described everyone's relationships, darling,' she said aloud. 'Families are lovely, and families are hard. Don't let guilt get to you. Our family isn't perfect. I miss your dad every day but I am managing. I didn't think I could, but I can. Our relationship—yours and mine—has been rocky, but it's still rock-solid. I love you and your sister more than life itself.'

'Yes. I know you do.'

Miriam couldn't sit still after that. She got up and hugged her daughter, tightly. Then, a little awkwardly, she went back to her seat. *I wish I was better at showing affection*, she thought to herself. *Pete was so easy about all that. I wish I had the knack.*

'What did the nurse say?' she asked.

'Not much; she just sat and listened.'

'Is she coming back again?'

'Yes, she said she'd come next week.'

'Are you happy about that?'

But before Ally could answer, Teddy woke up and started howling. His mother immediately looked panic-stricken.

'Look at me, I must be crazy! Even my little boy scares me!'

'But that's perfectly normal,' Miriam assured her. 'I remember whenever you or your sister cried, I used to get this feeling like a lift had just dropped ten floors through my belly!'

Ally's face relaxed a bit. 'That's exactly how it feels. It's all so new to me.'

She smiled for the first time that morning and got up to fetch the baby. Miriam sank back on the sofa and heaved a huge sigh. She'd been working very hard to listen, really listen to Ally, and not push or prod or pry. God, it was hard.

When Ally came back into the room, making soothing noises to the child in her arms, Miriam said, 'Things will get easier, Ally, I am sure.' Then, thinking of the baby on the way, she realised that was a rather bold promise to make. 'Just make sure you ask Nick for help when you need it, okay? I know having a new baby—two, soon—isn't the easiest thing to cope with so early in the marriage, but—'

'Thanks, Mum, but my marriage is not the problem—*I'm* the problem. I just need to get well. Nick is bewildered, of course. I'm not the woman he married, you see; I'm this sad sack of misery. But I'm determined to get back to my old self. And Nick's helping, he really is. He adores Teddy and he is wonderful with him. Teddy is always fussing when I try to comfort him but he settles the instant Nick picks him up. I almost feel jealous sometimes.'

'Your dad was the same. Used to drive me mad. I was doing all the work and he got all the fun! Anyway, look at Teddy now—you seem to be just what he needs.'

And the baby was looking very content—wide awake, but perfectly happy held close in his mother's arms. Ally dropped a kiss on his dark head.

'Thank you, Mum. It's good to have you here. I feel better than I have in ages.'

'I am glad of that—and remember, I'm not far away. If it ever gets too much for you, even if you just want a break, you can come home anytime. I've got plenty of room.'

And that, she supposed, meant she'd made her decision—Miriam wouldn't be selling the house in the near future.

CHAPTER 11

That afternoon, while Ally had a rest, Teddy lay happily on a blanket on the floor, fascinated by his own hands and kicking his legs. *He really is a very easy baby*, his fond grandmother thought, remembering her own two fussy daughters. Seeing him so contented, Miriam took the opportunity to tidy up a bit—not that the house was very messy; there was just the usual tide of detritus that gathers around a baby. As she unpacked the dishwasher, she noticed how obsessively neat and organised every cupboard and drawer seemed to be. It made her hesitate to put things away, as if there'd be a consequence if she put something in the wrong place. There could not have been a starker contrast with the Ally she had known when her daughter lived at home. Then she had been immune to chaos, oblivious to mess and dirt. Here there wasn't a speck of dust or a thing out of place anywhere. It made her wonder what on earth Nick had meant when he said the house was a tip. Perhaps Nick was a bit controlling, she mused, not quite the paragon of virtue he had always seemed. She remembered how he had taken over the phone call they'd had about Christmas—the missed Christmas—without, as far as she knew, so much as a by-your-leave. Yet Ally had spoken so highly of him, of the support he was giving her—and asking Miriam to come and stay was proof of his good intentions, surely. But something about the little temper tantrum Ally had described kept nagging at her. *Ridiculous*, she thought to herself as she put a load of washing into the machine. *There is nothing like inanimate objects to make even the most even-tempered person lose their cool.* Pete had been infuriated when confronted with things that didn't work, or failed to do what they were supposed to do, or were hard to open, or just got under his feet. He'd go around the house sometimes kicking things, especially if he was tired, thundering, *FOR FUCK'S SAKE*. If she'd ever told anyone that story in isolation, they might have thought badly of him too.

Ally was not asleep for long, but by the time she got up she looked better than she had all day. The black circles under her eyes had faded and she had a bit of colour back in her cheeks. *She just needed to get a bit more sleep*, Miriam thought. Sleep deprivation was not just a form of torture, it was also a brainwashing technique. No wonder Ally felt like she was losing her grip. Miriam made a mental note to gently suggest to Nick that he let the baby sleep with Ally for the time being, for all their sakes.

'Let's go to the brewery, Mum. Jeremy just texted me. He's going to be there and I haven't seen him for ages.'

It was lovely to hear some of the old energy back in Ally's voice. It was even nicer to know she had a friend.

'Why don't you go on your own? I'm quite content staying here with Teddy. I can't get enough of him at the moment.'

'No, no, you must both come. Jeremy loves Teddy and I want you to meet him. I think you'll get on. And, Nick's not here, so . . .'

Miriam decided to let the unspoken words remain that way.

'Well, if you're sure?'

To be honest she'd kill for a glass of wine or that nice porter, and it'd be good to get out and be among other people. Getting out put your own problems into perspective, she'd always believed. Something about so many other people living their own lives distracted you from your own.

As they drove past the dilapidated house with the broken-down verandah, Abbey the cattle dog came hurtling down the driveway like a ball of furious brown fur, barking aggressively and nipping at the tyres of Pete's old Merc. Miriam swivelled her head to watch the dog give up the chase while they left her in the dust.

'Do you know the people in that house?'

'I don't know anyone on this street.'

Of course you don't, thought Miriam, and decided there was no point saying anything more. She took one last look over her shoulder at the nasty dog, who was still sitting in the middle of the road, biting at her crotch.

Teddy, in his car seat, was wearing the expression she remembered so well from her own babies—a look of puzzled anxiety. And who could blame them? What a confusing world to be born into after the warm, safe environment of the womb. She shivered.

'Are you okay, Mum?'

'Yeah, someone just walked over my grave.'

Babies are tougher than they look, she thought. *I must remember that.* Then she turned and looked in the direction they were going. The outskirts of Dungog were just ahead. Hardly the Emerald City, but it would have to do.

∽

'Sonny! I've got a table over here, with room for the stroller!'

A plump, very fair young man was gesturing to them from inside the brewery. The young man's pleasure and enthusiasm at seeing her sad daughter made her like him immediately. *Here is an ally*, she thought. *An ally for Ally.* She smiled at her own lame joke. Louise the nurse might be an ally too, but it was always harder to tell with professionals.

Jeremy folded Ally in a big bear hug and pulled funny faces at an oblivious Teddy.

'This is my mum, Miriam,' Ally said, drawing Miriam forward.

'Of course she is. You two are like peas in a pod.'

This pleased Miriam very much. She'd always thought her daughters resembled their father and—though she'd never said—she felt slightly wistful about it.

'Do you think so? Most people think Ally—sorry, Sonny—looks like her dad.'

'Nonsense. I'd have known who you were anywhere. Now, drinks. How about champagne all round?'

'The champagne's crap here, Jez. Mum'll have a rosé and I suppose I'd better have bloody mineral water.'

Poor Ally, now she was pregnant again, she couldn't even have the comfort of a drink to take the edge off. No wonder she was *all* edge.

'Are you sure, darling? I used to let myself have the occasional glass of wine when I was pregnant with you.'

'What about a low-alcohol beer?' Jeremy suggested. 'That's more fun than mineral water, at least.'

'Would that be okay?' Ally was looking at her mother for permission.

'Of course! Your father called them brewed soft drinks. Go ahead. Jeremy is right.'

'Alright, but just one. And whatever you do, don't mention anything to Nick; he's a stickler about it.'

Miriam saw Jeremy raise an eyebrow.

Ally must have seen it too, because she said, 'You two should be grateful! You've got a designated driver without any argument.'

Jeremy opened his mouth as if he was going to object.

Ally put her hand up to cut him off but grinned as she did so. 'No time for discussion. Watch Teddy for me. Alcohol or no alcohol, I have to pee. I'll order the drinks on my way. Damn this being knocked up!'

As Ally disappeared towards the bar, Jeremy pulled his stool closer to Miriam's. It seems they were confidential already.

'Is she alright?' he asked.

'I don't know. She seems livelier this afternoon than she was this morning.'

'I worry about her, you know. Her husband makes it hard for me to stay in touch. God knows why. I mean, look at me—he has nothing to fear. And every girl needs a gay friend.'

Miriam laughed. She liked this young man. Encouraged, he leant in still closer and dropped his voice. 'He's an arsehole, you know. I hope you don't mind me saying.'

'That's what Fiona said . . . my eldest daughter.'

Ally's phone started to buzz. It was on the table where she had left it.

'Speak of the devil!' said Jeremy, picking it up and looking at the caller ID. 'I swear he has us under surveillance.'

Miriam laughed again. Jeremy didn't.

Their drinks arrived. Miriam gulped her rosé far too quickly.

'Looks like you needed that,' Jeremy observed.

'Well, I have gone a whole twenty-four—no, make that forty-eight hours without a drink!'

'How ghastly! Drink up, then, and I'll get you another.'

Miriam was tempted to unburden herself to Jeremy but, delightful as he was, she'd only met him minutes before.

'Did Louise come?'

'She did. That seemed to help a bit. You know her?'

'Yeah, she's great. Got me through a few tough times, I can tell you.'

He took a long swig of his Pale Ale and then looked pointedly at Miriam's almost-empty glass and drained his.

'My shout.'

He'd just stood up to go to the bar when Ally reappeared. The first thing she did was look at her phone.

'Christ! I missed his call!'

'So what? Call him back later.'

'I can't. He's at a conference. They work them to death at those things. He's probably only got a short break.'

Work them to death? thought Miriam, remembering the annual real estate conferences she attended. Vets must be a very different breed.

'But you won't be able to hear yourself think in here,' she said. 'Take the phone outside and we'll watch Teddy.'

'He'll want to know where I am.' The anxious Ally from this morning had suddenly made another appearance.

'For fuck's sake, Sonny, ring him back and tell him you're here,' Jeremy urged. 'You're a grown woman—you can go out for a drink with friends if you want to.'

'Never mind friends,' said Miriam. 'You are out for a drink with your mother! Who could possibly object to that?'

'You're right. I'm being silly. I'll call him now.'

And she was gone, slipping through the crowd, out the front door and down the side alleyway, where it was quieter.

Jeremy went to the bar and soon returned with drinks in hand.

'He's an arsehole, you said?' Miriam reached for the wineglass.

Jeremy shook his head. 'Yeah, but I was wrong. Actually'—he leant back in his chair and spoke louder than he needed to—'he's a cunt.'

Miriam threw back her head and laughed.

༄

By the time Ally came back to the table, Miriam and Jeremy were up to their third drink and feeling no pain.

'I fucking love your mother,' Jeremy said, throwing his arm around Ally's neck.

'Ditto!' said Miriam. 'Or vice versa!'

'You're pissed!' Ally sounded cross.

'Yep. I am. Pissed and in charge of a baby.'

Jeremy attempted a look of remorse. 'Me too. Sorry, Sonny.'

'He's fine, though,' Miriam assured her. 'We haven't heard a peep.'

They all looked at the baby in his stroller and, of course, he was sleeping peacefully under the white cashmere bunny rug—literally decorated with bunnies—that Miriam had brought with her as a gift the day before.

'He's snug as a bug in a bunny rug. It's cashmere, by the way,' she told Jeremy. She assumed it was the sort of detail that would interest him, because it was the sort of detail that interested her, and after less than an hour, she already felt that she and Jeremy were kindred spirits.

'I wish he wasn't so snug. I want him to wake up. Uncle Jez wants a cuddle.' Then Jeremy gave Ally a look of genuine kindness and concern. 'Cheer up, love,' he said. 'You've got time off for good behaviour, so enjoy it. Here, I'll get you another brewed soft drink. May as well throw caution to the wind.'

'Get me another too,' Miriam said, handing him her credit card. Bugger caution. Bugger the wind. Bugger tomorrow, too.

❦

Later, back in the little weatherboard cottage she and Ally sat in the lounge room while Ally got Teddy ready for bed. It was warm, and Miriam felt sleepy and pleasantly inebriated.

'Jeremy really doesn't like Nick, does he?' she ventured.

'No.'

'How come?'

'Nick killed his dog.'

Miriam sat up abruptly. 'What?!'

'No, not killed him—euthanised him. Jeremy has never forgiven him for it. It's ridiculously unfair. Nick was only doing his job.'

Miriam leant back again. 'People are very funny about dogs.'

Then, a strange thought hit her. Nick was a vet, yet he didn't have any pets. Miriam wondered what that was about. Then another thought. Why didn't Fiona, Liam and Jeremy like Nick? Okay, as Ally had just revealed, he wasn't always Mr Wonderful, but who was? Miriam shook her head, as if to shed the thoughts taking hold inside it. Ally loved him, Ally picked him. It was Miriam's job to support Ally in her choice.

CHAPTER 12

The next day passed quietly; well, as quiet as it is possible to be with a young baby in the house. It was well into Friday afternoon when Miriam heard the crunch of tyres on gravel, and saw Ally sit up straighter. Her movement disturbed Teddy, who pulled off the breast and began to wail.

A few seconds later, the front door opened, and Nick dropped his bag with a loud bang. As it hit the floor, Ally jumped. *Crikey*, Miriam thought, *you're still living on your nerves, aren't you?*

When Nick entered the room, it was clear that he was delighted to see his wife and child.

'Darling! Tedster! Have you managed alright while I've been gone? I missed you both so much.'

'We've managed fine, thank you, Nick. How was your conference?' It was Miriam who spoke.

Nick looked over to her. For a fleeting moment, it was clear he hadn't been expecting to see her. She could have sworn he looked irritated, maybe even alarmed, but perhaps Ally's anxieties were catching, and she had imagined it, because a nanosecond later he was the old easygoing Nick she remembered.

'Miriam! Of course, how silly of me—I forgot you'd be here.'

Nick sat down next to Ally and took a still-fussy Teddy out of her arms. The baby calmed down instantly. *Ally is right*, thought Miriam. *He has a knack.* She smiled warmly at him. It was hard to harbour dark suspicions about this man when he was being so tender with his son. And even though she had enjoyed her stay, there was a part of Miriam that was relieved to pass the responsibility for a brittle and jumpy Ally back to her husband.

'Well, here I am. And we've had a lovely time! Teddy is gorgeous, and I have been very impressed with what a wonderful mother Ally is. She's been coping brilliantly. All she needs is a bit more sleep, I think.'

She sounded too cheery, even to herself.

'Glad to hear it,' Nick said. 'I've been a bit worried about you, darling, haven't I?'

'I've been a bit worried about myself,' Ally said, scraping her hair back into a ponytail.

'I do have one suggestion,' Miriam said brightly. 'If Teddy sleeps better snuggled up to his mum, and you find it hard to sleep with him in the bed, Nick, maybe you could bunk in the spare room every few nights or so, to give Ally a rest?'

'Is that right, darling? Why didn't you say?'

'It's no big deal.'

Miriam could see that Ally was furious with her but that was too bad. Sleep was what she needed, and if Ally was too miserable or exhausted or anxious to say it, her mother would.

'Lack of sleep *is* a big deal, but it may be easy to fix. Anyway, if me being here makes any difference'—Miriam was remembering with pleasure what the mental health nurse had said to her the day before—'I'm happy to come and stay again anytime. I've had such a great couple of days, and I get lonely in that big old house'

'But if you're here, how can I bunk in the spare room?' Nick asked.

'I can stay in that Airbnb again, the one near Lovey's car park.'

They all sat in silence for a moment or two. Then Nick said casually, 'So, did you get out much?'

Sneaky bugger, thought Miriam. She had no idea whether Ally had told him about their evening at the brewery or not, so she kept her response vague.

'Not much. It's always hard with a little one. You feel like you have to pack to go on holiday just to pop to the shops. I did take Teddy for a walk yesterday and we got bailed up by one of your neighbour's dogs! That was a bit of an adventure.'

༄

Even though everyone was behaving perfectly reasonably, and Teddy was quiet and easy, Miriam felt a tension in the air. *Maybe Nick is a bit territorial or competitive*, she thought as she helped Ally prepare the evening meal; maybe that was the problem. She remembered a similar tension between Pete and her mother and stepfather. Pete had been perfectly charming, of course, he always was, but her mother had seemed shy with him—ill-at-ease—and Boris had occasionally been downright rude.

'Your dad doesn't like me,' she remembered Pete saying after one stilted evening.

'He's not my dad!' she'd replied, bristling. 'And if he did like you, I'd be worried.'

'What about your real dad? Is he still around? I'd like to meet him.'

Miriam had shrugged. 'No idea. I haven't seen or heard of him for more than twenty years. He could be dead and buried for all I know.'

'That's sad.'

'No, it isn't. I don't miss him at all. Hard to be sad about someone you have no memory of.'

'But maybe he misses you. I mean, when I become a father, I'd hate to think that I could just die or disappear and my kids wouldn't care.'

'Well then, don't take off and leave the mother of your children holding the baby. That's the best way to avoid that happening.'

Miriam was feeling quite cross with Pete. It felt like they were having a conversation about their own possible future. And she found it irritating to have to justify her lack of emotion around the father who had deserted her. Why the fuck should she feel anything about him, when he quite clearly felt nothing about her? He'd never even tried to get in touch. She'd had not so much as a birthday card from the man.

Then the thought struck her—Pete *had* left her, just like her father. One minute he had been there, and the next minute he wasn't. The idea was such a blow she almost dropped the plates she was carrying.

'Are you right, Mum?' Ally asked.

Miriam steadied herself. 'Yes, sorry—away with the pixies.'

✧

The evening passed without incident. Ally seemed subdued, so Miriam kept up the conversation, asking Nick endless questions about his conference; she'd watched her mother do this with her stepfather and had despised her for it. Now she felt a twinge of respect for the woman who had given birth to her. It took skill.

Miriam heard more than she'd ever wanted to about new treatments for some disease called 'scours' that killed calves like flies when the weather got too hot (due to climate change, this was becoming an increasing issue in Nick's practice), and by the time she finally made it to bed, the Nurofen she'd been using to keep her hangover from the night before in check had worn off, and her head was thumping. She took another couple of tablets, but she still felt wired and could not sleep. The walls in the little weatherboard cottage were thin. She could hear the low rumble of Nick's voice talking to Ally in the room next door. That was irritating enough, but when she heard the springs of their bed begin to creak rhythmically she had to put her pillow over her head and clamp it to her ears. *Leave her alone*, she thought. *Can't you see how exhausted she is?*

The next morning, Nick was clearly keen to see the back of his mother-in-law.

'We don't want to keep you any longer than necessary, Miriam,' he said over breakfast. 'You've been more than generous, and I'm sure you're keen to get back to the office. Saturdays are work days in real estate, I imagine.'

'As they are for vets.'

'Not this vet, thank God, not this weekend. Time off in lieu.'

No wonder Nick was in such a hurry to get rid of her. He'd actually fetched her overnight bag from the bedroom. Just as well she'd packed it. In his other hand he was carrying the roses from the bedside table, carefully wrapped in damp newspaper. As Miriam took the flowers from him, she was reminded of her husband.

'You do remind me of Ally's dad sometimes,' she said. 'He'd have wrapped the flowers just like that.'

'Architects and vets, we both have to be good with our hands. Anyway, I know they are not much of a thankyou, but still . . .'

'They're lovely and they smell divine, but I don't need to rush away. They can cope without me at work, and I thought I could keep Ally company a bit longer and get some more time with Teddy.'

But Nick was holding out her bag and, short of allowing it to fall on the floor, she couldn't think of anything to do but take it. It didn't help that Ally was standing behind her husband, nodding over his shoulder. If her daughter also wanted her to leave, she would have to go.

'It's fine, Mum. It'll be nice to have Nick to ourselves for a whole weekend.'

'Well, if you put it like that . . .'

There was an awkward pause.

'Oh, and I meant to tell you, Teddy and I will be going to the baby health centre on Monday. Louise thinks I should join the new mothers' group.'

'Great idea! I loved my mothers' group when you and Fiona were small. Kept me sane.'

'Great idea!' echoed Nick, as he started walking down the hall. 'Come on, Miriam, I'll walk you to your car.'

The next thing she knew, she was outside the cottage. *He really can't wait to see the back of me*, she thought. Well, she'd never much liked having Pete's parents to stay either. She'd been spoilt by Fiona and Liam; until now she'd never realised how hard it was being an in-law.

'Thank you so much for coming. I can see you have been a great help to Sonny.'

Nick had opened the car door and was giving her a peck on the cheek. With her hands full of bag and roses, she could do little but accept it.

'She's just exhausted and sick, and her dad died just over a year ago. They were very close, you know. I'm afraid I am a poor substitute.'

'I'm sure that's not true.'

But Nick was just being polite. He glanced at his watch. Just for a moment, she had some sympathy with Fiona, Liam and Jeremy.

Miriam put her bag on the back seat and the flowers on top, then opened the driver's-side door. 'Be kind to her, Nick,' she said as she slid behind the wheel. 'She's got a lot on her plate and she seems desperate to please you. She's wearing herself out worrying about keeping the house tidy, for example. What does it matter if it's a bit messy, if it means Ally can get a bit more of the rest she needs.'

Nick's smile had disappeared. 'Thanks for the advice.'

Ouch, thought Miriam, *he didn't like me saying that.*

'But it's not me who cares about the house. I told you, she's not herself at the moment. She's the one who's obsessive about it. Maybe it helps her to feel more in control to keep the house neat and tidy. Anyway, she's going to be seeing the mental health nurse almost daily. Maybe that'll help.'

'It's weekly.'

'What?'

'The visits from Louise—the mental health nurse.' She wanted Nick to know that she and the nurse were on first-name terms.

Nick's previous warmth had cooled. He remained perfectly civil, and his smile had returned, but something about his manner made her feel wary.

'Don't be annoyed with me, Nick. The last thing Ally needs is for the two of us to be at loggerheads. If she's going to get back to her old self again, we need to work together to support her.'

'That's very kind of you, but I think we can manage.'

Nick was not being rude, exactly, but Miriam felt dismissed.

'Great, but if you can't, don't hesitate to call me again. Or maybe I'll just pop up and surprise you.'

Nick had been just about to close the car door, such was his hurry to see her go, but this made him pause.

'Don't do that,' he said, in a tone that brooked no opposition. 'We don't like surprises.' Then he turned and walked back inside the house.

Miriam sat in her car and tried to digest what had just occurred. Nothing much, on the face of it, but she felt she had been told, in no uncertain terms, to stay away and not to come back until she was invited. *Where does that leave me?* she wondered, as she very much doubted there'd be another invitation anytime soon.

After a few moments, she started the car and accelerated away rather faster than she had intended. Her tyres were spinning, spraying gravel everywhere. She felt embarrassed, as if the wheels of her car had betrayed her feelings of helplessness.

※

'I'd drive up and march her out of there, if I were you.'

Miriam had braved the unfriendly greyhound next door that evening so she could confide in Julie. She was now rather wishing she hadn't. Maybe she'd overstated what had happened, because Julie's reaction was making her feel worse, not better.

'Don't be ridiculous! No one has done or said anything that would justify that. Ally just seems so vulnerable at the moment, and that has made her very dependent on him.'

'Ally? This is Ally we're talking about? Miss Independent, Miss Go Her Own Way?'

'Yeah. I think that's part of the problem. She needs help, but she hates asking for it. She always has.'

'Both your daughters were always determined to do everything themselves.'

Julie was right. Fiona had always been competent and independent, and Ally had always tried desperately to keep up with her older sister, even when she was very little. *Was that when I first started to feel so protective of her?* Miriam wondered.

'Maybe Nick reminds her of her dad.'

Miriam looked at her neighbour sharply. She might have noticed a few superficial similarities between the two men, like how they wrapped flowers, but fundamentally Pete and Nick were like chalk and cheese.

'I know you have always thought Pete was pretty perfect, Miriam, but . . .'

'I never thought he was perfect, but I was never scared of him. *Never.*'

Miriam realised that was the first time she had acknowledged that Ally did seem frightened of her husband.

'No, I know. That's not what I meant.'

'What exactly did you mean?'

'Well, it's just . . . Pete was always pretty controlling. Everything had to be his way or else. Remember how he'd never let anyone else cook the sausages on a barbecue? They all had to be lined up perfectly, turned at just the right moment, and pricked in just the right way. He'd get steamed up if anyone tried to interfere.'

'He was pernickety, yes,' Miriam conceded, 'but controlling? That's a bit extreme.'

While she tried to keep her tone mild, Miriam was furious. Really angry with her friend. Pete was *not* controlling; he was supportive and helpful.

'Look, I'm sorry if I upset you, I didn't mean to. I know you and Pete were very happy together—really tight—and you loved how he protected and adored you. Anyone could see you thrived on that, and who could blame you?'

'Sounds like you are!'

Julie looked crestfallen. 'No, no, I'm sorry, this is obviously coming out all wrong. All I'm trying to say is that he protected the girls in the same way. Maybe he gave them a false idea by trying to make the world safe. That's all I'm suggesting. Maybe Ally sees Nick as another man like her dad, someone who will adore her and protect her and make her feel safe, like Pete did with you.'

'I can't believe you're blaming Pete like this!'

'I'm not! I'm not blaming anyone. But why was she attracted to a man like Nick in the first place?'

'I don't know. Anyway, she loves Nick, apart from her depression . . .'

'And anxiety,' interrupted Julie.

'Okay, and anxiety. They seem to have a pretty good relationship. He's just a bit possessive, that's all. And if Ally really is falling apart, and it's not just post-partum depression, then it's my fault, not Pete's! I was a crappy mother. I never did know how to cope with Ally.'

'You were no crappier than the rest of us. And anyway, why does it have to be anyone's fault? It's hormones if it's post-partum depression. And even if it isn't, and Ally or Nick—or the pair of them—are unstable and headed for misery, it's still not your fault, or Pete's. After all, do you take credit for Fiona and her relationship with Liam?'

'No, of course not.'

Except Miriam did. She was proud of her eldest daughter's stable and supportive marriage, almost smug about it. She'd silently congratulated herself and her husband for being such positive role models. Maybe Julie had a point.

'Well, if you don't take credit when things go right for your kids, why should you assume the blame when they go wrong?'

'Why do we put such angst and effort into bringing them up, then, if what we do doesn't matter?' Miriam countered.

'I'm not saying it doesn't matter, just that we can only do what we can do. We teach them good things and bad things. So I just wondered if Nick's controlling behaviour reminded her of Pete's and . . . well, we're all trying to find someone to protect us, I think, especially when we're young.'

'Is that why you have that nasty greyhound?'

The dog raised its head from its blanket and bared its teeth at her. Miriam shrank back. She'd had more than enough of dogs.

'It's as if the bloody thing can understand what I'm saying!'

'Nah. You just looked at him. He doesn't like that. But yes, to answer your question, it probably is why I got him. He protects me and—because he's a rescue—I protect him.'

'And you're saying that's what Pete and I did for one another.'

'Maybe, but I don't think you need protecting. I don't think you ever did. You just enjoyed it when it was available. Now, I think you've found your true calling.'

'What on earth do you mean?'

This conversation was bizarre. She'd never heard Julie talk like this before. They usually just gossiped about neighbours or argued about politics. This whole day had got out of control. Miriam took a large gulp of her chardonnay.

'You're the protector now, and it suits you. Just remember one thing—protection can become control. I think that's where Ally is right now.'

'You mean she wanted to be protected—like I was, and all of us were, by Pete—but now she is being controlled?'

'Maybe, or maybe she just feels like she is, because she's gone from single-career-girl-about-town to wife and mother in little more than a year. I reckon anyone would feel like things had got a bit out of control in that situation. Maybe Nick is just responding to Ally's need to feel safe.'

'What should I do to help, then, given you seem to know all the answers?'

'I think you just have to hang in there.'

'You were telling me to march her out of there just a few minutes ago!'

'Yeah, that was silly.'

It was an unsatisfactory response. Forget Ally feeling out of control; it was Miriam who could do nothing.

She held out her now-empty wineglass. 'I'll need another after all that truth-telling.'

'I'm sorry. I hope I didn't overstep the mark. I know how much you loved Pete.'

Miriam nodded. 'Yes, but I never thought he was perfect.'

'Yes, you did.'

But Julie was smiling at her as she leant forward to fill her glass. Miriam smiled back. She knew she ought to be grateful for a friend who would tell her the truth, but just at that moment what Miriam really wanted was to be wrapped in comforting lies.

CHAPTER 13

For a while, everything went back to normal, or, at least, what Miriam had come to accept as normal. She rang Ally as often as she dared, though she still felt as if she was interrupting her daughter when she did. As if her desire to speak to Ally meant just another duty Ally had to perform. She enjoyed FaceTiming with her grandson, of course, but there really is only so much you can say to a baby. And whenever she hung up the phone, she felt bereft. As she had said to Prisha, it really was like her daughter and grandson lived a million miles away, rather than a few hours' drive. Miriam tried to remind herself of what the mental health nurse had said about Ally needing her support, but her daughter always seemed so cool or distracted on the phone that she began to think the woman had just been flattering her. The phone conversations she did have with Ally were often repetitive.

'It's just I haven't got any news, beyond Teddy's getting a new tooth, and I am still cooking his sister . . .'

'His sister? So you're not keeping this baby's gender a secret then?'

'Obviously.'

Miriam ignored this.

'Well, that's news!'

'Yes, I should have rung you. I'm sorry. I can't seem to raise much enthusiasm for anything these days. I know I should be excited, I know I should, but I just feel so . . . Everything seems like an effort. Louise says it's part of the depression.'

'Are there any medications you can take while you're pregnant?'

'The shrink—Dr Singh—sent me a script for Zoloft, but I don't want to take it if I don't have to.'

'But if it helps you feel better, maybe you should think about it? Having a depressed mum can't be good for Teddy, surely—'

Ally cut her off. 'Don't, Mum, I feel bad enough already.'

Miriam made a mental note to put more energy into her FaceTiming with Teddy; she'd have to pull more faces, sing more songs, play more peekaboo. If Ally's exhaustion was exhausting for her mother, how much worse must it be for her small son? In the meantime, Miriam tried to ignite a little bit of joy.

'A girl! How lovely. A pigeon pair.'

'Yes. Nick was pleased. I'm pleased too, of course.'

Except she didn't sound pleased. She sounded . . . hassled.

∽

Even Fiona was worried, Miriam discovered.

'She sounds so flat on the phone. I can hardly get anything out of her. I've offered to go up with Molly one weekend and take Teddy out for the day to give her a break, but she just gets all vague about dates and somehow we hang up without having organised anything definite.'

Fiona was sitting at the dining table at Greenwich after Sunday lunch. Liam was playing with Molly in the corner of the room and Julie had just headed home.

'I've got to feed Sinbad and give him his medication,' Miriam's neighbour had said as she got up from her place. 'And don't roll your eyes at me, Miriam Duffy. Sinbad's all I've got these days. You should get yourself a pet—it's another beating heart in the house, if nothing else.'

Miriam might have rolled her eyes at Julie's early departure, but she was actually grateful. Julie leaving meant that she and her eldest daughter could have an unguarded conversation. Miriam did confide in Julie about Ally, but she felt a bit disloyal. She didn't feel that way with Fiona.

'That's a great idea!' she said now. 'Taking Molly up, I mean. I'll come with you. There are some lovely spots around Dungog.' Miriam was thinking about the picnic area at the Chichester Dam.

'Why don't you go up Saturday fortnight? I've got that golf day with some Japanese clients.' Liam looked up from the game of Snap he was playing with Molly on the floor.

'Saturday fortnight?' Miriam was looking at the calendar in her phone. 'I've got a couple of viewings, but I'll see if I can get one of the others to take them.' Not Prisha; she'd been leaning on her too much recently.

'Well, we'd better get up there soon,' Fiona said. 'That baby is due to be born in a couple of months.'

But they didn't get up there soon. First the date they'd settled on did not suit Ally and Nick, then Liam and Fiona couldn't get away.

'Honestly, it's like herding cats!' Miriam said to Fiona. 'I'll just have to go up and take Teddy out for the day on my own. Ally needs at least one child-free day before she has two of them! And it will give me a chance to catch up with Jeremy.' Miriam had a feeling that Ally confided in her friend much more than she did in her mother. Maybe he'd have a better idea of how her daughter was faring.

⁂

'I'll bring him back by five at the latest, I promise.'

Miriam was putting Teddy into his car seat in the Merc. She and Ally had agreed it was easier to swap cars than move the cumbersome baby capsule, particularly as Nick was on call at the surgery and not around to help. Ally had loaded her mother down with nappies and bottles of expressed breast milk, baby food—all homemade, Miriam noticed; nothing mass-produced for Teddy—extra clothes, cardigans, booties and two sunhats.

'Two, Ally? As far as I can see Teddy only has one head.'

'But one might blow away . . .'

Miriam raised both eyebrows, expecting Ally to laugh at how ridiculous she was being, but then she realised that her daughter was deadly serious. Miriam's heart sank. She really was in a bad way.

'It's okay, darling. I have looked after babies before and they all lived to tell the tale.'

Ally looked both bereft and relieved. 'I know, Mum, I know. I just haven't been apart from him since he was born.'

'Well, it's about time you were. He's almost ten months old, and you are about to have another one . . .' Miriam glanced at her daughter, who looked as if she was about to pop any minute. 'So take these few hours on your own and enjoy them, even if it means just sleeping the day away.'

'Oh, I've got so much to do.'

'Don't do it.' Miriam put as much authority into her voice as she could while trying not to sound too aggressive. 'I didn't come all this way so you can do some bloody housework. I did it to give you a break—and so I could spend time with my grandson, of course.'

༄

It felt strange driving Pete's car. He'd almost never let her take the wheel when he'd been alive. Unless he'd had a few too many drinks, of course, and it was her turn to be the designated driver.

'Oh, Teddy,' she said, glancing at him in the rear-view mirror, 'you'd have loved your Pop. I'm so sorry you never got to meet him. I miss him very much. I think your mummy does too.'

Jeremy was waiting for her outside the bistro. He had a great big bag with him. Not as big as Teddy's, but almost. He opened the back door when she pulled in beside him and heaved it onto the back seat before getting into the passenger seat beside her.

'I've got champers—pink, in your honour, madame—pâté, cheese, crusty bread from the famous Dungog Bakery and a quiche I made with my own fair hands.'

'Yum! You'll have to drink most of the champagne yourself, though. I'm driving back tonight and I cannot possibly be drunk in charge of this baby again.'

'Oh, I fully intend to. That's precisely why I bought the most expensive bottle they had in Lovey's Liquor. It might be in your honour, but it's for my pleasure.'

'Well, also for your pleasure I have brought my famous chicken sandwiches—'

'Never heard of them.'

'—my *famous* chicken sandwiches. I can't help it if you live in a backwater.'

'Ouch. Below the belt, Ms Duffy.'

'And a lemon syrup cake. I bought that, admittedly, but it's awesome. Plus a thermos of coffee and some freshly baked scones with butter and jam. I did make those.'

'I intend to put on kilos this afternoon!' Jeremy rubbed his plump belly unselfconsciously and Miriam laughed. Teddy joined in, chortling from the back seat. This day out had been a good idea. Miriam felt better than she had in she didn't know how long. She could see why Ally was so fond of this young man. He was fun! *So few people are*, she thought. *It's what I miss most in my life as a widow.*

༄

Despite their best intentions, they left most of their picnic uneaten. It was hardly surprising, because they'd brought enough food to feed six. However, Jeremy had been true to his word and downed most of the expensive champagne. Miriam had a discreet glass. It was delicious. She had hoped he might leave a little in the bottle for her to finish at whatever ungodly hour she made it home that night, but alas not. Never mind, every sip just made him more entertaining. And Teddy was a delight. He was crawling about on the grass, eating dirt and investigating every seed and acorn he could lay his chubby hands on. They all went straight in his mouth, so Miriam had to spend half the time prising apart his few teeth to stop him swallowing whatever it was he'd found.

'Here, Nanna, let me.'

Jeremy scooped Teddy up off the grass confidently and popped him into the little portable seat Ally had provided that clamped to the end of the picnic table. Miriam looked at him and widened her eyes. Jeremy shrugged.

'I'm the eldest of nine. If there is one thing I know how to handle, it's babies.'

'Nine?'

'I know. It was awful. Big Catholic family and my father was a bastard . . . Let's not go there.'

Teddy protested loudly as Jeremy did up the safety strap around his waist. The baby went rigid, arching his back in indignation at being restrained. He yelled loudly until Jeremy gave him a bit of scone smothered in jam. That shut him up fast.

'Jeremy!'

'Oh, it's your job to spoil him. I'm just helping.'

'Don't you dare tell his mother.'

'Scout's honour.'

'Don't tell me you were a scout?'

'Anything to get out of home.'

Miriam's face must have given her away because Jeremy immediately guessed what she was thinking.

'And don't be such a cliché, Ms Duffy! It was all good clean fun, and the only camp thing about it was the tents. Honestly, a gay man can't mention scouts or priests these days without everyone immediately imagining a complete backstory.' Jeremy paused for a moment. 'If you'll pardon the expression.'

Miriam threw a scone at him. 'Alright, alright,' she said, grinning. 'Point taken.'

Later, after they'd packed away the gargantuan amount of food they hadn't been able to eat, and Jeremy had expertly rocked Teddy to sleep in his stroller, the adults lolled about on the picnic blanket, enjoying the last of the afternoon sun.

'I still can't get over you being the eldest of nine,' said Miriam. 'Your poor mother.'

'Yes. Maybe that's why I feel so protective of Ally. She reminds me a bit of my mother.'

Miriam pulled her cardigan around her shoulders. The sun had gone behind a cloud and she felt cold suddenly.

'What do you mean?'

'My mother has sort of faded away. She's still got my youngest four siblings at home, as well as regularly minding her grandchildren, and she's become almost wraith-like. She just works—washing the clothes, cleaning the house, cooking meals, minding my sister's kids. Her only recreation is mass on Sunday and picketing the local abortion clinic on Saturday . . .'

Miriam gave a yelp of shocked laughter.

'And as a reward for all this devoted self-sacrifice, God gave her an openly gay son.'

'I am sure she is proud of you and loves you.'

'She loves me alright. I don't think she's proud, though. And my father hates me. I can only visit when he's not there.'

'I'm sorry to hear that. I'm getting to the point where I feel I can only see or speak to Ally when Nick's not there.'

'Well, you know how I feel about Nick.'

'He's a cunt, I think you said.'

'Look, that was probably the booze talking, but he reminds me of my dad, especially the way he is around Ally.'

'What do you mean?'

'I've always thought of my dad as a bit of a vampire. He sucked the life out of my mum. Well, him and all us kids, but we couldn't help it and he could. The more exhausted and faded she got, the bigger and more robust he became—as if he was feeding off her life force or something. He's the size of a fucking house, these days.' Jeremy rubbed his belly again. 'I take after him.'

'But how does he remind you of Nick?'

'It's sort of the same dynamic, don't you think? She gets more and more insubstantial and unstable, and he gets bigger and stronger and more dominant. Look, I'm probably just projecting my own experience onto her. Don't mind me. I really don't know anything.'

'What did your dad do to your mum, apart from saddle her with nine kids?'

'He wouldn't let her wear make-up. He insisted she wear what he called "modest" clothes. If she laughed at something on the TV, he'd tell her off like she was a child. She learnt to laugh behind her hand. I hated seeing her do that. He insisted on the house always being in order, that the meals be on the table at a certain time, and with a family of eleven that was just about impossible. Then, when she failed, he'd belittle her and tell her how useless and incompetent she was. I stood up to him once and told him he was a lazy selfish sod who should help out. He punched me and threw me out of the house. She didn't say a word. That's when I knew she was totally his creature. I don't go back home very often anymore.'

'Do you think that's what Nick does to Ally?'

'How would I know? She doesn't tell me any more than she tells you, but she sure as hell isn't happy. Any fool can see that.'

'And I haven't seen her wear so much as lipstick since her dad's funeral.'

Miriam was about to say more, when she felt rain drops hit her head. 'Shit!' she said, looking up. The clouds had gathered while they were talking. 'We'd better get Teddy into the car!'

᪇

Later, driving home down a darkened M1, Miriam thought about everything Jeremy had told her. None of it added up to much. Maybe he was projecting, like he said, but it was true Ally was fading away. The only signs of the old Ally were in her exasperation, her grumpiness with her mother. That was something Miriam recognised from long before Nick had entered her life.

'But if he's making her so miserable,' she said out loud, 'why doesn't she just leave?' *I've already told her she's welcome in Greenwich anytime*, Miriam thought. *Then again, I've always been the last person she seems to turn to when she needs help.*

CHAPTER 14

A couple of Saturdays later Miriam was weeding her herbaceous border getting it ready to plant her spring annuals when her phone rang. It was Nick. Ripping her gardening gloves off, she answered the phone as quickly as she could. She knew that Ally was due any time now.

'Hi, Nick, is everything okay?'

'Better than okay, Miriam. Sonny and I are now the proud parents of a beautiful baby girl!'

'Oh, that's wonderful. A sister for Teddy. A pigeon pair.'

It's what she had said to Ally, but Miriam had no idea whether she ought to keep the fact that she'd known that the baby was a girl quiet or not.

'How is Ally doing?'

'Right as rain. Isla just popped out. No need for any stitches this time.'

'Isla? That's lovely.'

'Isla Allison Carruthers.'

'Lovely,' she repeated.

But Miriam was disappointed. It was silly of her, and she felt ashamed. Why would Ally want to call her daughter after her mother? She wasn't dead, like Pete, and they had never been as close as Ally and her father. She tried to keep the disappointment out of her voice.

'I-S-L-A?'

'Yes. It's got a kind of Irish feel, don't you think?'

'Yes. I suppose so. It's very pretty.'

'Anyway, the birth was so easy and Sonny is managing so well, they're only keeping her and the baby in overnight. She'll be home tomorrow.'

'Tomorrow! Oh, I must come up to help out. Easy or not, labour is a big thing, and managing a newborn and a toddler is hard yakka.'

'Thanks, but there's no need. I've taken a month's parental leave from the surgery so I'll be there as 2IC.'

'But . . . I want to meet Isla, and I know Fiona and Liam will too. Molly will be beside herself to have a girl cousin.'

'I'll talk to Sonny. We'll organise something.'

Miriam sighed as she ended the phone call. She immediately texted Ally—*Congratulations, darling, and loving welcome to Isla Allison Carruthers*—then rang Fiona to tell her the news.

As soon as she'd told her eldest daughter about Isla's arrival, Miriam burst into tears. She should've been feeling overjoyed, but instead she felt awful, and she wasn't sure why.

'What is it, Mum? What's the matter?'

Fiona sounded concerned.

'I don't know.' Miriam struggled to put her feelings into words. 'I just feel so shut out, so far away, and I don't know what to do about it.'

'She's always been able to make you cry.' Now there was resentment in Fiona's voice.

'What do you mean?'

'Remember when you made that joke about how she had burst the button on her new jeans—she must have been, what fifteen? Sixteen?—and she absolutely went up you about calling her fat? I mean she was probably all of a size six at the time; I felt like a lump of lard next to her. She went on and on until you gave up trying to explain that you meant no such thing—which obviously you didn't, because it was patently ridiculous—and burst into tears in frustration? You apologised and apologised, but she held it over you for ages. I really hated her back then. She was such a bitch and she had such power over you.'

Miriam was genuinely dumbfounded. She had only the vaguest recollection of the incident. At that point in their life, she and Ally were constantly having tearful bust-ups and that one had obviously meant little to either of them. It seemed to have meant a lot to Fiona, though. She had always been bigger than Ally and was quite chubby at the time. Miriam felt awful that she had never realised how teenage Fiona must have felt about it.

'I'm so sorry, darling. I never realised how much that hurt your feelings.'

'Too late to worry about that now.'

A response, Miriam thought, that was no comfort at all.

✑

The bad feeling didn't leave her. She rang her daughter daily, but their conversations were just as unsatisfactory as they had been before Isla's arrival. She could hear Nick in the background, clattering about, and there was always a baby wailing or a toddler crying. Now, when Ally answered the phone, Miriam felt even more like just another person her daughter had to please.

'How are you, darling?'

'I'm fine. A bit tired and sore, but at least I'm not sick as a parrot anymore, and according to the lactation consultant my breasts have developed tone.'

Miriam laughed. 'That's right, I remember them telling me that after you were born. The milk coming in and the feeding is just nowhere near as horrendous the second time around.'

'Tone! It made me feel like my breasts were a tuning fork, or something.'

Miriam was so relieved to hear Ally make any kind of joke, she laughed rather too hard.

'It's not that funny, Mum.'

'It's so good to hear you sound a bit better.'

'I'm glad that me sounding a bit better makes you feel a bit better.'

There was something about that reply that made Miriam feel uneasy. Did Ally really mean she had to pretend to be happy to keep her mother sweet, or was she genuinely glad that her happiness made her mother feel the same? Miriam felt unsure. Nevertheless, she brushed the thought aside and ended that phone call feeling a little brighter than she had for ages.

'I was worrying about nothing,' she said to Pete as she walked past the linen cupboard. 'You were right, as always. I was letting my imagination run away with me. Ally's had a shocker of a pregnancy, given birth to two kids in just over a year and she also lost you. It's not surprising she's been feeling like shit. Nick's a bit controlling, perhaps, a bit territorial, but so were you, Mr Franklin. So were you.'

※

One afternoon when Isla was about twelve weeks old, Miriam's phone rang with a call from an unknown number. It was Monday, the day she took off if she'd worked on Saturday. She had been binge-watching a detective drama on Netflix, eating chocolate-covered liquorice bullets and thoroughly enjoying herself in a way she could not remember doing since Pete died. She didn't feel guilty or lonely or anxious. She wasn't ruminating about anything. She was just relaxed.

When her phone vibrated on the coffee table, she contemplated declining the call, but instead she paused the drama and answered her phone.

'Hello? Miriam Duffy.'

'Oh, is that Mrs Franklin?'

A woman's voice. One she did not recognise.

'Yes, this is she.'

'Sonny's mum?'

Now Miriam was on alert.

'Yes, that's right.'

'This is Louise Sarkov. We met briefly at Sonny's house a while ago.'

'Yes, yes, I know who you are. Is everything alright?'

'Hopefully. Sonny and the children are on their way to you right now. She's left her husband.'

'*What?*'

'She's taken the children and left her husband. She's on her way to you and she asked me to call and let you know.'

'Why? How? For good? I mean . . . what happened?'

'I can't tell you that. Sonny might if you ask her.'

Miriam's brain was not keeping up with what the woman was saying. She was still trying to absorb the meaning of her words.

'What time should I expect them?'

Maybe they'd just had a fight or something—but if that's all it was, why was the mental health nurse ringing her? Surely that meant something bad had happened. Was Ally on the brink of collapse or had Nick . . . was Nick . . .? Miriam's head was buzzing.

'In about an hour, depending on traffic. But I don't think she's out of the woods yet. I've seen this sort of thing before, too many times. I need to warn you what you're in for. He won't give up easily.'

'Well, no, I mean, he loves her and the kids, he'll be devastated.'

'Yes. He will.'

There was a lot of weight in those three words. Miriam couldn't help thinking about Fiona saying, 'I don't like him,' and Jeremy saying, 'I've always thought of my dad as a bit of a vampire. He sucked the life out of my mum.' Had she been a fool all this time, thinking it was Ally who was the problem? Well, whatever had happened, whoever was to blame, Ally was her daughter and Miriam would be on her side.

'Well, she'll be safe here with me,' she told Louise. 'It's my house and I decide who gets let in.'

'That might work with someone who was rational—but he isn't.'

Nick *isn't rational?* Miriam was completely confused now. *Isn't Ally the one Louise was counselling?*

'But he always claims she's the crazy one.'

'She's not crazy. She's an abused woman who has been subjected to a relentless campaign of terror—we call it "coercive control". He won't give up that control without a fight.'

'What? I've never seen any evidence of violence—never. What do you mean she's abused? What has he done to her?' Then she was struck by a dark suspicion: 'What has she been telling you? She can be very dramatic, and she hasn't been well for a long time.'

'You'll need to talk to Sonny about that.'

'Has he committed any sort of crime?'

'Again, you'll have to speak to Sonny. I can't really tell you anything more than I already have.'

'I don't understand.'

Miriam must have sounded as awful as she felt, because the nurse did not hang up the phone, and, after a pause, she spoke again.

'Mrs Franklin, I just want you to know that you'd be surprised how common this is. I might be the mental health nurse, but I see a lot of people who are not crazy, just abused.'

'No doubt, but I just don't believe . . . I mean, I'm sure I'd have noticed . . .'

'Not necessarily. Perpetrators are very good at keeping their behaviour hidden.'

But Miriam was still unconvinced. *Maybe you just see this behaviour everywhere because of your job*, she was thinking about the woman with the calm, professional voice on the other end of the phone. *Maybe you've just filled Ally's head with stupid ideas.* But this was not the moment to have a fight, nor was this the person to fight with.

'Well, whatever has happened, Ally and the kids always have a haven here. Thank you for letting me know.'

'No problem. It's my job.'

Miriam hung up and immediately rang Fiona.

'She's left him!'

'Shit! That's a bit out of the blue!'

'Not according to the mental health nurse. She says Ally's not crazy—she's been abused.'

'I told you I never liked him. Shall I come over?'

Fiona did not seem as blindsided by the accusation as her mother. But much as she would've liked to have her sensible older daughter with her for support, she had no idea what Allison would want.

'No, let's see how she is first.'

'Okay. Call me if you need me.'

~

An hour later, almost to the minute, Miriam, who had been sitting at her front window watching the driveway anxiously, saw Pete's old Merc—looking a bit dusty and neglected—swing through the front gates. For a moment or two, she didn't know how to react. She didn't know if she was pleased to see this prodigal daughter, or horrified that her marriage had broken up in what to Miriam seemed such a shocking and abrupt manner. Next minute, she was on her feet and out the door, running towards the car. She was so pleased to see her daughter and grandchildren, and yet so filled with dread, she found she was both laughing and crying.

'Hello! Hello! Louise told me you were coming!'

Ally looked so sad and so lost standing beside the car that Miriam threw her arms around her. For a moment Ally slumped against her mother, and then Miriam felt her stiffen and pull away. It took every ounce of self-control she had to release her daughter. They stood there facing each other in the middle of the landscaped garden, filled with blooming hydrangeas and artfully scattered clumps of old-fashioned bulbs. So much hung unspoken in the air between them that Miriam hardly knew where to start. She squared her shoulders.

'It's okay, darling, it's okay. Whatever's happened—'

'Don't, Mum.' Ally held up her hand as if to ward off her mother.

Don't what? Miriam wondered. *I'm not doing anything!*

'Don't make a big fuss. I—I just can't cope with anything right now.'

Miriam nodded, because Ally did look as if she was only just managing to hold herself together. Her face was white and taut and she was breathing hard.

'Okay. Should we get the children out of the car?'

The babies slept on in their car seats, no doubt because Ally had not yet turned off the engine. The Merc's familiar hum gave Miriam the oddest feeling, as if somehow Pete was with them.

As Miriam gently extracted a sleeping Isla from her baby capsule, she realised that this was the very first time she had met her new granddaughter.

'Hello, Isla,' she said to the still-sleeping newborn. 'I'm your nan.'

'I'm so glad to get out of there,' Ally declared.

'I had no idea things had got so bad. I knew you weren't happy, but . . .'

'How could you know? I didn't even really know myself. But I can't talk about it now. Let's get the kids inside.'

And Ally looked over her shoulder, as if she feared someone might be coming after them. Miriam remembered what the nurse had said over the phone—that Nick would not give up easily.

Ally turned away and lifted Teddy from his car seat. He wriggled and grumbled a little as she hoisted him over her shoulder, but mercifully he stayed asleep.

'Isla is gorgeous—even more beautiful than her pictures.'

Ally nodded mutely. She looked done in, as if she did not even have the energy to form any words.

※

Miriam helped her daughter tuck the children up in the double bed in Fiona's old room (three-month-old Isla looked impossibly tiny sleeping under her bunny rug on the big expanse of bed), then she tactfully left them. She didn't know whether

Ally would stay with her children and sleep herself, or join her mother and explain.

Miriam heated up some soup she had left over in the freezer—enough for the two of them—served herself a bowl and left the rest to keep warm on the stove. She settled down in front of the crime drama she'd been absorbed in so recently, but it seemed like she'd been watching it a lifetime ago. She could no longer follow its labyrinthine plot. Instead, she began searching for something to distract but not distress her. She settled on old episodes of *The Great British Bake Off*. There was something so soothing about watching a diverse group of people putting ingredients in a bowl and making them into something delicious. It calmed her to the extent that she must have nodded off herself. She woke to find Ally leaning over her in the half-light.

'Is that soup for me?'

Miriam sat up, feeling a bit groggy. 'Yes, yes . . . shall I get it for you?'

'No, stay where you are, I can get it. May I have a glass of wine?'

'Of course. Pour me one while you're at it.'

Ally carried the wine and soup to the dining table, and Miriam got up to join her.

'The kids are still asleep,' Ally said. 'I had a little kip myself.'

'Me too, it seems.'

'We're all exhausted, I think.'

Miriam smiled, nodded and sipped her wine. For a few minutes they sat in silence, Ally seemingly focused on her soup, while Miriam tried to summon the courage to ask her daughter what was going on. *It's now or never*, she thought. *Surely I have a right to know what is happening.*

As if Ally had read her mother's mind, she broke the silence. 'I am sorry about . . . turning up out of the blue like this.'

'No need to be sorry. I've told you before you'll always have a home here.'

'I just . . . I couldn't . . . anyway, I feel better now.'

'I'm so glad, but you don't have to tell me anything, not unless you want to.'

It cost Miriam quite a lot to say that.

'I know. But Louise thinks it's better if I do talk about it, and I think if you're going to have to put us up and put up with'—Ally paused and looked over her shoulder again—'well, God knows what . . . I owe you an explanation.'

'I must admit, I am confused,' Miriam said. 'I didn't know you were thinking of leaving Nick.'

'Nor did I, until last night. And then Louise told me I had to go.'

'What happened? I mean, I know you were no longer as happy as you were at first, but I had no idea things had got so bad.'

'Of course you didn't. We both put a huge effort into making sure no one had any idea what was really going on. I didn't even admit the truth to myself until now.'

Ally got up and walked to the window. It was dark outside, so there was nothing much to see but the dim glow of streetlights and the occasional pendulum swing of a passing car's headlights. If Nick was out there looking in at them, they would not know.

Ally put her hand up to her neck, then turned and faced her mother. She looked tense and overwrought.

'It was bad, but I thought I could still make things work. Then, after Isla was born, it all got so much worse, so fast.'

Ally glanced over her shoulder again as she spoke, as if Nick might be right there in Miriam's kitchen, hiding in the shadows. Almost against her will, Miriam looked too.

'He'd been frightening me on and off for ages, ever since we brought Teddy home. He'd always been a bit volatile, right from when we first met. He'd be showering me with kisses one day and blowing up the next, but I confess at first I found it really exciting—sexually exciting, if you know what I mean.'

Miriam did not know what Ally meant, but she knew better than to say so.

'He seemed to love me so much. More than I had ever felt loved before.'

A dagger ran through Miriam as Ally said that, but she kept her face impassive.

'When he lost his temper he turned into a man I hardly recognised, but he'd explain afterwards that it was just terror, his fear that things could not continue to be as perfect as they were forever. If I got upset, he'd scream at me that I was not the victim. Later, when he'd calmed down, he'd explain that it was me acting so pathetic—like an entitled little princess, he called it—that enraged him. And I believed him. I am—well, I *was*—an entitled little princess. So I accepted the criticism, and I tried to change. And that continued right up until Isla was born.'

'Did he hurt you?'

'Not until last night. He didn't have to. If I tried to deny him anything, he raged so much it was easier just to give in and do what he wanted, whether it was have sex or wear dowdy clothes or drop out of my PhD. We used to have terrible, terrible fights, but I presumed it was me; I know how difficult I can be to live with. You and I used to have terrible fights, remember? I could make you cry just like that. I was a bitch. I *am* a bitch. You know that better than anyone. And when I got depressed and turned into such a sad sack, I couldn't blame him for getting impatient with me and telling me I was boring and dreary and a bad mother. And he'd get me so confused. I'd get up in the morning and find the house was a mess, when I was sure I had cleaned it all up before I went to bed, and he'd convince me that I was imagining things and that my brain wasn't working properly. I'd think I could hear music but he'd deny there was anything playing and I never could find where it was coming from. And he always knew where I was going, who I'd seen and who I'd spoken to, even though I didn't remember telling him about any of it. But how else would he know? I really did feel like I was losing my mind.' Ally's eyes filled with tears.

Pieces were falling into place now. Nick's claim on the phone to her that the house was a tip, when in fact it was obsessively orderly. Ally's panic when she thought Miriam had told someone that her daughter had revealed Teddy's gender before the birth. *What had Ally been going through?* she wondered, a cold feeling spreading through her. *And how could I not have seen?*

Miriam reached for her daughter's hand and squeezed it. 'Oh, Ally, you're not crazy at all. Louise said as much. She said you weren't crazy, you were just abused. She called it coercive control.'

There was something else that had troubled her, Miriam recalled. 'When you told me you were pregnant again, you said something about it being deliberate. What did you mean?'

Ally dabbed at her eyes with a serviette. 'We'd agreed not to rush into having another baby. Both my obstetrician and my psychiatrist had said we should wait until I'd recovered from Teddy's birth, and that another pregnancy could be harmful both physically and mentally. But Nick . . .' She hesitated. 'He wouldn't even wait the six weeks after Teddy's birth before having sex. He—he raped me, I suppose, even though I didn't fight. There wasn't any fight left in me. He said it was because he desired me so much, but now I wonder . . . Anyway, from then on, I knew I didn't love him anymore. Even when he was charming, even when he was trying, even when he was being lovely with Teddy, I just felt nothing for him. Then, when I realised I was pregnant with Isla, that's when I started to hate him. But I didn't know what to do about it. I have two babies, no money of my own, and I'm just . . . I'm just so tired. And he'd make threats, about what he might do . . .'

Miriam's alarm must have shown on her face.

'. . . to himself, not us, if I tried to leave. I thought that maybe I could just stick it out—until last night.'

'What happened last night?'

Ally put her hand back up to her neck. 'He strangled me, Mum. He put his hands around my neck and squeezed. He squeezed until I thought I was going to die, until everything went black and I saw stars.'

'My God.'

Miriam was so horrified at how close she had come to losing this beloved daughter, she hardly dared breathe herself.

'When I woke up, he gave me a glass of water and smiled like nothing was wrong. "Why did you do that to me?" I asked him. I could hardly speak my throat was so sore—it still is. And do you know what he said? *Do you know what he said?*'

Ally's voice had become high and urgent.

'No, what did he say?'

'He said, "Do what to you, darling? You've just had a little nap. Maybe you've had a bad dream." That's when I knew I had to leave. If he could do that to me and then just deny it . . . he could have killed me—he almost *killed* me—and it seemed to mean nothing to him. Like it was a game, or something. It made me wonder, if he could do that to me, what could he do to the children?'

CHAPTER 15

BANG! BANG! BANG!
Someone was hammering on the front door, pounding their fists against the wood. As she pulled on her dressing-gown, Miriam felt dizzy with exhaustion. She wondered how on earth she had managed to fall asleep at all.

Ally was already standing by her mother's bedroom door. She looked panic-stricken.

'It's Nick!' she whispered, as if scared that he'd hear her. 'I knew he would come. I've been lying awake dreading it.'

'You stay here. I'll get rid of him.' Miriam found herself whispering too.

'Be careful, Mum. He's . . . he's out of control.' She took a breath, and the words she spoke seemed to come from deep in her gut. 'I hate him! I hate him! I HATE him!' She was standing with both her fists clenched, breastmilk staining her nightie, breathing hard.

'Sonny!' Nick yelled. 'Sonny, I know you're in there! Come out or I'll . . .'

As she and Ally looked at each other, Miriam's heart was thumping in her chest. She was afraid, she realised. Physically afraid.

She grabbed her phone from her bedside table. 'I'll film him,' Miriam said, brandishing the device at her daughter. 'That should make him think twice.'

The phone made her feel a tiny bit safer, but it wasn't a weapon. *That's what I really need*, she thought, as she scurried down the stairs.

'SONNY! GODDAMN IT, OPEN THIS DOOR!'

Christ, she thought, *he must be waking everyone for miles around. I hope Julie calls the police.* Why it never crossed her mind to call them herself—she had her phone in her hand, after all—she would never know, but it didn't. *Fear and panic*, she supposed later. *It fucks with your head.*

When Miriam got to the door, she didn't open it. Instead, she turned on the outside light and peered at her son-in-law through the old-fashioned peephole located beneath a panel of glass. She held her phone up to the window above her head and started filming. She had absolutely no idea whether she was getting anything on camera or not.

'Stop that!' she yelled at him through the door in her rich-lady voice. She sounded much more confident than she felt. 'Stop it immediately!'

'I won't stop until you let me see my wife and my children! I know they are here!'

Through the peephole, she could see Nick's face only inches away. She tried to keep her voice steady and firm. 'That's not happening. Not while you are in this state. Go away and leave us alone. And I'm filming you, by the way, just so you know.'

The effect of her words was remarkable. Almost instantly, his manner grew calm.

'Look, I'm sorry, Miriam, but I'm devastated. I came home to an empty house and a note from Sonny saying she'd left me and taken the kids!' He ran a hand through his hair; the anguish on his face was clear. 'Can you open the door, please? It's ridiculous shouting at each other like this.'

For a moment Miriam was tempted to relent and let him in; maybe he and Ally could talk this through in a reasonable manner. Then she remembered that this was the man who had strangled her daughter until she had passed out.

'No, Nick, I'm not letting you in now. It's the middle of the night. If you want to talk in a civilised fashion, you must come around at a civilised hour.'

'Alright, alright, I'll go.'

There was the distant sound of a siren. Perhaps Julie had called the police. Perhaps Ally had.

'Good. And call *me* before you come, not Ally.'

Then, hearing a sound behind her, Miriam turned to see Ally running down the stairs, her hair and dressing-gown flying, her face flushed pink. Before Miriam could stop her, Ally was wrenching the front door open. She flew outside and rushed at Nick with such force and determination he staggered backwards.

'Go away, Nick! I never want to see you again! Never, do you hear me? *Never!* Just *fuck off!*'

Nick continued to back away. By now she was pushing at his chest with both her hands.

'You tried to kill me and *I will never forgive you*!'

'Don't be ridiculous,' Nick blustered. 'I did no such thing.'

He was trying to stay calm, but it was clear his much smaller wife had taken him by surprise.

'LIAR! I know what you did and *you* know what you did. *Everything* you did!'

Ah, thought Miriam, *there is more than she has told me.*

The distant siren sounded as if it was getting closer. Nick glanced in the direction of the sound, then turned on his heel and began to stalk away. He stopped once he was at a safe distance and yelled back at them.

'You are a crazy bitch, Sonny! You are an unfit mother! You are fucking *nuts*!'

Then, his feet crunching on the gravel as he ran to the gate, he disappeared down the street. Their street, the one they had lived on for over thirty years, where the loudest disruption they had ever created previously was a teenage party. Miriam felt embarrassed as she imagined the neighbours lying awake in the dark, listening. No one would ever say a word about it to her face—well, except Julie, perhaps—but it'd be the talk of the neighbourhood.

Ally was still standing on the driveway. She wrapped her arms around her body as if she were cold and yelled into the dark, 'And don't call me Sonny! My name is *Ally*! It's *Ally*, you bastard!' She bent and picked up a handful of stones from the gravel driveway and hurled them as hard as she could at the spot where her husband had been standing. Then she turned to Miriam. 'That nickname always made me feel like I was a goofy adolescent boy in some American sitcom, not like an adult woman.'

They heard his jeep starting up behind the hedge. It was good his car had such a distinctive sound, Miriam thought; they'd always know when he was coming.

Mother and daughter stood in the dark, every nerve straining, until they heard the car pull away. Only then did they relax. Miriam felt as tired as she could ever remember feeling. As tired as the day Pete had died. Was this how life was going to be from now on?

'Are you alright, Mum?'

Ally was standing beside her. She seemed calm enough.

'Yes. I think so. Are you?'

'Yes. I feel better than I have in months.'

Lucky you, thought Miriam. *I feel like a balloon after all the air has been let out.*

The siren was very close now and they both turned towards the sound, waiting for whatever would happen next, but it blared right past them, hurtling noisily through the dark. Apparently the vehicle—whether it was a cop car, an ambulance or a fire engine, Miriam couldn't be sure—was attending to someone else's crisis in the night. Nevertheless, Miriam gave silent thanks for it. Ally's ferocity notwithstanding, the siren had helped chase Nick away.

'He'll be back,' Ally muttered. 'He won't give up.'

'No, but he does deserve an explanation, surely?'

Even in the dark, Miriam could sense Ally's fury.

'Did you not hear a word I said?'

Christ, thought Miriam, *I am such an idiot.*

'No, I did, I did. I'm sorry—it's just hard to go from who I thought Nick was to who you now tell me he is. I need time.'

'There is no time,' Ally said fiercely. 'Either you believe me, or you don't.'

'I believe you.' And Miriam did.

Ally's arms were still wrapped around her body, and Miriam saw she was shivering.

'You're cold. Let's go in.'

༄

'We should go to the police. We need to get an AVO.'

Miriam looked up, startled. She was helping Teddy eat his rice cereal. She still felt as if she had been run over by a truck.

'An apprehended violence order? Is that necessary?'

'Louise made me promise to do it straight away.'

Ally's face was rigid, emotionally closed down. She seemed a million miles away, businesslike and cold.

'Okay. Do you know how?'

'I go to the nearest police station and tell them how he strangled me. I don't know if they'll believe me . . .'

Miriam flushed.

'. . . because he left no marks. That's why they do it that way, Louise said.'

Ally held her hand against her neck with her fingers splayed to demonstrate. Miriam was guiltily aware that she had snuck a few surreptitious glances at Ally's neck earlier, trying to see if there were any finger marks or bruises. *Doubt is a terrible and powerful thing*, she thought to herself, *I must not indulge in it.*

'But I did get him on film last night,' Miriam said. 'They'll have to believe that.'

She played back for her daughter what she had managed to record through the window the night before. The mottled glass made it hard to identify who was standing on their front doorstep, but there was no mistaking Nick's words and the tone of his voice.

Ally watched without changing expression then said, 'Send it to me. We should have two copies.'

'I should talk to Julie too,' Miriam said. 'She'll have heard something.'

'Yes, when I heard the siren, I thought she must have called the cops—or you had.'

'I never thought of it,' Miriam confessed.

'No, nor did I. Seems Julie didn't either.'

'I wonder why not?'

'You should talk to her,' Ally suggested.

'If you're okay with it, I will.'

'It's funny, yesterday I couldn't bear the idea of anyone knowing what he was doing to me. Today I don't care. Maybe I'll feel differently tomorrow. Anyway, I doubt there's anyone in the vicinity who hasn't got a pretty clear idea already, after that little display last night.' Ally smiled bitterly.

And I suspect you haven't told me the half of it, thought Miriam.

❦

'I'd like to report some threatening behaviour towards my daughter and take out an AVO against my son-in-law. I have it recorded on here, if you want to see.'

Miriam waved her phone at the young copper behind the glass screen at their local police station. And he was *very* young. He looked to her as if he should still be at school. Miriam hadn't known what to expect from her first visit to the police, but it wasn't this pimply stripling with nails bitten to the quick. She felt very uncertain about his ability to offer any kind of protection.

'Are you the person I should be speaking to?' she asked.

That posh lady voice again. She hadn't meant to use it. She was starting to think it was a product of her nerves. The more inadequate she felt, the more pompous she sounded.

'Your son-in-law? The DV liaison officer isn't in this morning, I'm afraid,' the stripling said. 'So, yes, you can report it to me.'

'When will the DV person be in?'

'This afternoon, possibly, but I can't say for sure. She's at court. Frankly, I wouldn't waste time if you need an AVO. If we make the report now, you should be able to get it in a day or two.'

'A day or two?' Miriam echoed in dismay.

She turned to look at Ally, who was rocking the double pram back and forth in the small waiting area while her mother fronted the desk. It'd been quite an exercise just getting the bloody thing into the station, even though it was a modern building designed to be accessible. Nothing was very accessible for a double pram, it seemed.

'Yes, it has to go to a magistrate, who will grant an AVO on the basis of a police report.'

Miriam felt like they were about to step off a precipice into a world she had no inkling about and no desire to enter. She had a sudden urge to get out of there. Maybe it would all be okay. Maybe Nick would never come back. Maybe Ally could just get a divorce, they could work out custody like reasonable people and get on with their lives. Then she remembered the fear on Ally's face as she described how close her husband had come to killing her. No, there could be no turning back now.

'He strangled her.'

The constable looked up. 'Who? You?'

Now, Ally stepped forward. 'No, me. My husband strangled me until I lost consciousness.'

Ally spoke matter-of-factly, but it was obvious from the constable's reaction that he took the charge very seriously. As Ally recounted her story, he took careful notes. Eventually, Teddy ran out of patience.

'I'll take the kids for a walk.'

Miriam had to raise her voice to be heard over Teddy's wailing. She was feeling useless and unnecessary anyway. *It's funny*, she thought, as she struggled to get the large pram out the door, *sometimes I feel central to this drama, and other times completely peripheral.*

Outside, wandering down the busy street, it was a relief to see ordinary people going about their ordinary business. There was something claustrophobic about being in a crisis, something that made you feel as if you were set apart from everyone else, from normality. She'd felt the same after Pete had died.

'And here I am again,' she said aloud to Teddy. He grinned back at her companionably.

When she returned after half an hour or so, she was relieved to see that Ally was signing her statement.

'What happens now?' her daughter asked.

'We serve the application on your husband.'

Ally looked up from the document. 'What?'

'Yes, he has to attend court same as you.'

'But I'm doing this to keep him away from me and the kids, not so I can see more of him!'

'I know. It's hard, but you are not protected by the provisional AVO until it is served on him. After that, if he comes near you, even before you've gone to court and it is approved by a magistrate, he is in breach.'

'How quickly can you serve it on him?'

'Do you know where he is?'

'At his mother's probably. She lives in Lane Cove.'

Uncomfortably close to Greenwich, Miriam thought.

As Ally gave the police officer—Constable Moran, as she now called him—the address, Miriam found herself feeling sorry for Sally Carruthers. This surprised her, as she'd taken an almost instant dislike to the woman. *But what a shock it would be for any mother*, she thought, *to have the cops turn up on your doorstep to serve your son with an AVO.*

Now Isla started to cry. No doubt she was hungry. It felt as if they had been in the station for hours. Miriam picked up the baby and put her over her shoulder, holding the little belly firmly against her collarbone, a trick she'd learnt during her own mothering.

'You cause us all sorts of trouble, you little ones,' she whispered to the baby, 'but it's nothing to the trouble you cause us when you get older.'

Her thoughts returned to Nick's mum. *We're both helpless in this, caught in a drama between our two children we neither started nor can stop. But maybe we are also both responsible in some way. We brought them up, after all.*

'We'll serve this on your husband as soon as we can,' Constable Moran was saying, 'and we will let you know when we have.'

'You'll call me?'

'Either the DV liaison officer or I will.' He handed Ally his card. 'Here's my number in case you need it.'

~

'Did you ever find your father a bit controlling?'

They were driving the short distance home, Ally at the wheel of the Merc. She turned her head to look sharply at her mother. 'What brought that on?'

'Just something Julie said.'

'He was a terrible fusspot and sometimes he'd drive me crazy trying to do stuff for me that I could perfectly well do myself, but he was nothing like Nick, if that's what you're driving at.'

'That's what I said.'

'Was Julie having a go?' Ally had turned back to the road.

'Not really. She just got me thinking.'

'Do you miss him?' Ally checked her side mirror before changing lanes.

'Every day.'

'Me too.' Then Ally accelerated quickly, nipping into a small gap in the traffic.

They lapsed into silence. Miriam was filled with yearning. If only Pete were still there to tell her what to do, to make the decisions, to protect her. No matter what Julie said, she did not feel capable of handling this on her own. But at least they now had an AVO, or had started the process anyway. That was something.

The first thing Miriam and Ally saw as they turned into their street was Nick's jeep parked outside their house.

'Shit, he's here.'

'They won't have had time to serve him with the AVO yet!'

Miriam felt terrified. She'd thought somehow that merely applying for an AVO would protect them from harm, like a magic spell, like waving garlic at a vampire. They'd spoken to the police and now the law would protect her and her daughter. *Wasn't that how it was meant to go?*

'I'll tell him to leave.'

'No.' Ally put her hand out to stop her mother. 'You get the kids. I'll go.'

They both got out of the car, and Miriam watched her daughter like a hawk while she struggled to get the giant double pram out of the boot. Leaving Nick seemed to have instilled Ally with a new determination.

As Ally walked towards the jeep, Nick and his mother climbed out of it. Miriam got such a shock at the sight of Sally that she straightened up without thinking and banged her head hard on the lid of the boot.

'Sally!' she exclaimed.

Nick's mother looked at Miriam with a cold expression. 'We've come for the children.'

Ally gasped and ran back towards her mother. She stood beside the Merc, arms spread wide, as if to ward them off. Any fellow feeling Miriam had been nurturing towards Nick's mother disappeared in an instant.

'You *what?*' Now it was Miriam's turn to step up. 'Don't be ridiculous. We've just applied for an AVO against Nick after his behaviour here last night.'

'And you actually got the cops to believe your lurid fantasies?' Nick scoffed.

'We have you on film, remember,' Miriam put in.

'And you strangled me,' Ally cried, 'until I blacked out. You know you did. The cops said that was a red flag.'

'Don't be ridiculous, Sonny!' Sally snapped. 'Nick would never do such a thing. That's why we need to take the children. You are clearly not well.'

Ally said nothing. She just looked long and steadily at her husband and mother-in-law. Then she took out her mobile phone and dialled a number.

'Constable Moran? It's Ally Franklin . . .'

Miriam's heart leapt at hearing her daughter take back control *and* her own name.

'Yes, I was just in applying for an AVO against my husband, Nick Carruthers. He's here at my mother's house—you have the address, if you want to serve it on him now . . . Thank you, we'll see you soon.'

The change in Nick's demeanour made Miriam hold her breath and take a step backwards. Something very dark emanated from him.

He stepped towards his wife. 'You are delusional, Sonny. This is all in your mind. If you keep this up, we *will* have to take the children.'

But Sally was plucking at her son's sleeve. 'Come on, Nick, we'd better go home.'

Nick allowed his mother to take him by the elbow and lead him away.

'Now is not the time,' she continued. 'You have done nothing wrong, so you have nothing to fear. The police will soon find out the truth. She won't be allowed to keep my grandchildren for long. She's in no fit state.'

'They are my grandchildren too.'

Miriam had Isla in her arms by this time, and Ally was holding tight to Teddy.

'Then you must see that they'd be safer with us,' Sally countered.

'I see no such thing. Your son is abusive. If he abused my daughter, what is to stop him abusing his children?'

'I would *never* . . .!' Nick was suddenly looming over her.

Miriam stood firm. In fact, she felt a small sense of triumph. If he was this easy to provoke, there was no chance he'd be awarded custody.

She looked from her furious son-in-law to his mother. 'See? It's not Ally who's the problem. If you want access to the children, you'll have to fight us in court.'

Miriam smiled to herself. Oh, yes. She'd love to see him try. They would fight him alright. And they would *win*.

PART TWO

CHAPTER 16

Four years later, Miriam was staring blankly at the pile of papers on Ally's desk under the window. The desk that once was Pete's was now well and truly her daughter's. The letter on the top of the pile was from Ally's lawyer notifying them of yet another custody application filed by Nick and his lawyers. Miriam sighed. How many such applications would this be? She'd lost count. It was just as well Duffy Real Estate continued to be profitable and that she'd received a good price for Pete's share of BPF, lawyers were eye-wateringly expensive.

Maybe it was weariness that kept her emotions in check but she was surprised how calm she felt as she turned back to her computer and typed, *Where can I buy a gun?* into the search engine. Until recently, it would have been beyond her wildest imaginings to ever consider doing such a thing. She'd always hated guns of any kind. She and Pete had been such supporters of gun control they had donated money regularly to the group that vigilantly defended the tight restrictions Australia had implemented after the Port Arthur massacre. Yet, given what she had lived through in the years since Pete had died, typing such words now felt as reasonable as googling *tastiest salad recipes* or *best cafe near me*.

Everyone else in the house was either asleep or watching TV. When Pete had died—was it really nearly six years ago?—she'd had to learn to cope with her big house and garden on her own. Over the last few years, thanks to her younger daughter and two small grandchildren, she'd had to learn to share it all over again.

As the names of gun shops and gun dealers loaded onto her screen, she saved the relevant links into a file she had created after Pete had died. It was called Spring Annuals and last year that was what it had contained—links to online gardening retailers who carried the spring flowers she liked to plant in her herbaceous border. Miriam knew how much a well-maintained garden could add to the value of a property. She also knew that life was temporary. She would not let the garden go to rack and ruin, no matter how much stress she was under. She now understood all too well that she could never know when she might pop her clogs—as Pete used to say—and she wanted her daughters to get the best price possible for the major asset they would inherit—the house she was currently sitting inside, glass of rosé at hand, as she calmly researched how to buy a gun.

Since Ally and the children had moved in, Miriam's life had been turned upside down. She had learnt to live with a constant level of dread that occasionally rose to a pitch of panic. Nick had proved adept at making their lives a misery. Despite the AVO, which had been extended and then extended again, he had found ways to haunt them. Miriam could not believe how naive they had been at the beginning of this ordeal. She had assumed at first, and for far longer than she should have, that the police and the law would be able to protect them. She now understood that they could not.

She remembered how angry she had been with Julie about her failure to call the cops that first night after Ally had finally left Nick. Her anger was intense because she thought that if he had been stopped by the cops that night—arrested, perhaps—his campaign of terror might have been nipped in the bud. As she closed the Spring Annuals folder on her computer, she snorted out loud at her own idiocy.

'Why didn't you call the cops when Nick was bashing our front door down the other night?' she had demanded of her neighbour.

Julie just gave Miriam a puzzled look. 'He did what? I didn't hear anything.'

'Have you gone temporarily deaf or something?'

She had not meant to sound so aggressive, but fortunately Julie ignored it.

'No, but I wear earplugs at night now.' She smiled sheepishly. 'It's Sinbad. He's started sleeping on my bed, and he snores. If I didn't wear earplugs, I wouldn't get a wink.'

'He sleeps on your bed? Oh, Julie. I hope he doesn't have fleas.'

'Not so far, but he's getting old and his arthritis bothers him, and he cries when I try to insist he sleep in his basket. I think the cold gets to him.'

Miriam simply did not have the energy to sympathise with a bloody dog.

'Just as well we got the AVO then; you'd be worse than useless.'

As it turned out, just about everything was worse than useless. Nick had breached the AVO numerous times. Whenever a story about a husband or father killing his partner and/or his family appeared in the media, he never failed to use it to ratchet up the threat. After a man burnt his wife by dousing her with petrol, they found a box of matches in the letterbox. Of course, Nick denied all knowledge of the matches when confronted by police. After a woman drove her car into a lake and drowned her children, they found one of Teddy's toy cars in a puddle in the driveway. Did Teddy leave it out and then it rained? It was perfectly possible. When a man gassed himself and his wife and kids while they slept, they found a length of hose rolled up on the footpath outside their house. Had it fallen off a tradie's ute? Been left by the landscaper working next door? Maybe. Eventually they had stopped going to the police. It wasn't that the cops weren't sympathetic; it was just that they could not do anything.

Such provocations had largely ceased when they got the CCTV installed, because they'd been able to prove he'd breached the AVO, even when all he'd left was a bunch of flowers. But the one or two times it got to court—and that took long enough—it was judged a 'minor' breach and no action was taken. It seemed Nick knew just how far he could go to keep them on edge while not getting himself into strife. He'd turn up in places outside the boundaries of the order when Ally was there. A coincidence that happened so often they began to realise something else had to be going on.

'Is he watching me all the time?' Ally asked.

It turned out he was.

It took them a long time to work out that Nick had installed some kind of software on Ally's phone that meant he knew every move she made and every word she said. It had been the DV liaison officer—Rebecca—who had gently suggested they get Ally a new phone. The minute she mentioned it, Miriam felt like a fool. Why hadn't she thought of that? It was also Rebecca who suggested that they install the CCTV system around the house. It was meant to ensure their safety, and maybe it did, but it didn't make them *feel* safer. After all, who would go to all that expense (Miriam had gulped when she'd received the quote) if they were not actually in danger? Miriam wondered what people with fewer resources did in this situation. And by people, of course, she meant women. Installing their own system reminded her of the elaborate security system Nick had set up in the little house in Dungog.

'God!' she said to Ally one evening after they had tucked the children into bed. 'How could we have been so naive? Believing his claim that he had never turned it on! Of course he had—he had you under surveillance from the start!'

'Who is this "we" you are referring to?'

'Well, you seemed to have accepted what he said.'

'Not quite, but I was still trying to convince myself that he was only overprotective because he loved me so much.'

'You never said.' Miriam felt aggrieved. Had they both colluded to deceive her?

'No. Like I said, I was trying to convince myself. The sane part of me knew it sounded batshit crazy, but it's weird the games you can play with yourself when you really, really want to believe something.'

Miriam had really, really believed that, following the divorce, the custody and access arrangements for the children would be an open-and-shut case, but in the last four years she had discovered the reality was far different.

'The Family Court is often biased against mothers who allege abuse, I'm afraid. They call it parental alienation, and it can put your own battle for access and even your current arrangements at risk.'

Nerida Ong was Ally's lawyer and she came highly recommended, but this remark in one of their early meetings with the woman had shocked Miriam to the core.

'Well, what do I do?' Ally had asked. 'How can I safeguard my children? He strangled me until I lost consciousness and he did more—you *know* what else he did . . . Surely that ought to preclude him having unsupervised access?'

Ally always hated listing all the things Nick had done to her, particularly the controlling behaviour and sexual humiliation. She was ashamed of what she had tolerated. Ashamed to tell anyone how utterly degraded she had been. Miriam was sure she still did not know the half of it.

'And how many awful, awful things have to happen before they believe us? I've heard about older kids pleading with their lawyers to tell the court how afraid they are of their dad, only to find their lawyers have done nothing! What the fuck do we have to do? Must we just die without a fight? Without even protesting or seeking help? I am sure the mothers of all the dead kids did everything they could to protect them—it's our fucking job—but how do we do it alone?'

'But as far as we know, he has never hurt the children,' Nerida said. 'That's the way the court will look at it. They see this as a fight between the two of you that has nothing to do with the kids.'

'But surely hurting their mother is damaging to kids,' Ally argued. 'Surely the court understands that. And if he has the capacity to be violent, they ought to at least take that into account.'

'You'd think so, but that's not how it works.'

Miriam felt enraged. Why must Ally have to suffer in this way and why must her safety be of so little account? The justice system, which she'd believed in all her life, not only didn't help, it made everything worse. Abusive men knew they could get away with intimidation and power plays. They knew the court would do nothing. *Christ*, thought Miriam, *I believe in innocent till proven guilty, of course I do, but they still operate as if women and children are owned by their husband and father!*

Fortunately, Miriam rarely set eyes on her ex-son-in-law these days. It was Sally who came to pick up the children whenever it was Nick's access weekend. He was now living with his parents a few suburbs away in Lane Cove.

Despite Ally's agitation about Nick's intentions regarding the children, Miriam still hoped that despite all the awful and threatening things he did—the matches, the toy car, the garden hose—he would never seriously contemplate hurting them. He was just trying to frighten their mother—and succeeding. Miriam's own fear was that somehow Nick would persuade a judge to give him sole custody. That outcome didn't bear thinking about. She had seen how vengeful and unpredictable Nick could be, and she knew from Ally how cruel and controlling he was. That did not make for good and stable parenting. It was a relief that the children's paternal grandparents were in the house on access weekends. It was a relief that both Teddy and Isla seemed very fond of them. *Mind you*, Miriam told herself, *they also love their dad.* And sometimes, Miriam had a chilling thought: *Sally and Maurice raised Nick. Maybe they're not such a safe pair of hands.* But she tried to keep these anxieties at bay. After all, what choice did they have? The legal system just closed its eyes and folded its arms in the face of their fears for the children. They were his kids, and apparently that gave him a right to them, whatever he had done to their mother. It wasn't just the unfairness of this Miriam found so shocking; it was the refusal to recognise the risk it posed.

Now, months after that exchange with the lawyer, Miriam leant back in her chair. These days, her back always ached if she sat too long at her computer. Too bad. She had a task to finish.

Applying for a gun licence, she typed into the search engine. After all, she was a law-abiding citizen and had no intention of doing anything illegal. But she needed to do something. She could no longer bear feeling so powerless.

A few weeks ago, she had begun taking a couple of hours out of the office regularly, telling Prisha she had appointments. Mondays, Wednesdays and Thursdays, she drove across the bridge to a gun club in the city's southern suburbs. No way did she want to be recognised, and the problem with having been a real estate agent in her area for so long was that everyone who lived locally knew her face, even if they had never actually met her. Her immaculately made-up features smiled benignly from all her For Sale and Sold signs and on all the ads she ran in the local papers.

This 'project'—whatever it was—was hers and hers alone. She would confide in no one. She knew if she did, they would only try to stop her. If Pete had still been alive she might have confided in him; it might even have become his project rather than hers. But, just like the garden, the fuse box, the bills, bin night and blown light bulbs, this was just something else she'd now have to take care of herself. Why she wanted a gun exactly, she did not know. She just did. *For insurance*, she thought. *So we don't have to sit here, defenceless, waiting like ducks in a shooting gallery.*

She wasn't much of a shot—not that it mattered—but as she had discovered through her research, if she wanted to own a pistol legally, she had to be a member of a gun club and she had to participate in a minimum of eight competitive target shoots a year. When she first read that restriction, she almost questioned her commitment to strict gun controls. Then she took herself in hand. She'd always been a thorough and hard-working person, and if that's what it took, then that's what it took. She hadn't built a business from scratch, starting in an era when professional women were regarded at best with patronising amusement and at worst with hostile suspicion, without learning how to overcome hurdles.

As a result, she was now working quite hard on her shooting technique and getting her eye in, as the instructor put it. And, she had to admit, she was improving. The one time she'd hit the bullseye she got quite excited. For a moment, she'd let herself enjoy her increasing skill for its own sake.

Then she reminded herself that she didn't want to win any competitions; she just wanted to be able to buy a handgun legally and shoot straight—if ever, God forbid, it came to that. *A Smith and Wesson 9 mm*, she thought after listening to her fellow gun club members. It was easy to get them to give her advice. Such was the hostility to guns in urban Sydney, enthusiasts were delighted to help a beginner. Miriam supposed it made them feel less like pariahs. They even recommended nearby gun shops where she might buy her own weapon rather than hire one at the range. But she hadn't been ready until now. Now she wanted to have a gun here, in the house. Safely stored, of course. Unlike the elaborate security system, she hoped a gun would make her feel safer—or less helpless, anyway.

But she did not want to buy a gun too close to home or too close to where anyone might recognise her, including members of the gun club. That's why she was searching for gun shops outside the Sydney metropolitan area, so the chances of meeting anyone she knew were small. She could not imagine how she would explain her presence in such a place to anyone who knew her from her real life.

Miriam drained her glass of rosé, closed the computer and went around carefully checking the locks on all the doors and windows—a habit that had become an obsession since Allison and the children had taken refuge with her. She also checked the CCTV was on.

When she was sure the perimeter of the house was secure, she set the alarm and went upstairs to bed. The children were asleep, but Allison was either still awake or had fallen asleep with the TV on. She walked past her daughter's room, resisting the impulse to check. She'd made that mistake before, treating her daughter as if she was still a little girl. Allison was a grown woman. She could run her life as she chose. Miriam just wished she hadn't made such a hash of it.

'Did you remember to set the alarm?' Allison had opened her own door and was standing silhouetted against the light in an oversized t-shirt.

Miriam could hear the anxiety in her daughter's voice and that made the now-constant knot in her own belly tighten. 'Yes. Everything is secure. Sleep well, darling.'

Her daughter snorted. 'As if.'

CHAPTER 17

'I ran into Nick at the pub near my work.'

Liam was sitting at the lunch table in Greenwich. Molly was playing with Teddy and Isla on the other side of the room, and there had been a pause in the conversation. It was unusual for quiet, logically minded Liam to be the centre of attention. The other adults at the table turned to look at him. They had been talking about the upcoming custody case. Miriam had indulged in a rant about how much she and Ally were dreading yet another battle in court and how frightened they were that Nick could gain custody, or even just more access.

'"Ran into him?" I doubt that.' Ally no longer believed in coincidences where her ex-husband was concerned.

'Yeah, I doubted it too. I tried to make an excuse and leave, but he kept badgering me to let him buy me a beer. I didn't want to, but I was frightened if I didn't he'd cause a scene. I told him I could only stay for a few minutes, because I had a meeting.'

'What did he want?'

'To justify himself,' said Fiona. Liam had obviously already confided in his wife.

'How'd he do that exactly?' Ally was leaning forward.

'He got all weepy and maudlin. I think he'd had a few already. He went on about his marriage vows and how he regarded them as sacred. How if he made a promise, he always kept it, come what may. That it was a point of pride for him.'

'What did you say?'

'Nothing. I just kept my eyes on my beer and hoped I could get away soon.'

'No such luck.' Fiona was prompting her husband.

'Then he got really intense, and he went on about how even when Sonny—sorry, Ally—went nuts he stuck by her. It never even crossed his mind to leave, he said. He'd sworn to love her in sickness and in health—he repeated that quite a few times. He yelled it eventually, right in my face, and everyone looked at him. By this time I just wanted the floor to open up and swallow me.'

'Jesus,' Miriam whispered.

'Yeah. He kept trying to get me to agree with him. Lots of "you know, mate, these women, mate, what would they know, mate" stuff. I wasn't playing. Then he went on about how he was a man of honour—he yelled that a couple of times too and pounded his fist on the bar; the barman came over and told him to keep it down. Honestly, I'll never be able to show my face in that pub again, and it's where we all go for a drink after work . . .'

Liam worked for a large construction company in the city.

'What else did he say?' Ally wasn't interested in how this encounter would affect Liam's drinking habits.

'He said he would never break his vows, that despite the divorce, he regarded marriage as lasting till death us do part. Anyway, I'd had enough by then, so I got up to leave, but he grabbed my arm to stop me.'

'What did you do?' asked Miriam.

'I pulled away and then I leant into *his* face and said loudly, so everyone could hear, "An honourable man would let his wife leave if she wasn't happy anymore—that's what an honourable man would do." And then I got out of there fast.'

Ally rose from her seat and gave her brother-in-law a hug. 'Thank you, Liam. My sister has good taste in men. I just wish mine had been better.'

Miriam said nothing. It was the phrase 'till death us do part' that was reverberating in her head. Then she remembered another part of the marriage service: 'to have and to hold'. She'd never realised before how sinister the vows were.

༄

The pub where Liam drank with his colleagues was not the only sanctuary Nick had managed to invade; Miriam's own work had suffered. She was not paying as much attention to her business as she used to. Prisha was really running Duffy Real Estate now. Miriam had upped her salary a few times in gratitude and was considering offering her a partnership. Quite apart from the stress of protecting her daughter and grandchildren from harm, she was getting older and feeling it. Maybe, at sixty-two, it was time to pass the business on to someone younger. But it wasn't just her age that was an issue, she knew; it was the sense of apprehension that had overtaken her.

Whenever Miriam held an open house, she lived in fear that Sally or Maurice would wander through the property. The first time Sally had appeared at a gate beside an Open for Inspection sign, Miriam had been unable to believe her eyes.

'What are you doing here?' She cornered Nick's mother as she signed the form by the front door, put there so Miriam could capture the details of potential buyers.

'Hello, Miriam. It's nice to see you too.'

'Don't play games, Sally.'

'Games? I don't know what you are talking about. Maurice and I are thinking of investing or maybe even moving. This place fits our search criteria, so here I am.'

Her tone reminded Miriam of a smart-arse teenager daring an authority figure to take her on. It took all of Miriam's self-discipline not to scream abuse at her and throw her out. Instead, she forced herself to be civil, though her voice was cold.

'It's an open house. You have as much right to be here as anyone else—except your son, of course. He's banned.'

'Ridiculous!'

But Miriam was already hurrying off to welcome a family of four who'd just walked through the front gate.

Later, when she looked at the inspection sheet, she saw that Sally had signed herself in as 'mother of a wronged son'. She picked up one of the Duffy Real Estate branded pens she kept in a little beaker beside the book and scribbled over the entry so hard she tore the paper.

That evening, feeling even more edgy than usual, the upcoming custody hearing was hanging over her head, Miriam had grabbed a bottle of chardonnay from the fridge in the garage and gone over to Julie's place. She knew where Julie hid the key, so she let herself in and called out her usual greeting.

'It's only me!'

She put the key back in its hiding place and closed the door behind her. She was surprised to find the house quite dark and wondered why Sinbad had not come creakily up to her to growl out his usual warning.

'Julie? Are you okay?'

There was a wail from the back of the house. 'Nooooo!'

Julie sounded like she had been crying. Miriam found her curled up on the sofa in the TV room in the dark drinking Scotch. She was a picture of misery and obviously half-pissed.

'What on earth has happened?'

'Sinbad was put down today . . . by your horrible son-in-law!'

It was an accusation.

When Nick came to Sydney and moved in with his parents, he'd found a job at a vet clinic in a nearby suburb. His job had cut Miriam and Ally off from their usual shopping street and forced them to change all their habits. Again, Miriam had wondered why it was that the person who was wreaking the havoc was deferred to, why he seemed to still have the power to make them shape their lives around him.

'Why were you taking the dog to him? I didn't know Nick was your vet.'

Miriam felt betrayed by her friend. Surely she should have changed vets the minute she found out Nick was working there, out of solidarity, if nothing else. Julie had always seemed sympathetic when Miriam had told her tales of Nick's latest outrage, but maybe she didn't believe them either. Meanly, Miriam almost felt pleased that the old dog was gone. She'd never liked the animal and it served Julie right for taking him there. Anyway, Sinbad was demented, smelly and riddled with arthritis, and now—an added bonus—Julie could take out her earplugs at last.

'He wasn't, but Omar is on leave, so Nick was standing in. He pushed me and pushed me to do it. Told me it was cruel to keep Sinbad alive when he was suffering. He even took out this carved wooden box that had his euthanasia kit in it—syringes, vials of drugs, needles—and explained the whole process. He just kept at me until I gave in. I hate your son-in-law.'

'Well, that makes two of us—three if you count Ally.'

Julie sniffed. 'You don't really care. You never liked Sinbad.'

'I liked him a lot better than I like Nick. Here, pour me one of those, let's we two miserable old ladies drown our sorrows together.'

A few weeks later, Sally turned up at another of Miriam's open houses, this time with Maurice in tow. Miriam decided to cut them off at the gate. She stepped in front of them as they walked down the front path. Sally looked at Miriam with real hatred, but Maurice smiled vaguely at her, as if he had no idea who she was. Miriam noticed that Sally had hold of him by the hand. *He's not all there*, she realised. His pale blue eyes—so like his son's—were vacant and unfocused. She felt pity for him for a moment, but then Sally tried to push past her and Miriam's heart hardened.

'Forget it, you're not viewing this house. There is no way I'd sell it to you.'

'You would if we offered enough. You've got a calculator where your heart should be. I saw you during the divorce.'

This was such an unfair accusation—Miriam had many faults but being obsessed with money was not one of them—it left her open-mouthed. It was particularly outrageous given how much money defending her daughter and grandchildren against Nick's constant litigation was costing her. Like the fast-approaching custody hearing, for instance.

'There is no way the courts would let you buy a house so close to Ally.'

'Why not? You've got an AVO out against Nick, not me and Maurice.'

'It can be extended. You know that. Why don't you just leave quietly? Why must you and I fight our children's battles?'

'Because you've got our grandchildren, that's why.'

'You old cunt!' Maurice was suddenly looming over Miriam. The vacant stare of a few moments ago had been replaced by a look of pure hatred.

Christ, thought Miriam, *so this is where Nick gets it from!*

Even Sally looked startled. She took her husband's arm and began to steer him out of the garden, speaking soothing words to him in a low voice.

He allowed himself to be manoeuvred away, but not without another parting shot. 'OLD CUNT!' he roared. 'STINKING OLD CUNT!'

'I feel sorry for you, Sally, having to deal with two abusive men!'

Nick's mother looked at Miriam with a face that had turned to stone. Yet as their eyes met, Miriam could have sworn she saw Sally's fill with tears. She took a step towards the woman. Maybe they could talk to one another; maybe there was a chance they could make a connection after all. But at that moment a young couple approached, potential buyers. Miriam hesitated and Sally turned away. The young couple stood back to let Sally and the crazy old man pass, giving them a wide berth. Miriam hurried up to them, best placatory smile plastered to her face.

'I am so sorry. Advanced dementia, I think. Very sad. You see all sorts in this job. I think he might have lived here once—just wandered in . . .'

Miriam was making it up as she went along. The couple made sympathetic noises, but Miriam wasn't fooled. She'd said the first thing that came into her head and it had been the wrong thing. People were strange about houses. They liked to imagine that everything had been sweetness and light in a place before they bought it. Any hint of past tragedy could see prices fall. *As if suffering is contagious*, Miriam thought. The young couple were polite, but they were unlikely to buy the place now.

Although she had not seen either of Nick's parents since, she now approached open houses with trepidation. She knew that Sally and poor, demented Maurice only came at their son's instigation. He was stalking her by proxy. She supposed she could have applied for an AVO against them too, but it seemed absurd, an overreaction. Nonetheless, Nick's tactics had their intended result. If she was ever alone in a property, which sometimes happened on Wednesday showings when the market was slow, her heart was in her mouth. Recently, she had begun delegating more of the open house supervision to Prisha and the rest of her staff. She hated the feeling that her son-in-law had intimidated her out of doing her job properly, but he had—it was no use pretending otherwise. And it seemed he'd chased Liam out of his usual drinking hole as well.

※

'Look, Nan, I've put the giraffe in with the lion, but that's okay because he's a really nice lion.'

Teddy, a sweet-faced, serious-minded, five-year-old, was looking up at her with his big, round, trusting eyes. He was playing with his Duplo zoo. She loved it when he explained his motives for his games. He could rationalise anything.

'That sounds sensible.'

'Daddy won't let me, he says lions eat giraffes, but my one doesn't. Daddy says he knows because he's a vet and so he's an expert about animals.'

Miriam resisted the temptation to say that she was sure Daddy was an expert on everything.

'Well, it's your game, so I think you can do just what you want.'

'I don't want to go to Daddy's anymore.'

'Why? Because he won't let you play your games the way you want to?'

Teddy shook his head. 'Why do I have to go?'

'Because the judge says so.'

'But Daddy wants to give me and Isla a needle, and I don't like needles.'

Miriam sat forward and grasped her knees. She held them so tightly, her fingers were digging into her flesh. She held them to stop herself from leaping up and screaming, from grabbing this precious little boy and running away as fast and far as she could. She sat like this for what seemed like a long time, while her brain tried to make sense of what Teddy had said. When at last she spoke, she kept her voice as low and as calm as she could.

'Do you mean he wants to take you to the doctor for a vaccination?' she suggested. 'Like Mummy does sometimes?'

Teddy shook his head, his mouth turned down at the edges as if he were trying not to cry. 'No, Daddy has his own needle. He showed it to me once. It's in a box. It's very big and sharp. I cried and ran away and Daddy smacked me.'

All the air went out of Miriam's lungs and terror gripped her bowels. A thousand and one terrifying news stories chimed at once in her head. Children thrown off bridges, women and children burnt alive, drowned in lakes and baths, shot as they cowered in fear, gassed as they slept, strangled, stabbed, smothered, beaten and run over . . . on and on the stories went. Watching the nightly news now meant holding the remote control in both hands, finger poised to hit the mute button as fast as possible. Each of the stories dragged on for weeks over the news cycle. First there was the horror of the event itself, with the perpetrator described as a 'good bloke' who must have been 'pushed too far'; no one who knew him ever saw it coming. Then there were demands for action—more laws, more policing and occasionally a pious campaign by governments encouraging 'respect'. Then it all died down again, until the next one, or until the coroner's inquest. And still Nick wanted custody. He wanted to increase the time he had with his children whose lives he had now directly threatened. What was wrong with the world? How could this be happening? Why did the courts continually allow him—and all those other men—to get away with it, time after time? Miriam was damned if any of her family was going to end up making headlines like those. Not while she was still standing upright and had money in her bank account.

That night, before she went to bed, Miriam returned to the Spring Annuals file on her desktop. She found a gun shop down the coast in Wollongong. She could easily drive there and back in a day, and she didn't know a soul in the place. The next morning, she made her excuses to Prisha and headed south.

CHAPTER 18

In the days that followed her impetuous purchase, Miriam considered the step she had taken with a mix of wonder and horror. Yes, it had been in the back of her mind, but as a possibility not a probability. While she had taken the idea seriously enough to go to the gun club and learn to shoot, and had investigated the legalities of gun ownership, she had done so because it gave her a sense of power and control; buying a gun had been a fantasy, not something she'd ever contemplated in reality.

Now, when she walked past the linen cupboard, it wasn't simply Pete's ghost she was eerily aware of; it was the box that now lay next to his ashes containing the Smith and Wesson 9 mm. Why she had chosen to store it there, she was not sure. It was safe from the children and that was important. All those stories of toddlers accidentally shooting themselves with handguns in the US scared her rigid. Up there, it was out of harm's way. It was also hard for her to reach, which, no doubt, made it impractical for self-defence, but she didn't really expect that she would have to use it against Nick defensively. What, were they going to have a shootout or something? Not likely. If Nick intended to do something, he would do it quietly, slyly. And he wouldn't use something messy and obvious, like a gun. He was a vet. He was expert in the taking of life. He did it regularly. He had the means, the motive and the opportunity. As Teddy had told her, as Teddy had been meant to tell her, Nick would do it with a needle.

Maybe she had placed the gun next to Pete, or what was left of him, for safekeeping. As if his ghost could look after it for her while she made up her mind about what she should do. She didn't want to *do* anything. She just wanted her fear to recede, the threat to go away. But if it was a choice between the lives of her daughter and her grandchildren and anyone else's life, it was no contest—she would do whatever she had to do to protect them. She could hear fate approaching sometimes, like a runaway train heading towards them as they stood frozen on the tracks.

She still ached for Pete and she often searched hungrily for reminders of her husband in her small and beloved grandson. What she saw instead were flashes of his father. Sometimes, when Nick had left them alone for a while and so had receded a little from the front of her mind, she was able to wonder what had happened to her son-in-law to make him the man he had become. Once, he must have been just as trusting and big-hearted as the little boy she had heard explaining to each of his plastic jungle animals why they had to share a certain cage with another animal.

'Be nice,' he said to them sternly. 'Be kind and don't squabble.'

What had made Nick into the possessive and terrifying person he had become? When had he stopped being sweet and gentle, like his son, and become someone she now thought of as a monster? She had asked Ally if she knew anything about her husband's past, or some awful event that might explain how his personality had become so warped.

Ally just shrugged. 'According to him he had an idyllic childhood straight out of a storybook.'

'But something must have happened to him. He was a cuddly baby once, a cute toddler, a sweet little boy who loved animals. He wasn't born like this, surely?'

Miriam could see that she was making her daughter uncomfortable.

'I don't know, Mum,' she said impatiently. 'I can only deal with the man I know now. And that's more than enough.'

Miriam shut up after that. The last thing she wanted to do was increase her daughter's stress. But sometimes she wondered what had happened to fuck Nick up; she wanted to make sure nothing like that ever happened to her grandson. She wanted Teddy to stay just as he was.

What would Pete make of the situation? she wondered. What would he have done if he had lived? Would it have made a difference to Nick's behaviour if Ally had had a protective dad still around to look out for her? Would he have been so brazen in his desire to intimidate them? Or would it have made no difference? Sometimes she'd let herself hope that Ally would meet someone else, someone good and kind and sweet, like

Liam or a straight version of Jeremy. Maybe then, if Ally was in another relationship, Nick would back off. *Or would it have the opposite effect*, she wondered, *and simply inflame him further?* Anyway, as Ally hardly went anywhere much anymore, and never without the children, the whole idea was academic.

And, Miriam asked herself sternly, what had she and Pete done to Ally to make her such an easy victim? They hadn't abused Fiona or Ally, of that she was sure, but they must have got some important stuff wrong for Ally to be attracted to a man like Nick in the first place. The idea nagged at her.

We're all fucked up, she thought, *so how can we not pass on some of our own shit to our kids? I guess my dad shooting through the way he did must have fucked me up, particularly about men. Maybe I passed some of that stuff on to Ally without realising it. But why to Ally and not Fiona? And Pete was a wonderful father. I know that for sure.*

No, Miriam reminded herself, the fault did not lie with Miriam and Pete and their daughter—it was all Nick. She wondered again what might have happened to him. His parents seemed—well, pretty ordinary, really. Maybe Maurice had been abusive behind closed doors. Or maybe the aggression she had witnessed had just been the Alzheimer's talking. *Christ*, thought Miriam, *maybe I need to talk to a shrink to sort all this out.*

One of the few excursions Ally made every week was to her psychiatrist. Not Dr Singh, who'd been found by Nick, but a woman Ally referred to as Yasmin. She didn't talk about her therapy much, but she kept going, which Miriam assumed was a good sign. But, she conceded with an inward sigh, talking to a psychiatrist would not help them to deal with the crisis at hand. Once again, they would have to turn to the law—and hope that this time something would come of it.

※

'You have to talk to your lawyer.'

Ally and Miriam were in the kitchen. Miriam was chopping carrots, onions and celery for the casserole she was making for their meal later. Ally was pan-frying chicken schnitzels for the children, who were staring goggle-eyed at *Paw Patrol*, blaring noisily from the TV in the corner. Both were clutching their soft toys and their comfort blankets. Four-year-old Isla was crouched on all fours like a small animal, while Teddy sat with his legs crossed on the couch in best preschool manner.

'What now?'

Miriam had been dreading telling Ally what Teddy had said to her because she knew the effect it would have. But what else could she do? If they were going to protect her grandchildren, they would need help.

'Teddy told me that he doesn't want to go to Daddy's because Daddy wants to give him and Isla a needle. Nick showed him the needle. Teddy said it's big and he keeps it in a box.'

Ally gasped and then stood silently for what seemed a long time. Her face was working but she said nothing. When she finally spoke, the words poured out of her.

'It's one of the needles he uses to put animals down. He keeps it as a kind of display. He showed it to me once too. He was explaining how he used it to reassure owners of terminally ill pets when he was explaining the euthanasia process . . . then he suddenly changed tack and told me he could use it anytime, like when someone—and I knew he meant me—was asleep, and no one would ever know.'

'Of course they'd know! Surely an autopsy would show the lethal substance in your bloodstream—and who else but your vet husband would have access to that kind of thing?'

'I know, I know, but I wasn't thinking straight at the time. And anyway, he also put the needle against his own arm and told me it was the easiest way to commit suicide.'

'I wish he would!'

Ally looked at her. 'Me too.'

'Is that bad?'

Ally shrugged. 'He won't.'

Miriam was about to ask how she knew, but Ally held up her hand to stop her.

'I can't talk about this now. I feel really sick.'

It was true her face had turned a pale greenish colour. She looked awful. Miriam was starting to wish she'd never told her what Teddy had said. But she'd had to; it was a threat, and Ally had to tell her lawyer.

'Go to bed,' she urged. 'We can deal with it tomorrow. I can look after all this in the meantime.'

Ally handed the spatula she'd been using to her mother. Miriam attended to the chicken schnitzels, of course, but she also did a whole lot more. Not just the dinner, but the bathing, putting on pyjamas, story-reading, soft-toy finding and all the other bedtime rituals, made doubly exhausting by the children continuously clamouring for their mother.

'I want Mummy to do it!'

Isla looked stubborn, her jaw was set, and Miriam's heart sank. She did not want to have a fight with her granddaughter. Not ever, but particularly not now. She was tired. She was badly frightened. She wanted someone else to do it too—whatever 'it' might be. None of this situation was of her making. Miriam had not chosen to marry a psychopath. She had not stayed in a terrifying relationship until she'd had two children. *Two, for Chrissake!* And yet here she was, her whole life turned upside down by decisions that she had not made.

Isla's set face suddenly crumpled and she began to cry. Now Miriam felt bad about the angry and resentful thoughts that had been running through her head, even though she had not voiced a word of them. She swept Isla up and hugged her tight, gratified that the little girl snuggled back. *She's just exhausted, poor little mite, and she is living in this atmosphere of tension as much as I am*, thought Miriam, as she rocked the little girl in her arms, *but she has even less idea why.*

'Mummy's not feeling well, baby, so Nan will do it tonight. Is that okay?'

Isla nodded, sniffing back her tears and graciously allowing her grandmother to get her into her pyjamas. Once Miriam finally got the child into bed, Isla was asleep in seconds, her ginger curls splayed out across the pillow. Isla was a redhead and Miriam had no idea where that gene came from. They were all conventionally fair or brunette in the Duffy and Franklin families. Miriam's carefully coiffed blonde locks were thanks to outrageously expensive hairdressing appointments every six weeks. Beneath the bleach, the toner, the products and the hairspray her hair was dead straight and mousy brown—or it had been the last time it'd been its natural colour. It was probably pepper and salt by now, unless Nick had sent it snow white!

Miriam looked at Isla's face, wiped clean by the magic of sleep, and felt a wave of love so fiercely protective it almost frightened her. *If that bastard so much as touches a hair on this little girl's head*, she thought, *I will kill him.*

'Nan?'

'Yes, love?'

Teddy was still awake in his big boy bed on the other side of the room.

'I can't get to sleep.'

'Can't you, darling? Would you like me to tell you a story?'

Teddy nodded.

'What do you want it to be about?'

He shrugged and stuck his thumb in his mouth.

'How about a story about a giraffe and a lion who are best friends?'

'Yes! The ones in my zoo, sharing a cage!'

Teddy snuggled under the covers, clutching his teddy bear, and she began to spin a tale. Within minutes, he began to yawn and his eyelids drooped. Once she was sure he was asleep, she pulled the doona up under his chin and kissed him gently on the forehead. Teddy's hair had turned out to be a thick dark brown, like his dad's. As she listened to the child's peaceful breathing, she thought the same as she had about his sister. *If Nick so much as threatens you, I will kill him.* Then a cold, sick feeling washed over her as she remembered—according to Teddy, his father had done just that.

A thin, white-faced Ally came into the kitchen the next morning and dropped her car keys on the bench. She'd been out and bought them both coffees.

'Look at this. I found it in the letterbox.'

She was holding a newspaper clipping in her hand. It was a picture of a woman and her two children smiling at the camera. Miriam recognised them immediately. The picture had been splashed all over the media after the family had been murdered by their husband and father as they slept.

'Read what he's written.'

On the back of the clipping in thick black texta Nick—it could only be Nick—had written: *Which picture of you should I choose?*

Miriam yelped and bile rose in her throat. 'We have to take this to the police! We have to.'

'I know. I know.' Ally's voice was flat.

'And we have to tell them what Teddy said about the needle. You need to call Nerida this morning too, as soon as her office is open.'

Ally nodded wearily and sipped her coffee.

'You're taking it rather calmly,' Miriam observed.

Her daughter gave a weary shrug. 'It's like I don't have the energy to feel afraid anymore. I mean, he just bombards us with this stuff. It's like my nerves have run out of puff.'

Miriam hated to see all the stuffing knocked out of Ally like this. It made her feel even more determined to take action. Someone had to.

'We have to take this seriously. Deadly seriously. We need to make the courts recognise it and do something.' Miriam was trying to make Ally see how urgent, how vital this was. 'At least see if it can affect his access,' she urged. 'That picture has kids in it—surely that will be seen as a direct threat to them? *Surely?*'

Now, at last, Ally fired up. 'I don't know! How would I know? If you ask me, I believe he's capable of anything. He cannot bear the thought that I have escaped from his control, and he can't tolerate any kind of rejection. It makes him crazy. But he's brilliant at convincing the authorities that he is nothing but a loving father, pushed too far out of grief for his lost children. And his lawyers are equally brilliant at tying everything up in knots. Even if we get someone to take this seriously, it will take months before they do anything. And we might not *have* months! Yasmin says he's escalating.'

'Would she be prepared to say that in court, do you think?'

'Probably, for all the good it will do.'

'Mummy, look, Nan made me arches!'

Isla held up her peanut butter toast to show Ally the shape Miriam had made when she cut off the crusts. It immediately sagged and tore, causing Isla to collapse into theatrical tears. It took her mother and grandmother a few minutes to placate her and give her another piece. Ally, used to interrupted conversations after five years of motherhood, picked up exactly where she'd left off.

'Anyway, my problem is, I don't know what I can do to keep my children safe. I have tried everything—*everything*—but he's still there, lurking in the shadows, biding his time. Sometimes

I wonder if it wouldn't be better if he just did it and got it over with.'

Miriam gasped. Then something inside her clicked into place. She was suddenly certain that was never going to happen. Not while she had breath in her body and a gun in the linen cupboard.

'You're exhausted. You didn't sleep at all last night, did you?'

Ally shook her head.

'Why don't you take a sleeping pill and go back to bed. I'll take care of the kids.'

'What about work?'

'That place can run perfectly well without me. It mostly does these days.'

Ally nodded and took a last sip of her coffee. 'What a fuckwit he is.'

'We don't say the "f" word!' Teddy piped up. He had become the language police, at his mother's request. Both Ally and Miriam were terrified that any negative reports about either child's behaviour or language would find their way straight to Nick's lawyers or the Family Court's report writers. It was embarrassing for any parent if their toddler swore at childcare, but Ally worried that such a lapse by either of her kids could be fatal. Miriam, seeing the way the Family Court policed parenting, had to agree with her.

'Quite right, Teddy. We don't. Mummy is very naughty. Ally, you owe the swear jar a gold coin!'

Ally reached for her wallet and paid her penalty. 'Thanks, Mum,' she said. 'I'm sorry I'm so useless.'

Miriam put her arm around her daughter's shoulders and gave her a squeeze. 'You're not useless, Ally. Not remotely. Just worn to a frazzle.'

She was rewarded with a wan smile.

'And anyway, if you're worried about swearing, it's not just us. Maurice called me a'—she lowered her voice to a whisper so the children wouldn't hear—*'stinking old cunt*, remember?'

'He's been diagnosed with Alzheimer's, apparently. Poor old bugger.'

That used to be my worst fear, thought Miriam. Now she felt entirely unmoved by that old anxiety. It turned out there were so many worse things that could happen to you.

CHAPTER 19

'Will you be there for the whole weekend?' Ally asked. Sally was picking the children up as usual. Ally always dreaded giving her children into the care of the man who continued to stalk and abuse her, but today she was even jumpier than usual. *Quite understandably*, Miriam thought.

'I have no other plans.'

'Okay. Please keep an eye on them and don't . . . don't let anything happen to them.'

'Oh, for goodness sake, Sonny, your paranoia is absurd,' her former mother-in-law snapped. 'They are perfectly safe with their father. You have to stop filling their heads with your nonsense. It's one of the reasons Nick is still fighting for custody. Your delusions can't be good for them!'

Ally was biting her lip, as if to literally stop herself from saying anything. So Miriam said it for her.

'And yet the courts haven't seen fit to award it to him, have they?'

'Everyone knows the Family Court is biased towards mothers.'

'Except mothers.'

∾

Miriam didn't think either she or Ally slept for more than a few exhausted hours that whole weekend. They filled the evenings with the silliest TV programs they could find, while Miriam spent the daylight hours ripping weeds out of her herbaceous border. She pruned any straggly plants within an inch of their life. She fantasised about what she might do with the gun sitting in the linen closet as she sliced viciously into their green branches. Gardening was a relief. The physical work helped her stress and tired her out. And, as a bonus, she got a much neater and better cared for garden at the end of it.

'Win, win,' she said out loud as she inspected her handiwork at the end of the day. But who was she kidding? She still felt like shit.

'Mum! Mum! Turn it off! Turn it off!'

It was later that evening. Dinner had been made and served and sort of eaten. Miriam and Ally were sitting in front of the TV watching the ABC news. A few minutes earlier, Prisha had called for some advice about a pre-auction offer she'd just received for a house that had been open for inspection that afternoon. Miriam was distracted by the call and had not noticed that Juanita Phillips was presenting a story about yet another horrifying domestic murder. It was in the US this time, but the details were so horrendous it had made news bulletins worldwide. Phone to her ear, Miriam was sitting with the remote beside her. When she looked up in response to Ally's frantic words, she saw that the screen was filled with weeping people placing flowers, balloons and soft toys outside an otherwise perfectly ordinary looking suburban house. She knew immediately what that signified. It was a scene that had become so commonplace it was almost a cliché.

'Hold on, Prish!' Cutting across her friend mid-sentence, she grabbed the remote and stabbed at the off button, but Ally had already seen enough. She was rocking back and forth on the sofa with her head in her hands, making a horrible keening sound.

'Sorry, Prish. Something's come up.'

'You okay?'

'We're never okay anymore, but I'll call you back.'

Miriam hung up, then she scooted across the sofa to her distressed daughter and put a hand on her arm. She was still tentative about offering physical affection. Ally either stiffened or fought her off. At first, Miriam had felt rejected by her behaviour. Slowly she realised that Ally's distress was often so intense she needed to deal with it alone. Miriam had come to recognise it as the same instinct she'd had when Pete died. Just like Ally, she'd not been able to bear anyone making a fuss. She'd needed all the energy she possessed to deal with her own pain. Ally was living in such a state that she could just about summon what she needed for herself and her children, but everyone else, including her mother, would have to take care of themselves.

'Oh God, Ally, I'm so sorry.'

Ally turned a stricken face towards her. 'He's going to do something like that to Teddy and Isla, I know he is—he's as much as said so! But I can't get anyone to believe me!'

'I believe you,' said Miriam, thinking about the gun in the linen closet. 'I believe you.'

Later, when Ally got up to go to bed, she leant over her mother and put a hand on her shoulder. 'You are a wonderful mother. You always have been. I honestly do not know what the children and I would do without you.'

※

'They're here.'

Ally was at the front window, where she had been for the last half-hour, watching the driveway. Before Miriam had a chance to answer, she was out the front door. Teddy and Isla broke into a run. Sally was behind them, carrying their overnight bags. Teddy reached his mother first.

'Are you okay?' There was anxiety in Ally's voice.

It was Sally who answered. 'Of course they are! Honestly, what did you think we were going to do? Beat them?'

Isla was still running towards them, red curls flying. Miriam loved those curls.

Teddy was flushed with excitement. 'Mum! Mum!'

'What, darling?' It was clear he had something momentous to say.

'Daddy bought us kittens! One for Isla and one for me! We get to see them whenever we go to his house.'

Isla was just as excited as her brother. 'My one is black! Her name is Island—like Isla!'

'And mine is orange and splotchy. Her name is Tebby because Daddy says she's a tabby and I'm a Teddy, so he put them together to make her name.'

'They're very cute,' Sally said smugly.

'How wonderful!' said Ally, sounding strained.

That bastard, thought Miriam. *That clever, conniving, manipulative bastard.* She turned to the bastard's mother. 'Don't let us hold you up, Sally. I'm sure Maurice needs looking after.'

Sally shot Miriam a look of loathing but said nothing. Instead, she bent down, kissed the children and walked away up the gravel driveway.

'See you in a fortnight!' she called out. 'The kittens will be missing you.'

Miriam ushered Ally and the kids inside, and shut the front door with a bang.

'Can we live at Daddy's place now, with the kittens?' Isla was jumping up and down.

Ally gasped. Miriam knew she had to do something, fast.

'We can get some kittens too—or even a puppy.'

Miriam could not believe what she was saying. She did not want a pet. She had enough to contend with already. And she'd been doing a lot of reading on the subject of domestic violence and coercive control (a term much more familiar to her now than when she'd first heard Louise use it) and knew that abusers often hurt the family pet. When she'd read that fact, she'd actually congratulated herself on not having one. And yet here she was, bloody volunteering!

'Why don't you bring the kittens home from Daddy's with you?' she suggested hastily. 'They can have two homes, like you do.'

'But I don't like having two homes,' Teddy said. 'Why should they? Anyway, I already asked if we could bring them home, but Daddy says cats like to have their own territory and don't like travelling about.'

He'll never hand them over, thought Miriam, *and I really can't bear the idea of having a fight with him in front of the children.* There was nothing for it. She would have to bite the bullet.

'Alright, I'll tell you what—we can drive out to the RSPCA and get a puppy this afternoon.'

Both children immediately began jumping up and down. 'A puppy! We're getting a puppy!'

'Oh, Mum, I know you don't want a pet . . .' Ally had to raise her voice to be heard over the excited din her two children were making.

Miriam shrugged. 'What other option do we have? You know what he's doing and why as well as I do, and we cannot let him get away with it. The safety of these two is worth a puppy. But *you* can pick up its shit, okay?'

※

They brought home a wriggly little black-and-white creature, part Jack Russell, part God-knew-what. It was far too boisterous for Miriam's liking. She'd wanted a dog that was just like a cat. But the kids had their hearts set on this lively little mongrel the moment they saw her, mainly because she had jumped up and barked at them both as they'd walked along looking at all the puppies available for adoption. The little dog's eagerness had made both the children squeal with such joy that Miriam's unwilling heart softened. When it piddled all over the back seat of Pete's prized leather upholstery on the way home, it had hardened up again. But while Miriam was scrubbing at the seats with paper towels later, back in Greenwich, she heard Ally and the kids laughing as the little dog raced around the garden, yapping with delight. It was a sound she was not sure she could remember hearing ever since they had arrived, a thought which made her teary. She was relieved she was out of sight, cleaning up dog wee, so she could let her emotions flow in private. It was her job to stay strong, she knew that.

Once she had dried the seats and her tears, she pulled herself together and emerged from the car with an arm full of damp paper towels and a determined smile on her face.

'What are you going to call her?'

This was Ally and the children's dog, not hers.

'Piddler?' Ally laughed.

'Harsh.' Miriam shoved the paper towel in the bin. (*Should it be the recycling bin?* she wondered. *Does the fact that it's soaked with dog wee make a difference?* She dropped them in anyway.)

'Wriggler?' Miriam watched as the little dog wagged its tail so hard its entire back end seemed to twist and turn.

'Brachiosaurus!' yelped Teddy.

'He's not a dinosaur!' said Ally. 'He's a dog.'

'She's a girl, Mummy, not a boy!' said Isla crossly. 'Like you and me . . . and Nan.'

'Yes, ma'am,' said Miriam. 'That's a good name—what about Ma'am?' Despite everything, she was beginning to enjoy herself.

'She doesn't look like a Ma'am to me,' Ally objected. 'More like a flirt, or a good-time girl.'

They were all having fun now. They hadn't had fun since . . . Miriam couldn't remember. She was beginning to think this puppy thing hadn't been such a bad idea after all.

'Goody. Let's call her Goody.' Isla spoke decidedly, as if it was she who'd have the final word.

'I like Goody,' said Miriam. It seemed to suit the animal. She was so joyous and enthusiastic, everything and everyone seemed good to that little dog. And she was making them all feel good in return.

'Nice one, Isla,' said Miriam. 'What do you think Teddy?'

Teddy looked solemn. He walked up to the dog, who was panting from the exercise, pink tongue hanging out, sitting on her haunches. The little boy got onto his own haunches (how Miriam envied him that effortless flexibility) so he was down at the dog's level. He looked her in the eye.

'Goody? Do you want to be called Goody?'

By way of an answer, Goody jumped up, put both her paws on Teddy's shoulders and licked him on the face. He squealed and fell backwards, overcome by laughter as the dog jumped all over him. It made Miriam's heart sing to watch them.

'Goody it is, then,' declared Ally. 'Well done, Isla!'

Isla went pink with delight.

'I picked it!' she said. 'Me. It was my name!'

*

Later, as the children sat on the couch and watched their afternoon allocation of *Paw Patrol*, interspersed with the occasional episode of *Bluey*, Goody was curled up between them. Ally sipped a glass of wine as Miriam prepared dinner. It was the most peaceful evening they'd had for ages. Somehow, the little dog had managed to disperse some of the dread that permanently hung over them.

'Are you really okay about the dog, Mum? We have turned your life upside down.'

'I think Goody is a really good idea. And anyway, what else could we do? We have to keep the children with us. Him winning custody is something I cannot bear thinking about, and you know why he got the kittens. You know exactly why. He wanted the kids to say how much they love going to Daddy's, especially to the Family Court report writer. He's a fucking clever bastard.'

'We don't say the "f" word,' Teddy yelled at them over the back of the couch.

Immediately both women lowered their voices.

'Fuck!' whispered Miriam, and Ally was relaxed enough to just laugh.

'Anyway,' she continued, 'we've outsmarted him. Goody will beat the kittens any day of the week—and like I said, if the worst thing I have to do to protect you and the children is get a puppy, that's fine with me.'

And then they both went quiet. *It won't be the worst thing, though, will it?* said a nasty little voice inside Miriam's head, and her thoughts flew immediately to the gun upstairs in the linen cupboard. *He will never go away and he will never give up. He will never let his ex-wife and children live in peace or feel safe. If he ever does that, he will have admitted defeat, and that is something he will never do.*

Later, after the children had gone to bed, Miriam picked a stray hair off her jumper. It was Isla's. She'd been brushing the little girl's fine curls just a few minutes ago, before bedtime.

'Where did Isla's red hair come from, I wonder?'

'Nick's hair was red when he was young.'

'Ah, that would explain it. No sign of it now. Not even in his colouring.'

'But he was quite ginger when he was young, apparently.' Then Ally sat forward, as if she was remembering something. 'He told me a weird story about it once. Apparently, his red hair drove his mother crazy. She hated it, saw it as lower class or something. Anyway, she kept his hair in a crew cut until he was a teenager, giving it the once-over with a number two clipper every month. She said it was to prevent him getting lice. She only let him grow it to a normal length when the red had turned to brown.'

'What? That's quite mad!'

'Yes. Bonkers. But it may not be true. I referred to the story at the vet's later, in front of his colleagues. I can't remember why, but it seemed appropriate. We were having a conversation about mad things our parents had done—and some of them were hair-raising.'

I wonder what story you told about me? thought Miriam.

'Everyone was laughing and having a good time, so I threw in Nick's story. I tried to get him to tell it, but he wouldn't, and so I did. When I'd finished he looked at me like I was a crazy person and flatly denied it. It was awful. Everyone stopped laughing and just looked really uncomfortable. I felt completely humiliated. I assumed he was embarrassed about the story and that's why he denied ever telling me about it, so I felt even worse because I'd betrayed him. I hadn't realised it was a secret. When I asked him about it later and apologised, he still denied it—not only that it ever happened, but that he'd ever told me about it. He did things like that to me all the time. I stopped telling anecdotes, eventually. I worried constantly about whether what I thought had happened really had happened.'

Miriam had thought there was nothing left that could shock her. She was wrong.

'So you see, it may not be true. Though when Isla was born with red hair, it did make me think.'

CHAPTER 20

A week later, Miriam was woken at some ungodly hour by Goody barking furiously at the front door. For such a little dog, she sounded ferocious. Miriam knew immediately who Goody must be warning off. The dog's ability to hear what human ears could not was very useful.

Christ, she thought, as she pulled on her dressing-gown, *why didn't we think to get a dog before?* And then a stab of guilt. *Because of me,* she thought, searching for her slipper, *because I made it so clear I did not want one.* Once she'd found the missing footwear, Miriam made straight for the CCTV. She was just in time to see a hooded figure run up the driveway and disappear. She could also see that Nick (who else could it be?) had left a small white box on their front step.

'Has he gone?'

Miriam looked up to see Ally standing by the door. She nodded. 'But he's left a parcel. I'll go down and see what it is.'

Ally took a step towards her mother, holding out a cautionary hand. 'Be careful! Maybe it's a bomb!'

A bomb! thought Miriam. *That's a new one.*

'Don't make that face, I'm serious. It's not like it hasn't happened before! You remember—like that guy who bombed all those judges from the Family Court back in the eighties.'

Poor Ally really was paranoid—for perfectly understandable reasons, but Miriam was pretty sure Nick would not have a clue how to build a bomb. (*But aren't there instructions on the internet? Can't you make one easily with household ingredients like fertiliser?* the little voice in her head reminded her.) And besides, she reassured herself, a bomb was far too unsubtle. Nick did things on the sly, on the quiet. He had always, so far, given himself plausible deniability. That's what made him so hard to beat in a court of law.

'No,' Miriam said decisively. 'A bomb's too melodramatic, even for Nick.'

Nevertheless, Miriam hesitated after she'd opened the front door and saw the small white cardboard box on the front step. Brave words or not, she did not want to pick it up. It looked like one of those boxes that you get from patisseries with a cake or French pastries inside. *If it does contain anything like that*, she thought, *no matter how tempting they look, they're going straight in the bin*. Who knew what he might have laced them with?

She risked poking the box gently with her foot, moving it an inch or two. Nothing happened. As she looked around cautiously, she noticed a movement by the front gate. Looking up, she saw a man in a hoodie looking back at her—Nick. Something snapped inside her head. Instinctively, she began to run towards him, rage coursing through her body. She did not know what she intended to do. Punch him? Claw his eyes out? Scream abuse?

Nick ran out onto the street, and she followed. But when she reached the road she stopped. The street was quiet, deserted, and she didn't know which way he had gone. She was still hesitating when, suddenly, she was caught in the full glare of high beams. She put her arm up to shield her eyes and heard the distinctive sound of Nick's jeep revving. With a squeal of tyres on asphalt, the car started heading towards her at high speed. *Move!* she urged herself, but her legs seemed incapable of obeying. She stood frozen like a deer in the headlights. Then there was a screech of brakes and the jeep stopped, mere inches from knocking her down. She put both hands on the bonnet of the car. She was breathing heavily, shaking all over. Suddenly, the car revved again and sped backwards, so quickly, she almost fell over. Then the driver shifted gears and accelerated towards her again, skidding to a halt alongside. Still dazzled by the headlights, she saw Nick lean out of the window. He was smiling his familiar, charming smile.

'You need to watch where you're going.'

And then he cruised away, slowly, into the dark.

Miriam had no idea how long it took her to collect herself. As Nick drove off, her legs started to give way, and she had to sit down on the gutter to stop herself from collapsing. Breathing hard, she reminded herself that she could not afford to fall apart. There was still the box to be dealt with. Maybe it did contain a bomb. Maybe that had all been a ruse to get her outside so he could take her family from her in one fell swoop.

Steeling herself, Miriam walked back towards the house. She felt as if she was all that stood between her family and disaster. When she arrived on the front step, she again had to stop and catch her breath, holding the portico post for support. She felt like she'd just climbed Mount Everest. Then she bent down and gingerly picked up the box. What else could she do? It wasn't like she could call the bloody bomb squad.

It was surprisingly light; so light, she almost dropped it. There was something inside, she could feel the contents slide about as the box wobbled in her hands. Steadying it and herself, she carried it into the kitchen and placed it on the counter. It was sealed with tape. She opened the kitchen drawer and found a sharp knife. Carefully she ran it around the lid. She was about to open it when her daughter entered the room. Miriam looked up at her and tried to smile. 'Well, it hasn't exploded yet.'

'What was all that going on outside?' Ally asked.

Miriam was on the verge of describing what had just happened, then she paused. *What good would it do?* It would just terrify her daughter even more, and Ally was already hanging by a thread.

'Just Nick being an arsehole.'

'Are you okay?'

'Yes. He'd gone by the time I got outside.'

They both looked down at the box.

'Are you sure you want to see what's in it?' Miriam asked. 'I doubt it's delicious baked goods.'

Ally closed her eyes, but she nodded.

Slowly, still frightened the bloody thing might be booby-trapped, Miriam lifted the lid.

Inside were two kittens. One was black and the other a mottled tabby. Written on the box beneath them were the words *Island* and *Tebby*. The little creatures were both quite dead.

The two women recoiled.

'Jesus!' said Miriam.

'We'd better get rid of them before the kids see.' Ally's voice was trembling.

'Hang on, there's a note.' Miriam picked it up and peered at it; she didn't have her glasses.

'Here, let me.' Ally read Nick's message aloud. *'Euthanised due to feline distemper, infected by their mother.'* She gasped. 'That fucking bastard! I hate him, I hate him, *I hate him.*'

Ally had dropped the note onto the kitchen bench, but Miriam could see there was more. 'Read the rest, Ally.'

'I don't want to,' her daughter whimpered. 'You read it.'

Ally gave her mother an imploring look but she did what she was told.

'I think Teddy and Isla should see the kittens and bury them. It's a good way for children to learn how to deal with loss. Owners often like to see their pets after death and either bury them or scatter the ashes. I thought the kids ought to have that chance too. He's signed it *Daddy.*' Ally turned to her mother with a look of disbelief. *'Learn to deal with loss?* What does he mean by that?'

'I have no idea.' But so many sinister possibilities were running through Miriam's head that she felt faint.

'My loss? His loss? Whose loss?' Ally was obviously thinking along the same lines.

'Or maybe nobody's loss. Maybe he's just enclosed the note so that if we show the dead kittens to the cops he can act all wounded innocence and bring out some research paper that says it's helpful for children to participate in the disposal of their dead pets' remains.'

'Well, he can go fuck himself,' Ally said fiercely. 'No way am I showing them this.'

'I'll get rid of them.'

Except Miriam didn't. She took the box, complete with kittens and note, outside to the garage. Up the back was an old chest freezer. It still worked and there were some ancient steaks and God knew what else buried in the ice at the bottom. Miriam had looked in there many times and thought she must clean it out, but she hadn't quite got around to it. She lifted the rusting lid and placed the box inside. *Evidence*, she thought to herself. Tebby and Island were dead, and she didn't believe for one moment it was because they were suffering. This was no mercy killing. This was a second direct and unequivocal threat to the lives of her grandchildren—and their mother. *Till death do us part*, he had said to Liam. *Whether he kills them tomorrow, next week or next year*, Miriam realised, *he is telling us that he can do what he likes and that no one can stop him.* Her stomach heaved, and she clapped her hand over her mouth. She wanted to vomit, to release everything she had held inside for so long— her fear, her fury, her hatred, his words, his madness that had plummeted them all into this living hell. But she did not.

He knows if we take this to the police, nothing will happen, she reasoned. *He might get a fine for breaching the AVO, but no one is going to convict a vet for putting down two sick kittens, and no one is going to bother doing an autopsy to find out if they really were sick. Ally will just look hysterical if she tries to take it further. And if I go to the police about him almost running me over, he will have some story about how I ran straight out in front of his car and he just managed to stop in time. I'll be the madwoman, the idiot, and he will be the hero.*

And if he is escalating, like Ally's shrink thinks, maybe he doesn't care about deniability anymore, maybe he doesn't care if he is exposed as the lunatic he clearly is. And he doesn't care because he has a plan, and what other people or the law might think or do no longer matters.

If she was right, they were nearing the end game. The idea terrified her.

Miriam looked up at Julie's window next door and thought about how her neighbour and everyone else within earshot had failed to call the police when Nick had practically bashed the door down. She thought about Ally begging Nerida to do something and being told that including Nick's abusive behaviour and threats in any custody application might actually work against her. She thought about the horror stories she had heard and read about women and children trying desperately to escape an obsessed and murderous husband and father but to no avail. There was nowhere to run; she and Ally could not leave the country or even move further away, because the court would rule that it interfered with Nick's access to his children. What options were they left with? Did she and her daughter just have to sit and wait for the inevitable, hoping against hope that the AVO and the CCTV would be enough to keep him at bay?

And, suddenly, Miriam was no longer frightened. She was angry—as angry as she could ever remember being in her life. Her veins and arteries felt as if they were filled with molten lava and that, any minute now, like a volcano, she would explode. Would she just sit and wait while her ex-son-in-law threatened the lives of three people whom she held most dear? No, she would not. If no one else could stop him, she would.

CHAPTER 21

Miriam arrived early. She sat on a low step beside the pink granite portico in front of the grey stone Lionel Bowen Building in Goulburn Street. Her position allowed her to see who was approaching while remaining unobtrusive herself.

Miriam wondered why they had named the edifice that housed the Family Court of Australia after the rather colourless Lionel Bowen rather than Lionel Murphy, the Whitlam government's attorney-general who had revolutionised family law in Australia. It felt like a deliberate slight, and the fact the two politicians had the same first name made the rejection seem even more pointed. While she couldn't recall Bowen at all, she had a clear image in her mind of Murphy. He'd had a particularly magnificent nose. It made him look like a boozer. Whether he was one, Miriam had no idea. Men didn't have noses like that nowadays, but they'd been quite common when she was young, even on famous faces. She supposed they all had their noses fixed these days, their teeth straightened and their clothing styled. When she was a girl, debating the Vietnam War at Beacon Hill High, all the politicians were hideous, except Gough himself; Henry Bolte, Robert Askin, Joh Bjelke-Petersen, Russ Hinze, Billy McMahon. They were part of that post-war generation of Aussie blokes instantly identifiable by their walk shorts, long socks and beer bellies. They were the codgers who continued to wear hats long after everyone else had gone bareheaded. They were the men who yelled, 'Get a haircut, son,' at the boys they called 'draft-dodgers'. They supported conscription, law and order, and hierarchy. They were vehemently, absurdly, defensively homophobic. By the early 1970s, when Whitlam was elected, they were already relics of a bygone era.

Murphy had a very pretty wife. Miriam couldn't remember her name. A lot of those ugly blokes had pretty wives. Murphy had been brought low, she recalled, by some scandal or other. Maybe that was why they didn't call the building after him. She couldn't remember much about it, except for the phrase 'my little mate'. Revenge, she supposed, for bringing in no-fault divorce, which was bitterly opposed by those men who strode about in their walk shorts and long socks decrying the modern world. As she mused over all this ancient history (anything to distract herself), she wondered whether the court Murphy had established when he was full of reforming zeal back in the day didn't now disproportionately punish the women who came before it. *We sowed the wind*, she thought, *and now I am about to reap the whirlwind.*

It helped to lose herself in recollections of the lost world of her girlhood. Youth may not have been a particularly happy time for her, but it was a bloody sight better than what she faced now.

The gun in the pocket of the long line black cardigan she was wearing banged against her thigh as she crossed her legs. The weight of it brought her back to the present. She was about to do something that as recently as three months ago she could never have imagined doing. Abandoning the beliefs of a lifetime, she was about to take the law into her own hands, as the saying went. She was about to become a vigilante. It was so absurd to use that word about herself—a respectable North Shore real estate agent, mother of two, grandmother of three—that it felt as if it could not possibly be true. But however surreal it sounded, her mind was made up. After Nick's veiled threat two nights ago, she had known what she must do. It was Ally, Teddy and Isla, or Nick—and that was no contest.

She was no longer filled with rage, as she had been the night her demented son-in-law had delivered a box of dead kittens to their doorstep and almost run Miriam over. She hated him alright. How could she not? But her feelings towards him had gone from red hot to ice cold. She felt methodical, determined, more in control now than perhaps she had ever been. She had an unpleasant job to do that just had to be done. She pulled the hood of the cardigan up over her head and continued to scan the passers-by. She hadn't seen Ally yet; she was dropping the kids at day care before heading to the court and had no idea her mother was already there. She hadn't seen Nick either . . .

Then the little voice started in her head again—the one she always tried to ignore. It was whispering doubts. *Is this just about protecting them? Is it? Or are you also protecting yourself? Didn't you fail to protect Ally before? You brought her up, you made her susceptible to this psychopath. Admit it,* hissed the voice—it felt like a snake, coiled around her cerebellum—*you were relieved when Nick came along, relieved to get this difficult daughter off your hands. Aren't you guilty too? And you believed Nick when he told you your daughter was crazy. You bought his story hook, line and sinker. You are a bad mother. You were a lousy wife. And now you are holding someone else to blame for your own mistakes. No wonder Pete has gone, no wonder your brother and stepsister have nothing to do with you, no wonder your dad took off without a backward glance. You might get rid of this man, but you can't obliterate your own culpability That will be with you forever.*

Miriam wanted to put her hands over her ears to shut out the snake, but she knew it was useless. No matter how much her own behaviour may have contributed to the horrible situation her daughter now found herself in, she would not fail her child this time. And she recognised something else. What she was about to do was not just personal. It was political. Yes, she wanted her daughter and grandchildren to live, and to live free of fear. But she was doing this to reclaim her own power too, and the power of all of those who found themselves in this terrifying situation. Yes, she was a vigilante, but she was also an assassin.

She sipped the coffee she had bought at the coffee cart that stood outside the Family Court. It was doing a roaring trade. There were always people in need of something to comfort them, distract them, keep them from melting into a puddle of despair. Her coffee had gone a bit cold. She looked around for a bin. She hadn't wanted to bring her keep cup, not for this. All she had with her—apart from the gun—was a small satchel slung across her chest with her ID and credit cards, some cash (she had no idea if she'd need money or not but better to be safe than sorry), her phone, reading glasses and the toothbrush she'd popped in at the last minute. Who knew how long she'd be away from home?

She was scanning her surroundings for the hundredth time when she saw Nick.

At the sight of him, the snake in her head almost won. Her guts churned and she felt the urge to turn and run. Instead, Miriam put the coffee cup down and slowly got up from the step. She kept her head low under the hood of her cardigan. She did not want Nick to see her until the last minute. Not that anyone would spare her a second glance anyway; it was one time when the invisibility that went with being an older woman was working in her favour. She was trembling, but she stood her ground, knowing that Nick would have to walk past her to enter the court. He was busy talking to his lawyer and not paying any attention to anything else. In fact, he was flirting with his legal adviser, flashing his attractive smile and making jokes. Miriam saw the blonde lawyer duck her head and flick her hair girlishly in response. *He's enjoying himself,* she thought with a spurt of anger. *This is all a game to him—a game he thinks he's won!*

As he got closer, she lifted the gun inside her pocket. She would not take it out till the last minute. The safety was off and she had her finger on the trigger. He was almost upon her. She stepped out into the middle of the footpath so she blocked his way. He looked down at her in irritation. She raised the gun. She saw a flicker of recognition in her son-in-law's eyes.

She aimed her weapon at his heart. He was very close. He stopped. She pulled the trigger. She watched him fall. Then all hell broke loose.

CHAPTER 22

There was a ringing in Miriam's ears. The gunshot had been loud, but not loud enough to deafen her, surely? *Maybe it's shock*, she thought. She could see people running and could tell they were screaming, but she could not hear them. It was as if she were behind a pane of glass. No matter; she had planned what she intended to do from beginning to end. She had rehearsed it over and over, both in her head and, late at night, in the garage, out of sight of anyone. She was glad she had prepared. Now that she had carried out her plan, she felt shakier than she'd anticipated, but she was still able to follow each step methodically.

She knelt down and put the gun—safety back on—on the ground beside the body. Then, still on her knees, she put both her hands behind her head and waited, head down, for whatever would happen next. She watched Nick's blood pooling around his body. There was so much of it—viscous and dark. She had not thought he'd have so much blood in him. She was watching it stain the pavement when she was shoved violently from behind, pushed flat onto her face. And though she had anticipated something like this happening, the shock of such rough handling was profound. The pain of her head meeting the pavement took her breath away.

'Keep your hands where I can see them!'

A man's voice. Police. He sounded breathless and panicky. She stretched her arms out wide, feeling the grit of the pavement under her fingers.

'Where is the gun?'

He was talking to someone else, someone she could not see. Not that she could see much with her head squashed against the pavers. Nevertheless, lifelong good-girl Miriam automatically turned her head, ready to help, to point out where she had put it. The habits of a lifetime die hard. The cop who now had his knee in her back reacted immediately. He shoved her head back down even harder. She felt sick. Something wet trickled down her forehead. *More blood*, she thought.

'It's here, Sarge, she's put it next to the victim. Safety is on.'

A woman's voice this time—young, also panicky.

Victim? They'd called Nick 'the victim'? That startled her. She hadn't expected such a reframe so quickly, but she supposed it was accurate enough. He was her victim. She rolled the idea around in her head to get the feel of it. It felt good. She knew it shouldn't, but it did.

'Secure the weapon. I'll secure the suspect.'

Suspect? She wasn't trying to hide anything. She'd done what she'd planned to do—shot him publicly, in broad daylight, surrounded by witnesses. There was nothing left to be suspected. It was all perfectly obvious.

Now, the knee between her shoulder blades was pressing down on her even harder. It hurt.

'Put your hands behind your back.'

It was an order.

She felt the cold metal of the handcuffs go around each wrist, one at a time. She heard them ratchet closed and click shut.

'Suspect in custody.'

Already her shoulders ached. The knee came off her back and she was yanked to her feet. She was unused to being treated with such disrespect, but she did not complain. It was a shock, that was all. Different in reality than in her imaginings. She was a 'suspect', a criminal now, a cold-blooded murderer. She deserved no better. That idea did not feel so good.

Now that she was on her feet again, she could look around her. Another police officer and a woman were kneeling over Nick, looking for a pulse or attempting to revive him or something. There was a wide circle of bystanders around them, many filming the scene on their phones. *They're all paying attention now*, she thought, and that made her wonder. Was that another motivation for doing what she had just done? To—at last—get someone to pay some bloody attention? If so, it had worked.

The strange silence that had blanketed her since she'd fired the shot had been broken and she could hear everything now, including a siren approaching. An ambulance had been called—more than one, she didn't doubt, given how many witnesses there were. Another two police officers were pushing the crowd back and cordoning off the area with crime scene tape. *Just like on TV*, she thought.

The ambulance drew up beside the kerb, its siren deafening. Then the noise died; someone must have hit a kill switch somewhere. The vehicle's lights kept flashing, though, even as the paramedics rushed to see what they could do for—what was it they'd called him?—her 'victim'. She could already see, however, that her aim had been true, that her training had paid off. Something about the demeanour of the people leaning over him, their sudden lack of urgency, the slump of their shoulders told her what she needed to know. At that range, he must've died almost instantly. A great weight lifted off her. Ally and the children were not just safe now, they were free. She rubbed her wrists against her restraints and smiled. The irony of her own predicament had not escaped her.

'The shooter, over there in the handcuffs and the hoodie—it's a woman!'

Someone standing nearby was speaking loudly and pointing an accusing finger at her. 'An *old* woman!'

She wasn't the kind of suspect they expected. Another stereotype bites the dust. She smiled again.

'She's smiling!'

Another voice, a woman's, curdled with disgust. *Of course*, Miriam remembered, *I'm meant to feel bad about this*. But she didn't quite know how she felt, not yet. Everything still had an air of unreality. She did feel bad in one way. What she had done was wrong, no doubt about that—but she had done it for the right reasons. Well—she remembered the snake—mostly right. She felt afraid of what was to come. She knew that what would happen next was specifically designed to be unpleasant, to be a punishment. She had been a privileged and protected woman most of her life, and she had no real idea how she would cope. Society would take its revenge, she knew that much. She took a deep breath.

'Maybe she's hysterical . . .'

'Or nuts!'

Miriam realised that everyone standing around was now looking at her. Every movement, every change of expression or intake of breath, was being minutely examined and judged. She squared her shoulders and lifted her head.

'She looks mean.'

A man's voice now.

Then a new sound, ripping through the air. A familiar voice, a woman, screaming the same word, over and over again. It was Ally.

'Mum! Mum! Mum! That's my mother! What's going on?'

Like everyone else, Miriam turned. Ally had arrived for the access hearing that no longer mattered. She was running full tilt, hair flying, shoulder bag banging on her back towards what was now a crime scene. A police officer stepped forward and caught her by the shoulders, stopping her from breaching the tape. There seemed to be ever-increasing numbers of cops at the scene now, and the press was arriving, by the look of the microphones that were bristling from the edge of the crowd. *I'm a suspect, a criminal, a murderer*, Miriam thought, as the camera's flashbulbs dazzled her eyes.

Ally kept struggling but the officer held her fast.

'Mum! Mum! What's going on?'

Part of her plan had been to stay silent, but she had to comfort her daughter.

'It's alright, darling. I did what I had to do. Nick will never bother you or the children again. Not ever. You are safe now.'

She watched as Ally turned her head and saw Nick's body on the ground. They'd covered him up while they erected some sort of tent to shield him from prying eyes. Could she get a tent too? she wondered. Ally looked from the body to her mother, from the victim to the suspect. Incomprehension was followed by a dawning understanding, and that was when the younger woman crumpled. It was just as well the copper had such a tight hold of her shoulders, or she would have hit the ground.

Miriam wanted to run to her daughter, to take her from the arms of the anonymous cop and reassure her that everything was alright now and that none of this was her fault. She took a step forward, but someone grabbed her from behind. Miriam watched helplessly as the media surged towards her youngest daughter, sticking their microphones in her face, their cameras feasting on her despair. She pulled hopelessly against the person who held her back.

'Stay where you are.'

Miriam obeyed. She had no choice. Her daughter was free, she was in custody. She had traded her freedom for Ally's. For a moment she felt something like pride. Then someone else grabbed hold of her hands. She looked around to see what was happening. A woman wearing plastic gloves was putting Miriam's hands into blue plastic bags one at a time and tying them closed. The woman wasn't in uniform, but she looked official. *A detective, probably,* thought Miriam, *or forensics, preserving evidence.*

'Miriam Duffy . . .'

How did they know her name? No one had asked her who she was, nor had they asked Ally as far as she could tell. There must be other people in the crowd who knew her. She looked at the faces surrounding her, searching for someone familiar. She spotted Nick's pretty blonde lawyer. She looked positively shattered. Miriam did not blame her, poor girl. What a terrible shock it must have been. She'd been standing right beside him. She may even have been splattered with his blood. She felt guilty for causing her such distress. It was that young lawyer who must have identified Miriam for the police, she guessed. It was her business, as Nick's legal representative, to know exactly who everyone was.

She felt very sorry that this young woman, who had only been doing her job, would now have to deal with such a traumatic memory. Jackie Kennedy in her blood-spattered pink suit flashed into her mind's eye. But she could not see how it could have been helped. She hadn't thought about any bystanders when she'd planned all this. Perhaps she should have.

'. . . I am arresting you for the murder of Nicholas Carruthers and we are taking you to the station where you will be formally charged. You do not have to say anything but anything you do say could be used as evidence against you.'

Evidence against me? Miriam looked at the scene around her. *What more evidence do you need?*

The detective who had bagged her hands had stopped speaking. She was standing directly in front of Miriam. The woman's face was expressionless; she was reciting her lines like a bad actor. Miriam craned her head to try to see what was happening to Ally.

'Do you understand?'

The woman sounded irritated.

Miriam nodded quickly. 'But my daughter—someone needs to look after her. I need to make sure she's alright.'

'Too late to think of that now. Anyway, she will be looked after.'

The woman's voice was neutral again, neither kind nor unkind. *She's done this before*, thought Miriam.

The woman had hold of Miriam's arm and was firmly pushing her in the direction of one of the police cars. Miriam took one last look at Ally over the heads of the crowd. Nerida Ong was with her. Miriam was relieved. Nerida would make sure her daughter was alright. She looked towards the blonde lawyer and saw that someone had given her a bottle of water and brought her a blanket. She'd be alright too. More alright than she knew, perhaps, if her relationship with Nick had gone beyond flirtation.

The detective got into the back seat of the car first, but before Miriam could follow her someone put a hand on her head and half-forced her into the car. *It's as if I've lost all my agency,* thought Miriam, *even the ability to get into the back seat of a car without bumping my head.* But she acquiesced. What else could she do? The person who owned the hand slid in beside her. It was a man. She was hemmed in by police officers. The woman put Miriam's seatbelt on for her. Miriam had been rendered helpless by the handcuffs. She felt almost childlike, now she was under arrest. None of the police said anything; they just stared straight ahead. It was Miriam who finally spoke.

'What happens now?'

'You will be formally charged and taken into custody.'

'Custody?' She snorted. 'That's what all this'—Miriam gestured towards the crime scene which was rapidly disappearing in the rear-view mirror—'was about.'

The woman looked at her but remained expressionless. Miriam decided to interpret her steady gaze as interest.

'My grandchildren . . .' Her voice cracked, so she paused and gathered herself. 'He was going to kill them, you see.'

'Wait till you're charged.'

It was the man on the other side of her. His voice was brusque. She looked at him. He was older, paunchy, his blue business shirt straining a bit at the buttons. His hair was combed over his bald spot. The air conditioning was going full blast in the car, but he was sweating. Miriam shivered a little from the cold, or maybe the shock. He looked at her for a moment and his pale eyes were full of disgust. *He thinks I'm making excuses*, she realised. *A lot of people will think that. Easier to blame me than acknowledge what a man can do to his children out of—what? Jealousy? Possessiveness? Spite?*

The car pulled off the road and into the car park of the police station. *Here we go*, thought Miriam.

⁂

'Greg?'

'Hello?'

'It's Miriam Duffy. Pete's Miriam.'

She was surprised how ordinary she sounded, how her 'social' voice had just kicked in.

'Of course, Miriam, how lovely to hear from you. How are you?'

Greg's voice was warm; as far as he knew, this was a social call from an old friend. He had no idea that his old friend was standing in a police station on the payphone—they'd already confiscated all her belongings—making the one phone call she was allowed. She turned towards the wall to try to keep her conversation private, because the station was buzzing with people and barely repressed excitement. She'd caused a stir. People were staring at her. There was a media pack outside the front doors. She was 'breaking news'.

'Are you still my lawyer, Greg?'

'That's up to you. Do you still want me to be? I'm semi-retired these days, but I'm always happy to do work for friends like you.'

Pete and Greg's friendship went back to their school days, and Greg and his wife, Jen, had been part of their social circle for decades, but she had not seen either of them since Pete's funeral, so they had no clue what had been going on. She was sorry for the shock she was about to give him.

'Thanks, Greg, but you may not be quite so happy when you hear what I need. I'm under arrest, you see. I'm at Surry Hills police station.'

There was a deathly silence at the other end of the phone.

'Under arrest?'

It was clear Greg thought he must have misheard. Miriam was surprised at the wave of shame that suddenly overwhelmed her. She hadn't felt that emotion at all until now—even in the face of all that pointing and staring. It was this voice from her old, safe, comfortable life with Pete that made her realise how far she had fallen. She dropped her voice and said what had to be said. 'Yes, for murder. My son-in-law. I shot him.'

Another long pause and a sharp intake of breath was followed by more silence at the other end of the phone. Miriam wondered for a moment what she would do if he just hung up on her.

'Fuck me, Miriam! You know how to shake up an old bloke's afternoon.'

She laughed out loud. Heads turned and she stifled her laughter quickly, but she was overwhelmed by relief. They had lots of lawyer friends, of course they did. She and Pete, especially Pete, had moved in those kinds of circles. She was glad that out of all of them she'd thought of Greg. He'd been the right choice.

'It's rather shaken mine up too.'

It was what she needed. The chance to make a joke about all . . . this. *Gallows humour*, she supposed. *How very appropriate*. His response grounded her, helped her to recover her bearings and feel like herself again.

'Don't tell me any more over the phone. You're at Surry Hills? I'll just cancel a couple of things and I'll be right there.'

'Oh, I don't want to put you out . . .'

Even as she said it, she was thinking how stupidly middle class she sounded.

'Put me out? Honey, my job is to get you out—though if it's murder . . . Anyway, no use speculating. I'll be there as soon as I can. Don't say anything to anybody until I arrive. Got that?'

'I won't. I promise.'

Now she was waiting in the holding cell for Greg to arrive so she could be formally charged. Miriam supposed the next step was to apply for bail, but given what she now knew about the speed of the courts, that would not happen until the next day at the earliest, so she faced at least one night inside. She was glad she'd packed her toothbrush, though whether they'd let her have it or not, she was not sure.

The feeling she'd had when they closed the door had been indescribable. Her guts had plummeted through her body to the floor as she heard the heavy locking device crunch into place. She'd thought for a horrible moment she was going to vomit but she had not. She'd had to put her head between her knees, however, until she had regained control over her composure, not to mention the scant contents of her stomach.

She looked around. She was sitting on the plastic-covered mattress that sat on a shelf-like bed at the far end of the cell. There was nothing else in the room. She'd wondered if there'd be a toilet, but there wasn't. She'd have to ask to go soon. She couldn't remember when she'd last peed. Back in her old life in Greenwich, she supposed, just after she got out of bed. When would she next see that bed again? she wondered. Maybe never. The thought made her feel nauseous. Christ, what had she done? But she couldn't think like that. Not now.

The cell was clean, too clean. It smelt of hospital-grade disinfectant and something else; something synthetic, cloying. Miriam could not identify it, but it was strangely familiar. The walls were painted an indifferent shade of grey. The ceiling and the floor were grey as well—concrete. At least the plastic on the mattress was blue. There was a barred window above her head letting in a thin greyish streak of natural light—not that it was needed. The cell was flooded with light from the fluoro tube above her head. Even when she closed her eyes, it burnt through her eyelids. She'd looked for a light switch to turn it off but there was none. Someone else controlled the light and the dark. *Like God*, she thought. She sat with her back against the wall, parallel with the window, and hugged her knees to her chest.

They'd taken the blue bags off her hands and then swabbed her fingers and palms for gunshot residue. When they'd put Miriam in the cell, they'd taken off the handcuffs. That was a huge relief. It wasn't that they'd hurt her, exactly, it was just that every time she forgot they were there she'd wrenched her wrists painfully. The only way to avoid it was to keep your hands still, and it was amazing how often she moved them without thinking. She let go of her knees and examined her hands carefully. *The things you have done*, she thought as she looked at them, *that I would never have imagined you would do*. Then Miriam pulled herself up. That was crap. Her hands hadn't done it; she had.

She looked up. There was a camera mounted in the corner of the ceiling to the right of the door, where it could survey everything. Even if she stood directly below it, it would still see half of her. Its unblinking eye stared at her coldly. She waved at it. God knew why.

Everything still had an air of unreality about it, as if she'd wake up soon and find her world had gone back to normal. Try as she might to get her head around her changed circumstances, she could not do it. She suddenly felt terribly, terribly tired, as if she'd climbed a mountain or been run over by a truck. Every particle of her seemed to ache. She put her head on her knees and closed her eyes; perhaps she should try to sleep.

She snapped her eyes open again. As soon as she had closed them, the events of the day had started to unspool in her mind, starting with her first sight of Nick strutting down the footpath towards the Lionel Bowen Building, Miriam reaching into her pocket for her gun . . . She couldn't go there again, not yet.

She got up and paced the cell. It was ten steps from the bed to the door, five steps across and ten steps back. She felt agitated now. She had no book to read, no phone to scroll through, no pen with which to draw or write. She was not used to being idle and the adrenaline was pumping through her veins, making her feel edgy and restless. She suddenly felt a wave of dread. *It is the boredom that will do me in*, she thought. *I'll never be able to deal with it. I had not thought about how boring incarceration would be.* She almost cried. Instead, she went to the door and opened the little slot they'd told her she could use to contact those outside. It was too tall for her and she had to stand on tiptoe. She called out to the custody officer.

'Excuse me?'

She still sounded timid, middle class, not like a cold-blooded killer at all.

Her voice echoed down the corridor but there was no answer.

'Hello? Is there anyone there? Can I speak to you for a minute?'

Then, her upbringing cutting in, she tried what her mother had always called the magic word.

'Please?'

It must have worked, because she heard heavy footsteps coming towards her and then there was a face at the little window.

'What do you want?'

She almost felt embarrassed, though she couldn't think why. All her dignity had long gone by now.

'I need to go to the bathroom.'

The man nodded and she heard him begin to unlock the door. A crazy impulse seized her—to hit this man on the head, scratch at his eyes, and then run away, back to her old life, to Ally, Fiona, the kids and Pete. Oh, dear God, how she longed for Pete.

Instead she stood there meekly, humble and compliant, clasping her hands together to make sure they didn't do anything rash.

⁂

'I don't think you'll get bail,' Greg told her straight away. 'We can apply, but the police will oppose.'

Greg was sitting opposite her in a small interview room. He was too large for the chair. His body stuck out from it in every direction, his legs and arms splayed out in front of him. By contrast, Miriam felt tiny. Her feet only just touched the floor, so she was forced onto tiptoes or had to let them swing in the air like a kindergartner. Yet Greg's size reassured her. In a shamefully old-fashioned way, she liked feeling this big man was on her side.

'Now, why don't you start from the beginning.'

And so she told him the whole bizarre story.

Greg listened intently, not interrupting except to ask for clarification. For that she was grateful. The hardest part was telling him about her actions of that morning. Telling him what Nick had done was one thing—they were the innocent victims in that part of the story—but talking about what she had done was quite another. The shame of her crime, her violent crime, surged over her again. She had committed the worst of sins. Maybe this kind-hearted man, this old friend, this man who had been so close to Pete that he had been a pallbearer at the funeral, would also cast her out.

'And so'—she stopped and swallowed, gathering what was left of her courage—'I shot him this morning, as he approached the Family Court for the access hearing. And that's how I ended up . . . here.'

She waved her arms to encompass the small room with its CCTV camera above the door, two-way mirror (she assumed) along one wall, and recording device on the table between them, and then she shrugged. She was done.

It took Greg a long time to respond, and his silence made her feel weary and vaguely ridiculous. Some of what she had told him was so extreme—Nick strangling Ally, the dead kittens, the needle, Sally and Maurice, the red hair being shaved monthly—that even she wondered if she was making it up or exaggerating. She had to fight the instinct to underplay what had happened or to constantly apologise for being so dramatic, for dumping her problems on him, for having made such a mess of everything. Even just for ruining his afternoon. She was ashamed and afraid of rejection, terrified that he would not believe her and would abandon her. It was fear of being considered a liar or of overdramatising that she felt most profoundly, even though she knew that every word she'd uttered was true. But there was another fear too—that Nick's behaviour had not been as bad as she and Ally had thought and she had done what she had done unnecessarily.

She dropped her head, almost too exhausted to hold it up. She was sitting right on the edge of the chair and its plastic rim was cutting into her thighs. She did not shift her weight. The pain was anchoring, it held her to the present, to this moment, this chair, this anonymous, indifferent room. But Miriam could not bring herself to look at her old friend. She half-expected him to get up and walk out in disgust, telling her to get another lawyer.

Instead, Greg sat back in his chair, put his hands behind his head and stretched out his legs. He seemed to be making up his mind about something. Then he reached across the table and put his hand over hers. The gesture brought her to tears. No matter what she had done, or what was about to be done to her, she had not been totally rejected. Not by this man, anyway.

'Oh, Miriam, what a time you have had. Why didn't you come to me? Maybe I could have helped.'

Miriam still did not look up. His question, kind and generous though it was, stung. Why hadn't she gone to him? Perhaps she should have. Perhaps she should not have taken this on by herself. What on earth had made her think she could be judge and jury? Yet even as she had that self-lacerating thought, she looked up and shook her head.

'No, no one could have helped. I thought at first that they could—that the police could stop him, that the magistrate could, the courts, the law, the AVO. But it turned out they couldn't. It wasn't until we'd exhausted every avenue that I gave up hope.

Nothing the law had to offer was going to stop him. And that's why I decided to do what I did.'

'Why didn't you come to me then? I could have advised you.'

'You would have stopped me, and Ally and I would still be living in dread. You have no idea what that is like, living on edge all the time, wondering when the axe is going to fall—and who it is going to fall on. Every time I looked at the children I wondered how long it would be until we'd make tragic headlines. Every. Single. Time. What I did was wrong, terribly wrong. I am not going to try to evade responsibility. I deserve to be punished. I know that, and I know it's not going to be pleasant, but at least I have a pretty good idea what's in front of me. And Ally and the kids are free and alive and likely to stay that way. They can get on with their lives.'

'Do you think they will feel very free with you facing decades in jail?'

The word 'decades' made her wince. That reality was hard to face.

'No, but it can't be helped. If I had not done what I did, I would still be living with the constant fear of losing my grandchildren and my daughter. I have traded my freedom for theirs. It's a Faustian pact, I know, but it was the only one on offer.'

Greg was silent again for a few long moments.

'Look,' he said finally, 'I am not a criminal lawyer. I think I should find someone who is.'

'No!' She was alarmed now. She felt safe with Greg. 'I don't want to tell that awful story all over again to a stranger.'

'Oh, Miriam, you should have thought of that before.'

Someone else had said that to her . . . the woman detective. She glanced at the mirror. Was she there now? Watching? All Miriam saw was her own reflection. She looked awful.

'You are going to be telling that story a thousand times before you are through. And it is going to become almost the only thing most people will ever know about you.'

He was right, of course.

'You are going to have to tell it again now, when the detectives come in to take your statement of evidence.'

She did not reply. She did not trust herself to speak. She just nodded.

'I am going to find you a criminal lawyer and barrister. I can stay involved in some capacity, if you like, but you need better representation than I can give you. You are sure you want to plead guilty to murder? You don't want to enter a plea of manslaughter due to diminished capacity? You're going to have to do a psych report either way.'

For a second, her heart leapt. Was there a way out of this? Then she shook her head.

'They're going to try to paint me as crazy. That's what Nick did to Ally right from the start. He almost got her to believe it. He *did* get me to believe it. But I know now that we're not crazy, neither of us. And I am not going to pretend I am to escape what I deserve.'

To Miriam's relief, Greg did not try to change her mind. He just nodded.

'In that case—mind you, more up-to-date lawyers may advise you differently—I think our best bet is to try to get you a reduced sentence by pleading provocation and so reducing your moral culpability. But you have to understand that you are looking at jail time, Miriam. Serious jail time.'

She nodded and swallowed hard.

'Shall I ask the police to come in?'

She put out her hand and caught his wrist to delay him. 'And Ally? Have you seen Ally? Is she okay?'

'She's outside. So is Fiona. They won't let them see you, not here, not until a magistrate has remanded you. Not till they have taken your evidence. I wouldn't say either of them are okay exactly—how could they be? They're both shocked and upset; we all are. But Ally said that I was to tell you that you are the bravest person she has ever known.'

A sob caught in Miriam's throat and she saw Greg's eyes fill with tears.

'I am so sorry this has happened to you,' he said. 'If only Pete were still alive, it never would have.'

She cried then, great heaving sobs that came up from her guts.

When she was calmer, Greg rose. 'It's time.'

CHAPTER 23

'Oh, Mum, oh, Mum, I am so sorry. I am so, so sorry.'
This time it was Ally who was sobbing. Two whole days had passed, during which Miriam had been fingerprinted, DNA-swabbed, strip-searched, had all her clothes and possessions taken away from her and been given a complete physical and psychological medical examination. She had been accused of lying, of special pleading, of trying to blacken her son-in-law's name by the police who questioned her. She'd been yelled at once or twice, but mostly she had been treated with cold, efficient indifference. The social status she had once taken for granted had evaporated. She was a prisoner, an inmate. No one gave a shit about her; all they cared about was getting their paperwork done and making sure she didn't top herself.

The evening of the day she had been arrested, she'd been taken in the back of a prison transport van to the Remand and Reception Centre where she would be held until her sentencing hearing. (As Greg had explained, since she was pleading guilty there would be no trial. Bail, as Greg had predicted, had been refused. You don't shoot someone in broad daylight and then get released a few days later, and much as Miriam longed to go home, she could see the logic of that.) There was only one other woman in the vehicle, and she was achingly young. Miriam had looked over at her and wondered what she might have done to bring her to this place. That was a mistake.

'What are you looking at, cunt?'

Miriam dropped her gaze. There were no windows in the transport vehicle, so the only safe place to look was at her hands, back in handcuffs.

Later, after all the processing was completed, she was allowed to take a shower. The cubicle offered little privacy, but she turned her face to the wall, and as the hot water ran over her hair and body, she allowed herself to weep again. She did it as quietly as she could, but sometimes the fear, shock and grief overwhelmed her and she sobbed out loud. She half-expected the bored prison officer who was guarding her to react in some way, but the woman said nothing. No doubt they were used to misery in here.

That same prison officer handed her the ugly green tracksuit that marked her out as an inmate. She put it on. It was old, but it was clean and not uncomfortable. Then she was given some bedding, a toothbrush, toothpaste, toilet paper, soap, tissues and deodorant.

'No need for these,' the guard said, putting a pack of sanitary napkins back on the shelf.

Miriam smiled wanly. She did not get a smile back.

Next, she was shown to her cell—double bunks, a toilet, sink, a desk, two chairs, bookshelves above the desk and a TV on the wall. As she stood in the middle of the narrow space, trying to get her bearings, the guard went to close the door.

'It's lights-out in a minute; you'd better make your bed while you can still see. Oh, and you've got a visitor coming tomorrow.'

'Who? Who is my visitor?'

But Miriam was speaking to a closed door.

❧

Her visitor—Ally, of course—was now sitting opposite her in the visiting room.

Miriam sat quietly, letting Ally cry for as long as she needed, before asking, 'How are the children?'

'Missing you. Fiona is minding them for me, which is saying something. She's hardly speaking to me at the moment, and she can't look at me at all.'

'Why?' Miriam was genuinely shocked. Why would Fiona take this out on her sister? They should be supporting one another.

'She blames me for . . . for . . . all this. And she's right, Mum! I blame me too! How I wish I'd never laid eyes on that bastard. It's all my fault for bringing him into our lives.'

Her voice had gone wobbly again. Miriam really did not want her to cry anymore.

'It's alright, you know. Remand isn't that bad.'

Miriam was lying.

'You're just saying that to make me feel better. You're in jail, for fuck's sake! How long are they going to keep you here? When is the trial going to be?'

'There won't be any trial.'

'What? Everyone is entitled to their day in court. They can't just lock you up without hearing your side of the story!'

'There will be a hearing. It's called a sentencing hearing. It's heard by a judge, not a jury, and you can call witnesses and there can be victim impact statements and so on, but it's just to decide what my punishment should be and how long it should last, not whether I should *be* punished or not. I'm pleading guilty, you see, so there's no need to spend public money on lawyers arguing about it.'

'But why are you pleading guilty?'

'Because I am. I shot Nick in broad daylight, in front of witnesses. It was premeditated and planned. There is no point pretending otherwise.'

Ally's face crumpled and she began crying again. 'But you did it for us, to save us! Surely that will count for something?'

'Greg says they will be looking at provocation and how it impacted on my "moral culpability" to help get me a shorter sentence. He's out looking for a top criminal barrister now. But I am a murderer. I killed a man in cold blood. It wasn't self-defence because he was not threatening me at the time.'

'What about when he tried to run you over?'

Greg had told Ally all about that incident. She had given him permission to tell her daughters whatever they wanted to know. She owed them that at least.

'That will go to provocation, Greg says, but as he was obviously trying to frighten me, not kill me, it's not enough on its own.'

'*I* should have killed him!'

'No way! Your kids need you. They've suffered enough and they're going to have to live with the fact that their nan killed their dad. It had to be me. I am simply not as important to anyone now as I once was.'

Miriam did not mean to sound self-pitying. But since Pete had died, it was true.

'That's not what Fiona says. She is so upset. She accused me of robbing Molly of her grandmother!'

'Better she lose her grandmother than her cousins and her aunt.'

'Nonsense. And you are just as important to me as you ever were. More so, maybe.' Ally was crying again.

'Nah. When you have kids of your own they become your focus. As they should. It's okay, I promise. I am managing.'

'But you, of all people, in jail for God knows how long! My law-abiding, North Shore matron of a mother! And all because of me.'

'Turns out I'm a badass.'

That shut her up. Ally looked at her mother open-mouthed, then burst out laughing. Miriam had to wait a second time for her daughter to calm down, but it was better to watch her cry with laughter than sob with despair.

'The media are calling you all sorts of names, that's for sure. Some of them are just plain silly—I heard some pundit call you the Ninja Nanna on the radio this morning. I snorted my coffee out of my nose when I heard that.'

'How undignified!'

Ally rolled her eyes. 'Some badass.'

'Maybe I'll get a prison tattoo . . .'

Her daughter looked so horrified that Miriam hastily retracted. 'Only kidding.'

'The press are camped outside our house and also outside Fiona's. It's bedlam every time I step out of the door. Goody is going insane barking at them and the kids are frightened, though also a bit excited. They keep asking when you are coming home, though.'

Miriam's eyes filled with tears, but she cleared her throat. No more tears. No. More. Tears. And no use speculating how long it might be before she could go home. She could not bear to think about that.

'Is that why Fiona is so upset with you—because of the media?'

'No! Of course not! She's upset because she loves you and can't bear to think of what you're going through.'

'I hope she comes to see me—and brings Molly.'

'She will. She's not mad at you. Just me.'

'That's silly. I'm the one who pulled the trigger. You had no idea what I was planning to do.'

'She knows that. She's not mad at me for any rational reason. She knows it's not directly my fault, but—and I agree with her—she knows that it is also *all* my fault.'

'It's HIS fault! No one else's!'

Miriam had spoken louder than she intended. The prison officer at the back of the room looked up and took a step towards them.

'Keep it down,' she warned.

Miriam placated her with a smile and an apologetic gesture and the woman leant back against the wall. But Miriam wasn't sorry she had reacted so strongly. She was sick of women taking the blame for what men did to them.

'I've been a bit shielded from what the media are saying in here. I've been avoiding the papers and the news, and we've no access to social media. There are computers in the library, apparently, but they've disabled Facebook and the others. It's a bit like being in a big boarding school, weirdly. Just with really awful uniforms. Anyway, I hope they are talking about Nick's part in all this, not just mine.'

'The media are knee deep at Sally's too, and she's talking to them, of course.'

Miriam felt a sharp pang of remorse at the mention of Sally. She felt ashamed of the pain she had brought to another mother.

'Who can blame her? She loved her son. She must hate me.'

'That'd be understating it.'

'What's she been saying?'

'That we're all insane—you, me, Fiona, the lot of us—and that her son was the sweetest, kindest, most loving son, husband and father the world has ever seen. She's getting a lot of traction too, Mum, and I'm scared it won't help your case. She's also threatening to apply for custody.'

'Access,' Miriam corrected her automatically.

'Whatever.' Ally would not be distracted.

'She won't get it. You've done nothing wrong. I have, and I am going to be locked up out of harm's way. That's another reason why it had to be me.'

'Yes, that's what Nerida said.'

'Nothing much is going to help my case, anyway. Greg's hoping that we can get a reduced sentence, but he's said upfront that I have to anticipate spending a long time in a place like this.'

Miriam and Ally both looked around. They were sitting in a largish room, with high barred windows, and some dilapidated couches along the wall. There were a few other people in the room, sitting, like them, on either side of the tables that were lined up like school desks. A few garish toys were piled in a corner and a small child was playing happily with them while his parents spoke in hushed tones at a table nearby. The bored-looking prison officer stood by the closed door. She was chewing at the skin around her fingernails. The contrast between Miriam's old home and this new one was stark. Miriam stared at the grubby doors, stained by decades of finger marks and the scratched and pitted floor. *And I used to fret about mascara on a bolster*, she thought.

'I'll bring Teddy and Isla next time,' Ally promised.

Again, Miriam teared up. *I am very raw*, she thought.

'If you're sure they'll cope?'

'It's not that bad.' Ally forced a smile. 'You're right about the boarding school vibe. They'll be pleased to see you and they'll just play with the toys. By the way, I've brought you some underwear, and some books and some photos, but I had to give them to one of the prison officers when I arrived. They said they'd pass them on to you.'

'That's okay. They buy us magazines and I can get all the newspapers.'

Ally pulled a face. Miriam knew what she was thinking.

'Like I said, I don't read what they're saying about me. I just turn the page. I can't quite cope with other people's opinions, not yet. And if it comes on the TV, I just turn it off.

Ally looked up at her mother and held her gaze steadily. 'Maybe you should read some of it, Mum. Not everyone thinks what you have done is so wrong.'

※

Prisha, sitting where Allison had sat a few weeks earlier, confirmed this. She had made the trek to the correction centre to talk about Duffy Real Estate and what was to happen to the business while its founder and proprietor was in jail. Miriam's friend was her usual, unruffled self. Judging by her demeanour, they could have been in any ordinary conference room.

'There are plenty of women speaking up for you,' she said, 'particularly those who work in domestic violence. And there are a few men too, some of whom have lost a sister or daughter to DV. And lots of people are talking about how the laws don't protect women and children properly. You've caused a storm, Miriam, but at least you've made people talk about it.'

'Thank you for always being in my corner, dear friend, but nothing you say can change the fact that I have put you, the business, our staff and clients in a bloody awful position.'

'Actually'—Prisha opened the compendium she had brought with her—'as these latest listings and sales figures show, you've done rather the opposite.'

Miriam scanned the spreadsheets Prisha put on the table between them. What she saw was astonishing. Business was up by twenty per cent!

'I had the devil's own time persuading the prison guards to let me bring all this in,' Prisha was saying. 'I had to take them through it all to prove there was nothing illegal about any of it.'

Miriam wasn't really listening to her. She was growing used to her freedoms being stripped away, used to having no privacy and no control over her own life. She had even adjusted to the unchanging rhythms of her day—lights on, breakfast, work detail, lunch, work detail, free time, showers, dinner, cells locked, lights out. She had gone from the height of anxiety to the depth of dullness. She knew which she preferred.

Miriam double-checked the figures to make sure that what she saw was accurate, then looked at Prisha in astonishment.

'I know!' said the other woman. 'Apparently notoriety is good for business! The fact that your face and name and the debate about what you have done is the talk of the town has put us on the map. Your actions even got a mention in parliament. Most of the new customers come out of curiosity, but some come out of solidarity.'

'Actually,' Miriam said, 'some of the women in here seem to be really pleased about what I have done too. One of them told me I was a badass.'

Prisha, like Ally before her, threw back her head and laughed.

The compliment had been paid on the first full day Miriam had spent behind bars.

'You're the woman who shot her wife-beating fuckwit of a son-in-law?'

A fellow prisoner had stopped beside her in the corridor as Miriam stood in the queue waiting to use the payphone. The woman was large, dark-haired, dark-eyed—an Islander by the look of her. Miriam nodded, smiling the way she did at a viewing when a potential purchaser asked her if she was the real estate agent.

'Yeah, I thought it was you. Your face is all over the papers and the TV. Sounds like he was a real cunt.'

That's what Jeremy had called him, back in that other life she'd once lived.

Miriam nodded, still smiling her idiotic, ingratiating smile. 'He was.'

The woman nodded back approvingly. 'You might act like butter wouldn't melt, but you are a badass, lady. Good job. We should shoot the fucking lot of them.'

Now, staring at the spreadsheets, she remembered how she had felt as she watched the woman saunter away. Miriam had felt as pleased as she had when she'd won Realtor of the Year. Someone had seen what she'd done and recognised it. If Ally and Prisha were right, it seemed it wasn't just her fellow inmates who felt that way.

'What are the other women like?' Prisha asked.

'I don't really know yet. I've pretty much kept myself to myself, but most of them seem sad rather than bad. Most are very young and almost all of them are black or Islander or Asian. I think I'm the oldest and the whitest. The girl I'm sharing a cell with looks about fifteen. She's hardly spoken to me, so I've just left her alone. She's got a picture of a baby blu-tacked to the wall above her bed and I can hear her crying in the night. I feel sorry for her.'

'And the food? What's that like?'

Miriam pulled a face. 'It's like hospital food. They deliver it to you in the same sort of plastic dishes covered in cling wrap. I keep thinking about when my mother was in North Shore before she died. It's just like that. I doubt I'll put on any weight.

We can buy stuff, though. There's a shop in the prison. In fact, Ally is going to put money in my account every month so I can draw down on it to pay for the things I need. There's usually some fruit available.'

Miriam was trying to put the best possible spin on her new reality, but it actually wasn't all that bad. She could even see how she might make a bearable life for herself, with the time to read and paint and study. She'd also noticed some of the women tending a vegetable garden in the exercise yard. She'd find out how to get involved in that. And the woman who had called her a badass was not an isolated case. Miriam had already picked up, even in the short time she'd been in this place, that not only were many of the inmates well-disposed towards her, the prison officers were too.

'Actually, thinking about my mother, prison—well, remand, anyway—is better than what a lot of my contemporaries put up with. I'd rather be here than in a nursing home.'

What she was not telling anyone was how she felt at lights-out. That moment when the guards came around and closed and locked the doors, that was when her guts dropped and her throat constricted. That was when the walls pressed in and the very air she breathed seemed so thick with unknowable terrors that she could hardly pull it into her lungs. But—terrible as being awake after lights-out might be—she dreaded closing her eyes. As soon as she did, the movie projector inside her brain began to play, unspooling her fatal act in every excruciating detail from beginning to horrible bloody end. But, of course, it was not the end. Not nearly. She knew perfectly well that there was a lot more horror and humiliation waiting for her. Remand was one thing; no one here had been convicted of anything yet. Prison would be quite another.

'Well, she should be able to top up your prison account nicely with the money I'll be depositing every month.'

Miriam had agreed to sell Prisha the agency, and she would be paying for it in monthly instalments. She'd tried to interest Ally in taking it over, but Ally had accepted a casual job as a tutor in the Economics faculty at the University of Sydney. Miriam had been thrilled when she'd heard. It seemed that Ally was finally taking back control of her own life, finally beginning to heal. There was much comfort in that.

Prisha had tried to talk Miriam into continuing their partnership, but Miriam was having none of it. She had no idea how long a sentence she was likely to get, but she knew she'd be too old to get back into the real estate game by the time she got out.

'Well, the money might help pay some of my legal bills, at least.' Miriam gave Prisha a rueful smile.

'How long do you think you'll be in here?'

'Remand? I'm not sure. It could be up to a year before the sentencing hearing, Greg says. Then it's proper jail after I've been convicted. Mind you, I might still be in here. There's a unit up the back they call the Cottages where the long-timers are kept . . .'

'Kept? Miriam! Honestly!'

'Alright—where the long-timers live. It's five individual cells with a communal lounge and kitchen, showers and loos—and they only lock the front door. That's where I may end up after sentencing. It sounds a bit like those share houses for people with disabilities or mental health issues—but behind very high walls.'

She smiled brightly, but the thought made her feel ill.

Nevertheless, it was wonderful to see Prisha, wonderful to talk business again and feel her old financial muscles flex themselves in a way they had not for a very long time. Anything that distracted her from ruminating over what she had done and why she had done it was welcome. Anything that stopped the waves of shame that flowed over and through her at regular intervals was something to be grateful for.

∼

Miriam's cellmate did finally speak, one morning (well, she supposed it was morning). Miriam woke with a start. She had dreamt she could not open her mouth, that her lips were glued shut. Rubbing her eyes, she got up to drink some water from the tap over the sink.

'You're a celebrity.'

It was the girl from the top bunk. Miriam couldn't see her in the dark, but she could hear her well enough.

'Infamous rather than famous,' Miriam said.

'What?'

'I'm not the kind of celebrity people want to be like.'

'I dunno. I wish my mum had been like you.'

There was such a weight of sadness in the girl's voice that it almost distracted Miriam from her own pain.

'I'm not sure my daughters see it that way.'

Fiona still had not come to visit her mother. They had spoken once or twice on the phone, but Fiona was uncommunicative, almost cold. She was still angry with her mother, with her sister, with the world. And who could blame her? Her life had been turned upside down too.

'I bet they do,' the girl said. 'They're just shocked and upset that you've ended up in here, and they're saying things they don't really mean.'

Miriam was surprised at how much sense this sad young woman was making. They were only sharing a cell because remand was packed at the moment. One of the officers had already explained that the girl had been put in here because Miriam seemed sensible and might help calm her down. Though it seemed that at the moment the boot was on the other foot.

'She's withdrawing, you see,' the officer had explained. Miriam must have looked as blank as she felt, because the woman added, 'From heroin. Makes 'em crazy. And you're a murderer. Murderers are always the most sensible inmates. It's mostly a one-off crime, especially with women. You react to a set of circumstances and do the wrong thing. I've never seen one of you ever do it again. We've never had a serial killer. Mostly with the murderers, I always think, *There but for the grace of God go I.* I never think that about the druggies.'

'I hope I can help,' Miriam said. 'It's all a bit new to me, of course.'

That was an understatement, but Officer Coleman just nodded.

Officer Coleman liked a chat and Miriam was content to listen and learn. She was astonished to hear that those who committed the worst of crimes were actually considered the best of prisoners. The officer's words helped lift a little of the burden of her shame.

CHAPTER 24

'Tell me why you are here.'

Miriam sat in the chair opposite the therapist. At that moment, she was remembering something she'd read once. Someone had pointed out that if you divide the word into two, 'therapist' becomes 'the rapist'. Miriam's mood mirrored her thought. Her legs, in their prison greens, were wrapped around one another and her arms were folded tightly across her chest. She felt like a sullen teenager whose mother had sat her down for what her own daughters used to call a 'deep and meaningful'. She wasn't sitting opposite this grey-haired woman dressed in boho-chic by choice, but because she had to. A psychologist's report was a mandatory requirement for the sentencing hearing, whenever that was likely to be.

Greg had found her a criminal law firm that was prepared to act for her and would allow him to work in a sort of liaison capacity. The barrister attached to the case—Veronica Henry QC, AO, BA LLB Hons—was extremely elegant; when Miriam had met her in the visitors' room the woman had almost shimmered in an expensive cream linen suit paired with a silk scarf in fuchsia pink. Miriam had never felt uglier. Her prison greens had reduced her status comprehensively, as they were designed to do.

'Our job is to get you the shortest sentence possible, and that is precisely what we will do,' the barrister told her. But the glamorous Ms Henry and her minions had agreed with Greg that she might have to wait as long as a year before her case was heard.

'There's always a backlog—funding cuts and all that—and they often like to wait until the fuss dies down when it's a high-profile case like yours.'

Miriam had forgotten the name of the young woman who had confirmed the delay. She was just one of the eager-to-please young associates who dashed about after the eye-wateringly expensive barrister. The last thing Miriam wanted to do at the moment was please anyone, especially those who held her future in their hands. She had moved through the shock that had paralysed her for months after her arrest and incarceration. Now she was filled with resentment and anger towards everyone in a position of authority. She knew it was irrational. She knew she deserved to be where she was and she knew she had forfeited her right to control her own destiny. But knowing it didn't make any difference to how she felt. If they treated her like a child, she found herself reacting like a child. And rebellion felt good. It gave her a semblance of control. They could control when she woke, ate, washed and slept, but *she* could control how she responded to it. There was something liberating about becoming a notorious criminal. Given what she had already done, what difference would it make if she was a bit grumpy or even downright rude? It was a strange relief to let go of the people-pleasing she had been trained to do all her life.

'So why do I have to go see this psych in such a hurry then?' she'd asked. 'Or see her at all?'

'It's to inform the judge,' Greg explained.

'And it's in your interests to cooperate,' the barrister added, 'as a sympathetic report can help to reduce your moral culpability, and like I said, that's your best chance for reducing your sentence.'

It seemed she would have to spend a few sessions with the court-mandated psychologist, whether she liked it or not—and so, here she was.

The woman repeated her question. 'Tell me why you are here?'

Miriam rolled her eyes; it was a stupid question. When she did speak, her voice sounded sulky and resentful.

'My name is Miriam Duffy. I am sixty-two years old. I run my own successful real estate agency—or I did—and a few months ago I shot and killed my abusive son-in-law and have been on remand awaiting sentencing for murder ever since.'

The therapist smiled wryly. Despite herself, Miriam softened towards the woman. There was much to like about the therapist's expression; Miriam detected warmth, compassion, even admiration for the rebellious spirit that had motivated Miriam's too-literal answer.

'Okay, I deserved that. Tell me how you feel about being here, talking to me, then.'

'Shitty.'

'Shitty how?'

It was a good question. Miriam didn't really have a good answer. She knew she felt reluctant and defensive, but she didn't know why. Instead of answering, she shrugged like a scornful teenager. *Christ*, she thought, *I feel about fifteen.*

'How old do you feel right now?'

Miriam was astonished. It was as if this woman could read her mind.

'I told you. I am sixty-two.'

The therapist tilted her head and narrowed her eyes as if examining an exhibit under a microscope.

'I'd say your body language reminds me of a rebellious teenager. Were you one?'

'A bit.'

Miriam was alarmed at the wave of emotion that welled up inside her as she said those two words. She could feel her face flush and her heart rate speed up. Boho-woman watched her intently but said nothing.

'I wish I had been worse.'

Miriam had not expected to say anything, let alone that. Her voice was very low and she almost hoped the therapist had not heard her. No such luck, of course.

'Do you? Why is that?'

'I felt like I had to be good. I couldn't let rip, like I wanted to, like some of my friends did. I had to help hold everyone together. I couldn't let it all fall apart like it had before.'

'What had?'

'My family. My father . . .'

Miriam stopped herself. She never spoke of her father. Never even thought about him. She'd been four, or maybe five, when he'd disappeared out of her life. One day she'd come home from school—or was it preschool?—and he was gone. No one said anything about his absence, not for days, so she'd wondered if he might just reappear as suddenly as he had left. She had very much hoped that he would not. The weight that had lifted from her was wonderful. The whole world had felt lighter. It suddenly dawned on her that this was how the world felt now Nick was no longer in it. She might have been incarcerated, she was angry and resentful, no doubt, but she was no longer living in fear. Sometimes, she caught herself feeling lighter and freer than she had in years. The fear about what might happen to Ally and the children had gone.

'What about your father?'

Miriam felt frustrated by the turn the conversation was taking. It was such a cliché, asking about her parents, and her father was irrelevant.

'Nothing. He left when I was little. I don't even remember him.'

But she did remember him. She didn't remember what he looked like or how he sounded, but she remembered little moments and impressions. Flashes of memory would come to her in dreams, sometimes, or if something occurred to remind her—a shadow falling in a certain way, a particular smell, a distant sound. Then she would again see him coming into her room at night, his silhouette looming in the doorway. She remembered the smell of his beery breath and the scratch of his face on hers. She remembered how he'd overwhelmed her, crushed her—not physically, exactly—but with something else. A need, a seeking of something from her that she did not understand and could not give. That was another reason she loved Pete. He was not needy. He gave her as much as she gave him. *More, probably*, she thought, with a sharp stab of guilt. *I took him for granted.*

'Yet you said you felt you needed to hold everything together, to stop it falling apart as it had before, so you must have felt something when he left.'

For the first time, Miriam looked properly at boho-woman (her name was Margaret Somers, she reminded herself); looked right into her eyes. They were pale blue and had deep lines around them that crinkled when she smiled. Miriam had indeed said that. What had she meant by it?

'Maybe—or maybe I just saw how my brother, Michael, felt.'

'How did he feel?'

'He felt like me: relieved. I heard him ask Mum one night if Dad was coming back. When she said she didn't think so, he just said, "Good." And I remember thinking that was exactly the right word. Him not being there made me feel good too.'

'Why do you think you felt good about him going?'

Miriam's heart rate went up again. This whole session was weird. When she'd tried to anticipate how it would go, talking about her father had never entered her head. Being taken by surprise meant she had no chance to think about her answers.

'I guess I didn't like him. I guess he made me feel bad.'

'I guess?'

'As I said, I was very little. I don't remember.'

'Yet you remember what your brother said to your mother very clearly.'

Miriam did not know quite what to say. Instead she reverted to another shrug, but a less scornful one this time.

'If you could remember, what do you think he might have done to make you feel bad?'

'He used to come into my room at night.'

Miriam watched Margaret carefully. Was she going to jump to the obvious conclusion? The woman's expression did not change and she remained silent.

'And no, it was nothing like that.'

'How can you be so sure if you don't remember?'

Was she trying to be clever? Miriam folded her arms again and leant back in her chair.

'I think I would remember if it was anything like that. I remember I didn't like him lying down next to me because of his beery breath and his scratchy face, but that's all I remember. He used to cry sometimes and hold on to me too tightly. I hated that, but he never hurt me.'

'Do you think he hurt Michael? Or your mother?'

Miriam had never thought about that—and now that the therapist mentioned it, Miriam was astonished that she hadn't. He must have hurt them in some way, mustn't he, if they were all so pleased to see the back of him?

'I . . . I don't know. Maybe.'

There was something nagging at her, a memory. It wasn't something she'd blanked out or anything dramatic like that; it was just a snippet, a moment that she did not think about very often. In fact, when she thought back to her childhood, which she did rarely, she couldn't remember much at all before she was in primary school, beyond the impressionistic flashes. Maybe that was significant, maybe it wasn't.

'I do remember hearing Mum crying sometimes late at night. I used to hate it. I'd go and get into bed with Michael. He'd always be awake too and we'd lie there and listen. I remember something Michael said to me once, as we heard her sobbing—that he'd never be mean to his wife when he grew up and got married. I'm not sure he lived up to it, though.' Miriam gave a gallows laugh.

'Where is Michael now?'

'He lives in Singapore.'

'Are you still close?'

'God, no. He hasn't even contacted me about . . . all this.'

She hadn't thought about his silence until this moment. It wasn't as if he wouldn't have heard about it. It was splashed all over the news, she knew, and not just in Australia; no doubt her brother had heard about it in Singapore. She had not questioned his silence until now. *Why not?* she wondered.

'Where is your father now?'

'God knows. I haven't heard of him again since the day he left. It's possible Michael has had some contact, but I haven't. I imagine he'd be long dead by now.'

'Have you never wondered about him? Never asked Michael? Or your mother?'

'No. Never.'

And it struck her for the first time how very odd that was. Maybe he had done something awful to her, after all. Then she suddenly remembered something else; she just hadn't associated it with the shadowy figure that was her father.

'He threw a plate against the wall once—at least, I think it was him. I can see it now—it was a full dinner plate with meat and veg and mashed potato and gravy on it. It hung on the wall for a minute, as if it was stuck there by the food, then it slid down, leaving this awful brown mark like a shit stain on the back of the toilet. It must have been him who threw the plate. I can't believe anyone else would have.'

'But you hadn't associated it with him, until now?'

'No. I hardly ever think about it to be honest. Except sometimes, when I'm furious about something, I have a little fantasy about doing the same thing. I see it then, on our old red-and-white kitchen wallpaper. I never have done it, of course. It's the sort of thing only a bloke would do, I reckon.'

'Why do you reckon that?'

'A woman has to clean up her own mess, so of course she thinks twice about making one. I'm sure Mum scrubbed all that food off the wall and cleared up the broken china. He certainly didn't.'

'Do you remember anything else about that incident? What it was that made him throw the plate against the wall?'

And suddenly she did. It came back to her in a rush, almost as if it was happening all over again.

'It was me! I did. I was sitting on his knee and I peed my pants, and he didn't just throw the plate against the wall, he threw me! He was so disgusted by me pissing all over him. I remember how ashamed I felt. But I'd been trying to get off his knee to go to the toilet for ages, and he wouldn't let me. He kept telling me off for wriggling and, in the end, I couldn't hold on any longer. I was only little.'

The words had poured out of her mouth as if something inside her had burst and she could not hold that in any longer either.

'He went to kick me as I lay on the ground, but Mum got between us and she copped it instead. "A filthy little shit," he called me. "Just like your mother!"'

Miriam had mimicked a man's voice as she roared her father's long-ago words. Then, frightened at her own vehemence, she covered her mouth with her hands. She looked up at the woman opposite. 'How could I possibly have forgotten all that?'

'It makes sense not to want to remember such an awful experience. A child's job is to grow up. It's quite common for children to protect themselves by forgetting. And he disappeared out of your life, so there was no need to remember.'

'But it makes me wonder what else happened. What else I have forgotten.'

That idea was terrifying. Miriam felt as if what she had always thought of as solid ground had just shifted beneath her feet. The past was not as she had thought. *She* was not who she had thought.

'Maybe you could ask your brother. He's older than you, I gather?'

Miriam nodded. 'Three years older.'

'He may remember.'

'Is that why I killed Nick? Is it my father coming out in me?'

That was an even worse thought—that she had not done it to protect her daughter and grandchildren. She wasn't righteous after all. She was just the bad seed of a bad seed.

But Margaret shook her head. 'No, no. The experience of violence in childhood does not mean you are predisposed to it in adulthood. You killed your son-in-law to protect your family, or you sincerely believed you did. I'm sure of that. But this is the sort of experience judges take into account when assessing your moral culpability.'

'Just as well my dad was a violent bastard, then, is that what you mean?'

Margaret Somers smiled ruefully. 'In this situation, it helps. And if it makes you feel better, I have almost never interviewed a person in your predicament who has not had some violence or abuse in their background, whether they have committed a violent crime or not. Even embezzlers and con artists. Our prisons are full of mistreated children who have grown up—but perhaps only physically.'

Miriam thought of the women she had met so far in remand. Were all of them survivors of abuse of some kind, even the culpable drivers?

'Child abuse must be very common in that case.'

'Doing this job, you start to think it may be the norm.'

'Pete and I didn't abuse our kids. Well, not on purpose anyway.'

But the snake uncoiled itself inside her brain and hissed at her, *You must have done something, mustn't you? What did you do to Allison that made her vulnerable to such a man? Julie was right all along. There was something about your relationship with Pete that was toxic. It's your fault you ended up here, not hers.* Miriam shook her head to silence the snake.

'What are you thinking about now?'

'I was doubting my own words. Going back over all the mistakes I made as a parent. I must have done something, mustn't I, for my daughter to get involved with such a man.'

'Did you parent alone? Your husband, the father of your daughters, died only a few years ago, I believe.'

'Pete was a wonderful, loving and supportive father! None of this is his fault. I sometimes think that if he was still alive, none of this would ever have happened.'

'That is something we can never know.'

Thanks for stating the bleeding bloody obvious, thought Miriam.

'But what about Nick? If you blame yourself, don't you also hold his parents responsible for who he became?'

'Of course I do! But, having done what I have done, I don't feel I have any right to think that way. In fact, his mum is one of the people I feel worst about. She must feel as bad about losing him as I would have if I'd lost Ally and the kids!'

Miriam suddenly found that she was crying.

Margaret, like Prisha, let her cry. Eventually she passed Miriam a box of tissues. Miriam took one and blew her nose.

'Don't forget, she would have lost her grandchildren too if her son had carried out his threats.'

Miriam hadn't thought about that. There was some comfort in the idea.

The psychologist went on, 'And the men who do kill their children—and often their ex too—usually then kill themselves, so she could have lost him and more besides.'

'Are you justifying what I did?'

'No. Just facing reality. It's actually my job.'

❧

That night, lying on her bunk, staring up at the lump her cellmate's bum made in the worn metal springs of the bed base above her, Miriam tried to remember all she could about the man who had left her nothing but his surname. The thought of his foot lashing out towards her small self—*How old was I when he did this?* she wondered. *Three?*—made her shudder. Worse, however, was the memory of it connecting with her mother's shin as she put herself between her daughter and her husband. Miriam felt sick. She had never thanked her mother and she had been a cold and resentful daughter. Unforgiving of her mother's every mistake and weakness, especially her utter reliance on the stepfather Miriam had despised. She felt terrible about that now. Boris had treated her mother like a queen; he'd fussed over her and protected her. She must have been desperate for a partner like that after being married to Charles Duffy.

'I'm sorry, Mum.' Miriam whispered the words, aiming them skywards, past her cellmate's lumpy bum. She did not really believe her mother was up in heaven somewhere or hovering above her like some ghostly spirit waiting to be forgiven, but it was oddly comforting to apologise to her out loud. 'I wish I had known you better.'

CHAPTER 25

'But you haven't answered me. Why do you think it was the kittens that pushed you over the edge?'

Miriam had been to a few sessions with Margaret by now. Far from dreading them, as she had initially, she looked forward to them. Talking to Margaret was helping her to make sense of things. Miriam trusted her. Dr Somers had asked about the kittens a couple of times already. This time the therapist was obviously determined to make Miriam answer.

'You remind me of Ally,' Miriam said, smiling wryly.

'In what way?'

'She says I always deflect the conversation away from myself.'

'You mean like you are doing right now?'

Miriam laughed. 'Yeah. Like right now.'

'The kittens?'

'I don't know, exactly, but I read it as a direct threat. I suppose it was because of their names—Tebby and Island. I mean, could they have been more obvious avatars for Teddy and Isla? It wasn't just the kittens, of course. It was him pretending that he was going to run me over, showing me how powerless I was against him. And it was the photo of those other poor people, and him asking what photo of Ally and the kids he should choose for the media to use after he'd . . . I mean, what was I meant to think he was threatening to do? And what was I meant to do in return?'

Margaret nodded. It was the intense attention she paid that helped Miriam to open up.

'But the kittens were the final straw because it was the first time he had actually carried out his threat. Okay, he'd done it by proxy—what's that syndrome all the thriller TV series love?'

'Munchausen by proxy?'

'Yeah, that one. So killing the kittens was like a practice run, or something. A practice run for us, not him. He wanted us to get a taste of what it would feel like if he really did . . .' But Miriam could not get the words out. 'He'd already made Teddy frightened about Daddy wanting to give them a needle, and made sure he was scared enough to tell us about it.'

'So you think Nick wanted Teddy to tell you?'

'Of course he did. Why scare him like that, otherwise?'

'It seems to me that Nick liked scaring people. He clearly got a huge kick out of terrifying you that night on the road. Why wouldn't he enjoy scaring his son?'

Miriam had never thought of that.

'I don't know. I suppose I thought he wouldn't stoop so low with the children.'

'Yet you were deathly afraid he intended to kill them. Surely scaring them pales in comparison to that?'

'Do you think I was wrong about Nick wanting us to know?'

'No, but people can have many motivations for a single action. In fact, I think we almost always do.'

'When I told Ally what Teddy had said about the needle, she said that Nick had once threatened her with it, or maybe he'd threatened to kill himself, or both of them. It was often hard to tell exactly what he meant.'

'A very powerful technique, being ambiguous and hard to pin down. Politicians use it all the time. It gives you room to deny just about everything and put the blame for any misunderstanding on the listener.'

'And then there was Julie and her dog. I didn't think that was a coincidence either. And, even if it was, I still got the message. He was a vet, for fuck's sake. He was like fucking James Bond!'

'What do you mean?'

'He was trained to kill.'

'And licensed to kill.'

'Yeah, that too.'

'Talking of messages . . .'

'Yes, the message that came with the kittens. It was so . . . sinister—and yet so plausible.'

'Is that why you didn't go to the police about it?'

'Partly, but it was mostly because we had reported him so many times before and nothing really happened. Maybe he'd have copped a fine, but mostly he got a slap on the wrist. You know—*Be a good boy from now on*—that sort of thing. And it takes such a long time to get anything to happen in the courts, and every time we did, he seemed to get angrier and his behaviour got worse. It was like poking a beehive. All we did when we tried to protect ourselves was get stung.'

'So you felt helpless.'

'Yes, utterly powerless. And it was wrong! So wrong! He was the one who terrorised us, yet there seemed to be nothing anyone could do to stop him. I began to think that the only thing that would get people to take notice was the kids' actual dead bodies. I used to see them like that in my imagination, especially if it was me who had put them to bed. Sometimes, I got so freaked out I'd get up in the night and make sure they were still breathing, like some kind of neurotic new mother.'

'I can see why the dead kittens were such a shock.'

Miriam looked up—she had been staring at her hands. Her therapist's words had awakened a flash of hope.

'I hope the judge sees it like that at the sentencing hearing.'

But Margaret's face gave nothing away.

'Anyway, it seemed obvious to me then that it was either us or him. And if that was the only choice I had left, then there was no choice.'

'When you first bought the gun, did you think you would use it?'

'No, not at first. Not really. But I liked how the gun made me feel.'

'How did it make you feel?'

'Not helpless. Like I wasn't just sitting there waiting for him to take from me everything that I cared about.'

'Not helpless? Or powerful?'

It was a very good question.

∽

Miriam often felt too wired to sleep after her sessions with Margaret. She would go over what they had talked about and everything she had said. She'd told Margaret things about herself she did not know she knew. And things about Pete and Ally and Fiona.

'You might not recognise me now, Pete,' she whispered into the dark. 'I think I have become quite a different person.'

※

'Fiona can you get something from home and post it to me?'

Miriam was making the regular weekly phone call she was allowed. She was quite comfortable now, standing in the queue. She and Nula—the woman who had called her a badass—often stood together as they waited, sharing a packet of lollies. Nula may have been a couple of decades younger than Miriam, but the two of them were the oldest women in the place. That alone had helped them to form a bond. They were the elder statesmen of remand. Nula was behind her now, waiting to call her son, who was in foster care.

'Sure, Mum. What is it? Some clothes, books, DVDs? All of the above?'

'None of the above. I want you to send me a photograph of the urn that holds your father's ashes. It's on the top shelf of the linen cupboard, up the back, next to a box of some other old photos.'

There was a long silence. Miriam waited patiently.

'You want me to take a photo of Dad's urn and post it to you?'

'Yes. Is that okay?'

'Why don't you ask Ally?'

It was a reasonable question. After all, Ally and the kids were living in the house. Fiona would have to make a special trip.

'Because I think she'll get upset.'

'Oh, and I won't?'

But Miriam was not falling into that trap.

'No, you won't.'

'Why do you want it?'

'I don't know. I just do.'

Fiona did as her mother asked, and soon the photo was blu-tacked above her bunk. She had another one of her husband stuck up there too. But in the second photo he was full of life, grinning at her, with the wind blowing his dark hair. They'd been out sailing when she'd taken it. It was her favourite picture of him, but both photos brought her equal comfort. Pete was dead but he was not gone. As long as she and the girls were alive, he was too.

∽

Miriam's sessions with Margaret were drawing to a close. She had come to depend on her therapist. Her fortnightly sessions got her from one end of the week to the next. She knew her therapist was a professional, employed by the court to write a report that would shape her future, but it made no difference to the affection Miriam now felt for the woman who had listened so carefully and helped her to unlock so much she had buried for so long.

Early on in the therapy, Miriam had agreed to write her brother a letter. She was to ask Michael if he could help her understand her childhood and particularly what had happened with her father.

'It's interesting, isn't it, how your father just dropped out of your life completely when you were small. Have you ever thought about how it's also what has happened to Teddy and Isla?'

Miriam felt as if she had been punched.

'But we won't keep quiet about what has happened. Ally and I have already agreed we will tell the kids everything. What was it you said? You are only as sick as your biggest secret? Well, we won't keep any.'

'Sounds as if you don't like thinking about how similar your grandchildren's circumstances are to yours.'

'No. It makes me worry that something else was driving me. Something awful and cruel and fucked-up.'

Margaret sat in silence for a while. Then she said, 'Well, maybe it's time you tried to uncover some of the secrets in your own family—about your father, in particular.'

Miriam hated the idea. She was genuinely frightened of what she might discover. But despite her reluctance, Miriam agreed to do as Margaret suggested.

Miriam had found writing the letter relatively easy, once she got started. It was putting it in the prison postbox that was the hard part. She almost tore it to pieces rather than put it through the slot. But she didn't. Then, just before her last therapy session, she saw an unopened airmail envelope on her desk. It was postmarked Singapore.

'Fuck!'

Miriam's hands were actually shaking as she picked up the letter. It was from Michael alright, but she could not bring herself to open it, not until she was safely in Margaret's office.

'Why don't you read it to me?' the therapist suggested when Miriam produced it.

'Can't you do it?'

Margaret smiled her warm smile. 'I think you should. It's addressed to you, after all.'

Dear Miriam,

Thank you for your letter. I am very sorry about the predicament you find yourself in. However, I am also glad that Ally and the children are now safe. I don't agree with what you did, but I can understand the reason why you did it.

Despite its personal contents, Michael's letter read like a business response. She could almost sense him keeping his distance through the print.

To answer your question, Dad died more than a decade ago now, after suffering with alcohol-induced dementia for years. It was a heart attack that killed him in the end. I was surprised the bastard had one.

Michael was warming up a bit now.

His second wife used to send me occasional reports on his progress, but I never actually saw him for myself. I had no desire to.

When he lived with us, he was an abusive alcoholic. He used Mum like a punching bag and was quick to thrash me for any misdemeanour. But you were his little princess. Apart from the incident you described, which I remember vividly, you did not cop any actual violence—or not that I can recall, anyway. This may have been in part because Mum and I tried to protect you from the worst of it, but it was also because he adored you. He often said you were the only person in the family who cared about him. I used to feel sorry for you then, oddly enough, because he used to hold on to you and hug you and kiss you, and sometimes you'd struggle and try to get away. Then he'd accuse Mum of turning you against him. I used to find you hiding from him sometimes, when I asked you why you'd say it was because he was being yucky and smelt funny.

Mum threw him out just after you started school. We were all relieved. He'd been like a dark cloud hanging over us. Mum did it tough, though, because he never paid any child support or anything like that, of course. That's when she got that job answering the phones in the mechanic's shop and met Boris.

I know you never liked Boris much, and neither did I, but he was very good for Mum. I sometimes think now that we were both very hard on him and that probably made things very hard on her. In a strange way, he was a bit like Dad, except he made Mum the exclusive object of his adoration. He kept the rest of us at arm's length—even his own daughter—which is probably why we didn't like him much. It was almost as if he feared what might happen if he let Mum pay too much attention to anyone else, particularly you, I think. I don't know why he felt so threatened by you, but he did.

Do you ever hear anything from Carmen? I haven't for years. Boris and Dad had their way in the end, I suppose. They managed to keep us all apart from one another. I am sorry I have been a rather distant brother, but I find it hard to be intimate with anyone—just ask Ming and the kids. We're separated but living in the same house at the moment, for financial reasons. It drives Ming crazy, but I quite like it, to be honest. I don't really like being close to people. I always thought you'd turned out okay, but I guess our weird childhood took its toll on us all in the end.

I hope your court case goes as well as it can. One thing I can say for you, Miriam—you are always full of surprises.

Michael

Miriam looked up from the letter. Margaret was watching her.

'How do you feel?'

'Better than I thought I would.'

'Was it helpful?'

'Yes, it was. I was scared he wouldn't reply or that he'd send me something short and dismissive that would make me feel bad.'

'Was that all that you feared?'

Miriam looked at her hands. 'No. I was terrified he'd tell me I made it all up.'

'And yet he "remembered it vividly".'

'Yes. I felt such relief when I read that.'

Now Miriam felt able to look at her therapist again. 'Like I could trust myself and my memories. Like, whatever else I have done, I didn't play myself false. My memory was not telling me lies. To be honest, I never expected anything as enlightening as this letter, not from him, and it's made me feel rather sorry for him. I feel like I understand better why he is as he is.'

'Do you understand better why you are as you are? And why you may have done what you did?'

'The first—maybe I am starting to. I think I was putting all my energy into moving forward, when I was actually still caught in the past. Well, how could I not be when I didn't understand it, didn't even know about it? The second—I always knew why I did it, in practical terms. I did the wrong thing—a terribly wrong thing—but I still believe I did it for the right reasons. I do really believe I had little or no choice. Of course I hope the judge takes my past into account and reduces my sentence; I have no desire to spend decades in jail. But I don't believe it really has much to do with why I killed Nick. I think I could have had a dad as loving and sane as Pete was to our girls, and, given the circumstances, I would still have pulled that trigger.'

CHAPTER 26

'*The court accepts the evidence given by various witnesses, including the victim's wife and offender's daughter, Allison Janice Carruthers, that the victim, Nicholas Maurice Carruthers, was an abusive and controlling partner, who exhibited a pattern of behaviour consistent with intimate partner violence. The court accepts that the offender sincerely believed, as a result of past behaviours and threats made by the victim, that her daughter Mrs Allison Janice Carruthers, and her grandchildren Theodore Nicholas Peter Carruthers and Isla Allison Carruthers, were in imminent danger of harm or death at the hands of the victim. The court accepts that, given the circumstances and the evidence presented to the court, this was not an unreasonable belief on the part of the offender.*'

Miriam's long-awaited sentencing hearing was at an end, and Justice Judith Hermann was reading from her judgement. Miriam's fate, the length of her sentence, rested entirely upon what this woman now decided.

Justice Hermann had begun by recapping the details of the case and her responses to the various witnesses she had heard in the course of the hearing. Now, she moved from her introduction to her conclusions. The judge was softly spoken and some in the courtroom had to lean forward to hear her better. The court received the opening paragraph of her judgement in silence, except for a stifled gasp from Sally Carruthers.

Veronica Henry QC had a different response. She turned her head quickly and flashed her client a look of encouragement—or was it triumph? Though she allowed the tension in her shoulders to ease, Miriam otherwise maintained as blank a face as she could manage. She was only too aware of the journalists in front of her scribbling furiously. There was even an artist scratching away on his art pad. He kept looking up at her, cocking his head and narrowing his eyes. She hated it.

As her lawyers had warned she would, Miriam had spent almost a year on remand, and it was a shock when at last the sentencing hearing was scheduled. It was even more of a shock to re-enter the outside world. Locked away, she had almost forgotten the furore around her case, and the intensity of press and public interest. Facing its hot glare, it was as if her time inside had robbed her of a layer of skin. She felt rubbed raw by the many eyes that peered at her, as if each gaze was as sharp as a razor. In prison she was safe—the novelty surrounding her case had worn off, and she had become just another inmate. Outside, though, she was notorious, infamous, the focus of everything; the prisoner in the dock. To some she was a hero, to others a vengeful lunatic. She did not know how to behave in the face of so many versions of herself, none of which she recognised. The best she could do was react as little as possible.

Every morning, as she left remand to travel to the court, hordes of reporters gathered at both ends of the journey. Their cameras lit up the windows of the prison transport vehicle as it drove out of the gates of the correction centre. The prison officers assured her she was invisible behind its tinted windows, but she shrank into the corner of the van anyway and covered her face with her hands. She felt like prey, the press like predators. The sound of them screaming her name was like the screeching of a flock of carrion birds. She had never intended to become a cause célèbre, a figure of debate and controversy or even, as some were heralding her, a feminist hero. All she had wanted to do was save the lives of her daughter and grandchildren and free them from living in fear. The threat of losing them had been so appalling she had not thought about anything else. She'd thought about the deed, certainly, and a little about what would come after. She had not thought about how her actions would ripple outwards, across what sometimes felt like the whole world.

Bad as the start of her journey to court was, arriving was much worse. Handcuffed to a prison officer, with a jacket over her head, she had to run the gauntlet (and that's how it felt, even though it was just a few steps) of the press, while they howled her name (her first name, as if they knew her!) and fired questions at her as a blizzard of cameras flashed. It was like running through an electric storm, or maybe the Somme. She almost expected to hear explosions above her head. By the time she reached the privacy of the holding cell, she was always badly shaken.

'The court accepts the evidence of Mrs Allison Carruthers regarding the abuse she suffered at the hands of the victim and the terror she felt for her own safety and that of her children even after she left the marital home. Mrs Carruthers impressed me as a truthful and reliable witness, especially given the intimate nature of the evidence she gave. The court also accepts that she sincerely believed that her husband would not stop his campaign of terror and that a likely outcome was a murder-suicide. Contrary to the claims made by Mrs Sally Carruthers in her victim impact statement on behalf of her family, we do not believe that Mrs Allison Carruthers—now known as Ms Allison Franklin—was suffering from any mental illness or impairment apart from reasonable fear and anxiety in response to the actions of her husband.'

Sally Carruthers sobbed loudly. Miriam resisted the impulse to look at the woman whose son had caused them all so much grief. She did not want to give the scribblers anything to write about or speculate on. Although her lawyers had prepared her, and she had steeled herself, she had still been angered by Sally's evidence. Sally had minimised Nick's actions and blackened her daughter's name. Of course she had. What else could she do? Now, Miriam's anger evaporated as she listened to the woman crying. Sally Carruthers was a mother who had lost her son. Miriam was a mother who had lived in terror of losing her daughter. They were not so very different.

∽

Allison's evidence had also unsettled Miriam. She had discovered things about her daughter's suffering that she had not known until now. It had been both terrifying and reassuring to listen to her—terrifying to hear what Ally had had to live through, and reassuring because it made Miriam feel even more certain that what she had done, she'd had to do.

'He used to hide what he called "the housekeeping" all over the cottage so I had to search high and low for it—mostly low. He had me crawling about on the floor, looking under furniture and into filthy corners. I used to beg him to hand it to me, but he refused. I know it's a small thing, but it made me feel so humiliated, so downtrodden, to have to grovel in front of him for the money I needed to buy groceries, nappies, things for the kids. He'd follow me around with his arms folded, grinning, while I scooped up the cash. He always made sure there were lots of coins scattered about, and I couldn't stop until I had found it all and he had counted it. It made me want to weep. And I had to keep receipts for everything, and he'd check them weekly to make sure I wasn't salting any cash away.'

'Your husband got you a job at the Dungog Vet Clinic, where he worked, though, didn't he?'

'Yes, but I was a volunteer. I didn't get paid anything. If I wanted a coffee, I had to beg Nick to give me the money for it, and when I say beg, I mean beg, and sometimes he gave it to me, and sometimes he didn't. Eventually I stopped asking and told the other vet nurses I had given up caffeine. I used to think about asking Mum for an allowance, but I was too ashamed, and I knew she'd ask questions and . . . and I didn't want to tell her what I was putting up with.'

Listening to Allison was gut-wrenching, particularly because Miriam had to acknowledge the truth of what her daughter said. She would have asked questions. She would have pushed and pried. And though motivated by love and concern, harm would have been done by her good intentions.

'Why didn't you want to tell her?'

'I don't know. I didn't want to worry her, but I also didn't want to admit—even to myself—what a nightmare my marriage had become. I was still desperate to make it work. And I knew how much she liked Nick. I was frightened she wouldn't believe me.'

That remark hit Miriam like a slap.

And there were worse revelations.

'How were sexual relations between you and your husband?'

It took every ounce of Miriam's strength to sit still. She badly wanted to grip the dock in front of her for support, or even just the edge of her chair, but she dared not move.

'He insisted we have sex every night.'

Ally was staring at her feet and her voice had fallen to a whisper.

The judge leant forward. 'I know this is very hard, Ms Franklin, but we need you to speak up.'

Ally looked straight at her mother and nodded, a determined expression on her face. *She's doing this for me*, thought Miriam, and despite herself, she felt tears pricking. She saw the scribblers from the media intensify their scribbling. *It was torture*, she thought, *but who exactly was being tortured?* Was it her? Was it Ally? Or both of them? She looked at the public gallery. Fiona was seated at the opposite end of it, next to Liam, Jeremy and Julie. Tears were streaming down her face.

'He insisted you have sex every night . . . against your will?'

Ms Henry was very good, Miriam thought to herself. She was firm but did not badger.

'Not at first, but eventually yes. If I ever tried to say no, he made such a fuss it was just easier to give in to him and get it over with so I could get some sleep.'

'How did that make you feel?'

'Worthless.' Ally's voice was suddenly much stronger. Her colour was high. 'Like I had no control over anything, not even my own body. I was his. I was owned by him, lock, stock and barrel. That's why Isla was conceived so quickly after I'd had Teddy. Forget about waiting the six weeks my obstetrician recommended; he wouldn't give me so much as a day. He even insisted on sex while I was in labour. It made me hate him and hate sex. Frankly, I don't care if I never have sex again.'

A ripple ran through the court, and people shifted in their seats. Ally was no longer looking at the floor. She was standing up straight and staring defiantly ahead, both fists clenched. She was in the grip of fury.

∽

'Your daughter is a brilliant witness.'

Veronica Henry, Greg and the rest of her legal team were gathered around Miriam in the holding cell. There was elation in her barrister's voice. As if their team was ahead at half-time. Miriam was pleased by her praise for Ally but also horrified. *This isn't a game, where the side with the best witnesses wins*, she thought. *This is our lives.* Then she corrected herself. *But, of course, it is a game, and I'm just lucky that I have the means to pay for the very best team.*

'She is just telling the truth.'

'Yes, that's what I mean. She vibrates with conviction. You can see the judge likes her.'

'Nick's mum was pretty devastating. I thought she vibrated with conviction too.'

'With pain and grief, I think, and that is different.'

∽

Sally had been white-faced throughout her deposition. She did not look at Miriam once. Miriam was grateful for that. She did not think she would have been able to maintain her composure otherwise.

'My son is none of the things these women are saying. He told me completely different versions from the evidence that is being put before this court. He loved his wife and children and would not harm a hair on their heads. He was a vet! His life's work was to cure and heal and stop suffering. He was terribly worried about Sonny . . .'

'Sonny is the name your son called his wife?'

Ms Henry had interrupted Sally. It sounded as if she was merely seeking clarification, but Miriam was aware that it also reminded the judge how utterly Nick had erased his wife's identity.

Sally was quick to realise the implication too. 'It was a pet name! He called me Matey or Mater. He had pet names for everyone he loved.'

Mims, thought Miriam to herself. *Pete called me Mims.*

Now it was Judge Hermann's turn to interrupt. She did it gently, kindly.

'You were saying that your son was terribly worried about his wife . . . ?'

'Yes, sorry, your Honour. He started worrying about her soon after Teddy was born. He was concerned about her mental health. He told me she was having delusions, that she had become paranoid, convinced he was trying to hurt her and the baby. He was worried she had postnatal depression or worse.'

'Worse?'

'Postnatal psychosis. I'd never heard of it, but he'd read about it somewhere.'

'And your son sought medical help for his wife?'

It was the Crown prosecutor prompting her this time.

'He did! He did! All he wanted was for her to get better and return to being the happy, delightful young woman he had fallen in love with.'

Didn't we all, thought Miriam. She remembered how Nick had managed to convince her that Ally was mentally ill. How easy it was to convince people that a woman was nuts—even other women, even their nearest and dearest. She knew there were lots of people who thought she was a crazy old woman. Sometimes, in her darkest moments, she wondered if they were right. Often, she wondered what Pete would make of what she had done. Would he applaud her for saving Ally and the children? Or would he point out some simpler, less violent solution that she had never thought of? She had dreams sometimes in which he sat in judgement high above her, wearing a wig and gown—just like Judge Hermann—while she desperately tried to explain herself.

'It was your son's idea that the Dungog mental health nurse visit his wife regularly?'

'No, that was the psychiatrist's idea, the one Nick sent her to. There isn't a permanent psychiatrist in Dungog, you see, and Nick felt Maitland was too far for Sonny—his wife—to travel.'

'Why was it too far? Maitland's less than an hour's drive away, isn't it?'

Judge Hermann had interrupted again.

Miriam saw Veronica Henry raise her eyebrows at Greg. The judge was doing their job for them.

Sally flushed. 'He may have been overprotective, given how delusional she was, and she'd have had to drive there with the baby in the car, don't forget—but overprotectiveness is not a crime in a loving husband and anxious new father, is it?' Her voice had risen.

It depends, thought Miriam, *on how far that 'overprotection' goes and exactly what it's protecting. Them? Or his control over them?*

'But we have also heard from Ms Franklin that she no longer had a car until the offender gave her Mr Franklin's old Mercedes.'

Miriam winced inwardly every time she heard herself referred to as 'the offender'. Had she not admitted her guilt, had she had a trial, she would have been referred to as 'the accused'. But her guilt or innocence was not the issue here, she reminded herself. It was *how* guilty she was and how severely she deserved to be punished.

'They couldn't afford two cars. They were living on one salary and young vets don't get paid much, unless they own the business.'

※

Sally had done her best, but in the face of all the other evidence, her effort seemed feeble. In fact, it may have been the evidence of the mental health nurse that finally undermined Sally's attempt to convince the court and the world of what she probably sincerely believed—that her innocent son had been cruelly murdered by a crazy woman in defence of her equally crazy daughter.

'You are Louise Teresa Sarkov, employed by Hunter Valley Health as the mental health nurse for the Dungog Shire?'

'That is correct.'

'And Mrs Allison Carruthers was referred to you as a patient by Dr Guneet Singh?'

'That is correct, but we prefer to call them clients.'

'What did you notice when you first arrived at the Carruthers household to see Mrs Carruthers?'

Louise was calm and composed in the witness stand. She was dressed smartly in a suit and patterned shirt. She wore a little make-up and had her hair swept back into a bun. She looked younger and prettier than Miriam remembered.

'The first thing I saw was the elaborate security camera set-up pointing towards the front door.'

'Why did that catch your attention?'

'It's very unusual in rural areas to be so concerned about security, and the fact that it was pointing towards the house and not the road was a bit of a red flag.'

'Red flag?'

'We're trained to look for signs of domestic abuse. Elaborate surveillance is right up there.'

❦

'I also found the local mental health nurse, Ms Louise Sarkov, to be a credible witness. And her evidence supported the evidence given by Detective Sergeant Fredericks about the complex surveillance systems employed by Mr Carruthers to track the movements of Mrs Carruthers, which included the footage shown to the court by lawyers for the offender. I also accept that Ms Sarkov sincerely believed that Mrs Carruthers' life was at serious risk when she advised her to flee and take the children with her.'

❦

'You told Mrs Carruthers to take her children and leave her husband, correct?'

'Yes. I did.'

'Why did you do that? You had been calling on your client for some months by the time you advised her to go. Why then? Why not before?'

'She told me he had strangled her until she became unconscious. I know from my DV training that strangulation is a sign that a woman is at serious risk of being killed. I made a professional judgement that there was no time to waste.'

'You did not suspect that Mrs Carruthers may have been delusional? Or lying or exaggerating?'

'No. I did not.'

'Yet there were no bruises or marks to back up her story?'

'It is perfectly possible to strangle someone without leaving any marks—you apply the pressure with an open hand, rather than your fingers. And I had always found Sonny . . . sorry, Mrs Carruthers . . . to be truthful. If she did try to avoid the whole truth, it was always to play down her husband's behaviour, never the opposite.'

*

'The court also accepts that the lawyers for the offender have established a pattern of abusive and controlling behaviour by the victim involving a previous intimate partner, Ms Michelle Ann Holder, with whom Mr Carruthers had a relationship before he met his wife.'

*

'The defence calls Michelle Ann Holder.'

As the clerk of the court's voice rang out there was a commotion in the public gallery. Like everyone else, Miriam turned her head to see what was going on. Sally had collapsed in her seat and was making a strange keening sound. Her companion, a woman from the witness support program, rose and helped Sally to her feet. When she had realised Sally's 'friend' was actually a paid professional, Miriam had been moved by how alone Nick's mother was. It took a huge effort to stay impassive as she watched the woman half-carry Sally out of the gallery.

The introduction of this new witness surprised everyone. It sent the scribblers into a frenzy, with some of them even dashing outside to use their phones. Miriam had known that her lawyers had contacted one of Nick's previous girlfriends and that she had agreed to give evidence. What she had not known was what this witness might say. Given Sally's reaction, she now had rather more of an idea.

'I lived with Nick—Mr Carruthers—for a year, and I've had to have ten years of therapy to get over the experience.'

A ripple of suppressed laughter ran through the court. Judge Hermann shot the public gallery a stern look and the moment passed quickly. The judge might be soft-voiced, but she had authority.

Miriam was surprised to find that the young woman in the witness box unsettled her, even though she appeared to be so firmly on Ally's side. Maybe it was the woman's appearance. She was blonde, like Ally, and lively and forthright—the way Ally had been before her personality had been crushed by her husband. Perhaps Nick had been attracted to girls with strong personalities. Perhaps there was an extra kick in breaking them.

'Can you take us through "the experience", as you call it?'

'It's weird—when you tell people about it, it doesn't sound as bad as it felt—but I now think of it as like living in my own personal North Korea. I really do feel as if I am still a bit of a refugee.'

'Can you be more specific? What did he do to make you feel like you were living in North Korea?'

Michelle Holder had read Jess Hill's book, thought Miriam. The copy of *See What You Made Me Do* she had borrowed from the prison library was dog-eared with use.

'He watched my every move, made me give up my job and change the way I dressed. He found reasons why I shouldn't see my friends, even my family. If I did go out without him, he'd call me every few minutes to check on me, and if I didn't answer . . . he could be terrifying.'

'Terrifying how?'

'He took my phone once and smashed it into smithereens. His anger was overwhelming. He'd smash anything I cared about, even the framed picture I had of my little sister who'd died of cancer—that's when I finally left him. I remember him screaming at me as he ground his heel into her photo that I didn't pay him enough attention because I was too busy weeping over my dead relatives . . .' It was clear that Ms Holder was still angry and upset about this.

Miriam's barrister waited for a respectful moment or two before she asked her next question.

'Anything else? What about your sexual relations?'

The poor young woman blushed. *It's horrible that women have to talk about this stuff in public*, Miriam thought.

'If I ever tried to say no—even if I was feeling really ill or had a headache—he'd keep me awake for hours, raving about how cold and selfish and frigid and unloving I was. I was so tired most of the time, I'd give in just to get some sleep. But he'd often wake me for no reason in the night, especially if he knew I was tired already. Sometimes I'd wake to find he was already—well, you know, having sexual relations, as you put it—and that was horrible.'

Had he done that to Ally too? Miriam wondered. She'd never said.

'I think it was the exhaustion that did me in. That and the unpredictability. He'd be a monster for days and then, all of a sudden, he'd be the charming, funny, sweet guy I'd fallen in love with. I never knew who I'd wake up with from one day to the next or what behaviour would set him off. That changed constantly too. Some days he loved to cook for me, then others he'd rant about what a lazy bitch I was if I didn't have a meal on the table the minute he came through the door. I walked on eggshells until I eventually walked out the door.'

The young woman suddenly looked directly at Miriam.

'If I'd stuck around, maybe I would have killed him—or myself. Or maybe he would have killed me. I was terrified when I left, and he followed me around for months afterwards. I'd see him outside my work. He'd suddenly get into the carriage I was in on the train, and if I tried to move to another, he'd follow me there. I'm sure he put some kind of bug on my car and my phone. He seemed to know everything I did, everywhere I went and everyone I saw. It only stopped when I moved to London, and I only did that to get away from him.'

'Is that where you live now?'

'No, I came back to Sydney after he married Ms Franklin. It felt safe to do that then. His attention was elsewhere.'

'Did you ever try to warn Ms Franklin?'

The young woman looked mortified.

'No. I thought about it, but I didn't know how to approach it and I was frightened of how he might react. And I thought that maybe he had only been like that with me, that maybe there was something about me, about the way I behaved, that set him off, and that he might be different with someone else. I couldn't bear the idea of her—Ms Franklin, I mean—reacting as if she didn't know what I was talking about. I am sorry

I didn't now. That's why I came forward. I felt I owed her that at least.'

Allison had cried silently throughout Michelle Holder's deposition, and when Justice Hermann told the witness she could step down, Ally stood and intercepted her on the way out. The two women hugged one another in full view of the court. Miriam wept, and the scribblers scribbled even faster.

'The court also accepts the offender's claim of provocation. We accept that Exhibit G—the clipping left in the letterbox—was a threat and deliberately designed to provoke fear in both Ms Duffy and her daughter. The court also accepts the offender's evidence about her terrifying ordeal when the victim drove his car straight at her outside her house. The court also takes into account the physical evidence presented by the offender's lawyers—namely Exhibit H the cake box containing the two euthanised kittens named Tebby and Island.'

'May I present Exhibit H to the offender, your Honour?'

'You may, Ms Henry.'

Greg handed the barrister the white cardboard box that Miriam had preserved so carefully in the freezer. Ms Henry took it and handed it to the judge. The judge opened the box and looked inside. Her expression did not change. Then she replaced the lid and passed the box to the bailiff, who carried it over to Miriam.

'Can you tell me how you received this item?'

'It was left on the front doorstep by my daughter's ex-husband—Nick Carruthers—on the sixteenth of September, last year.'

'That was two days before you shot him, is that correct?'

Miriam nodded.

'Could you answer yes or no, please?' Judge Hermann's voice was gentle.

'Yes.'

'How do you know it was left by Mr Carruthers?'

'We had installed CCTV by this time.'

'May I play the relevant footage, your Honour?' the barrister broke in.

The judge nodded.

The footage was played. Miriam was painfully conscious that the hooded man who appeared in flickering black and white was not identifiable. She could tell it was Nick, mostly by his height and the way he moved, but how could she explain that to a court of law?

'Do you accept that the man in the footage could be anyone?'

'No, I don't.'

'Why not?'

'Because I saw him with my own eyes when I ran after him onto the street and when he drove his car at me. And also because of what is inside the box.'

'Would you open the box and tell us what it contains?'

Miriam did as she was asked. The kittens had completely defrosted. They looked as if they were decomposing in front of her eyes. The sight of them still horrified her. She had to swallow hard before she could speak.

'It contains two dead kittens and some writing.'

'Can you read what is written?'

'"*Island*" is written above the black kitten. It was Isla's. "*Tebby*" is written above the tabby kitten. It was Teddy's.'

'And there is also a note?'

'Yes.'

'Can you read that aloud too, please?'

Miriam did.

Ms Henry signalled for a photograph of the contents of the box to be projected on the screen near the judge's bench. All heads turned, and those present gasped. Miriam was grateful that Sally had not yet returned to the courtroom.

'And it was this box, its contents and message that made you decide you had to take matters into your own hands?'

Miriam nodded.

'Yes. I understood the message perfectly, but it wasn't the kittens alone. It was everything else he had done, over the years. I could not ignore his threats any longer.'

'But you had already joined a gun club, trained for some considerable time—months, in fact—and bought a weapon. That is also correct?'

'Yes.'

'So, this was not a spontaneous act, but premeditated murder.'

'I had prepared, yes; I had wondered if I might one day have to defend my daughter and grandchildren, and I wanted to be ready. But it was not until the night we received the—the box, and he tried to run me down, that I made up my mind.'

'*The court also accepts the expert opinion of the court-appointed psychologist, Ms Margaret Somers, about the offender's violent and chaotic childhood, and agrees that these formative experiences impacted on Ms Duffy's moral culpability.*'

Miriam was trying not to feel too heartened by Judge Hermann's remarks. Veronica Henry, Greg and the others on her legal team had warned her over and over that she would not be acquitted or freed and must expect not just a custodial sentence, but a long period behind bars. Nevertheless, it was very hard not to feel hopeful when the judge clearly understood exactly what Miriam and Ally had been up against. She struggled to school her features and could only hope that no one in the court could hear how hard her heart was beating. With hope? With fear? She could not tell.

'*However . . .*'

Judge Hermann's expression was suddenly more severe.

'*. . . whatever the mitigating circumstances, however desperate the dilemma, however real the threat, this court cannot take lightly anyone taking the law into their own hands. A man has lost his life. He has not had his day in court. He has not been able to put his side of the story or explain his actions. He has not had the privilege that the offender has enjoyed of having his motives and moral culpability examined and understood. We will never hear from him. This crime does not fit any of the definitions that might allow me to be lenient. Despite the provocation, which the court acknowledges was real and terrifying, this crime was not manslaughter, nor was it self-defence. It was also, as the Crown prosecutor has made clear, premeditated. Although the offender was directly threatened by the victim, and no matter how we might* *sympathise with her, vigilantism can never be the answer. It is to the offender's credit that she has taken full responsibility for her crime and has admitted her guilt. That is not at issue. What is at issue is her sentence.'*

Miriam's heart was now beating so loudly she was surprised she could still hear the softly spoken judge.

'*I am satisfied beyond reasonable doubt of the facts which inform the offender's culpability in so far as they are adverse to the offender. I find the offender guilty of the murder of Nicholas Maurice Carruthers. I sentence the offender, Miriam Carol Duffy, to fifteen years prison with a minimum non-parole period of seven years, including time served. Take the prisoner down.'*

EPILOGUE

Miriam stood waiting, holding the plastic bags that contained the few items she had accumulated over seven years. She was waiting for Officer Coleman to unlock the door and let her out. She felt anxious and afraid. This was what she had been waiting for, dreaming of, dying for every single day. Yet now the moment had arrived, she was scared to death.

She had paid her debt to society, but what was waiting for her out there? she wondered. She was an old woman now, almost seventy, but did that change anything? Would she ever be forgiven for what she had done? Would she ever forgive herself?

As soon as she was sentenced, she had been moved to the Cottages, as she'd suspected she might be. The other prisoners—her flatmates, as she thought of them—had all, like her, been convicted of more serious crimes: murder, manslaughter, embezzlement and culpable driving occasioning death. But, whatever they had done, she did not think of any of them as criminals. She agreed with Margaret Somers. Jail was full of suffering, not evil. It was where society put the people it had failed.

On the second day of her life as a convicted felon she'd had a meeting with the prison governor. He had not wasted any time with small talk.

'It's a long sentence. How are you coping?'

'Alright, I think. My lawyers warned me to expect something like this and they were delighted with the non-parole period. Much shorter than usual, they told me.'

The governor snorted. 'Easy for them to say. Seven years is a long time.'

'It's six with time served; I've already been on remand for a year.'

'Six is a long time too, particularly for someone your age.'

The old Miriam would have been taken aback by his comment about her age, but the new one was grateful. Everyone else she'd spoken to, especially those outside (as she thought of it now), had been at pains to put the most positive possible spin on everything. All that did was make her feel more alone. It was a relief to be spoken to honestly.

'Yes. I'll be nearly seventy by the time I get out.'

'Would you like to do something useful while you're in here? Like peer support work? I reckon you'd be good at it, precisely because you are older. You'd need to do a short training course, but essentially it's about helping new prisoners settle in. Like you said, you've been here a year already, so you know the ropes. Often when women first arrive here, they're coming down off drugs—those can be the toughest ones to help. Sometimes you have to deal with people who are extremely traumatised, and every last inmate is in the grip of some sort of shock. The work requires a certain maturity. Do you reckon you're up for it?'

'I don't know, but I'd like to give it a try.'

It had been a very good decision. Miriam had always thought growing up meant getting more certain about things; now she knew it meant precisely the opposite.

Miriam came to realise that, like famous serial killers, she had fans. It was often the women she helped to 'settle in' who made her aware of her notoriety. As soon as they realised who she was, they'd become excited. She was famous and these young women liked her celebrity. At first, she'd expected to teach them something, but they had taught her. She'd learnt about deprivation, poverty, systemic abuse, addiction, racism, what it was like to grow up in an institution and more than she'd ever imagined possible about mental illness and PTSD. And she was grateful. Sometimes she felt like Sleeping Beauty. She'd only woken up in prison.

But now prison was over and she was to be cast out. Officer Coleman had finished the paperwork. She reached down for her keys and opened the locked metal door.

Miriam blinked, temporarily blinded by the light that streamed in. It was a blazing hot afternoon and the heavy metal door through which she was about to emerge was on the western wall of the correction centre. She would have shaded her eyes if she could, but her arms were full of the plastic bags.

'Good luck, Duffy.' Coleman spoke gruffly, but her voice was kind.

'Thanks Mrs Coleman, and thanks for all your help.'

'You can call me Maureen now.'

'And you can call me Miriam.'

Maureen shook her head. 'I'll miss you, Duff— er, Miriam. We'll all miss you. But I sincerely hope I never have cause to call you anything ever again.'

Miriam grinned. She hoped so too.

'And I'll miss you,' she said.

'No, you won't. You've got a life outside. Not everyone in here does. Look'—Mrs Coleman straightened her arm and pointed—'there it is—your life, parked over there. Go and enjoy it.'

Miriam stepped outside, still half-blinded by the bright sunshine. The heavy door clanged shut and Miriam felt a sudden wild desire to turn around, hammer on it and beg Mrs Coleman to let her back in.

But the impulse to flee passed as suddenly as it had arrived. As her eyes grew accustomed to the light, she saw who had come to meet her.

Ally was the first out of the car, her arms full of a wriggling and barking Goody. Ally put the dog down on the ground and straightened up to wave. The best Miriam could do in response was grin and jiggle the bags that filled her arms, but her gaze was fixed on the dog. The Goody she remembered was now grey of muzzle, wide of girth and stiff of leg. If she'd ever needed a visual representation of how long she'd been inside, this little dog was it. She knew that she looked much older too. She had let her hair go as grey as Goody's muzzle. She was also considerably wider of girth and much stiffer of leg, back and—particularly—knees. For a moment she felt a terrible grief for all the years she had lost, then she pulled herself together. They had not been lost. *I am a better person*, she thought, as she stood outside the jail, waiting to greet her family. *I have grown up at long last.*

Now, Teddy and Isla emerged from the back seat. Her grandson was a leggy twelve-year-old and Isla an equally gangly eleven. They would both be tall, like their father, Miriam observed. She hoped that was all they had inherited from him.

There was a second car parked next to Ally's. Beside it stood Liam, Fiona and a teenaged Molly. For a beat or two, everyone stood still. Then Miriam took the first steps forward and that seemed to release the others. The three children bolted towards her, arms outstretched.

'Nan! Nan!'

She hardly had time to put down the bags containing her possessions before they were upon her, throwing their arms around her like a swarm of beautiful, warm-blooded, sweet-smelling octopuses. She staggered back a little under the weight of their enthusiasm and then burst out laughing. Perhaps it had been worth being separated from them for so long just to experience this exuberant moment. *Yes, look at the life in them,* thought Miriam. *It was all worth it. All of it.*

ACKNOWLEDGEMENTS

This has been a tough novel to write. It took me to places that I did not want to go and made me imagine things I did not want to think about. I do not believe I could have done it without the encouragement and support of many people whose days are filled with just such darkness and difficulty. Having merely dipped my toe in the murky waters of domestic abuse, violence and control, I take my hat off to everyone who works every day to keep women and children safe.

I could not have begun to write this book without the invaluable help of Annabelle Daniel, the warm, funny and commonsensical CEO of Women's Community Shelters. She did two things, apart from take time to meet and chat with me. She encouraged me to undertake this project and her enthusiasm made me hope that a novel about this extremely difficult and sensitive area might be useful and constructive. She also sent me the transcript of the judgement of Simon Gittany, convicted of the horrifying murder of his partner, Lisa Harnum, in 2013.

It was an invaluable resource and reminded me that however dark a novel may be, real life can be so much worse.

I am also indebted to my old school friend, now leading family law practitioner Duncan Holmes, of Holmes Donnelly and Co., who gave me expert advice about the world in which he has worked all his life. Who knew, when we were classmates at Frenchs Forest Public School that we would one day collaborate on a project like this? He does not know what a difference he made to me when I reached out to him about some of the scenarios in this book. I was worried I had jumped the shark until he replied saying, 'Oh, Jane, you have just summarised the contents of half the files on my desk.' I am aware that while this was indeed comforting to a novelist struggling with the darkest edges of her imagination, this response is, of course, horrifying. It is awful to think that so many relationships embarked on with love and hope can become so toxic.

My friend Judge Megan Latham spent an afternoon giving me an expert tutorial on legal procedures, language and the workings of the courts. She also kindly read the courtroom chapter of the novel and corrected any errors that I had made. She was quite strict with me about the kind of defence Miriam could mount and the sort of sentence she could expect under our current laws. I may have been a little more lenient with her than Megan would have liked.

The NSW Police media unit were also helpful in their advice about procedures for arrest, apprehended violence orders and the work of domestic violence liaison officers. They were patient and informative, even though I got the feeling that they get pestered quite a lot by authors wanting information for their novels. My apologies for being yet another.

I am also grateful beyond measure to Kerry Tucker, who I met while making a documentary series for ABC's *Compass* 'The Upside of Shame'. Kerry's open and candid approach to her experiences when she was tried and convicted of serious embezzlement in Victoria is inspirational. She was—as always—warm and generous and upfront about sharing her experiences inside the Dame Phyllis Frost Centre in Melbourne and helped me, I hope, make Miriam's experience in jail believable. Kerry has written her own book about her experiences, *The Prisoner*. I recommend it.

I am also indebted to other authors who have written about domestic violence, abuse and coercive control, specifically Jess Hill, whose ground-breaking book *See What You Made Me Do* was both an inspiration and vital resource. Ginger Gorman's seminal work *Troll Hunting* was another source of courage and grit. Both authors helped me feel that exploring the dark is a writer's core task and that shining a light on toxic masculinity and what it can do to women and children is particularly important right now.

My agent, Jacinta di Mase, has been a support from the very beginning. She made me put pen to paper (or fingers to keyboard) and her encouragement and judicious commentary kept me going, particularly when I reached the parts of Miriam's story that made me want to give up. Jane Palfreyman, my publisher at Allen & Unwin, is a legend in the business, and now I know why. She has been kind and straightforward and that is not a combination that is always easy to pull off.

Ali Lavau, my editor, should have her name on the title page. She helped me see where I had gone wrong and how I could correct it. She was meticulous in her editing and allowed me to get away with nothing. When I earned a compliment from her it kept me going more than anything else. Christa Munns, who went over the manuscript with a fine tooth comb, correcting my errors and bad habits with patience and sensitivity. My wonderful friend Terry Ryan and my daughter Polly Dunning were both invaluable sounding boards and helped me immeasurably with their criticism and brilliant suggestions when I got stuck or felt disheartened.

Like Miriam, I have been lucky in my own relationship and family. As always, I must thank my patient and endlessly supportive husband, Ralph, and my daughters, Polly and Charlotte.

Finally, I must make a few apologies. Firstly, to my two sons-in-law, who are both delightful and bear no resemblance to Nick. Also to the Dungog Veterinary Clinic whose name and occupation I have used in vain. So sorry, Steve and staff.

Two final thank yous: first to the writer of the world's first novel Murasaki Shikibu. The novel gives writers a unique way to investigate imaginatively not just the facts of situations, but to get inside the hearts and minds of those who experience them. All of us who write fiction owe her a great debt.

And secondly and most importantly, to all the women, men and children who have lived in fear of a wounded and dangerous perpetrator—whether he (or occasionally she) directly threatened their safety or the safety of those they loved. Thank you for your courage and endurance. Thank you for (mostly) surviving.

Thank you for telling the world about what you endured and demanding we change and fix this.

To those who did not survive, I can offer nothing, of course, except my poor attempt to use what skills I have to communicate what it may feel like to face a madman.

And, finally, a disclaimer. This book is a work of imagination. The idea and the characters arrived in my brain whole and fully formed, insisting I pay them proper attention. Any resemblance to anyone either living or dead is entirely coincidental.